THE GOOD GIRL

A Novel

GIRL

NEW YORK TIMES BESTSELLER

MARY KUBICA

D0038471

"A TWISTY, ROLLER COASTER RIDE OF A DEBUT.
Fans of *Gone Girl* will embrace this equally evocative tale."
—LISA GARDNER, #1 *New York Times* bestselling author

MIRA®

$14.95 U.S.
$17.95 CAN.

ISBN-13: 978-0-7783-1776-0

51495

9 780778 317760

EAN

Mary Kubica is the national bestselling author of *The Good Girl*. She holds a bachelor of arts degree in history and American literature from Miami University in Oxford, Ohio. She lives outside Chicago with her husband and two children. Follow Mary on Twitter, @MaryKubica.

Praise for Mary Kubica and *The Good Girl*

Look for Mary Kubica's next novel
PRETTY BABY
available soon from MIRA Books

THE GOOD GIRL

MARY KUBICA

ISBN-13: 978-0-7783-1776-0

Recycling programs
for this product may
not exist in your area.

The Good Girl

For questions and comments about the quality of this book, please contact us at
CustomerService@Harlequin.com.

www.MIRABooks.com

Printed in U.S.A.

For A & A

THE
GOOD
GIᴙL

EVE

BEFOЯE

I'm sitting at the breakfast nook sipping from a mug of cocoa
when the phone rings. I'm lost in thought, staring out the back
window at the lawn that now, in the throes of an early fall,
abounds with leaves. They're dead mostly, some still clinging
lifelessly to the trees. It's late afternoon. The sky is overcast,
the temperatures doing a nosedive into the forties and fifties.
I'm not ready for this, I think, wondering where in the world
the time has gone. Seems like just yesterday we were welcoming spring and then, moments later, summer.

The phone startles me and I'm certain it's a telemarketer,
so I don't initially bother to rise from my perch. I relish the
last few hours of silence I have before James comes thunder-
ing through the front doors and intrudes upon my world, and
the last thing I want to do is waste precious minutes on some
telemarketer's sales pitch that I'm certain to refuse.

The irritating noise of the phone stops and then starts again.
I answer it for no other reason than to make it stop.

"Hello?" I ask in a vexed tone, standing now in the center
of the kitchen, one hip pressed against the island.

"Mrs. Dennett?" the woman asks. I consider for a moment

telling her that she's got the wrong number, or ending her pitch right there with a simple *not interested*.

"This is she."

"Mrs. Dennett, this is Ayanna Jackson." I've heard the name before. I've never met her, but she's been a constant in Mia's life for over a year now. How many times have I heard Mia say her name: *Ayanna and I did this...Ayanna and I did that....* She is explaining how she knows Mia, how the two of them teach together at the alternative high school in the city. "I hope I'm not interrupting anything," she says.

I catch my breath. "Oh, no, Ayanna, I just walked in the door," I lie.

Mia will be twenty-five in just a month: October 31st. She was born on Halloween and so I assume Ayanna has called about this. She wants to plan a party—a surprise party?—for my daughter.

"Mrs. Dennett, Mia didn't show up for work today," she says.

This isn't what I expect to hear. It takes a moment to regroup. "Well, she must be sick," I respond. My first thought is to cover for my daughter; she must have a viable explanation why she didn't go to work or call in her absence. My daughter is a free spirit, yes, but also reliable.

"You haven't heard from her?"

"No," I say, but this isn't unusual. We go days, sometimes weeks, without speaking. Since the invention of email, our best form of communication has become passing along trivial forwards.

"I tried calling her at home but there's no answer."

"Did you leave a message?"

"Several."

"And she hasn't called back?"

"No."

I'm listening only halfheartedly to the woman on the other end of the line. I stare out the window, watching the neighbors' children shake a flimsy tree so that the remaining leaves fall down upon them. The children are my clock; when they appear in the backyard I know that it's late afternoon, school is through. When they disappear inside again it's time to start dinner.

"Her cell phone?"

"It goes straight to voice mail."

"Did you—"

"I left a message."

"You're certain she didn't call in today?"

"Administration never heard from her."

I'm worried that Mia will get in trouble. I'm worried that she will be fired. The fact that she might already be in trouble has yet to cross my mind.

"I hope this hasn't caused too much of a problem."

Ayanna explains that Mia's first-period students didn't inform anyone of the teacher's absence and it wasn't until second period that word finally leaked out: Ms. Dennett wasn't here today and there wasn't a sub. The principal went down to keep order until a substitute could be called in; he found gang graffiti scribbled across the walls with Mia's overpriced art supplies, the ones she bought herself when the administration said no.

"Mrs. Dennett, don't you think it's odd?" she asks. "This isn't like Mia."

"Oh, Ayanna, I'm certain she has a good excuse."

"Such as?" she asks.

"I'll call the hospitals. There's a number in her area—"

"I've done that."

"Then her friends," I say, but I don't know any of Mia's friends. I've heard names in passing, such as Ayanna and Lauren and I know there's a Zimbabwean on a student visa who's about to be sent back and Mia thinks it's completely unfair. But I don't *know* them, and last names or contact information are hard to find.

"I've done that."

"She'll show up, Ayanna. This is all just a misunderstanding. There could be a million reasons for this."

"Mrs. Dennett," Ayanna says and it's then that it hits me: something is wrong. It hits me in the stomach and the first thought I have is myself seven or eight months pregnant with Mia and her stalwart limbs kicking and punching so hard that tiny feet and hands emerge in shapes through my skin. I pull out a barstool and sit at the kitchen island and think to myself that before I know it, Mia will be twenty-five and I haven't so much as thought of a gift. I haven't proposed a party or suggested that all of us, James and Grace and Mia and me, make reservations for an elegant dinner in the city.

"What do you suggest we do, then?" I ask.

There's a sigh on the other end of the line. "I was hoping you'd tell me Mia was with you," she says.

GABE

BEFORE

It's dark by the time I pull up to the house. Light pours from the windows of the English Tudor home and onto the tree-lined street. I can see a collection of people hovering inside, waiting for me. There's the judge, pacing, and Mrs. Dennett perched on the edge of an upholstered seat, sipping from a glass of something that appears to be alcoholic. There are uniformed officers and another woman, a brunette, who peers out the front window as I come to a sluggish halt in the street, delaying my grand entrance.

The Dennetts are like any other family along Chicago's North Shore, a string of suburbs that lines Lake Michigan to the north of the city. They're filthy rich. It's no wonder that I'm procrastinating in the front seat of my car when I should be making my way up to the massive home with the clout I've been led to believe I carry.

I think of the sergeant's words before assigning the case to me: *Don't fuck this one up.*

I eye the stately home from the safety and warmth of my dilapidated car. From the outside it's not as colossal as I envision the interior to be. It has all the old-world charm an English Tudor has to offer: half-timbering and narrow windows and a steep sloping roof. It reminds me of a medieval castle.

Though I've been strictly warned to keep it under wraps, I'm supposed to feel privileged that the sergeant assigned this high-profile case to me. And yet, for some reason, I don't.

I make my way up to the front door, cutting across the lawn to the sidewalk that leads me up two steps, and knock. It's cold. I thrust my hands into my pockets to keep them warm while I wait. I feel ridiculously underdressed in my street clothes—khaki pants and a polo shirt that I've hidden beneath a leather jacket—when I'm greeted by one of the most influential justices of the peace in the county.

"Judge Dennett," I say, allowing myself inside. I conduct myself with more authority than I feel I have, displaying traces of self-confidence that I must keep stored somewhere safe for moments like this. Judge Dennett is a considerable man in size and power. Screw this one up and I'll be out of a job, best-case scenario. Mrs. Dennett rises from the chair. I tell her in my most refined voice, "Please, sit," and the other woman, Grace Dennett, I assume, from my preliminary research—a younger woman, likely in her twenties or early thirties—meets Judge Dennett and me in the place where the foyer ends and the living room begins.

"Detective Gabe Hoffman," I say, without the pleasantries an introduction might expect. I don't smile; I don't offer to shake hands. The girl says that she is in fact Grace, whom I know from my earlier legwork to be a senior associate at the law firm of Dalton & Meyers. But it takes nothing more than intuition to know from the get-go that I don't like her; there's an air of superiority that surrounds her, a looking down on my blue-collar clothing and a cynicism in her voice that gives me the willies.

Mrs. Dennett speaks, her voice still carrying a strong British accent, though I know, from my previous fact-finding expedition, that she's been in the United States since she was eighteen. She seems panicked. That's my first inclination. Her voice is high-pitched, her fingers fidgeting with anything that comes within reach. "My daughter is missing, Detective," she sputters. "Her friends haven't seen her. Haven't spoken to her. I've been calling her cell phone, leaving messages." She chokes on her words, trying desperately not to cry. "I went to her apartment to see if she was there," she says, then admits, "I drove all the way there and the landlord wouldn't let me in."

Mrs. Dennett is a breathtaking woman. I can't help but stare at the way her long blond hair falls clumsily over the conspicuous hint of cleavage that pokes through her blouse, where she's left the top button undone. I've seen pictures before of Mrs. Dennett, standing beside her husband on the courthouse steps. But the photos do nothing compared to seeing Eve Dennett in the flesh.

"When is the last time you spoke to her?" I ask.

"Last week," the judge says.

"Not last week, James," Eve says. She pauses, aware of the annoyed look on her husband's face because of the interruption, before continuing. "The week before. Maybe even the one before that. That's the way our relationship is with Mia— we go for weeks sometimes without speaking."

"So this isn't unusual then?" I ask. "To not hear from her for a while?"

"No," Mrs. Dennett concedes.

"And what about you, Grace?"

"We spoke last week. Just a quick call. Wednesday, I believe. Maybe Thursday. Yes, it was Thursday because she called as I was walking into the courthouse for a hearing on a motion to suppress." She throws that in, just so I know she's an attorney, as if the pin-striped blazer and leather briefcase beside her feet didn't already give that away.

"Anything out of the ordinary?"

"Just Mia being Mia."

"And that means?"

"Gabe," the judge interrupts.

"Detective Hoffman," I assert authoritatively. If I have to call him *Judge* he can certainly call me *Detective.*

"Mia is very independent. She moves to the beat of her own drum, so to speak."

"So hypothetically your daughter has been gone since Thursday?"

"A friend spoke to her yesterday, saw her at work."

"What time?"

"I don't know… 3:00 p.m."

I glance at my watch. "So, she's been missing for twenty-seven hours?"

"Is it true that she's not considered missing until she's been gone for forty-eight hours?" Mrs. Dennett asks.

"Of course not, Eve," her husband replies in a degrading tone.

"No, ma'am," I say. I try to be extracordial. I don't like the way her husband demeans her. "In fact, the first forty-eight hours are often the most critical in missing-persons cases."

The judge jumps in. "My daughter is not a missing person. She's *misplaced.* She's doing something rash and negligent, something irresponsible. But she's not *missing.*"

"Your Honor, who was the last one to see your daughter then, before she was—" I'm a smart-ass and so I have to say it "—*misplaced?*"

It's Mrs. Dennett who responds. "A woman named Ayanna Jackson. She and Mia are co-workers."

"Do you have a contact number?"

"On a sheet of paper. In the kitchen." I nod toward one of the officers, who heads into the kitchen to get it.

"Is this something Mia has done before?"

"No, absolutely not."

But the body language of Judge and Grace Dennett says otherwise.

"That's not true, Mom," Grace chides. I watch her expectantly. Lawyers just love to hear themselves speak. "On five or six different occasions Mia disappeared from the house. Spent the night doing God knows what with God knows whom."

Yes, I think to myself, Grace Dennett is a bitch. Grace has dark hair like her dad's. She's got her mother's height and her father's shape. Not a good mix. Some people might call it an hourglass figure; I probably would, too, if I liked her. But instead, I call it plump.

"That's completely different. She was in high school. She was a little naive and mischievous, but..."

"Eve, don't read more into this than there is," Judge Dennett says.

"Does Mia drink?" I ask.

"Not much," Mrs. Dennett says.

"How do you know what Mia does, Eve? You two rarely speak."

She puts her hand to her face to blot a runny nose and for a moment I am so taken aback by the size of the rock on her finger that I don't hear James Dennett rambling on about how his wife had put in the call to Eddie—mind you, I'm struck here by the fact that not only is the judge on a first-name basis with my boss, but he's also on a *nickname* basis— before he got home. Judge Dennett seems convinced that his daughter is out for a good time, and that there's no need for any official involvement.

"You don't think this is a case for the police?" I ask.

"Absolutely not. This is an issue for the family to handle."

"How is Mia's work ethic?"

"Excuse me?" the judge retorts as wrinkles form across his forehead and he rubs them away with an aggravated hand.

"Her work ethic. Does she have a good employment history? Has she ever skipped work before? Does she call in often, claim she's sick when she's not?"

"I don't know. She has a job. She gets paid. She supports herself. I don't ask questions."

"Mrs. Dennett?"

"She loves her job. She just loves it. Teaching is what she always wanted to do."

Mia is an art teacher. High school. I jot this down in my notes as a reminder.

The judge wants to know if I think that's important. "Might be," I respond.

"And why's that?"

"Your Honor, I'm just trying to understand your daughter. Understand who she is. That's all."

Mrs. Dennett is now on the verge of tears. Her blue eyes begin to swell and redden as she pathetically attempts to suppress the tiny drips. "You think something has happened to Mia?"

I'm thinking to myself: isn't that why you called me here? *You* think something has happened to Mia, but instead I say, "I think we act now and thank God later when this all turns out to be a big misunderstanding. I'm certain she's fine, I am, but I'd hate to overlook this whole thing without at least looking into it." I'd kick myself if—*if*—it turned out everything wasn't fine.

"How long has Mia been living on her own?" I ask.

"It'll be seven years in thirty days," Mrs. Dennett states point-blank.

I'm taken aback. "You keep count? Down to the day?"

"It was her eighteenth birthday. She couldn't wait to get out of here."

"I won't pry," I say, but the truth is, I don't have to. I can't wait to get out of here, too. "Where does she live now?"

The judge responds. "An apartment in the city. Close to Clark and Addison."

I'm an avid Chicago Cubs fan and so this is thrilling for me. Just mention the words *Clark* or *Addison* and my ears perk up like a hungry puppy. "Wrigleyville. That's a nice neighborhood. Safe."

"I'll get you the address," Mrs. Dennett offers.

"I would like to check it out, if you don't mind. See if any windows are broken, signs of forced entry."

Mrs. Dennett's voice quavers as she asks, "You think someone broke into Mia's apartment?"

I try to be reassuring. "I just want to check. Mrs. Dennett, does the building have a doorman?"

"No."

"A security system? Cameras?"

"How are we supposed to know that?" the judge growls.

"Don't you visit?" I ask before I can stop myself. I wait for an answer, but it doesn't come.

EVE

AFTEя

I zip her coat for her and pull a hood over her head, and we walk out into the uncompromising Chicago wind. "We need to hurry now," I say, and she nods though she doesn't ask why. The gusts nearly knock us over as we make our way to James's SUV, parked a half-dozen feet away, and as I reach for her elbow, the only thing I'm certain of is that if one of us falls, we are both going down. The parking lot is a sheet of ice four days after Christmas. I do my best to shield her from the cold and the relentless wind, pulling her into me and wrapping an arm around her waist to keep her warm, though my own petite figure is quite smaller than her own and I'm certain I fail miserably at the task.

"We go back next week," I say to Mia as she climbs into the passenger seat, my voice loud over the clatter of doors slamming and seat belts locking. The radio shouts at us, the car's engine on the verge of death on this bitter day. Mia flinches and I ask James to please turn the radio off. In the backseat, Mia is quiet, staring out the window and watching the cars, three of them, as they encircle us like a shiver of hungry sharks, their drivers meddlesome and ravenous. One lifts a camera to his eye and the flash all but blinds us.

"Where the hell are the cops when you need them?" James asks no one in particular, and then blares the horn until Mia's hands rise up to cover her ears from the horrible sound. The cameras flash again. The cars loiter in the parking lot, their engines running, vivid smoke discharging from the exhaust pipes and into the gray day.

Mia looks up and sees me watching her. "Did you hear me, Mia?" I ask, my voice kind. She shakes her head, and I can all but hear the bothersome thought that runs through her mind: *Chloe. My name is Chloe.* Her blue eyes are glued to my own, which are red and watery from holding back tears, something that has become commonplace since Mia's return, though as always James is there, reminding me to keep quiet. I try hard to make sense of it all, affixing a smile to my face, forced and yet entirely honest, and the unspoken words ramble through my mind: *I just can't believe you're home.* I'm careful to give Mia elbow room, not quite certain how much she needs, but absolutely certain I don't want to overstep. I see her malady in every gesture and expression, in the way she stands, no longer brimming with self-confidence as the Mia I know used to be. I understand that something dreadful has happened to her.

I wonder, though, does she sense that something has happened to me?

Mia looks away. "We go back to see Dr. Rhodes next week," I say and she nods in response. "Tuesday."

"What time?" James asks.

"One o'clock."

He consults his smartphone with a single hand, and then tells me that I will have to take Mia to the appointment alone. He says there is a trial, which he cannot miss. And besides, he says, he's sure I can handle this alone. I tell him that of course

I can *handle it,* but I lean in and whisper into his ear, "She needs you now. You're her father." I remind him that this is something we discussed and agreed to and how he promised. He says that he will see what he can do but the doubt weighs heavily on my mind. I can tell that he believes his unwavering work schedule does not allow time for family crises such as this.

In the backseat, Mia stares out the window watching the world fly by as we soar down I-94 and out of the city. It's approaching three-thirty on a Friday afternoon, the weekend of the New Year, and so traffic is an ungodly mess. We come to a stop and wait and then inch forward at a snail's pace, no more than thirty miles per hour on the expressway. James hasn't the patience for it. He stares into the rearview mirror, waiting for the paparazzi to reappear.

"So, Mia," James says, trying to pass the time. "That shrink says you have amnesia."

"Oh, James," I beg, "please, not now."

My husband is not willing to wait. He wants to get to the bottom of this. It's been barely a week since Mia has been home, living with James and me since she's not fit to be on her own. I think of Christmas day, when the tired maroon car pulled sluggishly into the drive with Mia in tow. I remember the way James, nearly always detached, nearly always blasé, forced himself through the front door and was the first to greet her, to gather the emaciated woman in his arms on our snow-covered drive as if it had been him, rather than me, who spent those long, fearful months in mourning.

But since then, I've watched as that momentary relief shriveled away, as Mia, in her oblivion, became tiresome to James, just another one of the cases on his ever growing caseload rather than our *daughter.*

"Then when?"

"Later, please. And besides, that woman is a professional, James," I insist. "A psychiatrist. She is not a *shrink*."

"Fine then, Mia, that *psychiatrist* says you have amnesia," he repeats, but Mia doesn't respond. He watches her in the rearview mirror, these dark brown eyes that hold her captive. For a fleeting moment, she does her best to stare back, but then her eyes find their way to her hands, where she becomes absorbed in a small scab. "Do you wish to comment?" he asks.

"That's what she told me, too," she says, and I remember the doctor's words as she sat across from James and me in the unhappy office—Mia having been excused and sent to the waiting room to browse through outdated fashion magazines—and gave us, verbatim, the textbook definition of acute stress disorder, and all I could think of were those poor Vietnam veterans.

He sighs. I can tell that James finds this implausible, the fact that her memory could vanish into thin air. "So, how does it work, then? You remember I'm your father and this is your mother, but you think your name is Chloe. You know how old you are and where you live and that you have a sister, but you don't have a clue about Colin Thatcher? You honestly don't know where you've been for the past three months?"

I jump in, to Mia's defense, and say, "It's called *selective* amnesia, James."

"You're telling me she picks and chooses things she wants to remember?"

"Mia doesn't do it—her subconscious or unconscious or something like that is doing it. Putting painful thoughts where she can't find them. It's not something she's *decided* to do. It's her body's way of helping her cope."

"Cope with what?"

"The whole thing, James. Everything that happened."

He wants to know how we fix it. This, I don't know for

certain, but I suggest, "Time, I suppose. Therapy. Drugs. Hypnosis."

He scoffs at this, finding hypnosis as bona fide as amnesia. "What kind of drugs?"

"Antidepressants, James," I respond. I turn around and, with a pat on Mia's hand, say, "Maybe her memory will never come back and that will be okay, too." I admire her for a moment, a near mirror image of myself, though taller and younger and, unlike me, years and years away from wrinkles and the white locks of hair that are beginning to intrude upon my mass of dirty blond.

"How will antidepressants help her remember?"

"They'll make her feel better."

He is always entirely candid. This is one of James's flaws. "Well hell, Eve, if she can't remember then what's there to feel bad about?" he asks and our eyes stray out the windows at the passing traffic, the conversation considered through.

GABE

BEFORE

The high school where Mia Dennett teaches is located on the northwest side of Chicago in an area known as North Center. It's a relatively good neighborhood, close to her home, a mostly Caucasian population with an average monthly rent over a thousand dollars. This all bodes well for her. If she was working in Englewood I wouldn't be so sure. The purpose of the school is to provide an education to high school dropouts. They offer vocational training, computer training, life skills, et cetera, in small settings. Enter Mia Dennett, the art teacher, whose purpose is to add the nontraditional flair that's been taken out of traditional high schools, those needing more time for math and science and to bore the hell out of sixteen-year-old misfits who couldn't give a damn.

Ayanna Jackson meets me in the office. I have to wait a good fifteen minutes for her because she's in the middle of class, and so I squeeze my body onto one of those small emasculating plastic school chairs and wait. This is something that certainly does not come easy to me. I'm far from the six-pack of my former days, though I like to think I wear the extra weight well. The secretary keeps her eyes locked on me the entire time as if I'm a student sent down to have a chat with the principal. This is a scene with which I'm sadly accustomed, many of my high school days spent in this very predicament.

"You're trying to find Mia," she says as I introduce myself as Detective Gabe Hoffman. I tell her that I am. It's been nearly four days since anyone has seen or spoken to the woman and so she's been officially designated as missing, much to the judge's chagrin. It's been in the papers, on the news, and every morning when I roll out of bed I tell myself that today will be the day I find Mia Dennett and become a hero.

"When's the last time you saw Mia?"

"Tuesday."

"Where?"

"Here."

We make our way into the classroom and Ayanna—she begs me not to call her Ms. Jackson—invites me to sit down on one of those plastic chairs attached to the broken, graffiti-covered desk.

"How long have you known Mia?"

She sits at her desk in a comfy leather chair and I feel like a kid, though in reality, I top her by a good foot. She crosses her long legs, the slit of a black skirt falling open and exposing flesh. "Three years. As long as Mia's been teaching."

"Does Mia get along with everyone? The students? Staff?"

She's solemn. "There's no one Mia doesn't get along with."

Ayanna goes on to tell me about Mia. About how, when she first arrived at the alternative school, there was a natural grace about her, about how she empathized with the students and behaved as if she, too, had grown up on the streets of Chicago. About how Mia organized fundraisers for the school to pay for needy students' supplies. "You never would have known she was a Dennett."

According to Ms. Jackson, most new teachers don't last long

in this type of educational setting. With the market the way it is these days, sometimes an alternative school is the only place hiring and so college grads accept the position until something else comes along. But not Mia. "This was where she wanted to be.

"Let me show you something," she says and she pulls a stack of papers from a letter tray on her desk. She walks closer and sits down on one of the student desks beside me. She sets the mound of paper before me and what I see first is a scribble of bad penmanship, worse than my own. "This morning the students worked on their journal entries for the week," she explains and as my eyes peruse the work, I see the name *Ms. Dennett* more times than I can count.

"We do journal entries each week. The assignment this week," she explains, "was to tell me what they wanted to do with themselves after high school." I mull this over for a minute, seeing the words *Ms. Dennett* splattered over almost every sheet of paper. "But ninety-nine percent of the students are thinking of nothing but Mia," she concludes, and I can hear, by the dejection in her voice, that she, too, can think of little but Mia.

"Did Mia have trouble with any of the students?" I ask, just to be sure. But I know what her answer is going to be before she shakes her head.

"What about a boyfriend?" I ask.

"I guess," she says, "if you could call him that. Jason something-or-other. I don't know his last name. Nothing serious. They've only been dating a few weeks, maybe a month, but no more." I jot this down. The Dennetts made no reference to a boyfriend. Is it possible they don't know? Of course it's possible. With the Dennett family, I'm beginning to learn, anything is possible.

"Do you know how to get in touch with him?"

"He's an architect," she says. "Some firm off Wabash. She meets him there most Friday nights for happy hour. Wabash and...I don't know, maybe Wacker? Somewhere along the river." Sounds like a wild-goose chase to me, but I'm up for it. I make note of this information in my yellow pad.

The fact that Mia Dennett has an elusive boyfriend is great news for me. In cases like this, it's always the boyfriend. Find Jason and I'm sure to find Mia as well, or what's left of her. Considering she's been gone for four days, I'm starting to think this story might have an unhappy ending. Jason works by the Chicago River: bad news. God knows how many bodies are pulled out of that river every year. He's an architect, so he's smart, good at solving problems, like how to discard a hundred-and-twenty-pound body without anyone noticing.

"If Mia and Jason were dating," I ask, "is it odd that *he* isn't trying to find her?"

"You think Jason might be involved?"

I shrug. "I know *if* I had a girlfriend and I hadn't spoken to her in four days, I might be a little concerned."

"I guess," she agrees. She stands from the desk and begins to erase the chalkboard. It leaves tiny remnants of dust on her black skirt. "He didn't call the Dennetts?"

"Mr. and Mrs. Dennett have no idea that there's a boyfriend in the picture. As far as they're concerned, Mia is single."

"Mia and her parents aren't close. They have certain...ideological differences."

"I gather that."

"I don't think it's the kind of thing she'd tell them."

The topic is drifting, so I try to reel Ayanna back in. "You and Mia are close, though." She says that they are. "Would you say that Mia tells you everything?"

"As far as I know."

"What does she tell you about Jason?"

Ayanna sits back down, this time on the edge of her desk.
She peers at a clock on the wall, dusts off her hands. She considers my question. "It wasn't going to last," she tells me, trying to find the right words to explain. "Mia doesn't become
involved too often, never anything serious. She doesn't like
to be tied down. Committed. She's markedly independent,
perhaps to a fault."

"And Jason is...clingy? Needy?"

She shakes her head. "No, it's not that, it's just, he's not
the one. She didn't glow when she spoke of him. She didn't
gossip like girls do when they've met *the one.* I always had to
force her to tell me about him and then, it was like listening
to a documentary: *we went to dinner, we saw a movie....* And I
know his hours were bad, which irritated Mia—he was always
missing dates or showing up late. Mia hated to be tied down
to his schedule. You have that many *issues* in the first month
and it's never going to last."

"So it was possible Mia was planning to break up with
him?"

"I don't know."

"But she wasn't entirely happy."

"I wouldn't say Mia wasn't *happy,*" Ayanna responds. "I just
don't think she cared one way or the other."

"From what you know, did Jason feel the same?" She says
that she doesn't know. Mia was rather aloof when she spoke
of Jason. The conversations were nondescript: a checklist of
things they had done that day, details of the man's statistics—
height, weight, hair and eye color—though remarkably, no
last name. But Mia never mentioned if they kissed and there
was no reference to that tingly feeling in the pit of your stomach—Ayanna's words, not mine—when you've met the man
of your dreams. She seemed upset when Jason stood her up—
which, by Ayanna's account, happened often—and yet she

didn't seem particularly excited on the nights they planned a late-night rendezvous down by the Chicago River.

"And you'd characterize this as disinterest?" I ask. "In Jason? The relationship? The whole thing?"

"Mia was passing time until something better came along."

"Did they fight?"

"Not that I know of."

"But if there was a problem, Mia would have told you," I suggest.

"I'd like to think she would have," the woman responds, her dark eyes becoming sad.

A bell rings in the distance, followed by the clatter of footsteps in the hall. Ayanna Jackson rises to her feet, which I take as my cue. I say that I'll be in touch and leave her with my card, asking that she call if anything comes to mind.

EVE

AFTER

I'm halfway down the stairs when I see them, a news crew on the sidewalk before our home. They stand, shivering, with cameras and microphones; Tammy Palmer from the local news in a tan trench coat and knee-high boots on my front lawn. Her back is toward me, a man counting down on his fingers— *three...two...*—and as he points at Tammy I all but hear her broadcast begin. *I'm standing here at the home of Mia Dennett....*

This isn't the first time they've been here. Their numbers have begun to dwindle now, their reporters moving onto other stories: same-sex marriage laws and the dismal state of the economy. But in the days after Mia's return they were camped outside, desperate for a glimpse of the damaged woman, for any morsel of information to turn into a headline. They followed us around town in their cars until we all but locked Mia inside.

There have been mysterious cars parked outside, photographers for those trashy magazines peering out of car windows with their telephoto lenses, trying to turn Mia into a cash cow. I pull the drapes closed.

I spot Mia sitting at the kitchen table. I descend the stairs in silence, to watch my daughter in her own world before I intrude upon it. She's dressed in a pair of ripped jeans and a snug navy turtleneck that I bet makes her eyes look just amazing. Her hair is damp from an earlier shower, drying in waves down her back. I'm addled by the thick wool socks that blanket her feet, that and the mug of coffee her hands are united around.

She hears me approach and turns to look. Yes, I think to myself, the turtleneck makes her eyes look amazing.

"You're drinking coffee," I say, and it's the vague expression on her face that makes me certain I've said the wrong thing.

"I don't drink coffee?"

I've been treading carefully for over a week now, always trying to say the right thing, going over-the-top—ridiculously so—to make her feel at home. I've been on edge to compensate for James's apathy and Mia's disarray. And then, when least expected, a seemingly benign conversation, and I slip up.

Mia doesn't drink coffee. She doesn't drink much caffeine at all. It makes her nervous. But I watch her sip from the mug, completely stagnant and sluggish, and think—wish—that maybe a little caffeine will do the trick. Who is this limp woman before me, I wonder, recognizing the face but having no knowledge of the body language or tone of voice or the disturbing silence that encompasses her like a bubble.

There are a million things I want to ask her. But I don't. I've vowed to just let her be. James has pried more than enough for the both of us. I'll leave the questions to the professionals, Dr. Rhodes and Detective Hoffman, and to those who just never know when to quit—James. She's my daughter, but she's not my daughter. She's Mia, but she's not Mia. She looks like her, but she wears socks and drinks coffee and wakes up sobbing in the middle of the night. She's quicker to respond if I call her Chloe than when I call her by her given name.

She looks empty, appears asleep when she's awake, lies awake when she should be asleep. She nearly flew three feet from her seat when I turned on the garbage disposal last night and then retreated to her room. We didn't see her for hours and when I asked how she passed the time all she could say was *I don't know.* The Mia I know can't sit still for that long.

"It looks like a nice day," I offer but she doesn't respond. It does look like a nice day; it's sunny. But the sun in January is deceiving and I'm certain the earth will warm to no more than twenty degrees.

"I want to show you something," I say and I lead her from the kitchen to the adjoining dining room, where I've replaced a limited edition print with one of Mia's works of art, back in November when I was certain she was dead. Mia's painting is done in oil pastels, this picturesque Tuscan village she drew from a photograph after we visited the area years ago. She layered the oil pastels, creating a dramatic representation of the village, a moment in time trapped behind this sheet of glass. I watch Mia eye the piece and think to myself: If only everything could be preserved that way. "You made that," I say.

She knows. This she remembers. She recalls the day she set herself down at the dining room table with the oil pastels and the photograph. She had begged her father to purchase the poster-board for her and he agreed, though he was certain her newfound love of art was only a passing phase. When she was finished we all oohed and ahhed and then it was tucked away somewhere with old Halloween costumes and roller skates only to be stumbled upon later on a scavenger hunt for photographs of Mia that the detective asked us to collect.

"Do you remember our trip to Tuscany?" I ask.

She steps forward to run her lovely fingers over the work of art. She stands inches above me, but in the dining room she is a child—a fledgling not yet sure how to stand on her own two feet.

"It rained," Mia responds without removing her eyes from the drawing.

I nod. "It did. It rained," I say, glad that she remembered. But it rained only one day and the rest of the days were a godsend.

I want to tell her that I hung the drawing because I was so worried about her. I was terrified. I lay awake night after night for months on end just wondering, What if? What if she wasn't okay? What if she was okay but we never found her? What if she was dead and we never knew? What if she was dead and we did know, the detective asking us to identify decaying remains?

I want to tell Mia that I hung her Christmas stocking just in case and that I bought her presents and wrapped them and put them under the tree. I want her to know that I left the porch light on every night and that I must have called her cell phone a thousand times just in case. Just in case one time it didn't go straight to the voice mail. But I listened to the message over and over again, the same words, the same tone— *Hi, this is Mia. Please leave a message*—allowing myself to savor the sound of her voice for a while. I wondered: what if those were the last words I ever heard from my daughter? What if?

Her eyes are hollow, her expression vacant. She has the most unflawed peaches-and-cream complexion I believe I've ever seen, but the peaches seemed to have disappeared and now she is all cream, white as a ghost. She doesn't look at me when we speak; she looks past me or through me, but never at me. She looks down much of the time, at her feet, her hands, anything to avoid another's gaze.

And then, standing there in the dining room, her face drains of every last bit of color. It happens in an instant, the light seeping through the open drapes highlighting that way Mia's body lurches upright and then sags at the shoulders, her hand falling from the image of Tuscany to her abdomen in one swift movement. Her chin drops to her chest, her breathing becomes hoarse. I lay a hand on her skinny—too skinny, I can feel bones—back and wait. But I don't wait long; I'm impatient. "Mia, honey," I say, but she's already telling me that she's okay, she's fine, and I'm certain it's the coffee.

"What happened?"

She shrugs. Her hand is glued to the abdomen and I know she doesn't feel well. Her body has begun a retreat from the dining room. "I'm tired, that's all. I just need to go lie down," she says and I make a mental note to rid the house of all traces of caffeine before she wakes up from her nap.

GABE

BEFORE

"You're not an easy man to find," I say as he welcomes me into his work space. It's more of a cubicle than an office, but with higher walls than normal, offering a minimal amount of privacy. There's only one chair—his—and so I stand at the entrance to the cube, cocked at an angle against the pliable wall.

"I didn't know someone was trying to find me."

My first impression is he's a pompous ass, much like myself years ago, before I realized I was more full of myself than I should be. He's a big man, husky, though not necessarily tall. I'm certain he works out, drinks protein shakes, maybe uses steroids? I'll jot this down in my notes, but for now, I'd hate to have him catch me making these assumptions. I might get my ass kicked.

"You know Mia Dennett?" I ask.

"That depends." He turns around in his swivel chair, finishes typing an email with his back to me.

"On what?"

"On who wants to know."

I'm not too eager to play this game. "I do," I say, saving my trump card until later.

"And you are?"

"Looking for Mia Dennett," I respond.

I can see myself in this guy, though he can barely be twenty-four or twenty-five years old, just out of college, still believing the world rotates around him. "If you say so." I, however, am on the cusp of fifty, and just this morning noticed the first few strands of gray hair. I'm certain I have Judge Dennett to thank for them.

He continues the email. What the hell, I think. He couldn't care less that I'm standing here, waiting to talk to him. I peer over his shoulder to have a look. It's about college football, sent to a recipient by the user name dago82. My mother is Italian—hence the dark hair and eyes I'm certain all women are wooed by—and so I take the derogatory name as an insult against my people, though I've never been to Italy and don't know a single word in Italian. I'm just looking for another reason not to like this guy. "Must be a busy day," I comment and he seems peeved that I'm reading his email. He minimizes the screen.

"Who the hell are you?" he asks again.

I reach into my back pocket and pull out that shiny badge I adore so much. "Detective Gabe Hoffman." He's visibly knocked down a notch or two. I smile. God, do I love my job.

He plays dumb. "Is there a problem with Mia?"

"Yeah, I guess you can say that."

He waits for me to continue. I don't, just to piss him off. "What did she do?"

"When's the last time you saw Mia?"

"It's been a while. A week or so."

"And the last time you spoke to her?"

"I don't know. Last week. Tuesday night, I think."

"You think?" I ask. He confirms on his calendar. Yes, it was Tuesday night. "But you didn't *see* her Tuesday?"

"No. I was supposed to, but I had to cancel. You know, work."

"Sure."

"What happened to Mia?"

"So you haven't spoken to her since Tuesday?"

"No."

"Is that normal? To go nearly a week without speaking?"

"I called her," he confesses. "Wednesday, maybe Thursday. She never called back. I just assumed she was pissed off."

"And why would that be? Did she have a reason to be *pissed off?*"

He shrugs. He reaches for a bottle of water on the desk and takes a sip. "I canceled our date Tuesday night. I had to work. She was kind of short with me on the phone, you know? I could tell she was mad. But I had to work. So I thought she was holding a grudge and not calling back...I don't know."

"What were your plans?"

"Tuesday night?"

"Yeah."

"Meet in a bar in Uptown. Mia was already there when I called. I was late. I told her I wasn't going to make it."

"And she was mad?"

"She wasn't happy."

"So you were here, working, Tuesday night?"

"Until like 3:00 a.m."

"Anyone who can vouch for that?"

"Um, yeah. My boss. We were putting some designs together for a client meeting on Thursday. I met with her on and off half the night. Am I in trouble?"

"We'll get to that," I answer flatly, transcribing the conversation in my own shorthand that no one but me can decipher. "Where'd you go after you left work?"

"Home, man. It was the middle of the night."

"You have an alibi?"

"An alibi?" He's getting uncomfortable, squirming in his chair. "I don't know. I took a cab home."

"Get a receipt?"

"No."

"You have a doorman in your building? Someone who can tell us you made it home safe?"

"Cameras," he says, and then asks, "Where the fuck is Mia?"

I had pulled Mia's phone records after my meeting with Ayanna Jackson. I found calls almost daily to a Jason Becker, who I tracked down to an architectural firm in the Chicago Loop. I paid this guy a visit to see what he knew about the girl's disappearance, and saw the evident perception on his face when I said her name. "Yeah, I know Mia," he said, leading me back to his cube. I saw it in the first instant: jealousy. He had himself convinced that I was the other guy.

"She's missing," I say, trying to read his response.

"Missing?"

"Yeah. Gone. No one has seen her since Tuesday."

"And you think I had something to do with it?"

It irritates me that he's more concerned with his culpability than Mia's life. "Yeah," I lie, "I think you might have something to do with it." Though the truth is that if his alibi is as airtight as he's making it out to be, I'm back to square one.

"Do I need a lawyer?"

"Do you think you need a lawyer?"

"I told you, I was working. I didn't see Mia Tuesday night. Ask my boss."

"I will," I assure him, though the look that crosses his face begs me not to.

Jason's co-workers eavesdrop on the interrogation. They walk slower as they pass his cube; they linger outside and pretend to carry on conversations. I don't mind. He does. It's driving him nuts. He's worried about his reputation. I like to watch him squirm in his chair, becoming antsy. "Do you need anything else?" he asks to speed things along. He wants me out of his hair.

"I need to know your plans Tuesday night. Where Mia was when you called. What time it was. Check your phone records. I need to speak to your boss and make sure you were here, and with security to see what time you left. I'll need the footage from your apartment cameras to verify you got home okay. If you're comfortable providing me with that, then we're all set. If you'd rather I get a warrant..."

"Are you threatening me?"

"No," I lie, "just giving you your options."

He agrees to provide me with the information I need, including an introduction to his boss, a middle-aged woman in an office ridiculously larger than his, with floor-to-ceiling windows that face out onto the Chicago River, before I leave.

"Jason," I declare, after having been assured by the boss that he was working his ass off all night, "we're going to do everything we can to find Mia," just to see the expression of apathy on his face before I leave.

COLIN

BEFOЯE

It doesn't take much. I pay off some guy to stay at work a couple hours later than he'd like to. I follow her to the bar and sit where I can watch her without being seen. I wait for the call to come and when she knows she's been stood up, I move in.

I don't know much about her. I've seen a snapshot. It's a blurry photo of her stepping off the "L" platform, taken by a car parked a dozen or so feet away. There are about ten people between the photographer and the girl and so her face has been circled with a red pen. On the back of the photograph are the words *Mia Dennett* and an address. It was handed to me a week or so ago. I've never done anything like this before. Larceny, yes. Harassment, yes. Not kidnapping. But I need the money.

I've been following her for the last few days. I know where she buys her groceries, where she has her dry cleaning done, where she works. I've never spoken to her. I wouldn't recognize the sound of her voice. I don't know the color of her eyes or what they look like when she's scared. But I will.

I carry a beer but I don't drink it. I can't risk getting drunk. Not tonight. But I don't want to draw attention to myself and so I order the beer so I'm not empty-handed. She's fed up when the call comes in on her cell phone. She steps outside to take the call and when she comes back she's frustrated. She thinks about leaving, but decides to finish her drink. She finds a pen in her purse and doodles on a bar napkin, listening to some asshole read poetry on stage.

I try not to think about it. I try not to think about the fact that she's pretty. I remind myself of the money. I need the money. This can't be that hard. In a couple hours it will all be through.

"It's good," I say, nodding at the napkin. It's the best I can come up with. I know nothing about art.

She gives me the cold shoulder when I first approach. She doesn't want a thing to do with me. That makes it easier. She barely lifts her eyes from the napkin, even when I praise the candle she's drawn. She wants me to leave her alone.

"Thanks." She doesn't look at me.

"Kind of abstract."

This is apparently the wrong thing to say. "You think it looks like shit?"

Another man would laugh. He'd say he was kidding and kill her with compliments. But not me. Not with her.

I slide into the booth. Any other girl, any other day, I'd walk away. Any other day I wouldn't have approached her table in the first place, not the table of some bitchy-looking, pissed-off girl. I leave small talk and flirting and all that other crap to someone else. "I didn't say it looked like shit."

She sets her hand on her coat. "I was about to leave," she says. She swallows the rest of her drink and sets the glass on the table. "The booth is all yours."

"Like Monet," I say. "Monet does that abstract stuff, doesn't he?"

I say it on purpose.

She looks at me. I'm sure it's the first time. I smile. I wonder if what she sees is enough to lift her hand from the coat. Her tone softens and she knows she's been abrupt. Maybe not so bitchy after all. Maybe just pissed off. "Monet is an impressionist painter," she says. "Picasso, that's abstract art. Kandinsky. Jackson Pollock." I've never heard of them. She still plans to leave. I'm not worried. If she decides to leave, I'll follow her home. I know where she lives. And I have plenty of time.

But I try anyway.

I reach for the napkin that she's crumpled and set in an ashtray. I dust off the ashes and unfold it. "It doesn't look like shit," I say to her as I fold it and slide it into the back pocket of my jeans.

This is enough to send her eyes roving the bar for the waitress; she thinks she'll have another drink. "You're keeping that?" she asks.

"Yes."

She laughs. "In case I'm famous one day?"

People like to feel as if they're important. She lets it get the best of her.

She tells me that her name is Mia. I say that mine is Owen. I pause long enough when she asks my name for her to say, "I didn't realize it was a hard question." I tell her that my parents live in Toledo and that I'm a bank teller. None of it is the truth. She doesn't offer much about herself. We talk about things that aren't personal: a car crash on the Dan Ryan, a freight train derailing, the upcoming World Series. She suggests we talk about something that isn't depressing. It's hard to do. She orders one drink and then another. The more she drinks, the more open she becomes. She admits that her boyfriend stood her up. She tells me about him, that they've been dating since the end of August and she could count the number of dates he's actually kept on one hand. She's fishing for sympathy I don't offer. It's not me.

At some point I scoot closer to her in the booth. At times we touch, our legs brushing against one another without intent beneath the table.

I try not to think about it. About later. I try not to think about forcing her into the car or handing her over to Dalmar. I listen to her go on and on, about what, I don't really know, because what I'm thinking about is the money. About how far cash like that will go. This—sitting with some lady in a bar I bet my life I'd never step foot in, taking hostages for ransom—isn't my thing. But I smile when she looks at me, and when her hand touches mine, I let it stay because I know one thing: this girl might just change my life.

EVE

AFTEЯ

I'm looking through Mia's baby book when it hits me: in second grade she had an imaginary friend named Chloe.

It's there in the yellowing pages of the album, written in my own cursive in blue ink somewhere along the margin, sandwiched between a first broken bone and a wicked case of the flu that landed her in the emergency room. Her third-grade picture covers part of the name Chloe, but I can make it out.

I gaze at the third-grade picture, this portrait of a happy-go-lucky girl still years away from braces and acne and Colin Thatcher. She flashes this toothless grin with a mop of flaxen hair engulfing her head like flames. She's splattered with freckles, something that has disappeared over time, and her hair is shades lighter than it will eventually be. The collar of her blouse is unfolded and I'm certain her scrawny legs are cloaked in a pair of hot pink leggings, likely a hand-me-down from Grace.

There are snapshots lining the pages of the baby book: Christmas morning when Mia was two and Grace seven, sporting their matching pajamas while James's greasy hair stood on end. First days of school. Birthday parties.

I'm seated at the breakfast nook with the baby book spread open before me, eyeing cloth diapers and baby bottles and wanting it all back. I put in a call to Dr. Rhodes. To my surprise, she answers.

When I tell her about the imaginary friend, Dr. Rhodes takes off in psychological analysis. "Oftentimes, Mrs. Dennett, children create imaginary friends to compensate for loneliness or a lack of real friends in their lives. They often give these imaginary friends characteristics that they long for in their own lives, making them outgoing if the child is shy, for example, or a great athlete if a child is clumsy. Having an imaginary friend isn't necessarily a physiological problem, assuming the *friend* disappears as the child matures."

"Dr. Rhodes," I respond, "Mia named her imaginary friend Chloe."

She grows quiet. "That is interesting," she says and I go numb.

I become obsessed with the name Chloe. I spend the morning on the internet trying to learn everything there is to know about this name. It's a Greek name that means *blooming*...or *blossoming* or *verdant* or *growth,* depending on what website I search, but regardless, the words are synonymous with one another. This year it's one of the more popular names, but back in 1990 it ranked 212th among all American baby names, slipped in between Alejandra and Marie. There are approximately 10,500 people in the United States right now with the name Chloe. Sometimes you find the name with an umlaut over the *e* (nearly twenty minutes is lost trying to find the meaning of those two dots over the vowel, and when I do— its purpose simply to differentiate between the *o* and *e* sounds at the end of the name—I realize it's been a waste of time), sometimes without. I wonder how Mia spells it, though I won't dare ask. Where would Mia have come up with a name like

Chloe? Perhaps it was on the birth certificate of one of Mia's prized Cabbage Patch Kids, flown in from Babyland General Hospital. I go to the website. I'm astounded to find new skin tones for this year's babies—mocha and cream and latte—but no reference to a doll named Chloe. Maybe another child in Mia's second-grade class...

I research famous people named Chloe: both Candice Bergen and Olivia Newton-John named their daughters Chloe. It's the real first name of author Toni Morrison, though I highly doubt Mia was reading *Beloved* in the second grade. There's Chloë Sevigney (with the umlaut) and Chloe Webb (without), though I'm certain the first is too young and the second too old for Mia to have paid any attention to when she was eight.

I could ask her. I could climb the steps and knock on the door of her bedroom and ask her. That's what James would do. He'd get to the bottom of this. I want to get to the bottom of this, but I don't want to violate Mia's trust. Years ago I'd seek James's advice, his help. But that was years ago.

I pick up the telephone, dial the numbers. The voice that greets me is kind, informal.

"Eve," he says and I feel myself relax.

"Hello, Gabe."

COLIN

BEFORE

I lead her to a high-rise apartment building on Kenmore. We take the elevator to the seventh floor. Loud music pours out of another apartment as we make our way down the piss-stained carpeting to a door at the end of the hall. I open the door as she stands by. It's dark in the apartment. Only the stove light is on. I cross the parquet floors and flip on a lamp beside the sofa. The shadows disappear and are replaced with the contents of my meager living: *Sports Illustrated* magazines, a collection of shoes barricading the closet door, a half-eaten bagel on a paper plate on the coffee table. I watch silently as she judges me. It's quiet. A neighbor has made Indian food tonight and the scent of curry chokes her.

"You okay?" she asks because she hates the uncomfortable silence. She's probably thinking this was all a mistake, that she should leave.

I walk to her and run a hand down the length of her hair, grasping the strands at the base of her skull. I stare at her, placing her upon a pedestal, and see in her eyes how she wishes, if only for a moment, to stay there. It's a place she hasn't been for quite some time. She forgot how it felt to have someone stare that way. She kisses me and forgets altogether about leaving.

I press my lips against hers in a way that's new and familiar all at the same time. My touch is assertive. I've done this a thousand times. It puts her at ease. If I were awkward, refusing to make the first move, she'd have time to reconsider. But as it is, it happens too fast.

And then, as quickly as it began, it's over. I change my mind, pull away, and she asks, "What?" short of breath. "What's wrong?" she begs, trying to pull me back to her. Her hands drop to my waistband, her drunken fingers clumsily work my belt.

"It's a bad idea," I say as I turn away from her.

"Why?" her voice begs. She grasps at my shirt in desperation. I move away, out of reach. And then, it sinks in slowly— the rejection. She's embarrassed. She presses her hands to her face like she's hot, clammy.

She drops onto the arm of a chair and tries to catch her breath. Around her, the room spins. I can see it in her expression: she isn't used to hearing the word *no*. She rearranges a crumpled shirt, runs sweaty hands through her hair, ashamed.

I don't know how long we stay like that.

"It's just a bad idea," I say then, suddenly inspired to pick up my shoes. I throw them in the closet, one pair at a time. They smack the back wall. They fall into a messy pile behind the closet door. And then I close the door, leaving the mess where I can't see it.

And then the resentment creeps in and she asks, "Why did you bring me here? Why did you bring me here, if only to humiliate me?"

I picture us at the bar. I imagine my own greedy eyes when I leaned in and suggested, "Let's get out of here." I told her my apartment was just down the street. We all but ran the entire way.

I stare at her. "It's not a good idea," I say again. She stands and reaches for her purse. Someone passes in the hallway, their laughter like a thousand knives. She tries walking, loses her balance.

"Where are you going?" I ask, my body blocking the front door. She can't leave now.

"Home," she says.

"You're wasted."

"So?" she challenges. She reaches for the chair to steady herself.

"You can't go," I insist. *Not when I'm this close,* I think, but what I say is "Not like this."

She smiles and says that's sweet. She thinks I'm worried about her. Little does she know.

I couldn't care less.

GABE

AFTEЯ

Grace and Mia Dennett are sitting at my desk when I arrive, their backs turned in my direction. Grace couldn't look more uncomfortable. She plucks a pen from my desk and removes the chewed-up cap with a sleeve of her shirt. I smooth a paisley tie against my shirt, and as I make my way to them, I hear Grace muttering the words "slovenly appearance" and "unbecoming" and "Spartan skin." I assume she's talking about me, and then I hear her say that Mia's corkscrew locks haven't seen a hair dryer in weeks; there are neglected bags beneath her eyes. Her clothes are rumpled and look like they should be cloaking the body of someone in junior high, a prepubescent boy no less. She doesn't smile. "Ironic, isn't it," Grace says, "how I wish you'd snap at me—call me a bitch, a narcissist, any of those unpleasant nicknames you had for me in the days before Colin Thatcher."

But instead Mia just stares.

"Good morning," I say, and Grace interrupts me curtly with "Think we can get started? I have things to do today."

"Of course," I say, and then empty sugar packets into my

coffee as slowly as I possibly can. "I was hoping to talk to Mia, see if I can get some information from her."

"I don't see how she can help," Grace says. She reminds me of the amnesia. "She doesn't remember what happened."

I've asked Mia down this morning to see if we can jog her memory, see if Colin Thatcher told her anything inside that cabin that might be of value to the ongoing investigation. Since her mother wasn't feeling well, she sent Grace in her place, as Mia's chaperone, and I can see, in Grace's eyes, that she'd rather be having dental work than sit here with Mia and me.

"I'd like to try and jog her memory. See if some pictures help."

She rolls her eyes and says, "God, Detective, mug shots? We all know what Colin Thatcher looks like. We've seen the pictures. Mia has seen the pictures. Do you think she's not going to identify him?"

"Not mug shots," I assure her, reaching into a desk drawer to yank something from beneath a stash of legal pads. She peers around the desk to get the first glimpse and is stumped by the 11x14 sketch pad I produce. It's a spiral-bound book; her eyes peruse the cover for clues, but the words *recycled paper* give nothing away. Mia, however, is briefly cognizant, of what neither she nor I know, but something passes through her—a wave of recollection—and then it's gone as soon as it came. I see it in her body language—posture straightening, leaning forward, hands reaching out blindly for the pad, drawing it into her. "You recognize this?" I ask, voicing the words that were on the tip of Grace's tongue.

Mia holds it in her hands. She doesn't open it, but rather runs a hand over the textured cover. She doesn't say anything and then, after a minute or so, she shakes her head. It's gone.

She slouches back into her chair and her fingers let go of the pad, allowing it to rest on her lap.

Grace snatches it from her. She opens the book and is greeted by an influx of Mia's sketches. Eve told me once that Mia takes a sketch pad with her everywhere she goes, drawing anything from homeless men on the "L" to a car parked at the train station. It's her way of keeping a journal: places she went, things she saw. Take this recycled sketch pad, for example: trees, and lots of them; a lake surrounded by trees; a homely little log cabin that, of course, we've all seen in the photos; a scrawny little tabby cat sleeping in a smattering of sun. None of this seems to surprise Grace, not until she comes to the illustration of Colin Thatcher that literally jumps off the page to greet her, snuck in the middle of the sketch pad amidst trees and the snow-covered cabin.

His appearance is bedraggled, his curly hair in complete disarray. The facial hair and tattered jeans and hooded sweatshirt surpass grunge and go straight to dirty. Mia had drawn a man, sturdy and tall. She applied herself to the eyes, shadowing and layering and darkening the pencil around them until these deep, leering headlights nearly force Grace to look away from the page.

"You drew this, you know," she states, compelling Mia to have a look at the page. She thrusts it into her hands to see. He's perched before a wood-burning stove, sitting cross-legged on the floor with his back to the flame. Mia runs her hand over the page and smudges the pencil a tad. She peers down at her fingertips and sees the remnants of lead, rubbing it between a thumb and forefinger.

"Does anything ring a bell?" I ask, sipping from my mug of coffee.

"Is this—" Mia hesitates "—him?"

"If by *him* you mean the creep who kidnapped you, then, yeah," Grace says, "that's him."

I sigh. "That's Colin Thatcher." I show her a photograph. Not a mug shot, like she's used to seeing, but a nice photo of him in his Sunday best. Mia's eyes go back and forth, making the connection. The curly hair. The hardy build. The dark eyes. The bristly beige skin. The way his arms are crossed before him, his face appearing to do anything to conceal a smile. "You're quite an artist," I offer.

Mia asks, "And I drew this?"

I nod. "They found the sketch pad at the cabin with your and Colin's things. I assume it belongs to you."

"You brought it with you to Minnesota?" Grace asks.

Mia shrugs. Her eyes are locked on the images of Colin Thatcher. Of course she doesn't know. Grace knows she doesn't know, but she asks anyway. She's thinking the same thing as me: here this creep is whisking her off to some abandoned cabin in Minnesota and she has the wherewithal to bring her sketch pad, of all things?

"What else did you bring?"

"I don't know," she says, her voice on the verge of being inaudible.

"Well, what else did you *find?*" Grace demands of me this time.

I watch Mia, recording her nonverbal communication: the way her fingers keep reaching out to touch the images before her, the frustration that is slowly, silently taking over. Every time she tries to give up and push the images away, she goes back to them, as if begging of her mind: *think, just think.* "Nothing out of the ordinary."

Grace gets mad. "What does that mean? Clothes, food, weapons—guns, bombs, knives—an artists' easel and a watercolor set? You ask me," she says, pilfering the sketch pad from Mia's hands, "this is out of the ordinary. A kidnapper doesn't normally allow his abductee to draw the evidence on a cheap, recycled sketch pad." She turns to Mia and presents the obvious. "If he sat still this long, Mia, long enough for you to draw this, then why didn't you run?"

She stares at Grace with a stark expression on her face. Grace sighs, completely exasperated, and looks at Mia like she should be locked up in a loony ward. Like she has no grasp on reality, where she is or why she's here. Like she wants to bang her over the head with a blunt object and knock some sense in her.

I come to her defense and say, "Maybe she was scared. Maybe there was nowhere to run. The cabin was in the middle of a vast wilderness, and northern Minnesota in the winter verges on a ghost town. There would have been nowhere to go. He might have found her, caught her and then what? Then what would have happened?"

Grace sulks into her chair and flips through the pages of the sketch pad, seeing the barren trees and the never-ending snow, this picturesque lake surrounded by dense woodland and…she nearly passes by it altogether and then flips back, ripping the page from its spiral binding, "Is that a *Christmas tree?*" she implores, gawking at the nostalgic image on the inner corner of a page. The tearing of the paper makes Mia leap from her seat.

I watch Mia startle and then lay a hand briefly on hers to put her at ease. "Oh, yeah," I laugh, though there's no amusement in it. "Yeah, I guess that would be considered out of the ordinary, wouldn't it? We found a Christmas tree. Charming really, if you ask me."

COLIN

BEFORE

She's fighting the urge to fall asleep when the call comes in. She's said about a thousand times that she needs to go. I've assured her that she doesn't.

It took every bit of self-control to pull away from her. To turn my back to her pleading eyes and force myself to forget it. There's just something wrong with screwing the girl you're about to snatch.

But somehow or other I convinced her to stay. She thinks it's for her own good. When she's sober, I said, I'd walk her down for a cab. Apparently she bought it.

The phone rings. She doesn't jump. She looks at me with the implication that it must be a girl. Who else would call in the middle of the night? It's approaching 2:00 a.m. and as I move into the kitchen to take the call, I see her rise from the couch. She tries to fight the lethargy that's taken over.

"Everything set?" Dalmar wants to know. I know nothing about Dalmar other than he just hopped off a boat and is blacker than anything I've ever seen. I've done jobs for Dalmar before: larceny and harassment. Never kidnapping.

"Un-huh." I peek out at the girl who's standing awkwardly

in the living room. She's waiting for me to finish up the call. Then she'll split. I move away. I get as far away as I can. I carefully slide a semiautomatic from the drawer.

"Two-fifteen," he says. I know where to meet: some dark corner of the underground where only homeless men wander at this time of night. I check my watch. I'm supposed to pull up behind a gray minivan. They grab the girl and leave the cash behind. That easy. I don't even have to get out of the car.

"Two-fifteen," I say. The Dennett girl is all but a hundred and twenty pounds. She's lost in the midst of insobriety and a splitting headache. This will be easy.

She's already saying that she's gonna go when I come back into the living room. She's headed to the front door. I stop her with a single arm around her waist. I draw her away from the door, my arm touching flesh. "You're not going anywhere."

"No, really," she says. "I have to work in the morning."

She giggles. Like maybe this is funny. Some kind of come-on.

But there's the gun. She sees it. And in that moment, things change. There's a moment of recognition. Of her mind registering the gun, of her figuring out what the fuck is about to happen. Her mouth parts and out comes a word: "Oh." And it's almost an afterthought, really, when she sees the gun and says, "What are you doing with that?" She backs away from me, bumping into the couch.

"You need to come with me." I step forward, closing the gap.

"Where?" she asks. When my hands come down on her, she jerks away. I unknot the arms and reel her in.

"Don't make this harder than it has to be."

"What are you doing with that gun?" she snaps. She's calmer than I expect her to be. She's concerned. But not screaming. Not crying. She's got her eyes bound to the gun.

"You just need to come with me." I reach out and grasp her arm. She's trembling. She slips away. But I hold her tight, twisting her arm. She cries out in pain. She shoots me a dirty look—hurt and unexpected. She tells me to let go, to keep my hands off her. There's a superiority in her voice that pisses me off. Like she's the one running this show.

She tries to rip free but finds she can't. I won't let her.

"Shut up," I say. I grip her wrist tighter and I know it hurts. My grasp is hurting her, leaving red finger marks along the flesh.

"This is a mistake," she barks. "You've got this all wrong." There's this strange composure to her, though her eyes remain glued to the gun. I can't tell you how many times I've heard that line. Every so-called victim says I've made a mistake.

"Shut up," I snap this time. With more authority. I back her against the wall, bumping into a lamp as I do. It crashes to the floor, hitting the parquet with a nasty thud. The lightbulb shatters. But the lamp doesn't break.

I hold her there. I tell her to shut up. I say it over and over again. Just shut the fuck up.

She isn't saying a word. She's got on her poker face, though inside she must be going ballistic.

"Okay," she says then, as if this is her choice. As if she has any say in the matter. She nods her head scornfully. She'll come with me. Her eyes are steady. Tired, but steady. Pretty, I think. She has pretty blue eyes. But then I force the thought from my mind. I can't think about shit like that. Not right now. Not before I hand her over to Dalmar. I need to finish the job. Be through with it before I start to second-guess myself.

With the gun pressed to her head, I tell her how it's going to be. She's gonna come with me. If she screams, I'll pull the trigger. It's that simple.

But she's not going to scream. Even I can see that.

"My purse," she says as we step over the bag she dropped to the floor when we made our way into the apartment, hours ago, floundering with each other's clothes.

"Forget your fucking purse," I snarl. I drag her into the hallway, slam the door shut.

It's cold outside. The wind is sailing in from the lake, blowing her hair about her face. She's freezing. My arm is wrapped tightly around her torso. Not for warmth. I don't give a damn if she's cold. I don't want her to run away. I hold her so tight that her left side rubs against my right side and at times our feet collide and we trip. We walk quickly, hurrying to the car parked on Ainslie.

"Hurry up," I say more than once, though we both know it's me that slows us down. I look behind, make sure we're not being trailed. She's staring at the ground, trying to avoid the cutting wind. Her coat has been abandoned in the apartment. Goose bumps line her skin. Her flimsy shirt fails to ward off the cold, early October air. There's no one on the street tonight but us.

I open the door for the girl and she gets in. I don't take the time to fasten my seat belt. I start the car and take off down the street, doing a U-turn on Ainslie and heading the wrong way on a one-way street.

The streets are all but empty. I drive too fast, knowing that I shouldn't, but wanting this to be through. She's silent, her breathing steady. She's strangely sedate. Though out of the corner of my eye I see her shake: the cold, the fear. I wonder what she thinks. She doesn't plead with me. She huddles into a ball on the passenger's seat of the pickup and stares out at the city.

It won't be long before we pull up behind the minivan and Dalmar's men will tear her from the truck, their dirty hands all over her. Dalmar has a temper. I don't know what they

have planned for the girl. Ransom. That's all I know. Hold
her for ransom until her father coughs up a substantial debt.
When the debt is paid, I don't know what they'll do. Kill her?
Send her back home? I doubt it. And if they do, it's only after
Dalmar and his guys have had a little fun with her, made it
worth their while.

My mind starts racing in a million different directions. And
now I'm thinking what will happen if I get caught. It'll all be
for nothing. Kidnapping carries up to a thirty-year sentence.
I know. I checked. I thought about that more than once, after
Dalmar hired me. But it's one thing to think about it, and another to do it. Now here I am, with the girl in the car, thinking about thirty years in the pen.

She won't look at me. At a stoplight, I stare at her. She
stares ahead and I know she can see me. I know she can feel
my eyes on her. She holds her breath. She fights the urge to
cry. I drive with one hand, the gun on my lap in the other.

It's not so much that I give a shit about the girl. Because I
don't. It's that I'm wondering what happens when word leaks
back home that I did this. When my name is attached to a kid-
napping/murder. And it would be. Dalmar would never sign
his name to this. He'd set me up. If and when this goes bad, I'll
be the stooge, the scapegoat, the one on the chopping block.

The light turns green. I get off on Michigan. A bunch of
drunken kids stand on the corner waiting for their bus. They're
monkeying around, being stupid. One of them stumbles from
curb. I swerve out of the way and almost hit him. "Idiot," I
mutter beneath my breath. He gives me the finger.

I consider my backup plan. I always have a backup plan,
for if and when things get messy. I've just never had to use
it. I check the gas gauge. There's enough to get us out of the
city, at least.

I should get off at Wacker. The red numbers on the truck's

dashboard read 2:12. Dalmar and his guys are in place, waiting. He could do it by himself, but he wouldn't. Dalmar never wants to get his hands dirty. He finds someone, some outcast like me to do the shit work, so he can sit back and watch. This way, when things go south, he's clean of any misdeeds. No fingerprints at the scene, his face omitted from any photographic evidence. He lets the rest of us, his *operatives* he calls us, like we're in the damn CIA, take the fall.

There's probably four of them in the van, four thugs just waiting to restrain this girl who sits still beside me when she could be fighting for her life.

My hands slip on the steering wheel. I'm sweating like a pig. I wipe them on my jeans and then I pound a fist against the steering wheel and the girl lets out a stifled cry.

I should get off at Wacker, but I don't. I keep driving.

I know this is stupid. I know everything that can go wrong. But I do it anyway. I peer in the rearview mirror, make sure that I'm not being trailed. And then I floor it. Down Michigan, to Ontario, and I'm on 90 before the clock ever reaches 2:15.

I don't say anything to the girl because there isn't anything I could say that she'd believe.

I'm not sure at what point it happens. It's somewhere as we're driving away from the city, as the skyline starts to disappear into the blackness, as the buildings get swallowed up by the distance. She squirms in her seat, the composure starting to wane. Her eyes move: out the side window, turning around and staring out the rear window as the city melts away. As if someone finally flipped the switch and *now* she realizes what the hell is happening. "Where are we going?" she demands, her voice becoming hysterical. The poker face has given way to gaping eyes, to ruddy skin. I see it in the glow of streetlights we fly past, illuminating her face every five seconds or so.

For a split second she begs me to let her go. I tell her to shut up. I don't want to hear it. By now she's crying. Now the water works have begun and she's a blubbering mess, begging me to let her go. She asks again: *Where are we going?* And I pick up the gun. I can't stand the sound of her voice, blaring and shrill. I need her to shut up. I point the gun at her and tell her to shut the fuck up. And she does. She's quiet, but she continues to cry, wiping her nose on a too-short sleeve as we soar out of the city and into suburbia, trees swapping places with skyscrapers, the Blue Line snaking down the middle of the road.

EVE

AFTEЯ

Mia sits at the kitchen table, holding a legal-size manila envelope with her name written on the front in a very masculine all-caps script.

I prepare dinner for Mia and myself. The TV is on in the
next room for background noise, but the sound drifts into the
kitchen, compensating for the silence between us. Mia doesn't
seem to notice, but these days, it makes me a nervous wreck,
and so I make idle conversation to offset the silence.

"Would you like chicken breast with your salad?" I ask
and she shrugs. "Whole wheat rolls or white?" I ask but she
doesn't respond.

"I'll make the chicken," I say. "Your father would like
chicken." But we both know that James will not be home.

"What's that?" I ask, motioning to the item in her hands.

"What's what?" she asks.

"The envelope."

"Oh," she says. "This."

I set a frying pan on the stove, slamming it down without intent. She starts, and I'm quick to apologize, filled with
shame. "Oh, Mia, honey, I didn't mean to startle you," I say

and it takes a moment for her to settle, to attach the rapid heartbeat and beads of sweat to the sound of the frying pan.

She says that she doesn't know why she feels like this.

She says that she used to enjoy when darkness set in, when the outside world changed. She describes it for me: the way the streetlights and buildings twinkled in the night sky. She says that she liked the anonymity of it, and all the possibilities that developed when the sun went to sleep. But now the darkness terrifies her, all the nameless things on the other side of the silk drapes.

Mia never used to be afraid. She would wander city streets well after dark and feel perfectly safe. She confides that she often found solace in deafening traffic, obtrusive car horns and sirens that blared at all times of the night. But now the sound of a frying pan rattles her nerves.

I'm overly apologetic, and Mia tells me that it's all right. She listens to the television in the other room. The evening news has given way to a seven o'clock sitcom. "Mia?" I ask and she turns to me.

"What?" she asks.

"The envelope." I motion toward it and it's then that she remembers.

She turns it over in her hands. "That policeman gave it to me," she says.

I'm slicing a tomato. "Detective Hoffman?"

"Yes."

Mia usually only comes downstairs when James is gone. The rest of the time she hides. I'm certain this room must remind her of her childhood. The room is the same as it's been for a dozen years or more: the paint, the color of butter, the mood lighting. Candles are lit. The track lighting is dimmed. The table is a dark pedestal table with scrolled legs and matching upholstered chairs, where she spent too much time under a microscope as a child. I'm certain she feels like a child, unable to be left alone, having to be cooked for and constantly watched. Her independence is gone.

Yesterday she asked when she could go home, to her own apartment, and all I replied was *in time.*

James and I don't let her leave the house, not unless we're going to see Dr. Rhodes or to the police station. Running errands is out of the question. For days the doorbell rang from dawn to dusk, men and women with microphones and video cameras awaiting us on the front stoop. *Mia Dennett, we'd like to ask you a few questions* they'd demand, forcing their microphones at Mia, until I told her not to open the door, and started ignoring the chime altogether. The telephone rang relentlessly, and those infrequent times I did answer it, the only thing I ever said was, "No comment." After a day or so, I started letting it go straight to voice mail, and then, when the ringing became too much to bear, I unplugged the phone from the wall.

"Well, aren't you going to open it?" I remind Mia.

She slides her finger under the flap and lifts it open. There's a single sheet of paper inside. She draws it carefully from the envelope and takes a look. I set the knife on a cutting board and saunter to the table beside Mia, feigning only a little interest when I'm absolutely certain I'm the more attentive of us two.

It's a photocopy, a drawing from a sketch pad, with circles lining the top where the original was ripped from its spiral binding. It's a drawing of a person, a woman, I can only assume from the longish hair.

"I drew this," Mia says to me, but I slip the drawing from her hands.

"May I?" I ask, dropping into the chair beside her. "Why do you say that?" I ask, my hands beginning to tremble, my

stomach turning somersaults inside me. Mia has been drawing for as long as I can remember. She's a talented artist. I
asked her once why she loved to draw, why it was something
with which she was so enamored. She told me that she drew
because it was the only way she could bring about change.
She could turn geese to swans or a cloudy day to sun. It was
a place where reality didn't have to exist.

But this picture is something else entirely. The eyes are
perfectly circular, the smile the sort she learned to draw in
grade school. The eyelashes are upwardly pointing lines. The
face is malformed.

"It came from the same notebook, the one Detective Hoffman had. The one with my drawings."

"You didn't draw this," I say with absolute certainty.
"Maybe ten years ago. When you were first learning. But not
now. This is much too *ordinary* for you. It's mediocre at best."

A timer beeps and I rise to my feet. Mia reaches for the
page to have a second look. "Why would the policeman give
this to me then?" she asks, turning the envelope over in her
hands. I tell her that I don't know.

I'm setting whole wheat rolls onto a cookie sheet that will
bake in the oven, when Mia asks, "Then who? Who drew
this?" On the stove, the chicken sears.

I lower the cookie sheet into the bottom of the oven. I flip
the chicken, and begin dicing a cucumber as if perhaps it was
Colin Thatcher himself lying on the cutting board before me.

I shrug my shoulders. "That picture," I say, trying hard not
to cry. Mia sits at the table, examining that picture, and I see
it, clear as day: the long hair, the circular eyes, the U-shaped
smile. "That picture," I say, "it's you."

COLIN

BEFORE

We're on the Kennedy before I ever bother to turn on the heat. Somewhere into Wisconsin I turn on the radio. Static blares out of the rear speakers. The girl is watching out the side window. She doesn't say a thing. I'm certain a pair of headlights has followed us the entire length of Interstate 90, but they disappear just outside of Janesville, Wisconsin.

I exit the interstate. The road is dark and deserted and seems to lead to nowhere. I pull into a gas station. There isn't an attendant on duty. I kill the engine and get out to fill up the tank, bringing the gun with me.

I've got my eyes on her the entire time, when I see a glow from inside the truck, the light from a cell phone that's come to life. How could I be so stupid? I thrust open the door, scare the shit out of her. She jumps, tries to hide the phone under her shirt.

"Give me your phone," I snap, ticked I forgot to ditch her phone before we left.

The light from the gas station fills the truck. She's a damn mess, makeup down her face, her hair a catastrophe. "Why?" she asks. I know she's not this dumb.

"Just give it to me."

"Why?"

"Just give it to me."

"I don't have it," she lies.

"Give me the fucking phone," I yell as I reach over and yank it from beneath her shirt. She tells me to get my hands off her. I check the phone. She got as far as finding the contact list but that's all. As I go to fill up the tank, I make sure it's off, then dump it into the trash. Even if the cops trace the signal, we'll be nowhere around when they do.

I scavenge the back of the truck for something—rope, an extension cord, a piece of fucking string. I bind her hands together, tight enough that she cries out in pain. "Try that again," I say when I get back in the truck, "and I'll kill you." I slam the door and start the engine.

There's only one thing that's certain: when I didn't show up with the girl, Dalmar sent everyone he knows after us. By now they've torn apart my apartment. There's a hit out on both our heads. There isn't a chance in hell I'm going back. If this girl is dumb enough to try, she'll be dead. But I won't let that happen. She'll tell them where I am before they kill her, but I'll kill her first. I've already done enough good deeds.

We drive through the night. She closes her eyes, only for a couple of seconds, then jerks them open again and searches the truck to realize that it isn't a nightmare. It's all real: me, the dirty truck, its vinyl seats torn, cotton falling out, the static on the radio, the endless fields and the dark night sky. The gun sits on my lap—I know she doesn't have the guts to reach for it—and my hands clutch the steering wheel, as I drive slower now that I know we're not being followed.

She asks once why I'm doing this, her voice shaking as she speaks. "Why are you doing this to me?" she asks. It's somewhere around Madison. She'd gone all this time in silence, listening to some Catholic priest ramble on and on about original sin, his voice cutting out every third or fourth word. And then all of a sudden, *Why are you doing this* to me, and it's the *to me* part that really rubs me the wrong way. She thinks it's all about her. It doesn't have a thing to do with her. She's a pawn, a puppet, a sacrificial lamb.

"Don't worry about it," I say.

She doesn't like this answer. "You don't even know me," she accuses in a patronizing way.

"I know you," I say with a fleeting look her way. It's dark in the car. I can't see more than an outline, obscured by the blackness outside the window.

"What did I do to you? What did I ever do to you?" she pleads.

She never did a thing to me. I know it. She knows it. But I tell her to shut up anyway. "Enough." And when she doesn't I say it again. "Just shut up." The third time I scream, "Just shut the fuck up," the gun flailing about and pointing her way. I swerve off the road and slam on the brakes. I step from the truck and already she's screaming at me to leave her alone.

I reach in the bed of the truck for a roll of duct tape, tear off a piece with my teeth. There's a chill in the air, the sound of the occasional semitruck soaring down the road in the middle of the night. "What are you doing?" she asks, her feet kicking at me the minute I open her door. She kicks hard and gets me in the gut. She's a fighter, I'll give her that, but the only thing it does is make me pissed. I force my way into the truck, slap the duct tape over her moving lips and say, "I told you to shut up."

And she does.

I get back in the truck and slam the door, pulling blindly out onto the interstate, the wheels kicking up gravel from the shoulder of the road.

It's no wonder then that it takes a good hundred or so miles for her to tell me she has to pee, to get the guts to lay a trembling hand on my arm and get my attention.

"What?" I snap, pulling my arm away from her hand. It's approaching dawn. She's wiggling in her seat. There's a sense of urgency in her eyes. I rip off the duct tape and she lets out a moan. It hurt. It hurt like hell.

Good, I think to myself. That'll teach her to keep her mouth shut when I tell her to.

"I have to use the bathroom," she mumbles, afraid.

I pull into the gravel parking lot of some run-down truck stop outside Eau Claire. The sun is beginning to rise over a dairy farm to the east. A herd of Holsteins grazes along the road. It's gonna be a sunny day, but it's damn cold. October. The trees are changing.

In the parking lot I hesitate. It's all but empty, only one car, a rusty old station wagon with political bumper stickers plastered across the back, the rear headlight held to the car with packaging tape. My heart races. I stick the gun in the seat of my pants. It's not like I haven't been thinking about this since we left. I knew this was something I'd have to do. By now the girl was supposed to be with Dalmar, and I figured I'd be trying hard to forget what I'd done. I didn't plan for this. But if this is going to work, there are things we need, like money. I have some money on me but not enough for this. I emptied the girl's wallet before we left. Credit cards are out of the question. I pull a knife from the glove box. Before I cut the girl's restraints I say, "You stay with me. Don't try anything stupid." I tell her she can use the bathroom when I say so, only when I say it's okay. I cut her rope. Then I cut two feet of spare rope and stuff it in a coat pocket.

The girl looks ridiculous as she steps from the truck in the wrinkled shirt that doesn't even reach all the way to her wrists. She crosses her arms across herself and ties them into a knot. She shudders from the cold. Her hair falls down into her face. She keeps her head bent, eyes on the gravel. Her forearms are bruised, right across some stupid Chinese tattoo on her inner arm.

There's only one lady working, not a single customer. Just as I thought. I wrap my arm around the girl and pull her toward me, try to make it seem like we're close. Her feet hesitate and fall out of sync with mine. She trips but I stop her before she can fall. My eyes threaten her to behave. My hands on her are not a sign of intimacy. They're a show of force. She knows it, but the lady behind the register does not.

We walk up and down the aisles, make sure as hell we're the only ones in the place. I grab a box of envelopes. I check the bathroom to make sure it's empty. I make sure there isn't a window the girl could jump out of, and then I tell her to pee. The woman at the register gives me a strange look. I roll my eyes and tell her the girl's had too much to drink. Apparently she buys it. It seems to take forever for the girl to pee and when I peek inside again, she's standing before the mirror, splashing water on her face. She stares at her reflection for a long time. "Let's go," I say after a minute.

And then we head to the register to pay for the envelopes. But we don't pay for the envelopes. The lady's distracted, watching old 1970s reruns on a twelve-inch TV. I look around, make sure there's no cameras in the place.

And then I come up behind her, pull the gun from the seat of my pants and tell her to empty the fucking register.

I don't know who panics more. The girl freezes, her face filled with fear. Here I am, with the barrel of the gun pressed against some middle-aged lady's gray hair, and she's a witness. An accomplice. The girl starts asking what I'm doing. Over and over again. "What are you doing?" she cries.

I tell her to shut up.

The lady is begging for her life. "Please don't hurt me. Please just let me go." I shove her forward, tell her again to empty the register. She opens it, and starts jamming stacks of cash into a plastic shopping bag with a big smiley face and the words *Have a nice day.* I tell the girl to look out the window. Tell me if anyone's coming. She nods, submissively, like a child. "No," she chokes between tears. "No one." And then she asks, *"What are you doing?"*

I press the gun harder, tell the lady to hurry up.

"Please. Please don't hurt me."

"The quarters, too," I say. There are rolls of them. "You got any stamps?" I ask. Her hands start to move to a drawer and I bark out, "Don't touch a damn thing. Tell me. You got any stamps?" Because for all I know, there's a semiautomatic in that drawer.

She whimpers at the sound of my voice. "In the drawer," she cries. "Please don't hurt me," she begs. She tells me about her grandchildren. Two of them, a boy and a girl. The only name I catch is Zelda. What kind of stupid name is Zelda anyway? I reach into the drawer and find a book of stamps and toss them into the shopping bag, which I yank from her hands and give to the girl.

"Hold that," I say. "Just stand there and hold it." I let the gun point at her for a split second, just so she knows I'm not screwing around. She lets out a cry and ducks as if maybe— just maybe—I actually shot her.

I tie the lady to a chair with the rope from my pocket. Then I shoot the phone for good measure. Both of the women scream.

I can't have her calling the cops too soon.

There's a pile of sweatshirts beside the front door. I grab one and tell the girl to put it on. I'm sick and tired of watching her shiver. She slips it over her head and static takes control of her hair. It's about the ugliest shirt I've ever seen. *L'étoile du Nord.* Whatever the hell that means.

I grab a couple extra sweatshirts, a few pairs of pants—long johns—and some socks. And a couple stale donuts for the ride.

And then we go.

In the truck, I bind the girl's hands once again. She's still crying. I tell her to either figure out a way to shut up or I'll figure it out for her. Her eyes drop to the roll of duct tape on the dashboard and she goes quiet. She knows I'm not screwing around.

I grab an envelope and fill out the address. I stuff as much money as I can in there and stick a stamp in the corner. I jam the rest of the money in my pocket. We drive around until I find a big blue mailbox and drop the envelope inside. The girl's watching me, wondering what the hell I'm doing, but she doesn't ask and I don't say. When I catch her eye, I say, "Don't worry about it," and then I think, *It's none of your fucking business.*

It's not perfect. It's nowhere perfect. But for now it will have to do.

EVE

AFTEЯ

I've gotten used to the sight of police cars stalled outside my home. There are two of them there, day and night, four uniformed guards keeping an eye on Mia. They sit in the front seat of the police cruisers, drinking coffee and eating sandwiches that they take turns picking up from the deli. I stare from the bedroom windows, peering between the plantation blinds that I've split apart with a hand. They look like schoolboys to me, younger than my own children, but they carry guns and nightsticks and peer up at me with binoculars and just stare. I convince myself that they can't see me when, night after night, I dim the lights to change into a pair of flannel pajamas, but the truth is that I don't know.

Mia sits on the front porch every day, seemingly indifferent to the bitter cold. She stares at the snow that surrounds our home like the moat of a castle. She watches the dormant trees lurch back and forth in the wind. But she doesn't notice the police cars, the four men who study her all hours of the day. I've begged her not to leave the porch and she's agreed, though sometimes she makes her way across the snow and onto the sidewalk, where she strolls by the homes of Mr. and

Mrs. Pewter and the Donaldson family. While one of the cars crawls along behind her, the other sends an officer to get me, and I come running out the door with bare feet to snatch up my wandering daughter. "Mia, honey, where are you going?" I've heard myself ask countless times, gathering her by the shirtsleeves and reeling her in. She never wears a coat and her hands are ice-cold. She never knows where she's going but she always follows me home and I thank the officers as we pass by, on our way into the kitchen for a cup of warm milk. She shivers as she drinks it and when she's through she says she's going to bed. She's felt unwell for the past week, always longing to be in bed.

But today for some reason she sees the police cars. I pull out of the garage and onto the street, en route to Dr. Rhodes's office for Mia's first round of hypnosis. It's a moment of lucidity that passes by as she gazes out the window and asks, "What are they doing here?" as if they had arrived right then and there in that single lucid moment.

"Keeping us safe," I say diplomatically. What I mean to say is keeping *you* safe, but I don't want her to fear the reasons she's not.

"From what?" she asks, turning her head to watch the policemen through the back window. One starts his car and follows us down the road. The other lingers behind to keep an eye on the house while we're gone.

"There's nothing to be afraid of," I respond in lieu of an answer to her question, and she gratefully accepts it, turning around to watch out the front window and forgetting altogether that we're being trailed.

We drive down the neighborhood street. It's quiet. The kids have returned to school after two weeks of winter break and no longer loiter in their front lawns building snowmen and tossing snowballs at one another with high, shrieking laughter, sounds that are foreign in our uncommunicative home. Christmas lights remain on homes, those inflatable Santas unplugged and lying dead in mounds of snow. James didn't take the time to decorate the exterior of the house this year, though I went all out on the inside just in case. Just in case Mia came home and there was cause to celebrate.

She's agreed to hypnosis. It didn't take much coaxing. These days Mia agrees to most everything. James is against the idea; he thinks hypnosis is a bogus science, equivalent to reading palms and astrology. I don't know what I believe, though I'll be damned if I don't give it a try. If it helps Mia remember one split second of those missing months, it's worth the exorbitant cost and the time spent in the waiting room of Dr. Avery Rhodes.

What I understood of hypnosis a week ago was negligible. After awakening at night to research hypnosis on the internet, I became enlightened. Hypnosis, as I've come to understand it, is a very relaxed trancelike state similar to daydreaming. This will allow Mia to become less inhibited and tune out the rest of the world to allow herself, with the doctor's help, to arouse the memories she's lost. Under hypnosis, the subject becomes highly suggestible, and can recall information that the mind has locked in a vault. By hypnotizing Mia, Dr. Rhodes will be dealing directly with the subconscious, that part of the brain that's hidden Mia's memories from her. The goal is to put Mia into a state of deep relaxation so her conscious mind, more or less, goes to sleep and Dr. Rhodes can deal with the subconscious. For Mia's sake, the goal is to regain all or some part—some minute details even—of her time in the cabin so that, through therapy, she can come to terms with her abduction and heal. For the investigation's sake, however, Detective Hoffman is desperate for information, for any details or clues that Colin Thatcher might have aired in the cabin that would help police find the man who did this to Mia.

When we arrive at Dr. Rhodes's office, I, at James's insistence, am allowed inside. He wants me to keep an eye on the *nutcase,* what he calls Dr. Rhodes, in case she tries to *screw* with Mia's head. I sit in an armchair out of the way while Mia, squeamishly, sprawls out on the couch. Textbooks line floor-to-ceiling bookshelves on the southernmost wall. There is a window that faces the parking lot. Dr. Rhodes keeps the blinds closed, allowing in only a scant amount of light, so there's an abundance of privacy. The room is dark and discreet, the secrets revealed inside the walls absorbed by the burgundy paint and oak wainscoting. The room is drafty; I pull my sweater tightly around my body and hug myself as Mia's conscious mind begins to get drowsy. The doctor says, "We'll start with off with the simple things, with what we know to be true, and see where that leads."

It doesn't come back chronologically. It doesn't even come back sensibly and, to me, long after we escape into the piercing winter day, it's a puzzle. I had imagined that hypnosis would be able to unlock the vault and there, in that very instant, all the memories would topple onto the faux Persian rug so that Mia, the doctor and I could hover over and dissect them. But that's not the way it happens at all. For the limited time Mia is under hypnosis—maybe twenty minutes but no more—the door is open and Dr. Rhodes, with a kind, harmonious voice, is trying to pry away the cookie's layers to get at the cream filling. They come off in crumbs: the rustic feel of the cabin with the knotty pine paneling and exposed beams, static on a car radio, the sound of Beethoven's *Für Elise,* spotting a moose.

"Who's in the car, Mia?"

"I'm not sure."

"Are you there?"

"Yes."

"Are you driving the car?"

"No."

"Who's driving the car?"

"I don't know. It's dark."

"What time of day is it?"

"Early morning. The sun is just beginning to rise."

"You can see out the window?"

"Yes."

"Do you see stars?"

"Yes."

"And the moon?"

"Yes."

"A full moon?"

"No." She shakes her head. "A half moon."

"Do you know where you are?"

"On a highway. It's a small, two-lane highway, surrounded by woods."

"Are there other cars?"

"No."

"Do you see street signs?"

"No."

"Do you hear anything?"

"Static. From the radio. There's a man speaking, but his voice...there's static." Mia is lying on the couch with her legs crossed at the ankles. It's the first time I've seen her relax in the last two weeks. Her arms are folded against a bare mid-riff—her chunky cream sweater having hiked up an inch or two when she laid down—as if she's been placed in a casket.

"Can you hear what the man is saying?" Dr. Rhodes asks from where she sits on a maroon armchair beside Mia. The woman is the epitome of together: not a wrinkle in her clothing, not a hair out of place. The sound of her voice is monotonous; it could lull me to sleep.

"Temperatures in the forties, plenty of sun..."

"The weather forecast?"

"It's a disc jockey—the sound is coming from the radio. But the static... The front speakers don't work. The voice comes from the backseat."

"Is there someone in the backseat, Mia?"

"No. It's just us."

"Us?"

"I can see his hands in the darkness. He drives with two hands, holding the steering wheel so tightly."

"What else can you tell me about him?" Mia shakes her head. "Can you see what he's wearing?"

"No."

"But you can see his hands?"

"Yes."

"Is there anything on his hands—a ring, watch? Anything?"

"I don't know."

"What can you tell me about his hands?"

"They're rough."

"You can see that? You can see that his hands are rough?"

I scoot to the edge of my seat, hanging on to Mia's every last muted word. I know that Mia—the old Mia, pre-Colin Thatcher—would have never wanted me to hear this conversation.

This question she doesn't answer.

"Is he hurting you?" Mia twitches on the couch, pushing aside the question. Dr. Rhodes asks again, "Did he hurt you, Mia? There, in the car, or maybe before?" There's no response.

The doctor moves on. "What else can you tell me about the car?"

But Mia states instead, "This wasn't...this wasn't supposed... to happen."

"What wasn't, Mia?" she asks. "What wasn't supposed to happen?"

"It's all wrong," Mia replies. She's disoriented, her visions cluttered, random memories running adrift in her mind.

"What is all wrong?" There's no reply. "Mia, what is all wrong? The car? Something about the car?"

But Mia says nothing. Not at first anyway. But then she sucks her breath in violently, and claims, "It's my fault. It's all my fault," and it takes every bit of willpower I have not to rush from my seat and embrace my child. I want to tell her that no, it's not. It's not her fault. I can see the way it grieves her, the way her facial features tense up, her flattened hands turn to fists. "I did this," she says.

"This is not your fault, Mia," Dr. Rhodes states. Her voice is pensive, soothing. I grip the arms of the chair in which I sit and force myself to remain calm. "It's not your fault," she repeats, and later, after the session is through, she explains to me in private that victims almost always blame themselves. She says that often this is the case with rape victims, the reason that nearly fifty percent of rapes go unreported because the victim feels certain it was her fault. If only she had never gone to such and such a bar; if only she had never talked to such and such a stranger; if only she hadn't worn such suggestive attire. Mia, she explains, is experiencing a natural phenomenon that psychologists and sociologists have been studying for years: self-blame. "Self-blame can, of course, be destructive," she says to me later as Mia waits in the waiting room for me to catch up, "when taken to the extreme, but it can also prevent victims from becoming vulnerable in the future." As if this is supposed to make me feel relieved.

"Mia, what else do you see?" the doctor inquires when Mia has settled.

She's taciturn, initially. The doctor asks again, "Mia, what else do you see?"

This time Mia responds, "A house."

"Tell me about the house."

"It's small."

"What else?"

"A deck. A small deck with steps that lead down into the woods. It's a log cabin—dark wood. You can barely see it for all the trees. It's old. Everything about it is old—the furniture, the appliances."

"Tell me about the furniture."

"It sags. The couch is plaid. Blue-and-white plaid. Nothing about the house is comfortable. There's an old wooden rocking chair, lamps that barely light the room. A tiny table with wobbly legs and a plaid vinyl tablecloth that you'd bring to a picnic. The hardwood floors creak. It's cold. It smells."

"Like what?"

"Mothballs."

Later that night, as we hover in the kitchen after dinner, James asks me what in the hell the smell of mothballs has to do with anything. I tell him that its progress, albeit slow progress. But it's a start. Something that yesterday Mia couldn't remember. I, too, had longed for something phenomenal: one session of hypnosis and Mia would be healed. Dr. Rhodes sensed my frustration when we were leaving her office and explained to me that we needed to be patient; these things take time and to rush Mia will do more harm than good. James doesn't buy it; he's certain it's only a ploy for more money. I watch him yank a beer from the refrigerator and head into his office to work while I clean the dinner dishes, noticing, for the third time this week, that Mia's plate has barely been touched. I stare at the spaghetti noodles hardening on the earthenware dishes and remember that spaghetti is Mia's favorite meal.

I start a list and begin to archive things one by one: the rough hands, for example, or the weather forecast. I spend the night on the internet rummaging around for useful information. The last time the temperatures in northern Minnesota were in the forties was in the last week of November, though the temperatures toyed around in the thirties and forties from Mia's disappearance until after Thanksgiving day. After that they plunged into the twenties and below and likely won't creep up to forty for some time. There was a half moon on September 30th, October 14th and another on the 29th; there was one on November 12th and another on the 28th, though Mia couldn't be certain that the moon was exactly at half and so the dates are only suggestions. Moose are common in Minnesota, especially in the winter. Beethoven wrote *Für Elise* around 1810, though Elise was actually supposed to be Therese, a woman he was to marry in the same year.

Before I go to bed, I pass by the room in which Mia sleeps. I silently open the door and stand there, watching her, the way she is draped across the bed, the blanket thrust from her body at some point in the night where it lies in a puddle on the floor. The moon welcomes itself into the bedroom through the slats on the plantation blinds, streaking Mia with traces of light, across her face, down a set of knit eggplant pajamas, the right leg of which is hiked up to the knee and tossed across an extra pillow. It's the only time these days when Mia is at peace. I move across the room to cover her and feel my body lower to the edge of the bed. Her face is serene, her soul calm, and though she's a woman, I still envision my blissful little girl long before she was taken away from me. Mia's being here feels too good to be true. I would sit here all night if I could, to convince myself that it isn't a dream, that when I wake in the morning, Mia—or Chloe—will still be here.

As I climb into bed beside James's blazing body, the bulk of the down comforter actually making him sweat, I wonder what good this information—the weather forecast and phases of the moon—actually does me, though I've stuck it in a folder beside the dozens of meanings for the name Chloe. Why, I don't know for certain, but I tell myself that any details notable enough for Mia to recount under hypnosis are important to me, any scrap of information to explain to me what happened to my daughter inside the log walls of that rural, Minnesota cabin.

COLIN

BEFOЯE

There's trees and a lot of them. Pine, spruce, fir. They hold on tight to their green needles. Around them, the leaves of oaks and elms wither and fall to the ground. It's Wednesday. Night has come and gone. We exit the highway and speed along a two-lane road. She holds on to the seat with every turn. I could slow down but I don't because I just want to get there. There's hardly anyone on the road. Every now and then we pass another car, some tourist going below the speed limit to enjoy the view. There's no gas stations. No 7-Elevens. Just your run-of-the-mill ma-and-pa shop. The girl stares out the window as we pass. I'm sure she thinks we're in Timbuktu. She doesn't bother to ask. Maybe she knows. Maybe she doesn't care.

We continue north into the deepest, darkest corners of Minnesota. The traffic continues to thin beyond Two Harbors where the truck is nearly engulfed in needles and leaves. The road is full of potholes. They send us flying into the air and I curse every single one of them. Last thing we need is a flat tire.

I've been here before. I used to know the guy who owns the place, a crappy little cabin in the middle of nowhere. It's lost in the trees, the ground covered in a crunchy layer of dead leaves. The trees are little more than barren branches.

I look at the cabin, and it's just like I remember, just like when I was a kid. It's a log home overlooking the lake. The lake looks cold. I'm sure it is. There's plastic lawn chairs out on the deck and a tiny grill. The world is desolate, no one around for miles and miles.

Exactly what we need.

I glide the truck to a stop and we get out. Yanking a crowbar from the back, we make our way up a hill to the old home. The cabin looks abandoned, as I knew it would be, but I look for signs of life anyway: a car parked in back, dark shadows through the windows. There's nothing.

She stands motionless beside the truck. "Let's go," I say. Finally she climbs up the dozen or so steps to the deck. She stops to catch her breath. "Hurry up," I say. For all I know, we're being watched. I knock on the door first, just to make sure that we're alone. And then I tell the girl to shut up and I listen. It's silent.

I use the crowbar to jimmy the door open. I break the door. I tell her I'll fix it later. I slide an end table before the door to keep it closed. The girl stands with her back pressed to a wall made of red pine logs. She looks around. The room is small. There's a saggy blue couch and ugly plastic red chair and a wood-burning stove in the corner that doesn't give off an ounce of heat. There are photos of the cabin when it was being built, old black-and-whites shot with a box camera, and I remember being told by the guy about it when I was a kid, about how the people who built the home a hundred years ago picked this location not for the view, but for the row of pine trees just east of the cabin that shield it from the driving winds. As if he had any way of knowing what thoughts ran through their minds, those people, dead by now, who built the home.

I remember, even back then, staring at his greasy receding hairline and pockmarked skin and thinking he's full of crap.

There's the kitchen with mustard-colored appliances and linoleum floors and a table covered in a plastic tablecloth. Dust covers everything in sight. There are spiderwebs and a layer of dead Asian beetles on the windowsills. It smells.

"Get used to it," I say. I see the disgust in her eyes. I'm sure the judge's house would never look like this.

I flip the light switch and test the water. Nothing. The cabin was winterized before he took off for the winter. It's not like we talk anymore, but I keep tabs on him anyway. I know his marriage fell through, again, know he got arrested a year or so ago for a DUI. I know that a couple weeks ago, as he does every fall, he packed his shit and left, back to Winona, where he works for the D.O.T., clearing ice and snow off the roads.

I yank a phone from a phone jack and, finding a pair of scissors in a kitchen drawer, cut the wire. I glance at the girl, who hasn't moved from the door. Her eyes are fixed on the plaid tablecloth. It's ugly, I know. I step outside to pee. A minute later I return. She's still staring at that damn tablecloth.

"Why don't you make yourself useful and start a fire," I say.

She puts her hands on her hips and stares at me, with that god-awful sweatshirt from the gas station. "Why don't you?" she says, but her voice shakes, her hands shake, and I know she's not as fearless as she wants me to think.

I stomp outside and bring in three logs of firewood and drop them to the ground beside her feet. She jumps. I hand her some matches, which she lets drop to the floor, the carton opening and matches falling out. I tell her to pick them up. She ignores me.

She needs to understand that I'm the one in the driver's seat. Not her. She's along for the ride, so long as she keeps her mouth shut and does what I say. I yank the gun from a pocket and attach the magazine. And I point it at her. At those pretty blue eyes that go from sure to not-so-sure as she whispers to me, "You've got this all wrong," and as I cock the hammer, I tell her to pick up the matches and start a fire. And I'm wondering if this was a mistake, if I should've just handed her over to Dalmar. I don't know what I expected from the girl, but this sure as hell isn't it. I never figured I'd end up with an ingrate. She's staring at me. A challenge. Seeing if I have it in me to kill her.

I take a step closer and hold the gun to her head.

And then she caves. She drops to the floor and with those shaking hands, picks up the matches. One by one. And drops them in the cardboard box.

And I stand there with the gun pointed at her while she scrapes one match and then another against the striking surface. The flame burns her fingers before she can start a fire. She sucks on her finger and then tries again. And again. And again. She knows I'm watching her. By now, her hands are shaking so much she can't light the damn match.

"Let me do it," I say as I come up quickly behind her. She flinches. I start a fire without any trouble and brush past the girl, into the kitchen, looking for food. There's nothing, not even a box of stale crackers.

"What now?" she asks but I ignore her. "What are we doing *here?*" I walk around the cabin, just to make sure. The water doesn't work. Everything has been shut off for the winter. Not that I can't fix it. It's reassuring. When he winterized the house, he wasn't planning on coming back until spring, the time of year he goes underground, lives like a hermit for six months of the year.

I can hear her pacing about, waiting for someone or something to come barreling through the front door and kill her. I tell her to stop. I tell her to sit down. She stands there for a long time before she finally backs a plastic chair against the wall opposite the front door and drops down in the seat. She waits. It's apocalyptic, watching her sit there, staring at the front door, waiting for the end to come.

Night comes and goes. Neither of us sleeps.

The cabin will be cold by winter. It was never meant to be lived in beyond November 1. The only source of heat in the cabin is a wood-burning stove. There's antifreeze in the john. The electricity had been shut off. That I fixed last night. I found the main breaker and flipped it back on. I literally heard the girl thank God for the 25 watts given off by an ugly table lamp. I made my way around the periphery of the cabin. I checked out a shed out back that's filled with a bunch of crap nobody'd ever need, and a few things that might come in handy. Like a toolbox.

Yesterday I told the girl she'd have to piss outside. I was too tired to deal with plumbing. I'd watched her walk down the stairs as if she was walking the plank. She hid herself behind a tree and slid down her pants. She squatted where she thought I couldn't see, and then, because she wouldn't dare touch her ass with a leaf, she opted to air dry. She only peed once.

Today I find the main water valve and slowly let the water in. It sprays at first, then begins to flow normally. I flush the toilet and run the sinks to get rid of the antifreeze. I make a mental list of things we need: insulation and more duct tape for the pipes, toilet paper, food.

She's pretentious. Smug and arrogant, a prima donna. She ignores me because she's pissed off and scared, but also because she thinks she's too good for me. She sits on the ugly red chair and stares out the window. At what? At nothing. Just stares. She hasn't said more than two words since morning.

"Let's go," I say. I tell her to get back in the car. We're going for a ride.

"Where?" She doesn't want to go anywhere. She'd rather stare out that damn window and count the leaves falling from the trees.

"You'll see." She's scared. She doesn't like the uncertainty. She doesn't move, but watches me with fake courage and deluded defiance when I know she's fucking scared to death. "You want to eat, don't you?"

Apparently she does.

And so we head outside. We get back in the truck and take off for Grand Marais.

I make a plan in my head: get out of the country, soon. I'll leave the girl behind. I don't need her slowing me down. I'll get a flight to Zimbabwe or Saudi Arabia, some place where they can't extradite me. Soon, I tell myself. I'll do it soon. I'll tie her up in the cabin and hightail it to Minneapolis for a flight before she has a chance to spread my face all over Interpol.

I tell her that I can't call her Mia. Not in public. Soon enough word will leak out that the girl's missing. I should leave her in the car, but I can't. She'll take off. And so she wears my baseball cap and I tell her to look down, don't make eye contact. It probably doesn't need to be said. She knows more about the gravel than me. I ask what she wants me to call her. After enough hesitation to start to piss me off, she comes up with Chloe.

No one gives a damn that I'm missing. When I don't show up at work, they'll assume I'm lazy. It's not like I have friends.

I let her pick out chicken noodle soup for lunch. I hate it but I say okay anyway. I'm hungry. We get about twenty cans. Chicken noodle, tomato soup, mandarin oranges, cream corn. The kind of food you find in a survival kit. The girl realizes this and says, "Maybe you don't plan to kill me right away," and I say no, not until we've eaten the cream corn.

In the afternoon I try to sleep. These days it doesn't come easy. I get an hour here, an hour there, but most of all I'm awakened by the idea of Dalmar coming after me or the cops showing up at the door. I'm on the lookout, all the time, peeking out every window as I pass. Always looking behind me. I barricade the front door before I sleep, glad to find the windows sealed shut by some idiot with paint. I didn't think I had to worry about the girl trying to escape. I didn't think she had it in her. I let my guard down, left the truck keys out in plain sight, and that was all the encouragement she needed.

And so I'm sound asleep on the sofa, hugging the gun, when I hear the front door slam shut. I'm on my feet. It takes a minute to get my bearings. When I do I see the girl fall down the second half of the stairs down to the gravel drive. I run out the door, screaming, irate. She's limping. The truck door is unlocked. She gets in and tries to start the ignition. She can't find the right key. I can see her through the driver's window. I see her pound a fist on the steering wheel. I'm closing in on the truck. By now she's grown desperate. She slides across the front seat and out the passenger door. She takes off into the woods. She's fast, but I'm faster. The tree branches reach out, scraping her arms and legs. She trips over a rock and falls face-first into a pile of leaves. She gets up and continues to run. She's getting tired, losing speed. She's crying, begging me to leave her alone.

But I'm pissed.

I grab her by the hair. Her feet continue to run but her head snaps back violently. She lands on the hard earth. She doesn't have time to cry out before I'm on her, all two hundred and some pounds crushing her slender frame. She gasps, begging me to stop. But I don't. I'm mad. She's crying wildly. Tears stream down her face, mixing with blood and mud and my own spit. She squirms. She spits on me. I'm sure she sees her entire life float before her eyes. I tell her how stupid she is. And then I hold the gun to her head and cock the hammer.

She stops moving, becomes paralyzed.

I press hard, the barrel leaving a mark on her head. I could do it. I could end her life.

She's an idiot, a damn moron. It takes every ounce of goodwill I have not to pull the trigger. I did this for her. I saved her life. Who the hell does she think she is to run away? I press harder with the pistol, dig the barrel into her skull. She cries out.

"You think that hurts," I say.

"Please…" She's begging, but I don't listen. I should have handed her over when I had the chance.

I stand up, grab her by the hair. She bawls. "Shut up," I say. I drag her by the hair through the trees. I shove her ahead of me and tell her to move. "Hurry up." It's like her legs don't work right. She trips, falls. "Get up," I snap.

Does she have a clue what Dalmar would do to me if he found me? A bullet in the head would be the easy way out. A quick and easy death. I'd be crucified. Tortured.

I push her up the steps, into the cabin. I slam the door shut, but it bounces back open. I kick it shut and throw the table down to keep it closed. I yank her into the bedroom and tell her that if I hear her so much as breathe she will never again see the light of day.

GABE

BEFOЯE

I drive downtown again, the fourth time in a week, planning to bitch when I don't get reimbursed for all the miles I'm racking up on my car. It's only about ten miles each way, but takes nearly thirty minutes in the damn traffic. There's a reason I don't live in the city. I fork over another fifteen dollars to park—robbery if you ask me—because I've passed the intersection of Lawrence and Broadway nearly a dozen times and still can't find an open meter.

The bar doesn't open for a few hours. Just my luck, I think, knocking on the window to get the bartender's attention. He's stocking the bar and I know he hears me but doesn't budge. I knock again and this time, when his eyes gaze in my direction, I show him my badge.

He opens the door.

It's quiet in the bar. The lights are dim, few of the sun's rays making it in through the grimy windows. The place is dusty and smells of stale cigarette smoke, things you wouldn't necessarily notice when jazz music and candlelight set the mood.

"We open at seven," he says.

"Who's in charge here?" I ask.

"You're looking at him." He turns and begins a retreat to the bar. I follow and prop myself up on one of the torn vinyl stools. I reach into a pocket for the photo: Mia Dennett. It's a fascinating picture, one Eve Dennett let me borrow last week. I promised it wouldn't get lost or hurt, and I feel bad that my shirt pocket has already wrinkled a corner. To Mrs. Dennett, it was the photograph that was *all Mia,* or so she claimed, this image of a free-spirited woman with dirty blond hair that hangs too long, azure eyes and a straightforward, honest smile. She's standing before Buckingham Fountain, the water shooting out aimlessly and, in the Chicago wind, spraying the woman who laughs like a child.

"You ever seen this woman before?" I ask, sliding the photo across the bar. He snatches it in his hand to have a look. I tell him to be careful. I see the recognition right away. He knows her.

"She's here all the time—sits in that booth over there," he responds, motioning with a nod to a booth behind me.

"You ever talk to her?"

"Yeah. When she needs a drink."

"That all?"

"Yeah. That's all. What's this about?"

"Was she here last Tuesday night? Around eight o'clock?"

"Last Tuesday? Buddy, I can barely remember what I had for breakfast this morning. She's been here before, that's all I know for sure." He hands me back the photo. I hate that he called me *buddy.* It's denigrating.

"Detective," I say.

"Huh?"

"It's Detective Hoffman. Not buddy." Then I ask, "Can you tell me who was working last Tuesday night?"

"What's this about?" he asks again. I tell him not to worry about it. I ask him again who was working Tuesday night, this time with a militant tone that completely goes over his big head. He isn't too fond of my disrespect. He knows he could kick my ass if he wanted to. Only one problem: I carry a gun.

But he retreats into a back room anyway. When he returns he's empty-handed. "Sarah," he says.

"Sarah?"

"She's the one you need to talk to. She was serving *that* table," he says, pointing to a filthy booth at the back of the bar, "Tuesday night. She'll be here in an hour."

For a while I sit at the bar and watch him stock bottles of booze. I watch him refill the ice bins and count money into the cash register. I try to make small talk to throw him off as he tallies up what seems to be thousands of pennies. I lose track at forty-nine. I pace.

Sarah Rorhig appears within an hour, coming through the front door with an apron in her hands. Her boss engages her in a secret exchange, during which her eyes turn to mine. There's a worried look on her face, a forced smile. I'm at the table, pretending to be rummaging around for clues when all there is is the vinyl booth and a slab of wood masquerading as a table. That and a frilly little green candle I consider swiping for my own home.

"Sarah?" I ask and she says that she is. I introduce myself and ask her to have a seat. I hand her the photo of Mia. "Have you seen this woman?"

"Yes," she admits.

"Do you remember if she was here last Tuesday, around eight o'clock?"

It must be my lucky day. Sarah Rorhig is a full-time medical assistant and only works Tuesday nights to make a little extra cash. It's been a week since she was here and so Mia's image is fresh in her mind. She says with certainty that Mia was here last Tuesday; she says Mia is always here Tuesday nights. Sometimes by herself, sometimes with a man.

"Why Tuesdays?"

"Tuesday-night poetry slam," she says, "or so I assume that's the reason she's always here. Though I'm never entirely sure she's listening. She always seems to be distracted."

"Distracted?"

"Daydreaming."

I ask what the heck a poetry slam is. I've never heard of it. I imagine works of Whitman and Yeats being thrown on the ground; that's not the case. The idea of listening to people recite their own poetry on stage, however, has me even more baffled. Who the hell would want to listen to that? It appears I have a lot to learn about Mia Dennett.

"Was she by herself last week?"

"No."

"Who was she with?"

Sarah thinks for a minute. "Some guy. I've seen him around here before."

"With Mia?" I ask.

"That's her name?" she queries. "Mia?" I say that it is. She says that she was nice—the use of the past tense runs into me like a freight train—and always very friendly. She leaves a good tip. She hopes that everything is okay. She can tell from my questions that it's probably not, but she doesn't ask to know what happened and so I don't say.

"This man Mia was with last Tuesday night...they've come together before?"

She says that no, they haven't. This was the first time she's seen them together. He's usually at the bar, alone. She's noticed him because he's apparently cute, in an enigmatic sort of way—I write that down; I'll have to look that one up in the dictionary. Mia is always at this table, sometimes alone,

sometimes not. But Tuesday night they sat together and they
left together in a hurry. She doesn't know the man's name
but when I ask she can describe him: tall, sturdy, a mound of
messy hair, dark eyes. She agrees to meet with a sketch artist
later to see if they can come up with something.

I ask again, "Are you sure they left together? This is really
important."

"Yes."

"Did you see them leave?"

"Yes. Well, sort of. I brought them the bill and when I came
back they were gone."

"Did it seem she was leaving on her own free will?"

"Seemed to me she couldn't wait to get out of here."

I ask if they arrived at the bar together. She says no, she
doesn't think so. How did he come to be at Mia's table? She
doesn't know. I ask again: does she know his name? No. Would
anybody know his name? Probably not. He and Mia paid cash;
they left a fifty on the table, which she still remembers because, for five or six beers, it was a charitable tip. More than
her usual customers leave. She remembers bragging about it
later in the night and flashing Ulysses S. Grant's face for all
her co-workers to see.

When I leave the bar, I check up and down Broadway for
security cameras outside of restaurants, banks, the yoga studio, anything that will tell me who Mia Dennett was with
that Tuesday night she disappeared.

COLIN

BEFORE

She won't eat. Four times I've offered her food, dropped a bowl full of it on the floor in the bedroom. As if I'm her damn chef. She lies on the bed on her side, her back to the door. She doesn't budge when I come in, but I can see her breathing. I know she's alive. But if she keeps this up much longer she'll starve herself to death. Now wouldn't that be ironic.

She emerges from the bedroom like a zombie, her hair—a tangled rat's nest—hiding her face. She walks to the bathroom, does her thing, walks back. I ignore her; she ignores me. I told her to leave the bedroom door open. I want to make sure she isn't up to anything in there, but all she does is sleep. Until this afternoon.

I'd been outside, chopping firewood. I worked up a sweat. I was out of breath. I came barreling into the cabin with my mind on one thing: water.

There she stood in the middle of the room, stripped down to a lace bra and panties. She might as well have been dead. Her skin was drained of all color. Her hair was snarled, a bruise the size of a goose egg on her thigh. She had a busted lip and black eye, scratches from her run-in with the trees.

Her eyes were bloodshot and swollen. Tears seeped from her eyes, down the albino skin. Her body convulsed, goose bumps everywhere my eyes could see. She walked with a limp, moving closer. She said to me, "Is this what you want?"

I stared. At her hair, falling mindlessly over the ivory shoulders. At her pale neglected skin. At the hollow craters of her collarbone and her perfectly shaped belly button. At her panties, cut high, and her long legs. At her ankle, so swollen it might be sprained. At the tears that dripped to the floor before her bare feet. Beside ruby-red toenails. Beside legs that shook when they walked, so that I thought they might give. At the snot that dripped from her nose, her crying no longer containable as she reached out and placed a shaking hand on my belt and started to unfasten the clasp. "Is this what you want?" she asked again, and for the time being I let her get both hands on my belt. I let her take it off and drop it to the floor. Let her undo the button of my jeans and slide the zipper. I couldn't say that it wasn't what I wanted. She reeked, as did I. Her hands were like ice when she touched me. But that wasn't it. That wouldn't have stopped me.

I gently pushed her away. "Stop," I whispered.

"Let me," she begged. She thought it would help. She thought it would change things.

"Get your clothes on," I said. I closed my eyes. I couldn't look at her. She stood before me. "Don't—"

She forced my hands on her.

"Stop." She didn't believe me. "Stop," I said louder this time, with more potency. And then added, "Just stop it already," as I pushed her away from me. I told her to get her fucking clothes on.

I hurried out of the cabin, grabbed the ax and began chopping the firewood, vigorously, maniacally. I forgot all about the water.

EVE

BEFORE

It's the middle of the night and, as has been the case for a week now, I can't sleep. Memories of Mia visit me all hours of the day and night, an image of one-year-old Mia in an olive-colored bubble outfit, her chubby thighs bulging out while she tried, unsuccessfully, to walk; hot-pink toenails on precious three-year-old feet; the sound of her wail when her ears were pierced, but later, watching for hours as she admired the opal gems in the bathroom mirror.

I'm standing in the open pantry of our darkened home, the clock above the kitchen stove reading 3:12 a.m. I grope the shelves blindly for chamomile tea, knowing I'd hidden a box somewhere, but also certain it would take much more than chamomile tea to help me sleep. I see Mia making her First Communion, see the distaste on her face when she first laid the Body of Christ on her tip of her tongue; I hear her laugh about it later, alone in her bedroom, just she and me, about how hard it was to chew and swallow, about how she almost choked on the wine.

And then it hits me like a load of bricks, this realization that suddenly overwhelms me: my baby might be dead, and there, in the middle of the pantry, in the middle of the night, I begin to weep; falling to the floor, I press the ends of my pajamas to my face to stifle the sound. I envision her in that olive bubble, see her flash a toothless grin as she hangs on to the edge of the coffee table and laboriously makes her way to my outstretched hands.

My baby might be dead.

I'm doing what I can to help with the investigation, and yet it feels entirely trivial and frivolous because Mia isn't home. I spent an entire day in Mia's neighborhood, passing out *Missing* fliers to everyone I passed. I taped the signs to lampposts and in store windows, an image of Mia on hot-pink paper that was impossible to ignore. I met her friend Ayanna for lunch, and together we went through the details of Mia's last day, desperate for oddities that might explain Mia's disappearance, of which there were none. I rode into the city with Detective Hoffman, after he had secured a key for Mia's apartment and checked that it was not a crime scene, and together we sifted through Mia's belongings, through every circadian object— lesson plans and an address book, grocery lists and to-dos, hopeful for a clue. We found none.

Detective Hoffman phones me once, sometimes twice a day. Hardly a day goes by that we don't speak. I find his voice, his gentle nature, reassuring and he's always amicable even when James winds him up.

James says that he's an idiot.

The detective gives the impression that I'm the first to know any bit of information that crosses his desk, but I'm certain I'm not. He is proofreading the fine points before offering snippets to me. These snippets leave a thousand what-ifs running through a mother's mind.

I'm reminded of my daughter's dissolution with every breath I take. When I see mothers holding their children's hands.

When I see children climbing onto the school bus. When I see postings of missing cats taped to the street posts, or hear a mother call her child by name.

Detective Hoffman wants to know everything he possibly can about Mia. I rummage through old photographs in the basement. I come across old Halloween costumes, and size-four clothes, roller skates and Barbie dolls. I know there are *other* cases, other missing girls like Mia. I picture their mothers. I know there are girls who never come home.

The detective reminds me that no news is good news. Sometimes he calls to tell me nothing at all, no information, in case I was wondering, which I always am. He humors me. He promises to do everything he can to find Mia. I can see it in his eyes when he looks at me, or when he lingers just a moment longer than he should, to make certain I'm not about to crumble.

But I think of it all the time, about how hard it has become to stand and walk, about how impossible it's becoming to function and live in a world that still thinks of politics and entertainment and sports and the economy when all I think about is Mia.

I was certainly not the best mother. That goes without saying. I didn't set out to be a bad mother, however. It just happened. As it was, being a bad mother was child's play compared to being a good mother, which was an incessant struggle, a lose-lose situation 24 hours a day; long after the kids were in bed the torment of what I did or didn't do during those hours we were trapped together would scourge my soul. Why did I allow Grace to make Mia cry? Why did I snap at Mia to stop just to silence the noise? Why did I sneak to a quiet place, whenever I could? Why did I rush the days—*will* them to hurry by—so I could be alone? Other mothers took their children to museums, the gardens, the beach. I kept mine indoors, as much as I could, so we wouldn't cause a scene.

I lie awake at night wondering: what if I never have a chance to make it up to Mia? What if I'm never able to show her the kind of mother I always longed to be? The kind who played endless hours of hide-and-seek, who gossiped side by side on their daughters' beds about which boys in the junior high were *cute*. I always envisioned a friendship between my daughters and me. I imagined shopping together and sharing secrets, rather than the formal, obligatory relationship that now exists between myself and Grace and Mia. I list in my head all the things that I would tell Mia if I could. That I chose the name Mia for my great-grandmother, Amelia, vetoing James's alternative: Abigail. That the Christmas she turned four, James stayed up until 3:00 a.m. assembling the dollhouse of her dreams. That even though her memories of her father are filled with nothing but malaise, there were split seconds of goodness: James teaching her how to swim, James helping her prepare for a fourth-grade spelling test. That I mourn each and every time I turned down an extra book before bed, desperate now for just five more minutes of laughing at *Harry the Dirty Dog*. That I go to the bookstore and purchase a copy after unsuccessfully ransacking the basement for the one that used to be hers. That I sit on the floor of her old bedroom and read it again and again and again. That I love her. That I'm sorry.

COLIN

BEFORE

She hides in the bedroom all day. She won't come out. I won't let her close the door and so she sits on the bed. She sits and thinks. About what, I don't know. I don't give a shit.

She cries, tears spreading across the pillowcase until it's probably soaking wet. Her face, when she comes out to pee, is red and swollen. She tries to be quiet about it, as if she thinks I can't hear. But the cabin is small and made of wood. There's nothing to absorb the sound.

Her body aches. I can see in the way she walks. She can't put weight on the left leg, an injury sustained when she fell down the cabin steps and into the woods. She limps, holding on to the wall as she staggers to the bathroom. In the bathroom she runs a finger across a bruise, which is now engorged and black.

She hears me in the other room. I pace. I chop firewood, enough to keep us warm for the winter. But it's never really warm. I'm sure she's cold all the time, though she dresses in long johns and gets under the quilt. The heat from the stove doesn't reach the bedroom. But she refuses to be out here where it's warm.

I imagine the sound of my footsteps scare the shit out of

her. She listens to nothing but the footsteps, waiting for the worst to come.

I try to keep busy. I clean up the cabin. I wipe away the cobwebs and pick up the dead beetles. I toss them into the trash. I unpack the things we bought in town: canned food and coffee, sweats and soap and duct tape. I fix the front door. I wipe down the countertops with paper towels and water. It's all just to waste time. I pick up the girl's clothes from the bathroom floor. I'm about to yell at her for being a slob and leaving her dirty clothes lying around. But then I hear her cry.

I fill the bathtub with water. I clean the shirt and pants with the bar of soap and hang them outside to dry. We can't do this forever. This cabin is only a temporary thing. I'm wracking my brain to come up with next steps, wishing I would've thought this through before I decided to grab the girl and flee.

She shuffles by me to use the bathroom. She's beaten up and limping. I'm not one to feel guilt, but I know that I'm the one who did it to her, out there, in the woods, when she tried to run. I tell myself that she asked for it. I tell myself that at least now she's quiet, not so certain anymore.

Now she knows who's in charge. Me.

I drink coffee because the tap water tastes like shit. I've offered her some. I've offered her water but she's refused. She still won't eat a thing. Pretty soon I'm going to pin her down and jam the damn food into her mouth. I won't let her starve herself to death. Not after all this.

The next morning, I invite myself into the bedroom. "What do you want for breakfast?" I ask.

She's lying on the bed, her back to the door. She's half-asleep when she hears me come in. The unexpected sound of my feet, the explosion of words in the middle of silence, force her from the bed.

This is it, she thinks, too disoriented to hear what I'm saying.

Her legs get tangled in the sheets. Her feet are lost though her body runs away from the sound. She falls to the hardwood floor. Her feet fight the sheet to find the floors. Her body thrusts itself as far away from me as she can. She backs herself into the wall, the bedding clutched in a shaking hand.

I'm standing in the doorway, dressed in the same clothes I've worn for nearly a week.

She's staring at me with panic in her distended eyes, her eyebrows raised and mouth hanging open. She looks at me like I'm a monster, a cannibal waiting to eat her for breakfast.

"What do you want?" she cries.

"It's time to eat."

She swallows hard. "I'm not hungry," she says.

"Too bad."

I tell her she doesn't have a choice.

She follows me into the other room and watches as I pour what are called eggs—but look and smell like shit from a box—into the skillet. I watch them brown. The smell is enough to make me gag.

She hates everything about me. I know it. I see it in her eyes. She hates the way I stand. She hates my dirty hair and the stubble that now coats my chin. She hates my hands, watching the way they stir the eggs in the skillet. She hates the way I look at her. She hates the tone of my voice and the way my mouth forms the words.

Most of all, she hates seeing the gun in my pocket. All the time, making sure she behaves.

I tell her she's not allowed in the bedroom anymore. Only to sleep. That's it. The rest of the day she has to stay out here where I can keep an eye on her. Make sure she eats, drinks, pees. It's like I'm caring for a damn infant.

She eats about as much as a baby—a couple bites here, a

couple bites there. She says that she's not hungry, but she eats enough to survive. That's all that matters.

I keep an eye on her so she doesn't try to run, like last time. When we go to sleep, I slide a heavier table in front of the door so that I'll hear if she tries to escape. I'm a light sleeper. I sleep with the gun nestled beside me. I ransacked the kitchen drawers and made sure there were no knives. Just my own pocketknife that I carry all the time.

She doesn't have a damn thing to say to me, and I don't try. Why bother? I can't stay here forever. In the spring there will be tourists. Soon we need to go. Screw the girl, I think. Soon *I* need to go. Ditch the girl and get on a plane and go. Before the cops find me. Before Dalmar finds me. I need to go.

But of course there's something holding me back, something that stops me from getting on that plane and going.

GABE

BEFORE

I'm standing in the midst of the Dennetts' kitchen. Mrs. Dennett hovers over the sink, scraping away the remains of a pork dinner. I see the judge's plate licked clean, and hers still sports a tenderloin and a pile of peas. The woman is wasting away before my very eyes. The water runs hot, steam spewing forth into the room, though her hands are immersed in it and seem blind to the heat. She scrubs at the china with a ferocity I've never seen in a woman washing dishes.

We stand before the island in the center of the kitchen. No one offers me a seat. It's a swank kitchen with walnut cabinets and granite countertops. The appliances are all stainless steel, including *two ovens* for which my Italian mother would give an arm and a leg. I imagine Thanksgiving without the drama of how to keep everything warm until dinnertime, no tears when my dad mentioned the potatoes were a tad bit cold.

There's an image of a man set on the island before the judge and me. It's a forensic sketch, one that our artist down at the station constructed with the help of that waitress.

"So this is the man? This is the man who has my daughter?" Eve Dennett had cried as I slipped the sketch from a manila folder. Already she was in tears. She turned her back on the conversation and tried to lose herself in washing the dishes, crying quietly over the sound of running water.

"Mia was seen last Tuesday night with this man," I respond, though by that time her back is facing my direction. The image before us is one of a rough man. His appearance makes him seem lowbred, but it's not as though he resembles the masked men in horror films. He's just not of Dennett stature. Neither am I.

"And?" Judge Dennett implores.

"And we think he might be involved in her disappearance."

He stands on the opposite side of the island, sporting a suit equal in value to two or three months' worth my salary. His tie is undone and tossed over a shoulder. "Is there any proof Mia didn't go willingly with this man?"

"Well," I say, "no."

The judge is drinking already. Tonight's drink of choice: scotch on the rocks. I think he might be drunk. There's a slight slur in his speech and he has the hiccups.

"Suppose Mia is just off monkeying around with him. What then?"

He talks to me like I'm an idiot. But I remind myself that I'm the one in charge. I'm the one with the shiny badge. I'm leading this investigation. Not him.

"Judge Dennett, it's been eight days since the investigation began," I state. "Nine since Mia was last seen. According to co-workers, she rarely missed work. According to *your* wife, this behavior—shiftlessness, irresponsibility—is not in sync with Mia's character."

He sips from the scotch and sets it down too quickly on the island. Eve jumps from the sound. "Of course, there's the disorderly conduct. Trespassing and vandalism. Possession of marijuana," he says and then, to piss me off, adds, "to name just a few." The expression on his face is complacent, holier-than-thou. I stare at him, unable to comment. I despise his bravado.

"I checked the police records," I say. "There was nothing on Mia." In fact her record was squeaky clean. Not even a speeding ticket.

"Well, there wouldn't be, now would there?" he asks and I understand: he made them disappear. He excuses himself long enough to get a refill. Mrs. Dennett is still scrubbing away at the dishes. I stray to the sink and nudge the faucet toward cold so the poor woman's hands will no longer burn.

She glances at me, taken aback, as if she just caught the first whiff of burning flesh and whispers, "I should have told you," her eyes filling with sadness. *Yes,* I think, *you should have told me,* but I bite my tongue as she goes on. "I wish I could say he was in denial. I wish I could say he was so overcome with grief that he's refusing to believe Mia is really gone."

Judge Dennett returns just in time to overhear the last few words of his wife's confession. It's quiet in the room and for a split second I brace myself for the wrath of God. But there's none of it; it doesn't come.

"This behavior of Mia's isn't as unexpected as you've led the detective to believe, now is it, Eve?" he asks.

"Oh, James," she cries. She's drying her hands on a tea towel when she says, "That was years ago. She was in high school. She made her fair share of mistakes. But that was *years* ago."

"And what do you know of *this* Mia, Eve? It's been years since we've had a relationship with our daughter. We hardly know her anymore."

"And you, Your Honor," I say, to take Mrs. Dennett off the hot seat. I hate the way he stares at her, his eyes making her feel stupid. "What do you know of this Mia? Any misdemeanors that have recently been expunged from her record?" I ask. "Traffic citations? Prostitution? Public intoxication?" I don't have to think twice as to why her youthful transgressions disappeared from the record. "That wouldn't look good for the Dennett name, now would it? And this whole thing—*if* Mia is out there screwing around at the end of the investigation, *if* she's perfectly fine and just out for a good time, that doesn't look good, either, does it?"

I watch the news; I'm generally up on politics. This November Judge Dennett is up for reelection.

And yet I find myself wondering if Mia's misconduct is limited to her youth alone, or if there's more to it than that.

"You'd better watch yourself," the judge warns, but in the background, Eve whimpers, "*Prostitution? James?*" Though it was never anything more than a hypothetical.

He ignores her. I suppose we both do.

"I'm just trying to find your daughter," I say. "Because maybe she is off doing something stupid. But consider for a minute that maybe she's not. Just think about it. What then? I'm certain you'll be asking for my badge if she winds up dead."

"James," his wife hisses. She's nearly in tears from my use of *daughter* and *dead* in the same sentence.

"Let me get this straight, Hoffman," he says to me. "You find my daughter and you bring her home. Alive. You just make sure you cover your bases because there's more to Mia than meets the eye," he concludes and, with that, takes his scotch and walks out of the room.

COLIN

BEFOЯE

I catch her staring at herself in the bathroom mirror. She doesn't recognize the reflection: the wiry hair and dowdy skin, the bruises that are beginning to heal. They're yellow now with gaps between instead of bulging and purple.

When she comes from the bathroom, I'm waiting for her. I'm leaned against the frame of the door. She steps out and bumps into me, staring at me, like some beast hovering over her, stealing her air. "I wasn't going to hit you," I say, reading her thoughts, but she doesn't speak.

I brush a cold hand across her cheek. She winces and pulls back, away from my touch. "It's better," I say about the bruises. She moves past me and walks away.

I don't know how many days we do this. I've lost track. I tried to remember when it was Monday and when it was Tuesday. Eventually the days began to blur. Every day is the same. She lies in bed until I make her get up. We force down breakfast. Then she sits on a chair she pulls up to the window. She stares outside. Thinks. Daydreams. Longs to be anywhere but here.

I'm thinking all the time about how to get out of here. I've got enough cash to catch a flight somewhere and then it will be gone. But of course I don't have a passport on me, so the farthest I can go is Tecate or Calexico, California, but the only way I'm getting out of the country is if I hire a coyote or swim across the Rio Grande. But getting myself out of the country is only half the problem. It's everything else I can't quite figure out. I pace the cabin, wondering how in the hell I'm gonna get myself out of this mess, knowing I'm safe here, for now, but the longer we hide out, the longer *I* hide out, the worse it's gonna be.

We have rules, spoken and unspoken. She's not to touch my shit. We use only one square of toilet paper at a time. We air-dry when at all possible. We use as little soap as possible so we don't reek of B.O. We can't let things go to waste. We don't open windows. Not that we can anyway. If we run into someone around the cabin, she's Chloe, I tell her. Never Mia. In fact she might as well forget that was ever her name.

She gets her period and we learn the literal interpretation for being *on the rag*. I see the blood in a garbage bag and ask, "What the fuck is this?" I'm sorry I ask. We collect our garbage in some white plastic bags that got left behind. From time to time we drive and drop them off in a Dumpster behind some lodge, late at night when we're certain no one will see. She asks why we don't just leave them outside. I ask if she wants to be eaten by a fucking bear.

There's a chill from the window, but the heat from the stove helps keep us warm. The days are getting shorter. Night falls earlier and earlier until darkness takes over the cabin. There is electricity, but I don't want to draw attention to us. I only turn on a small lamp at night. The bedroom becomes nothing but blackness. At night, she lays and listens to the silence. She waits for me to appear from the shadows and end her life.

But during the day she sits beside the drafty window. She

watches the leaves tumble to the ground. Outside the earth is covered in decaying leaves. Nothing remains to block the lake's view. Fall is almost over now. We're so far north we can touch Canada. We're lost in an uninhabited world surrounded by nothing but wilderness. She knows it as well as I do. That's why I brought her here. Right now, the only thing of concern is bears. But then again, bears hibernate in the winter. Soon they will all be asleep. And then the only concern will be freezing to death.

We don't talk much. It's all of necessity—*lunch is ready; I'm taking a bath; where are you going? I'm going to bed.* There are no casual exchanges. Everything is mute. We can hear every noise for lack of conversation: a stomach growl, a cough, a swallow, the wind howling outside the cabin at night, deer passing through the leaves. And then there are the imagined sounds: car tires on gravel, footsteps on the stairs leading up to the cabin, voices.

She probably wishes they were real so she didn't have to wait anymore. The fear is certain to kill her.

EVE

BEFORE

The first time I laid eyes on James, I was eighteen years old, in the United States with some girlfriends. I was young and naive, and mesmerized with the enormity of Chicago, the sense of freedom that had crawled under my skin the moment us girls boarded the airplane. We were country girls, used to small villages of only a few thousand people, an agrarian life-style, a community that was generally narrow-minded and conventional. And suddenly we were whisked away to a new world, dropped in the middle of a roaring metropolis, and at first glance, I was swept off my feet. I was in love.

It was Chicago that first seduced me, all the promises it had to offer. These immense buildings, the millions of people, the confidence they carried in the way they walked, in the stead-fast expressions on their faces when they strut across the busy streets. It was 1969. The world as we knew it was changing, but truly, I couldn't have cared less. I wasn't caught up in all that. I was enraptured with my own existence, as is to be ex-pected when one is eighteen: the way men would look at me, the way I felt in a miniskirt, much shorter than my mother would have ever approved. I was dreadfully inexperienced, desperate to be a woman and no longer a child.

What waited for me at home, in rural England, had been fated by my birth: I'd marry one of the boys I'd known my entire life, one of the boys who, in primary school, pulled my hair or called me names. It was no secret that Oliver Hill wanted to marry me. He'd been asking since he was twelve years old. His father was a rector in the Anglican Church, his mother the kind of homemaker I vowed never to be: one who obeyed her husband as if his command was the word of God.

James was older than me, which was exciting; he was cosmopolitan and brilliant. His stories were impassioned; people hung on to every last word out of his mouth, whether he was talking about politics or the weather. It was summer where I first saw him at a restaurant in the Loop, sitting around a large circular table with a group of friends. His voice boomed over the sounds of the restaurant, and you couldn't help but listen. He drew you in with his poise and presumption, with his vehement tone. All around him, eyes waited expectantly for the punch line of some joke, then everyone—friends and strangers alike—laughed until they cried. A few broke out in applause. They all seemed to know his name, those dining at other tables, the restaurant staff. From across the room, the bartender called out, "Another round, James?" and within minutes, pitchers of beer filled the table.

I couldn't help but stare.

I wasn't alone. My girlfriends, too, ogled him. The women at his table weren't hesitant to touch him when they could: a hug, a pat on the arm. One woman, a brunette with hair that stretched to her waistline, leaned close to share a secret: anything to be close to him. He was more confident than any man I'd ever seen.

He was in law school at the time. That I'd later learn, the

following morning when I woke up beside him in bed. My girlfriends and I weren't old enough to drink, and so it was apparently my infatuation that was responsible for my reckless abandon that night: the way I found myself sitting beside him at his round table; the gluttonous expression on the woman with the long hair as he draped an arm around my shoulder; the way James fawned over my British accent as if it was the greatest thing since sliced bread.

James was different then, not the man he's become over time. His faults were much more endearing, his bravado charming instead of the unpleasant way it's grown to be. He was a master at flattery long before his choice words became insulting and ugly. There was a time in our lives when we were happy, completely bewitched by the other, when we couldn't keep our hands to ourselves. But that man, the one I married, has completely disappeared.

I call Detective Hoffman first thing in the morning, after James has left for work. I waited, as I always do, until I heard the garage door close, his SUV make its way down our drive, before emerging from bed, where I stood in the midst of our kitchen with my mug of coffee, the face of that man who has Mia engraved in my mind's eye. I stared at the clock, watched as the minute hand crawled its way around the circle and when 8:59 gave way to nine o'clock, I dialed the numbers that are becoming more familiar with each passing day.

He answers the phone, his voice professional and authoritarian as he announces, "Detective Hoffman." I imagine him at the police station; I hear the bustle of people in the background, dozens of officers trying to solve other people's problems for them.

It takes me a moment to gather myself and I say to him, "Detective, this is Eve Dennett."

His voice loses its edge as he says my name. "Mrs. Dennett. Good morning."

"Good morning."

I envision him standing in our kitchen last night; I see the vacant look on his kindhearted face when James told him about Mia's past. He left in a hurry. I hear him slam the front door over and over again in my mind. I hadn't attempted to withhold a thing about Mia from Detective Hoffman. To me, in all honesty, her past behavior didn't matter. But the last thing I need is for the detective to have misgivings about me. He's my only link to Mia.

"I had to call," I say. "I had to explain."

"About last night?" he asks and I say yes.

"You don't need to."

But I do anyway.

Mia's teenage years were difficult, to say the least. She wanted so desperately to fit in. She wanted to be independent. She was impulsive—driven by desire—and lacking in common sense. Her friends made her feel accepted, whereas her family did not. Amongst her peers, she was popular, she was *wanted,* and for Mia, this was a natural high. Her peers made her feel like she was on top of the world; there was nothing she wouldn't do for her friends.

"Maybe Mia fell into the wrong group of friends," I say. "Maybe I should have been more vigilant about whom she was spending her time with. What I noticed was that B-plus book reports more commonly became C-minus papers, and she no longer studied at the kitchen table after school, but retreated to her bedroom, where she shut and locked the door."

Mia was in the midst of an identity crisis. There was a part of her desperately yearning for adulthood, and yet the rest of her remained a child, unable to think and reason like she would later in life. She was often frustrated and thought little of herself. James's insensitivity only made things worse. He compared her to Grace relentlessly, about how Grace, now in her twenties and away at college—his alma mater, of course—was going to graduate magna cum laude; about how she was taking courses in Latin and debate in preparation for law school, to which she'd already been accepted.

Initially her misbehavior was typical teenage slips: talking out in class, not completing her homework. She rarely invited friends to our house. When she was picked up by friends, Mia would meet them on the drive and when I peeked out the window for a glance, she'd stop me. *What?* she'd ask with a harsh tone that had once belonged only to Grace.

She was fifteen when we caught her sneaking out of the house in the middle of the night. It was the first of many escapes. She'd forgotten to turn off the house alarm and so, in the midst of her escape, the house began to scream.

"She's a juvenile delinquent," James said.

"She's a teenager," I amended, watching as she climbed into a car parked at the end of our drive, not bothering to look back as the alarms blared and James cursed the darn thing, trying to remember our password.

Image meant everything to James. It always had. He'd always been worried about his reputation, about what people would think or say about him. His wife had to be a trophy wife. He told me this before we were married, and in some crooked way, I'd been happy to fill that role. I didn't ask what it meant when he stopped inviting me to work dinners, when his children no longer needed to attend firm Christmas parties. When he became a judge it was as if we didn't exist at all.

So one can imagine the way James felt when the local police dragged a sloppy, drunken sixteen-year-old girl home from a party, and he, in his robe, stood at our front door all but begging the police to keep this under wraps.

He screamed at her even though she was so sick she could barely hold her own head over the toilet while she vomited. He bellowed about how insatiable reporters *love* this kind of thing: Teenage Daughter of Judge Dennett Cited with Underage Drinking.

Of course it never made the paper. James made sure of that. He spent an arm and a leg making sure that Mia's name never graced the pages of the local paper, not this time or the next. Not when she and her unruly friends attempted to steal a bottle of tequila from the local liquor store, not when she and these same friends were caught smoking pot in a parked car behind a strip mall off Green Bay Road.

"She's a teenager," I said to James. "This is what they do."

But even I wasn't so sure. Grace, with all her difficulties, had never been in trouble with the law. I had never had so much as a speeding ticket, and here was Mia, spending time in a holding cell at the local precinct while James begged and blackmailed local law enforcement not to press charges or to have allegations removed from her record. He paid off parents not to mention Mia's misadventures with their similarly disobedient children.

He was never worried about Mia and the source of her discontent and, therefore, misbehavior. He was only worried about what impact her actions would have on *him*.

It didn't occur to him that if he let her pay the consequences like any *normal* child, Mia's havoc might cease. As it was, she could do anything she liked and not suffer the consequences. Her misdeeds irked her father like nothing else; for the first time in her life she had his attention.

"I overheard telephone conversations between Mia and her friends about earrings they'd stolen from the mall—as if we couldn't have just *paid* for them. My car would smell of cigarette smoke after Mia had borrowed it for this or that, but, of course, *my* Mia didn't smoke. She didn't smoke or drink, or—"

"Mrs. Dennett," Detective Hoffman interrupts. "Teenagers, by definition, are in a class all of their own. They give in to peer pressure. They defy their parents. They talk back, and experiment with anything and everything they can get their hands on. The goal with teenagers is simply getting through it alive, with no permanent damage. Your description of Mia is not that far from normal," he admits.

Though I sense he'd say anything to make me feel better.

"I can't tell you how many stupid things I did when I was sixteen, seventeen," he concedes. He rattles them off: drinking, fender benders, cheating on a test, smoking *pot,* he whispers into the telephone's receiver. "Even the good kids have the urge to lift a pair of earrings from the mall. Teenagers believe they're invincible—nothing bad can happen. It isn't until later that we realize that bad things do, in fact, happen. The kids that are flawless," he adds, "those are the ones that worry me."

I assure him that Mia has changed since she was seventeen, desperate for him to see Mia as more than a teenage delinquent. "She's matured." But it's more than that. Mia has blossomed into a beautiful young woman. The kind of woman that, as a child, I'd hoped to one day be.

"I'm sure she has," he says, but I can't leave it at that.

"There were two, maybe three years of utter carelessness, and then she turned herself around. She saw a light at the end of the tunnel—she would be eighteen and could be rid of us once and for all. She knew what she wanted. She started making plans. A place of her own, freedom. And she wanted to help people."

"Teenagers," he says and I'm silenced because, without having ever met her, I see that he knows my daughter more than me. "Those who were troubled and feeling misunderstood. Like herself."

"Yes," I whisper. But Mia never explained it to me. She never sat me down and told me how she could relate to these children, about how she, more than anyone, knew the difficulties that juveniles faced, all those mixed-up emotions, about how hard it was for them to swim to the surface to breathe. I never understood. To me it was all skin-deep; I couldn't fathom how Mia could communicate with *those* kids. But it wasn't about black and white, rich and poor; it was about human nature.

"James has never gotten that image out of his mind—his daughter in the holding cell at the local precinct. He dwells on all those years he fought to keep her name out of the paper, about how disappointed he was in her. How she wouldn't listen. The fact that she refused law school was the icing on the cake. Mia was a burden for James. He's never gotten past that fact—he's never accepted her for the strong independent woman she is today. In James's mind—"

"She's a screwup," Detective Hoffman remarks, and I'm grateful the words came from his mouth and not mine.

"Yes."

I consider myself at eighteen, the emotions that overcame all common sense. What, I wonder, would have become of me if I hadn't been in the little Irish pub in the Loop that July night in 1969? What if James hadn't been there, hadn't been giving a soliloquy on antitrust law, if I hadn't hung on desperately to every last word, if I hadn't been so consumed when his eyes turned to me, not only with the Federal Trade Commission and mergers and acquisitions, but also with the way he could make something so mundane sound arousing, the way his mahogany eyes danced when they met mine.

Without a mother's instinct to tell me otherwise, there's a part of me that could see James's point of view.

But I'd never admit it.

My intuition, however, tells me something has happened to my daughter. Something bad. It screams at me, awakens me in the middle of the night: something has happened to Mia.

COLIN

BEFORE

I tell her we're going outside. It's the first time I let her out of the cabin. "We need sticks," I say, "for the fire." Soon it will snow. Then they'll all be buried.

"We have firewood," she says. She's sitting cross-legged in the chair beside the window. She's staring outside at the oppressive granite clouds that hover just above the tops of the trees.

I don't look at her. "We need more. For the winter."

She stands slowly, stretching. "You plan to keep me around that long?" she asks. She slips that ugly maroon sweatshirt over her head. I don't satisfy her with a response. I'm right behind her as we head outside. I let the screen door slam shut.

She makes her way down the steps. She begins to gather sticks from the ground. There are tons of them, tossed from trees during a storm. They are wet. They cling to the muddy ground and moldy leaves that cover the earth. She tosses them into a pile at the bottom of the steps. She wipes her hands on the thighs of her pants.

Our laundry hangs over the deck rail. We wash our clothes in the bathtub and then hang them out to dry. We use a bar of soap. It's better than nothing. They're cold and stiff when we slip them on, and sometimes they're still wet.

A thick fog hangs over the lake and drifts toward the cabin. The day is depressing. Rain clouds fill the sky. Soon it will begin to rain. I tell her to hurry up. I wonder how long these sticks will last. There's already a wall of firewood lining the cabin. I've been out here day after day with an ax, splitting fallen trees and taking the limbs off the rest. But we gather sticks anyway so we don't get bored. So I don't get bored. She isn't going to complain about it. The air is fresh, and so she makes the most of it. She doesn't know if she'll ever get another chance like this.

I watch her gather sticks. She carries them in one arm as the other bends down to swipe more from the ground. It's one swift, graceful movement. Her hair is draped over a shoulder so it stays out of her eyes. She gathers until her arms can hold no more, then stops to catch her breath. She arches her back to stretch. Then down again. When her load is full she brings them to the cabin. She refuses to make eye contact with me, though I'm certain she knows I'm watching. With every passing load she ventures farther and farther away, her blue eyes locked steadfast on the lake. Freedom.

It begins to rain. It's one torrential downpour: one minute, nothing, the next, we're soaked. The girl comes running from the far end of the property with a bundle of sticks in her arms. She'd been working as far away as I let her. I kept my eyes on her the entire time, making sure I could catch her if I needed to. I don't think she'd be that stupid. Not again.

I've already begun to haul the sticks upstairs and into the cabin. I dump them into a pile beside the stove. She follows me inside, drops her load, and then down the stairs again. I didn't expect such cooperation. She moves slower than me. Her ankle is still healing. It's only been a day or so since I haven't seen her limp. We brush past each other on the stairs and it's without thought that I hear myself say *sorry*. She says nothing.

She changes her clothes and hangs the wet ones from a curtain rod in the living room. I've already brought in the clothes from outside and draped them around the entire cabin. Eventually the fire will help them dry. The cabin feels wet. Outside, the temperatures have dropped by as much as ten or fifteen degrees. We trekked wet footprints throughout the cabin. The sticks puddle rainwater onto the wooden floor. I tell her to find a towel in the bathroom and wipe what she can. Sooner or later the rest will dry.

I'm making dinner. She moves silently to her chair and stares out the window at the rain. It drums on the roof of the cabin, a steady rat-tat-tat. A pair of my pants, hanging from the curtain rod, disrupts her view. Ambiguity fills the earth, the world smothered by fog.

I drop a bowl and she jumps, glaring at me with an accusatory look. I'm loud, I know that. I don't try to be quiet. Bowls pound on the countertops; cabinets slam shut. My heavy feet stomp. Spoons fall from my hand and clatter on the burnt-orange countertops. The pot on the stove begins to boil, spilling over onto the stove.

Dusk falls. We eat dinner in silence, thankful for the sound of the rain. I watch out the window as blackness takes over the sky. I flip on the small lamp and begin to feed sticks to the fire. She watches me out of the corner of her eye, and I wonder what she sees.

Suddenly I hear a crash outside and I jump to my feet, hissing, "Shhh," though she hadn't said a word. I reach for the gun and grip it in my hand.

I peek out the window, see that the grill has blown over, and feel relieved.

She stares at me, at the way I part the curtains and look out into the yard, just in case. Just in case someone is there. I let the curtains close and sit back down. She's still watching me, staring at a two-day-old stain on my sweatshirt, the dark hairs on the backs of my hands, the casual way I carry the gun as if it doesn't have the ability to end someone's life.

I look at her and ask, *"What?"* She's slouched in that chair by the window. Her hair is long, rolling. The wounds on her face are healing, but her eyes still hold their pain. She can still feel me press the gun against her head and she knows, as she scrutinizes me from ten feet away, that it's only a matter of time before I do it again.

"What are we doing here?" she asks. It comes out intentional, forced. She finally gets the guts to ask. She's been wanting to since the minute we arrived.

My sigh is long and exasperated. "Don't worry about it," I say after a long time. Just some offhand answer to shut her up.

"What do you want with me?" she asks instead.

My face is plastered with a deadpan expression. I don't want anything to do with her. "Nothing," I say. I poke around at the sticks in the fire. I don't look at her.

"Then let me go."

"I can't." I remove a sweatshirt and lay it beside the gun on the floor at my feet. The fire keeps the cabin warm, here at least. The bedroom is cold. She sleeps layered, long johns and a sweatshirt and socks, and still she shivers until long after she's fallen asleep.

I know because I've watched her.

She asks again what I want with her. Of course I want *something* with her, she says. Why else would I snatch her from my apartment and bring her here?

"I was hired to do a job. To get you and bring you to Lower Wacker. To drop you off. That's it. I was supposed to drop you off and disappear."

Lower Wacker Drive is the bottom part of a double-decker street in the Loop, a tunnel that goes on for I don't know how long.

I see it in her eyes: confusion. She looks away, out the window into the dark night.

There are words she doesn't understand: *a job, drop you off and disappear.* It was far more realistic for her to believe that this was random. That some madman chose to kidnap her for the hell of it.

She says the only thing she knows about Lower Wacker is that she and her sister used to love to drive down there when they were kids, back when it was lit with fluorescent green lights. It's the first personal thing she tells me about herself.

"I don't understand," she says, desperate for an answer.

"I don't know all the details. Ransom," I say. I'm getting pissed off. I don't want to talk about it.

"Then why are we *here?*" Her eyes beg for an explanation. She's looking at me with this blend of complete disorientation and frustration and conceit.

That's a fucking good question, I think.

I checked her out, online, before I nabbed her. I know a few things about her, though she doesn't think I know shit. I've seen photos of her socialite family in their designer clothes, looking rich and uptight all at the same time. I know when her father became judge. I know when he's up for reelection. I watched news clips of him on the internet. I know that he's a prick.

The apple doesn't fall far from the tree.

I want to tell her to forget it. To shut up. But instead I say, "I changed my mind. No one knows we're here. If they did, they'd kill us. Me and you."

She stands up and begins to traipse around the room. Her feet are light on the floor, her arms tangled around herself.

"Who?" she begs. Those words—*kill us, me and you*—take her breath away. The rain comes down harder, if possible. She leans in to hear my voice. I'm staring at the wooden floorboards of the cabin. I avoid her expectant eyes.

"Don't worry about it," I say.

"Who?" she asks again.

And so I tell her about Dalmar. Mostly so she'll shut up. I tell her about the day he tracked me down and handed me a photo of her. He said I was to find and deliver her to him.

She turns her back to me and asks with this accusatory tone, *"Then why didn't you?"*

I see the hate covering her from head to toe and think that I should have. I should have handed her over to Dalmar and been through. I would've been home by now, plenty of money to pay for food and bills, the mortgage. I wouldn't have to be worrying about what I left behind, wondering how things are going back home, how she's going to survive, how I'm going to get to her before I run. I find myself thinking about it all the time. It keeps me up at night. When I'm not worrying about Dalmar or the cops, I'm thinking about her, in that old house all alone. If I would've just turned the girl over like I was supposed to do, this would've all been through. Then the only thing I would've been worrying about is if and when the cops were gonna catch me. But of course that's nothing new.

I don't answer the girl's stupid question. That's something she doesn't need to know. She doesn't need to know why I changed my mind, why I brought her here.

Instead I tell her what I know about Dalmar. I don't know why I do it. I guess so she'll know I'm not screwing around. So she'll be afraid. So she'll see that being here with me is the best alternative, the only alternative.

Much of what I know about Dalmar is hearsay. Rumors about how he's believed to be one of those child soldiers back in Africa, the ones that are brainwashed and forced to kill. About him beating a businessman in an abandoned warehouse out on the west side because he couldn't pay a debt. About how he killed a boy, nine, maybe ten years old, when his folks couldn't pay the ransom for his return, about how Dalmar shot the kid, sent photos to his parents to rub it in, to gloat.

"You're lying," she says. But her eyes are filled with terror. She knows I'm not.

"How can you be so sure?" I ask. "Do you have any idea what he would've done if he got his hands on you?"

Rape and torture come to mind. He's got a hideout in Lawndale, a house on South Homan where I've been once or twice. This is where I figure he'd keep the girl, a brick home with busted steps leading up to the front door. Stained carpet. Appliances ripped out of the wall when the last owner foreclosed. Water damage and mold creeping along the ceiling, down the walls. Broken windows covered with plastic wrap. Her, in the middle of a room, on a folding chair, bound and gagged. Waiting. Just waiting. While Dalmar and his guys had a little fun. And even after the judge paid the ransom, I figure Dalmar would tell one of the guys to shoot her. To get rid of the evidence. Ditch her in a Dumpster somewhere, or maybe the river. I tell her this and then I say, "Once you get into this kind of mess, there's no getting out."

She doesn't say a thing. Not about Dalmar, though I know she's thinking about him, Know she's got that image of Dalmar shooting a nine-year-old kid glued to her mind.

GABE

BEFORE

The sergeant gives me the green light to air John Doe's face on the news Friday night. The tips start rolling in. People begin calling the hotline to say that they've seen our John Doe. Except to some people he's Steve and others he's Tom. Some lady says she thinks she rode the "L" with him last night, but can't be entirely sure (Was there a lady with him? No, he was alone). Some guy thinks he saw John Doe working as a janitor in his office building on State Street, but he's sure the man is Hispanic, which I assure him he's not. I have a couple of rookies answering the hotline, trying to differentiate real leads from the dead ends. By morning, the gist of the calls is this: either no one has a damn clue who he is, or he's known by enough aliases to send every rookie on wild-goose chases for the remainder of the year. This realization pains me. Our John Doe might be more experienced than I'd like to think.

I spend a lot of time thinking about him. I could guess a lot about him without having ever met him, without even knowing his name. There isn't any one factor in a person that causes violent or antisocial behavior. It's an accumulation of things. I could guess that his socioeconomic level doesn't place him

in the same neighborhood as the Dennetts. I could guess that
he never went to college, or had trouble finding and keeping
a job. I can guess that, as a child, he didn't have meaningful
relationships with many adults. He may not have had meaningful relationships at all. He may have felt alienated. There
may have been a lack of parental involvement. There may have
been marital problems. He may have been abused. There was
probably little emphasis placed on education, and not a whole
lot of affection in his family. His parents probably didn't tuck
him into bed at night; they didn't read him books before bed.
They probably didn't go to church.

He didn't have to be abusive to animals as a child. Maybe he
was hyperactive. Maybe he had trouble concentrating. Maybe
he was depressed or delinquent or antisocial.

He probably never felt like he was quite in control. He
didn't learn to be flexible. He doesn't know what empathy is.
He doesn't know how to solve a conflict without throwing a
punch or pointing his gun.

I've taken sociology classes. I've run across enough convicts
in my lifetime, headed down the very same line.

He didn't have to take drugs, but he might have. He didn't
have to grow up in a housing project, but he might have. He
didn't have to be in a gang, but I wouldn't put that past him,
either. His parents didn't have to own a gun.

But I can assume he wasn't hugged a whole lot. His family
didn't pray before dinner. They didn't go camping or snuggle
together on the couch for movie night. I can assume his father never helped him with his algebra homework. I can guess
that at least once, someone forgot to pick him up from school.
I can guess that at some point in his life, no one was paying
attention to what he watched on TV. And I can guess that
he's been smacked across the face by someone who should've
known better, someone he trusted.

I flip through the stations on the TV: the Bulls have an off day, Illinois just got beat by the Badgers. Not a good TV night for me. Before settling on *It's the Great Pumpkin, Charlie Brown,* I do a final run-through of the hundred-plus channels on my TV—who says money can't buy happiness?—and, as luck would have it, come across Judge Dennett's face, giving a press conference on the six o'clock news. "What the hell," I snap, turning the volume louder so I can hear. You'd think the lead detective would be there, at the press conference, or at least know the damn thing was going on. But there, in my place, is the sergeant, friends with Judge Dennett ever since the judge's stint in the D.A.'s office, long before he went into private practice. Must be nice to have friends in high places. The illustrious Eve stands by Judge Dennett's side, holding his hand—I'm sure that was prearranged since I've never seen any hint of affection between the couple—with Grace beside her, giving goo-goo eyes to the camera as if this might just be her acting debut. The judge seems truly pained by his daughter's disappearance and I'm certain some lawyer or political advisor told him what to say and what to do, down to every last, minute detail: the hand-holding, for example, or brief lapses and efforts to regain composure that I, for one, know was never lost. It's all a sham. A journalist attempts to ask a question but is denied as the family spokesman steps in and the judge and his family are ushered off the sidewalk and into their stately home. The sergeant steps on air long enough to let the world know he's got his best detectives on the case, as if that's supposed to appease me, before the scene jumps to a studio on Michigan Avenue where some news anchor recaps the Mia Dennett case—flashing an image of our John Doe across the screen—before jumping to a high-rise fire on the South Side.

COLIN

BEFORE

I hate to do this, but there just isn't any other way. I don't trust her.

I wait until she's in the bathroom and then follow her in with a rope. I thought about the duct tape we'd picked up in Grand Marais, but there's no need for it. There's no one around who would hear her scream.

"What are you doing?"

She's standing before the sink, brushing her teeth with a finger. Terror fills her eyes, just the sight of me coming unsolicited into the bathroom with the rope.

She tries to run, but I trap her in my arms. It's easy. She's fragile these days; she doesn't even try to fight. "There's no other way," I say and she's raving about what a liar and an asshole I am. I tie the rope to each of her wrists, then around the base of the sink. Boy Scouts. She's never getting out of there.

I make sure the front door is locked before I leave, and then I go.

I learned most everything I know from Scouting as a kid. My fourth-grade teacher was a leader, back when I actually gave a shit what teachers thought about me.

I can't remember how many merit badges I earned—archery, hiking, canoeing, camping, fishing, first aid. I learned how to fire a shotgun. How to tell when a cold front was coming. How to survive outside in a blizzard. How to build a fire. I learned how to tie knots, a figure eight follow-through and a water knot and a safety knot. You never know when that might come in handy.

When I was fourteen Jack Gorsky and I attempted to run away. He was this Polack who lived down the street. We were gone for three days. We made it all the way to Kokomo before the cops found us, camping out in an all-but-abandoned cemetery beside hundred-year-old graves. They found us drunk on a bottle of Mrs. Gorsky's vodka that Jack stuffed in a backpack on his way out the door. It was March. We'd built a fire from nothing but wood. Jack had tripped over a rock and scraped the shit out of his knee. I bandaged it up with a first-aid kit I'd brought, bandages and gauze I took from home.

I tried hunting once, with Jack Gorsky and his dad. I spent the night at their house, woke up at 5:00 a.m. the next day. We dressed in camouflage and headed out into the woods. They were professionals with all the gear, crossbows and rifles, binoculars, night vision, ammunition. I was the amateur, dressed in forest-green sweats I picked up at Wal-Mart the day before. Jack and his dad wore combat clothes from when Mr. Gorsky was in the Vietnam War. Mr. Gorsky spotted a whitetail deer. The damn thing was gorgeous, a male with antlers I couldn't take my eyes off. It was my first time hunting. Mr. Gorsky thought I should have the first shot. It was only fair. I crouched into position and stared it down, into these black eyes that dared me to shoot.

"Now take your time, Colin," he told me. I was sure he could see my arm shaking like a pansy. "Steady."

I missed on purpose, scaring the buck to safety.

Mr. Gorsky said it happened to everyone; next time I'd have more luck. Jack called me a sissy. Then it was Jack's turn. I watched him shoot a fawn right between the eyes while the doe watched her baby die.

The next time they invited me to tag along I said I was sick. It wasn't long before Jack was sent to juvie for threatening a teacher with his father's pistol.

I'm driving down County Line Road, just past Trout Lake Road when it hits me: I could keep driving. Straight past Grand Marais, out of Minnesota and onto the Rio Grande. I've got the girl tied up. There's no way she's getting out of there. No way she can call the cops and snitch. Even if she got her hands untied, which she won't, it would be hours before she could walk to civilization. By then, I'd be in South Dakota or Nebraska somewhere. The cops would put out an APB, but all the girl knows me as is Owen, so unless she got a good look at the license plate I might just stand a chance. I toy around with the idea in my mind, the notion of abandoning that crappy cabin and running. But there are about a million things that could go wrong. Chances are by now the cops know I'm with the girl. Maybe they've figured out my name. Maybe there's an APB out on me already. Maybe Dalmar turned me in himself for revenge, retribution.

But that's not the only thing that keeps me from going. I see the girl, tied to the bathroom sink, in the wilderness, off season. No one would find her. Not until she starved to death. Not until springtime, when tourists returned, drawn to the cabin by the smell of rotting flesh.

That's one thing that keeps me on track. One of many that make it impossible to cut and run, though I want to. Though I need to. Though I know that every day I stay is just another nail in my coffin.

I don't know how long I'm gone. Hours at least. When I

come back, I slam the door shut. I appear in the bathroom doorway with a knife. I see the girl start to panic but I don't say a thing. I drop down beside her and cut the rope. I reach out a hand to help her to her feet. But she pushes me away. I lose my balance, reaching for the wall. Her legs are weak. She runs fingers across a rope burn on each wrist, raw and red.

"What did you do that for?" I ask, grabbing her hands for a closer look. She sat there all day and tried to get out of the rope.

She pushes me as hard as she possibly can. It isn't much. I grab her by the arm and block the blow. It hurts, I can tell, the way I seize her and don't let go.

"You think I could just *leave* you here?" I ask. I throw her away from me. I'm already walking away. "Your face is all over the TV. I couldn't bring you with me."

"You did last time."

"You're famous now."

"And you?"

"No one gives a shit where I am."

"You're lying."

I stand in the kitchen, unpacking. The empty paper bags fall to the floor. Firewood. She eyes the new fishing pole that's leaned against the door.

"Where were you?"

"Getting all this shit." I'm short. I'm getting mad. I slam the canned food into the cabinet, bang the doors shut. And then I stop. I stop unpacking long enough to look at her. It doesn't happen often. "If I wanted you dead, you'd be dead. There's a lake out there close to freezing. They wouldn't find you until spring."

She looks out the window at the frigid lake in the afternoon haze. It makes her shudder, the thought of her own lifeless body submerged below the surface.

And then I do it.

I reach into the cabinet and pull the gun. She turns to run. I grasp her by the arm and force the gun into her hands. It surprises us both. The feeling of the gun, the heavy metal in her hands, immobilizes her. "Take it," I insist. She doesn't want it. "Take the gun," I scream. She holds it in her shaking hands and it nearly drops to the floor. I grab her hands and bind them around the gun. I force her finger onto the trigger. "Right there. You feel that? That's how you shoot it. You point it at me and shoot. You think I'm lying to you? You think I'm going to hurt you? It's loaded. So you just point it at me and shoot."

She stands, comatose, with the gun in her hands. Wondering what the hell just happened. She raises it for a second, the weight of it much heavier than she ever expected. She points it at me and I stare at her, daring her. *Shoot it. Shoot the gun.* Her eyes are skittish, her hands wobbly on the weapon. She doesn't have it in her to shoot that gun. I know that. But still, I wonder.

We stand like that, twenty seconds, thirty seconds, maybe more, before she lowers it before herself and walks out of the room.

EVE

AFTER

She tells me about her dream. The old Mia would never do this. The old Mia would never tell me much of what was on her mind. But this dream is really bothering her, a reoccurring dream that she says she's had night after night for I don't know how many nights now, but it's always the same, or so she says. She's sitting on a white plastic lawn chair inside the all-encompassing great room of a tiny cabin. The chair is pressed up against the wall opposite the front door and she's curled up on the chair, a scratchy blanket enveloping her legs. She's freezing cold, shaking to the point of uncontrollable, though she's sound asleep, her exhausted body toppling over the arm of the chair. She's wearing a frumpy maroon sweatshirt with an embroidered loon on the front, the words *L'étoile du Nord* stitched beneath.

In the dream she watches herself sleep. The darkness of the cabin closes in around her, smothering her. She can feel the apprehension and something else. Something more. Fear. Terror. Foreboding.

When he touches her arm she winces. His hand, she tells me, is as cold as ice. She feels the gun on her lap, bearing down on legs that are now numb, having been curled into a knot all night. The sun is up, gleaming through the filthy windows, the outdated plaid curtains that remain drawn. She seizes the gun, points it at him and cocks the hammer. Her expression is cold. Mia knows nothing about guns. Everything she knows, she says, he showed her.

The gun feels awkward and heavy in her shaking hands. But she can feel the resolve in her dreams: she could shoot him. She could do it. She could end his life.

He is unruffled, motionless. Before her his posture straightens until he is upright. He looks rested though his eyes still show distress: the furrowed eyebrows, the pessimism that returns her immovable stare. His skin is unshaven, days of stubble multiplying into a mustache and beard. He's just rolled out of bed. His face is covered with creases and in the corner of his eyes is sleep. His clothes are rumpled from having been slept in all night. He stands beside the lawn chair and even from the distance she can smell morning breath.

"Chloe," he says with this tranquilizing voice. She says that it is gentle and reassuring and even though she's certain they both know he could yank the weapon from her convulsing hands and kill her, he doesn't try. "I made eggs."

And then she wakes up.

There are two things that jump out to me: the words *L'étoile du Nord* on the sweatshirt, and eggs. Well, that and the fact that Mia—nom de plume Chloe—is holding a gun. I find my laptop in the afternoon, after Mia has retreated to her bedroom for one of many daily naps. I find a search engine and type in the French words I should know from a high school class about a million years ago but I don't. It's one of the first hits on the page: Star of the North, the Minnesota state motto. Of course.

If the dream is a memory, not a dream at all, a recollection of her time in *L'étoile du Nord,* then why is she holding a gun? And more importantly perhaps, why didn't she use the gun to shoot Colin Thatcher? How did this incident end? I want to know.

But I reassure myself that this dream is only symbolic. I search for the meaning of dreams, specifically eggs. I come across a dream-interpretation dictionary and it's in the definition that everything begins to make sense. I picture Mia at that very moment, lying on her bed, curled up in the fetal position under the covers. She said she didn't feel well when she went up to bed; I can't recall how many times I've heard that now and I've repeatedly chalked it up to fatigue and stress. But I understand now that it may be more. My fingers freeze on the keyboard, I begin to cry. Could it be?

They say that morning sickness is hereditary. I was sick as a dog with both girls, worse so with Grace. I've heard that it's often worse with a first child, and rightly so. I spent many days and nights hunkered down over the toilet, vomiting until there was nothing to throw up but bile. I was tired all the time, the lethargy like nothing I'd ever known before; it exhausted me just to open my eyes. James didn't understand. Of course he didn't; how could he? It was something I never understood until I lived through it, though over and over again I wished to die.

According to this dream-interpretation dictionary, eggs in one's dreams may represent something new and fragile. Life in its earliest form.

COLIN

BEFORE

I woke up early. I dragged that fishing pole outside, out to the lake with a tackle box I picked up at the store. I spent a small fortune on fishing supplies—an auger and skimmer, too, for when the lake freezes over. Not that I plan to be here that long.

She pulls a sweatshirt over her head. She hikes out to the lake. Her hair is still wet from a bath and the ends become crisp in the cold air. Until she arrives, it's quiet outside. The sun is just beginning to rise. I'm lost in thought, trying hard to convince myself that everything back home is okay. Trying to satisfy the guilt by brainwashing myself into believing that there's plenty of food in the fridge, that she hasn't fallen down and broken a hip. And just as I start to believe it, some new fear comes to mind: that I forgot to set the heat and she'll freeze to death, that she leaves the front door open and some critter lets itself in. And then the rationalization sets in, the excuses: I did set the heat. Of course I did. I spend ten minutes picturing myself setting the damn heat at sixty-eight degrees.

At least by now the cash should've arrived, enough money to get her through. For a while.

I brought a lawn chair down from the cabin and sit with a

mug of coffee by my feet. I stare at what the girl's wearing as she approaches the lake. Her pants do nothing to block the wind. There are no leaves left in the trees to slow it down. It drives her frozen hair around her face. It slips up the leg of her khakis and down the neck of her shirt. She's already shaking.

I did set the heat. Of course I did. Sixty-eight degrees.

"What are you doing out here?" I ask. "You're going to freeze your ass off."

And yet, she sits down, uninvited, on the banks of the lake. I could tell her to go back inside, but I don't.

The ground is damp. She pulls her legs into her and wraps her arms around them to keep warm.

We don't talk. We don't need to. She's just thankful to be outside.

The cabin smells awful, like mold or mildew. It pierces the nose even after all these days when you think we'd be used to it. It's as cold inside as out. We have to conserve as much wood as we can until winter. Until then, we only light the stove at night. During the day the temperature in the cabin must plummet to the fifties. I know she's never warm, though she bundles layer over layer. The winter this far north is harsh and unforgiving, cold like we've never known before. In days it will be November, the final calm before the storm.

A small group of Common loons soars above the lake heading south. The last few that remain this far north. It's the chicks who leave now, those who were born this spring and are only now gaining enough strength for the long journey. The others are gone.

I'm guessing she's never fished before, but I have. I've been fishing since I was a kid. I hold the rod, my body still. I watch the bobber on the surface of the water. She knows enough to keep her mouth shut. She knows the sound of her voice will scare the fish away.

"Here," I say, balancing the rod between my knees. I take off my coat, a big insulated rain jacket with a hood. I hand it to her. "Put it on before you freeze to death."

She doesn't know what to say. She doesn't even say thanks. This isn't something we do. She slips her arms into crevices that are two times too big for her and after a minute, she stops shaking. She drapes the hood over her head and takes refuge for winter. I'm not cold. If I was, I wouldn't admit it.

A fish bites. I stand to my feet and jerk the fishing line to set the hook. I begin reeling, pulling on the line to keep it tight. She turns her back when a fish comes flying out of the water, its fin kicking for dear life. I drop it to the ground and watch its body thrash about until it's dead.

"You can look now," I say. "It's dead."

But she can't. She doesn't look. Not until my body blocks the view. I hover over the fish, and I slide the hook out of its mouth. Then I slip a worm onto the end of the hook and hold the rod out for the girl.

"No, thanks," she says.

"You ever fish before?"

"No."

"Not the kind of thing they teach you where you come from?"

She knows what I think of her. Spoiled little rich girl. She has yet to prove otherwise.

She snatches the rod from my hands. She isn't used to people telling her what to do. "You know what you're doing?" I ask.

"I can figure it out," she snaps. But she doesn't so much as have a clue so I'm forced to help her cast the line. She drops down onto the shoreline and she waits. She wills the fish away. I sit down on my chair and sip from the mug of coffee, cold by now.

The time passes. I don't know how much time. I go inside

for more coffee and to take a piss. When I come back, she tells me she's surprised I didn't tie her to a tree. The sun is up, trying hard to warm the day. It's not working.

"Consider yourself lucky."

In time I ask about her father.

At first she's quiet, staring at the water, deathly still. She takes in the trees' long shadows on the lake, the twitter of birds. "What about him?" she asks.

"What's he like?" I ask. But really, I know. I just want to hear her say it.

"I don't want to talk about it."

We're quiet for a moment. Then she breaks the silence.

"My father grew up rich," she says. "Old money," she says and then tells me: his family's always had money. For generations. They have more money than they know what to do with. "Enough to feed a small country," she says, but they don't. They keep it all to themselves.

She tells me how her father's career is high-profile. I know this. "People know him," she says. "All this goes to his big head. My father's never-ending desire for more money has made him corrupt. I wouldn't put much past him—accepting bribes, for one. He's just never been caught.

"Image is everything to him," she says. Then she tells me about her sister. Grace. She says that she, like her father, is pretentious and hollow and hedonistic. I give her a look. Grace is not the only one who's all these things. She's the daughter of a wealthy bastard. Her life's been delivered on a silver platter.

I know more about her than she'd like to think.

"Think whatever you want," she says. "But my father and I are different people." Very different, she says.

She tells me that she and her father never got along. Not when she was a child, not now.

"We don't talk much. Occasionally, but it's all a ruse. In case someone's keeping tabs."

Grace, a lawyer, is her father's protégée. "She's everything I never was," the girl says. "She's his mirror image. While my father never financed my college education, he put Grace through both college and law school. He bought her a condo in the Loop, which she could have paid for herself. Myself, I pay eight hundred and fifty dollars every month in rent and most months, that about breaks the bank. I asked my father to donate to the school I work at. Start a scholarship fund, maybe. He laughed. But he has Grace working at a top firm downtown. She charges clients over three hundred dollars for an hour of her time. Within a few years she'll likely make partner. She's everything my father ever wanted me to be."

"And you?"

"I'm the *other* one, the one whose mistakes he had to cover up."

She says that she was never of interest to her father. Not when she was putting on an impromptu show at the age of five. Not when she was hanging her first piece in a gallery at the age of nineteen. "Grace, on the other hand, her very presence could change his mood. She's bright, like him, and articulate, her words wrought with efficacy rather than—as my father liked to call it—delusion. These *grand delusions* I had of one day being an artist. My mother's *deluded* sense of reality."

What pisses me off is that she talks like she got the short end of the stick. Like *her* life is full of hard knocks. She doesn't have a fucking clue what tough luck is like. I think of the mint-green trailer home, of sitting out a storm in a makeshift shelter while we watched our home blow over. "I'm supposed to feel sorry for you?" I ask.

A bird begins to warble. In the distance, another returns its call.

Her voice is quiet. "I never asked you to feel sorry for me. You asked a question. I gave you an answer," she confides.

"You're just full of self-pity, aren't you?"

"It isn't like that."

"Always the victim." I'm unsympathetic. This girl doesn't know a damn thing about tough luck.

"No," she hisses at me. She thrusts the fishing rod into my hands. "Take it," she says. She unzips the coat and cringes at the cold air that envelops her. She drops it to the ground beside me. I let it lay there. I don't say a thing. "I'm going in."

And she walks past the dead fish whose eyes stare at her with contempt for letting it die.

She's not twenty feet away when I say, "What about the ransom?"

"What about it?" she snaps. She stands in the shade of a big tree, her hands on her hips. Her hair whirls around her in the cold October air.

"Would your dad have paid the ransom?" I ask. If he hates her as much as she makes believe, he wouldn't pay a penny for her return.

She's thinking about it. I know she is. It's a damn good question.

If her father didn't pay the ransom, then she'd be dead.

"I guess we'll never know," she says, and then she goes. I hear her feet smashing the leaves on the ground. I hear the squeal of a screen door opening in the distance. And then I hear it slam shut. I know that I'm alone.

GABE

BEFOᴙE

I'm driving down the world's most perfect, tree-lined street. Red maple and yellow aspen trees canopy over the narrow street, their leaves raining down. It's too early for trick-or-treaters, the little misfits still in school for an hour or two. But the million-dollar homes wait for them, tucked behind impeccable landscaping and lawns that actually necessitate a riding lawn mower...though no one around here dares mow their own lawn. They're all decked out with hay bales and corn stalks and perfectly round pumpkins with the unblemished stalks.

The mailman is closing in on the Dennetts' mailbox when I pull into the brick drive. I settle my piece-of-shit car beside Mrs. Dennett's sedan and wave a friendly hello as though I might just live here. I make my way to the brick mailbox, more spacious than my own john.

"Afternoon," I say as I thrust out a hand for today's mail.

"Afternoon," he replies as he sets a stack of mail into my hand.

It's cold out here. And gray. It always is, every single Halloween that I can ever remember. The gray clouds descend to the earth's surface until you can no longer tell the difference between land and sky. I tuck the mail under an arm and plunge my hands into my pockets as I make my way up the drive.

Mrs. Dennett has this way of thrusting open the front door every time I arrive. There's a great gusto about it, her face awash with enthusiasm until she sees me. The smile disappears. Her wide eyes vanish. Sometimes there's a sigh.

I don't take it personally.

"Oh," she says. "Detective."

Every time the doorbell rings, she's sure it's Mia.

She's wearing an apron the color of mustard over a whole yoga ensemble.

"You're cooking?" I ask, trying not to choke on the smell. She's either cooking or a small animal has crept into the basement and died.

"Trying." She's already walking away from me, leaving the front door hanging open. There's a nervous laugh as I follow her into the kitchen. "Lasagna," she says, slicing a mound of mozzarella cheese. "Ever make lasagna before?"

"I specialize in frozen pizza," I say, setting the mail on the island. "Thought I'd save you the trip."

"Oh, thank you," she says, dropping the cheese slicer and reaching for an "explanation of benefits" from the insurance company. She wanders off in search of a letter opener while, on the stove, Italian sausage begins to burn.

I do know a thing or two about lasagna. I watched my mother cook it about a million times as a kid. She'd trip over me in our tiny kitchen, while I hounded her—*Is it ready yet? Is it ready yet?*—while playing with my Matchbox cars on the kitchen floor.

I find a wooden spoon in the drawer and give it a whirl.

"What was I..." she asks mindlessly as she returns to the kitchen. "Oh, Detective, you don't have to," she says, but I tell her that I don't mind. I set the spoon beside the skillet. She's sorting the mail.

"Have you ever seen so much junk?" she asks me. "Catalogs. Bills. Everyone wants our money. Have you ever even heard of—" she holds up the envelope for a closer look at the name of the charity "—Mowat-Wilson syndrome?"

"Mowat-Wilson syndrome," I repeat. "Can't say that I have."

"Mowat-Wilson syndrome," she says again, settling the envelope on a pile of mail that eventually works its way into a fancy-schmancy organizer on the wall. I would have thought for sure the Mowat-Wilsons were going to be recycled; turns out they just might get a check. "Judge Dennett must have done something special to deserve lasagna," I say. My mother cooks lasagna all the time. There's nothing special about it. But for someone like Eve Dennett, I gather that a home-cooked meal, one like this, is a rare treat. Depending, of course, on if ones lives through the meal; based on the looks of this, I'm rather happy I haven't been invited to stay. I'm an expert at stereotypes, sure that Mrs. Dennett is a one-trick pony in the kitchen. She's probably got a chicken recipe and chances are she can boil water. But that's all.

"It's not for James," Mrs. Dennett says as she moves behind me to the stove. The sleeve of a black spandex top grazes my back. I'm sure she doesn't notice. But I do. I can still feel it, seconds after she's gone. The woman tosses a pile of onions into the skillet. They hiss.

I know that it's Mia's birthday.

"Mrs. Dennett?" I ask.

"I'm not going to do this," she vows, completely absorbed in cooking the charred meat, quite a turn of events for someone who, two seconds earlier, didn't give a shit. "I'm not going to cry."

And then I notice the balloons, a whole slew of them covering the house, all in lime-green and magenta. Apparently a favorite.

"It's for *her*," she says. "Mia loves lasagna. Any kind of pasta. She's the only one I could always count on to eat what I'd cooked. It's not that I expect her to show up. I know that won't happen. But I couldn't..." And she lets her voice trail off. From behind, I see her shoulders quake, and watch as the Italian sausage absorbs her tears. She could blame the onions, but she doesn't. I don't stare. I lose myself in the mozzarella cheese. She finds a clove of garlic and begins to smash the damn thing with the palm of her hand. I didn't know Mrs. Dennett had it in her. Seems to be amazingly therapeutic. Into the skillet the garlic goes, and she yanks jars of seasoning—basil and fennel, salt and pepper—from a cabinet and slams them to the granite countertop. The acrylic salt shaker misses the edge of the countertop and tumbles to the hardwood floor. It doesn't break, but the salt spills. We stare at the collection of white crystals on the floor, thinking the same thing: bad luck. Is it seven years? I don't know. Regardless, I insist, "Left shoulder."

"Are you sure it isn't the right?" she asks. There's a panic to her voice, as if this little salt incident might very well determine whether or not Mia will come home.

"Left," I respond, knowing I'm right, but then to pacify her, I say, "Oh, what the heck, why not toss a little over both. Then you know you're covered."

She does, then wipes her hands on the front of the apron. I stoop to pick up the salt shaker, and she lowers herself to collect the remaining salt in the palm of her hand. It happens in an instant and before we know it, we clunk heads. She presses a hand to her wound. I find myself reaching out to her. I ask if she's okay, then say I'm sorry. We rise to our feet and for the first time, Mrs. Dennett begins to laugh.

God, she's gorgeous, though the laughter is uneasy, like she might just burst into tears at any moment. I dated a girl once who was bipolar. Manic highs one minute, so that she wanted to conquer the world, so depressed the next she could hardly get out of bed.

I wonder if Judge Dennett has once—just one time since this all happened—put his arms around the woman and told her that it was going to be okay.

When she settles I say to her, "Can you imagine if Mia did come home? Tonight. If she just showed up at that door and there was *nothing.*"

She's shaking her head. She can't imagine.

"Why did you become a detective?" she asks me.

There is nothing profound about this. It's embarrassing almost. "I was appointed this position because, apparently, I was a good cop. But I became a cop because I had a friend in college that was headed to the academy. I had nothing better to do than follow."

"But you like your job?"

"I like my job."

"Isn't it depressing? I can hardly watch the news at night."

"It has its bad days," I say, but then I go on to list as many good things as I can possibly come up with. Putting down a meth lab. Finding a lost dog. Catching some kid who'd gone to school with a pocketknife in his bag. "Finding Mia," I conclude and though I don't say it aloud, I think to myself: if I could find Mia and bring her back home, if I could wake Mrs. Dennett from this horrible nightmare she's trapped in, that would make it worth it. That would override all the open, unsolved cases, all the wrongdoing that goes on in our world every day.

She returns to her lasagna. I tell her that I wanted to ask her a few questions about Mia. I watch as she spreads the noodles and the cheese and meat into a pan, and we talk about a girl of whom photographs magically appear, scattered in more abundance every time I come through the door.

Mia on the first day of school, smiling though half her teeth are gone.

Mia with a goose-egg bump on her head.

Mia with scrawny little legs hanging out of a one-piece bathing suit, floaties on her arms.

Mia preparing for the high school prom.

Two weeks ago one might not have known that Grace Dennett had a younger sister. Now it's as if she's the only presence in this home.

COLIN

BEFORE

I have the advantage of a watch with the date on it. Without it we'd both be lost.

I don't do it first thing in the morning. She hasn't spoken to me in over twenty-four hours. She's pissed that I pried, but even more pissed that she talked. She doesn't want me to know a damn thing about her, but I know enough.

I wait until after we've eaten breakfast. I wait until after lunch. I let her be mad and sulk. She mopes around the cabin feeling sorry for herself. She pouts. It never crosses her mind that there are a million places I'd rather be than here, but this is her misfortune and hers alone. Or so she thinks.

I'm not one for grand displays. I wait until she's done cleaning the dishes from lunch. She's drying her hands on a terry-cloth towel when I more or less drop it on the counter beside her.

"It's for you."

She glances at the notebook on the counter. A sketch book. And ten mechanical pencils.

"That's all the lead there is. Don't use it all at once."

"What's this?" she asks stupidly. She knows what it is.

"Something to pass the time."

"But—" she begins. She doesn't finish right away. She takes the notebook into her hands and runs a hand across the front of it. She flips through the blank pages. "But…" she stammers. She doesn't know what to say. I wish she wouldn't say anything. We don't need to say anything. "But…why?"

"It's Halloween," I say for lack of a better answer.

"Halloween." She mutters it under her breath. She knows it's more than that. It isn't every day you turn twenty-five. "How did you know?"

I show her my secret, the tiny 31 on a watch I stole from some schmuck.

"How did you know it was my birthday?"

Time spent on the internet before I took her, that's the honest answer. But I don't want to tell her that. She doesn't need to know how I tracked her for days before the abduction, following her to and from work, watching her through her bedroom window. "Research."

"Research."

She doesn't say thanks. Words like that—*please, thank you, I'm sorry*—are signs of peace and we're not there yet. Maybe we'll never be. She holds the notebook close to her. I don't know why I did it. I was sick of watching her stare out the damn window, so I spent five dollars on paper and pencils and it seems to have made her fucking day. They don't sell sketch pads at the local outfitters, so I had to drive all the way back to Grand Marais, to some bookstore while I kept her tied to the bathroom sink.

EVE

BEFORE

I plan a party for her birthday, just in case. I invite James and Grace and my in-laws: James's parents, and his brothers with their wives and children. I make a trip to the mall and buy gifts I know she would adore: clothes mostly, those peasant blouses she likes and a cowl-neck sweater, and the big bulky jewelry the girls are wearing these days. Now that Mia has been on the television news, I can barely leave home without everyone wanting to know. In the grocery store, women stare. They whisper behind my back. Strangers are better than friends and neighbors, those who want to *talk* about it. I can't talk about Mia without being reduced to tears. I hurry through the parking lot to avoid news vans that have begun to stalk us. At the mall, the saleslady looks at my credit card and wonders if *Dennett* is one and the same with the girl on TV. I lie, feign ignorance because I can't explain without coming unglued.

I wrap the gifts in Happy Birthday paper and stack the boxes with a big red ribbon. I make three pans of lasagna and buy loaves of Italian bread to make garlic bread. I make a salad and pick up a cake from the bakery, with chocolate buttercream icing, Mia's favorite. I get twenty-five latex balloons from the grocery store and dribble them around the house. I hang an infamous Happy Birthday banner we've hung on to since the girls were kids and fill the CD player with relaxing jazz.

No one comes. Grace claims to have a date with the son of some partner, but I don't believe it. Though she wouldn't dare admit it, she is on pins and needles these days, knowing that what she swore was only a ploy for attention is likely something more. But Grace being Grace disengages herself from the situation rather than acknowledging it. She puts on a casual display, as if unaffected by Mia's situation, but I can tell, by the sound of her voice when we speak, when Mia's name slips from her tongue—and she lingers there, appreciating it—that she is truly afflicted by her sister's disappearance.

James insists that I can't plan a party when the guest of honor isn't here. And so, without my knowledge, he called his parents and Brian and Marty and told them the whole thing was a farce, there was no party. But he didn't tell me, not until eight o'clock, at least, when he finally strolled in from work and asked, "Why in the hell is there so much lasagna in here?" while staring at the display on the kitchen island.

"The party," I say naively. Perhaps they're only late.

"There is no party, Eve," he says.

He makes himself a nightcap as he always does, but before retreating to his office for the night, he stops suddenly and looks at me. It's rare that he does, actually look at me. The look on his face is unmistakable: the rueful eyes, the pleats of his skin, the taut mouth. It's in the sound of his voice, in the secretive, sedate speech.

"Do you remember Mia's sixth birthday?" he asks and I do. I had sat down earlier today and looked through photographs: all those birthday parties that came and went in the blink of an eye.

But what surprises me is that James remembers.

I nod. "Yes," I say. "That was the year Mia wanted a dog." A Tibetan mastiff, to be exact, a loyal guard dog with an abundance of thick, shedding fur that ordinarily weighed well over a hundred pounds. There would be no dog. James made that clear. Not that birthday; not ever. Mia replied with tears and hysterics and James, who typically would have ignored the rant, spent a fortune on a plush Tibetan mastiff, which had to be special ordered from a toy store in New York City.

"I don't think I've ever seen her so happy," he says, recalling the way little Mia's arms wrapped around that 36-inch stuffed animal, her hands like a padlock at the other end, and I begin to understand: he's worried. For the first time, James is worried about our child.

"She still has that dog," I remind him. "Upstairs. In her room," I say, and he says that he knows.

"I can still see her," he admits. "I can still see the *elation* when I came into the room with that dog, tucked behind my back."

"She loved it," I say, and with that, he walks to his office and solemnly closes the door.

I forgot altogether to buy Halloween candy for the neighborhood kids. The doorbell rings all night and, stupidly hoping to see my in-laws on the other side, I throw it open every time. Initially I'm the crazy lady passing out change from a piggy bank, but by the end of the night I'm slicing the birthday cake and giving it away. Parents who don't know give me dirty looks, and those who do examine me with pity.

"Any news?" asks a neighbor, Rosemary Southerland, who trick-or-treats with tiny grandchildren, too small to ring the doorbell alone.

"No news," I say, with tears in my eyes.

"We're praying for you," she offers, helping Winnie the Pooh and Tigger down the front step.

"Thank you" is what I say, but what I'm thinking is *Fat lot of good it's doing.*

COLIN

BEFOЯE

I say she can go outside. It's the first time I let her out alone. "Stay where I can see you," I say. I'm covering the windows in plastic sheeting in preparation for winter. I've been at it all day. Yesterday I caulked all the windows and doors. The day before, insulated the pipes. She asked why I was doing it, and I looked at her like she was stupid. "So they don't burst," I said. It's not like I want to stay here for the winter. But until I figure out a better option, it's not like we've got a choice.

She pauses before the door. She holds the sketch pad in her grasp. "You're not coming?"

"You're a big girl," I say.

She lets herself outside and sits about halfway down the stairs. I watch out the window. She better not press her luck.

It snowed last night, just a little. The ground is covered with brown pine needles and mushrooms, but soon they will die. Patches of ice form on the lake. Nothing substantial. It will all melt by noon. A sign that winter will arrive soon.

She dusts the step free of snow, sits down and spreads the sketch pad across her lap. Yesterday we came out together and sat beside the lake. I caught trout while she drew a dozen or so trees with raggedy lines protruding through the earth.

I don't know how long I watch her through the window. It isn't so much that I think she's gonna run away—she knows better than that by now—but I watch her anyway. I watch the way her skin becomes red from the cold. The way her hair blows around in the breeze. She tucks it behind an ear, hoping to contain it, but it doesn't work. Not all things like to be contained. I watch her hands move across the page. Quickly. Easily. With a pencil and paper she is the same way I feel with a gun: in charge, in control. It's the only time she's sure of anything about herself. It's that assurance that keeps me at the window, on guard but also hypnotized. I imagine her face, what I can't see when her back is in my direction. She's not so hard on the eyes.

I open the door and step outside. It slams shut and she startles, turning to see what the hell I want. On the paper before her, there's a lake, the ripples gliding across the surface on the gusty day. There's a handful of geese perched on a gauzy patch of ice.

She tries to pretend I'm not there, but I know, my presence makes it hard for her to do anything but breathe.

"Where'd you learn to do that?" I ask. I look at the exterior doors and windows, searching for leaks.

"Do what?" she asks. She sets her hands on top of the picture, so I can't see.

I stop what I'm doing. "Ice-skate," I snap sarcastically. "What the hell do you think?"

"I taught myself," she says.

"Just for the hell of it?"

"I guess."

"Why?"

"Why not?"

But she tells me anyway how she has two people to thank for her *artistic talent*: some junior high teacher and Bob Ross.

I don't know who Bob Ross is so she tells me. She says that she used to set up her paints and easel before the TV and paint with him. Her sister would tell her to get a life. She'd call her a loser. Her mom would pretend not to hear. She says that she started drawing early on, when she could hide in her bedroom with a coloring book and crayons.

"It's not bad," I say. But I'm not looking at her. Or the picture. I'm scraping old caulk from the window. It falls to the deck beside my feet, scraps of the white caulk that build up on the ground.

"How do you know?" she asks. "You didn't look."

"I looked."

"You didn't," she says. "I know indifference when I see it. I've been staring at it my whole life."

I sigh and mutter some curse under my breath. Her hands are still covering the picture. "What is it, then?" she asks.

"What the hell do you mean?"

"What's it a picture of?"

I stop what I'm doing and stare out toward the geese. One by one, they leave. "That," I say and she gives it a rest. I move onto another window.

"What did you do this for?" she asks, holding up the notebook.

I stop what I'm doing long enough to look. I'm going after that caulk with some brutality and I know what she thinks: *Better the caulk than me.*

"Why do you ask so many fucking questions?" I snarl and she goes silent. She begins to sketch the sky, low stratus clouds that wander just above the ground. At some point I say, "So I didn't have to babysit you. So you'd shut up and stay out of my hair."

"Oh," she says. She stands up and lets herself back inside.

But it isn't entirely the truth.

If I wanted her out of my hair I would have bought more rope to tie her to the bathroom sink. If I wanted her to shut up, I would have used duct tape.

But if I wanted to atone, I would have bought her that sketch pad.

Growing up, anyone could have guessed that I'd end up this way. I was always getting in trouble. For beating up kids, telling off adults. For failing and skipping classes. In high school the guidance counselor suggested to Ma that she take me to a shrink. She said I had an anger management issue. Ma told her that if she'd been through what I'd been through, she'd be angry, too.

My dad left when I was six. He stayed long enough for me to remember him, but not long enough for him to actually take care of Ma and me. I remember the fights, not just yelling. Hitting each other and throwing things. The sound of breaking glass when I pretended to sleep at night. Doors slamming and four-letter words screamed at the top of their lungs. I remember empty beer bottles and the caps that showed up in his pant pockets long after he claimed he was dry.

I got in fights at school. I told my math teacher to go to hell because he said I'd never amount to anything. I told my high school biology teacher to screw herself because she thought she could help me pass her class.

I didn't want anyone to give a shit about me.

I found this life by accident. I was washing dishes at some pretentious restaurant in the city. There was the filth of other people's leftovers on my hands, the scalding hot water as I stacked the clean plates from the conveyor dishwasher. My fingers would burn, my head drip with sweat. All for minimum wage and a share of the waitresses' tips. I asked if I could get some extra hours. I said I was tight on cash. My boss said to me, "Aren't we all." Business was slow, but he knew somewhere I could get a loan. It wasn't a bank. I thought I could handle it. I'd borrow a little, pay it back the next time I got paid but it didn't work out that way. I couldn't even cover the interest. We worked out a deal. Some bigwig owed about ten times as much as me. If I could get him to pay up, we'd be even. So I showed up at his Streeterville home, tied his wife and daughter to their antique dining room chairs and, with a borrowed gun to the wife's head, watched him withdraw the crisp dollar bills from a family safe hidden behind a reproduction of Monet's *Water Lilies*.

I was in.

A few weeks later Dalmar tracked me down. I'd never met Dalmar. I was in a bar minding my own business when he wandered in. I was the new kid on the block, their plaything. Everyone seemed to have something to hold over my head. And so it was out of necessity that when Dalmar claimed some dude had stolen his stuff, I went in to get it. I was paid generously. I could cover the rent. Take care of Ma. Eat.

But with every dollar I earned was also the knowledge that I belonged to someone other than me.

Every day she moves a little farther from the cabin. One day she goes to the bottom of the stairs. Another day her feet touch grass. Today she moves onto the dirt, knowing all the while that I sit at the window and watch her. She sits on the cold, hard earth, becoming numb as she draws. I imagine the air closing in on her, her fingers stiff. I can't see what she's drawing, but I imagine: bark and branches, what's left of the trees now that the leaves are completely gone. She draws tree after tree. She doesn't waste an inch of the precious paper.

She closes the notebook and starts to walk down to the lake, where she sits on the banks alone. I watch as she finds rocks and attempts to skip them across the surface of the lake.

They all sink. She lets her feet take her along the lake's shore. Not too far. A dozen or so feet to a spot that she's never been before.

It isn't that I think she's gonna go. It's that suddenly I don't want to be in the cabin alone. She turns at the sound of crunching leaves behind her. I'm tromping out toward the lake, my hands stuffed into the pockets of my jeans, my neck buried into the scruff of the coat.

"Checking on me?" she asks impassively before I arrive.

I stop beside her. "Do I need to?"

We stand side by side without saying a thing. My coat brushes her arm and she steps away. I wonder if she could ever get this right. This scene. In her sketch pad. The shape of the blue lake and the leaves spilled across the ground. The forest-green pine and evergreen trees. The enormous sky. Could she ever get the wind whipping through the remains of trees? Could she draw the cold air that eats at our hands and ears until they burn?

I start to walk away. "You want to walk, don't you?" I ask when she doesn't follow. She does. "Then let's go," I say, though all the time I stay two steps ahead. Between us, there's nothing but dead air.

I don't know how big this lake is. It's big. I don't know how deep it gets at its deepest point. I don't know what its name is. The shoreline is rugged, with rocky overlooks that peek down on the water. The evergreen trees come right up to the shores. There's no beach. They circle the entire periphery of the lake, huddled close together, fighting each other for a view.

The leaves crunch beneath our feet like foam chips. She fights to keep her balance on the jagged ground. I don't wait for her. We continue for a long time, until we can no longer see the cabin through the trees. I'm sure her feet are killing her in those stupid shoes, the ones she had on when we left.

Fancy work shoes. But the cold air and the exercise feel good. A change from sitting around in the cabin feeling sorry for ourselves.

She asks something but I don't hear. I wait for her to catch up. "What?" I ask sharply. I'm not one for small talk.

"You have any brothers?"

"No."

"Sisters?"

"You always have to *talk*?" I ask.

She passes ahead and takes the lead. "You always have to be so rude?" she asks. I don't say a thing. This is the gist of our conversations.

The next day she's outside again, moving aimlessly around the lot. She isn't stupid enough to go where I can't see her. Not yet, because she knows she'll lose this privilege.

She's afraid of the unknown. Of Dalmar, maybe, of what I'd do if she tried to run. It's fear that keeps her within my line of sight. She could make a run for it, but there's nowhere to go.

She has the gun. She could shoot me. But of course she hasn't figured out how to shoot the damn thing. As far as she's concerned, I'm worth keeping around just for that.

But with the gun in her possession, I don't have to listen to the bitching anymore. For the time being she's content. She can go outside and freeze her ass off. She can draw God-knows-what all day long.

She comes back in sooner than I expect. In her arms there's a filthy cat. It isn't that I hate cats. It's just that food is scarce. Heat is scarce. There isn't enough room for the two of us in here, much less three. And I'm not sharing.

Her eyes beg *please*.

"If I see that cat in here again," I say, "I'll shoot it."

I'm not in the mood to be a Good Samaritan.

GABE

BEFORE

After waiting for what seemed an eternity—in reality it's about three weeks—we finally get a good tip: an Indian woman living in a high-rise on Kenmore is certain our John Doe is her neighbor. Apparently she had been out of town for a while and this is the first time she's seen his face on TV.

So I bring backup and make my way downtown—again. The high-rise is located in Uptown, certainly not the best neighborhood in the city; not the worst, either. Far from it. It's a mix of people who can't quite afford the classier areas like Lakeview or Lincoln Park, and an eclectic mix of men and women who just stepped off the boat. It's very diverse. Ethnic restaurants line the streets, and not just Chinese and Mexican; there's Moroccan and Vietnamese and Ethiopian joints. Regardless of its diversity, nearly half the population of Uptown is still white. It's relatively safe to walk around at night. Uptown is known for its nightlife of historic theaters and bars. Many well-known names have made the trip to Uptown to perform for nobodies like me.

I find the apartment building and double-park; last thing I'm going to do is donate another penny to the city of Chicago to park my car. The butch cop and I head inside and take the elevator to the unit. There's no answer and the door is locked. Of course. So we beg the landlord to let us in. She's an old lady who hobbles along beside us and refuses to let us borrow the key. "You can't trust anyone these days," she says. She tells us that the unit is rented by a woman named Celeste Monfredo. She had to look it up in her files. She knows nothing about the woman other than she pays her rent on time.

"But of course the unit could be a sublet."

"How would we know?" I ask.

The old lady shrugs. "We wouldn't. Tenants are required to sublet their own units or pay to break the lease."

"There's no paperwork?" I can't pick up Sudafed at the pharmacy without having to sign away my life.

"None that I keep. The tenants are still required to pay rent. Anything happens, it's their problem. Not mine."

I take the key from her hands and let myself in. The landlord pushes her way into the apartment beside Butch and me. I have to ask her more than once not to touch anything.

I'm not sure what strikes me first: an overturned lamp, lights on in the middle of the day, or the contents of a woman's purse scattered across the floor. I reach into my pocket for a pair of latex gloves and roam the apartment. There's a stack of mail on the kitchen counter, hidden beneath an overdue library book. I check out the address label; every single one of them has been sent to a Michael Collins at a P.O. box in the city. Butch slips her hands in latex and heads for the purse. She delves in and finds a wallet, and inside, a driver's license. "Mia Dennett," she says aloud, though of course we both knew exactly what it would say.

"I want phone records," I say. "And fingerprints. And we need to canvass the building. Every unit. Is there a security camera?" I ask the landlord. She says that there is. "I need everything you have from October 1."

I examine the wall: concrete. No one would have heard a thing that happened inside this room.

COLIN

BEFOЯE

She wants to know how much I got paid for this. She asks too many questions.

"I didn't get paid a damn thing," I remind her. "I get paid for finishing a job."

"How much were you offered?"

"None of your business," I say.

We're in the bathroom, of all places. She's on her way in. I'm on my way out. I don't bother to tell her the water is ice-cold.

"Does my father know about this?"

"I told you already. I don't know."

The ransom was to be collected from her father. That I know. But I don't have a damn clue what Dalmar did when I didn't show up with the girl.

She smells of morning breath, her hair a labyrinth of dirty blond.

She closes the door on me and I hear the water begin to run. I try not to imagine her stripping away her clothes and stepping into the piercing water.

When she comes out she's drying the ends of her hair with a towel. I'm in the kitchen eating granola and freeze-dried milk. I've forgotten what it tastes like to eat real food. I've got all the cash spread out on the table, and I'm counting what we've got left. She eyes the cash. We're not broke. Not yet. That's a good thing.

She tells me how she always thought some disgruntled convict would shoot her father on the courthouse steps. In her voice I hear a different story. She didn't *think* it would happen. She hoped.

She's standing in the hallway. I can see her shiver, but she doesn't whine about being cold. Not this time.

"He was a litigation lawyer before becoming a judge. He got involved in a number of class-action suits, asbestos cases. He never protected the good guy. People were dying of these horrible things—mesothelioma, asbestosis—and he's trying to save the big corporations a buck or two. He never talked about his work. Attorney-client privilege, he said, but I know he just didn't want to talk. Period. But I'd sneak into his office at night when he was asleep. At first I was snooping because I wanted to prove he was having an affair in the hopes my mother might actually leave him. I was a kid—thirteen, fourteen. I didn't know what mesothelioma was. But I could read well enough. Coughing up blood, heart palpitations, lumps under the skin. Nearly half of those infected died within a year of diagnosis. You didn't even have to work with asbestos to be exposed—wives and children were dying because their fathers brought it home on their clothes.

"The more successful he was, the more we were threatened. My mother would find letters in the mail. They knew where we lived. There were phone calls. Men hoping Grace, my mother and I would die as painful a death as their wives and children had.

"Then he became a judge. His face was all over the news. All these headlines with his name. He was harassed all the time, but after a while we stopped paying attention to these unsubstantiated threats. He let it go to his head. It made him feel important. The more people he pissed off, the better he was doing his job."

There's nothing to say. I'm not good at this kind of crap. I can't handle small talk and I certainly can't handle sympathy. The reality is that I know nothing about the scumbag who thought it would be in his best interest to threaten some bastard's kid. That's the way this business works. Guys like me, we're kept in the dark. We carry out an assignment without really knowing why. That way we can't point fingers. Not that I'd try. I know what would happen to me if I did. Dalmar told me to nab the girl. I didn't ask why. That way, when the cops catch me and I'm in the interrogation room, I can't answer their underhanded questions. I don't know who hired Dalmar. I don't know what they want with the girl. Dalmar told me to get her. I did.

And then I changed my mind.

I stare up from my bowl and look at her. Her eyes beg me to say something, some grand confession that's going to explain it all to her. That's going to help her understand why she's here. Why her instead of the bitchy sister. Why her instead of the insolent judge. She's desperate for an answer to it all. How is it that in the blink of an eye everything can change? Her family. Her life. Her existence. She searches in vain, thinking I know the answer. Thinking some lowlife like me might be able to help her see the light.

"Five grand," I say.

"What?" This wasn't what she expected to hear.

I stand from the chair and it skids across the wooden floors. My footsteps are loud. I rinse the bowl with water from the faucet. I let it drop to the sink and she jumps. I turn to her. "They offered me five grand."

EVE

BEFORE

I let my days go to waste.

Oftentimes it's hard to get out of bed and when I do, the very first thought on my mind is Mia. I wake up sobbing in the middle of the night, night after endless night, hurrying downstairs so I don't wake James. I'm stricken with grief at all waking hours; in the grocery store, I'm certain I see Mia shopping the cereal aisle, stopping myself only moments before throwing my arms around a complete stranger. Later, in the car, I go to pieces, unable to leave the parking lot for over an hour as I watch mothers with their children enter the store: holding hands as they cross the lot, mothers lifting small children into the basket of the shopping cart.

For weeks I've seen her face flash across the TV screen and a sketch of that man. But now there are more important things happening in the world. It's both a blessing and a curse, I suppose. The reporters are less intrusive these days. They don't hound me in the driveway, follow me on my errands. The harassing phone calls and interview requests are on sabbatical; I can open my curtains without seeing a flood of reporters line the sidewalk before our home. But their withdrawal worries me as well; they've grown apathetic to the name Mia Dennett, tired of waiting for a front-page headline that may never come: Mia Dennett Returns Home, or maybe, Dennett Girl Found Dead. It settles upon me, like dark clouds descending on a winter day, that I will never know. I think of those families who are reunited with their loved one's remains, ten, sometimes twenty years later, and wonder if that will be me.

When I tire of the crying, I let the fury take control, shattering imported Italian crystal goblets against the kitchen wall, and when they're done, James's grandmother's dinnerware. I scream at the top of my lungs, a barbaric sound that certainly doesn't belong to me.

I sweep the mess before James arrives home, tucking a million pieces of shattered glass in the garbage bin beneath a dead philodendron so he won't see.

I spend an entire afternoon watching the robins en route to places south, Mississippi and such, for the winter. They arrive one day on our back porch, dozens of them, fat and cold, stocking up on whatever they can find for the journey ahead. It rained that day and the worms were everywhere. I watch them for hours, sad when they leave. It will be months before they return, those red bellies that beckon spring.

Another day the ladybugs arrive. Thousands of them, soaking up the sun on the back door. It's an Indian summer day, warm, with temperatures in the upper sixties and plentiful sun. The kind of day we long for in the fall, the colors of the trees at their peak. I try to count them all, but they scatter away, and more come, and it's impossible to keep track. I don't know how long I watch them. I wonder what the ladybugs will do for the winter. Will they die? And then, days later when a frost covers the earth, I think of those ladybugs and cry.

I think of Mia when she was a child. I think of the things we did. I walk to the playground I used to take Mia to while

Grace was in school for the day, and sit on the swings. I rake my hand through the sand in the sandbox and sit on a bench and stare. At the children. At the fortunate mothers who still had theirs to hold.

But mostly I think of the things I didn't do. I think of the time I stood idly by when James told Mia that a B wasn't good enough in high school chem, and the time she brought home a breathtaking impressionist painting she'd spent more than a month on at school, he scoffed, "If only you'd spend that kind of time on chemistry, you might have gotten an A." I think of myself, watching out of the corner of my eye, unable to say a thing. Unable to point out the vacant expression on our daughter's face because I was afraid he might get mad.

When Mia informed James that she didn't plan to go to law school, he said she didn't have a choice. She was seventeen, hormones raging, and she pleaded, *"Mom,"* desperate, just this one time, for me to step in and intervene. I'd been washing dishes, trying my hardest to evade the conversation. I remember the desperation on Mia's face, the displeasure on James's. I chose the lesser of two evils.

"Mia," I said. I'll never forget the day. The sound of the telephone ringing in the background, though none of us paid it the time of day. The smell of something I'd burnt in the kitchen, cold spring air wafting in a window I'd opened to get rid of the smell. The sun was staying out later, something we might comment on if we weren't so preoccupied with upsetting Mia.

"It means so much to him," I said. "He wants you to be like him."

She stormed out of the kitchen and, upstairs, she slammed a door.

Mia dreamed of studying at the Art Institute of Chicago.

She wanted to be an artist. It was all that had ever mattered to her. But James refused.

Mia started a countdown that very day to her eighteenth birthday, and she started packing a box of things she would take with her when she left.

The ducks and geese fly overhead. Everyone is leaving me.

I wonder if somewhere Mia is looking toward the sky, seeing the same thing.

COLIN

BEFORE

What we have is time to think. And a lot of it.

That damn cat keeps hanging around now that the girl is sacrificing scraps of her own dinner for it. She found a moth-eaten blanket in the closet and, with an empty box from the back of my truck, created a makeshift bed for the stupid thing. She has it set up in the shed out back. Every day she takes it a few bites of food.

She has a name for the damn thing: Canoe. Not that she bothered to tell me. But I heard her call to it this morning when it wasn't sleeping in its bed. Now she's worried.

I sit by the lake and fish. I'll eat trout every day for the rest of my God-given life if it means I don't have to eat something that's been freeze-dried.

Most often I come up with northern pike. Then walleye. Sometimes trout. I can tell from the light spots on the northern, that and the fact that they're always the first bastards to take the bait. The fish are stocked every year, mostly fry and fingerlings, sometimes yearlings. The smallmouth bass give me the most damn trouble. Until I get them on the ground,

I'd bet my life they're twice the size they turn out to be. Strong bastards.

I spend most of my time thinking about how we're going to pull this off. About how I'm going to pull this off. Food is running low, which means a trip to the store. I have the money. I just don't know what it will take for someone to recognize me. And what do I do with the girl when I'm gone? The disappearance of a judge's daughter—that's breaking news. I'd bet my life on it. Any store clerk is going to recognize her and call the cops.

Which makes me wonder: have the cops figured out I was with her the night she disappeared? Is my face, like hers, all over the fucking TV? Maybe that's a good thing, I tell myself. Not for me; not if it means I get caught. But if Valerie sees my face on the TV, sees that I'm a person of interest in the disappearance of a Chicago woman, then she'll know what to do. She'll know I'm not there to make sure there's food on the table and the doors are shut. She'll know what needs to be done.

When the girl isn't paying attention, I pull a photo from my wallet. It's worn with time, shriveled around the edges from all the times I've pulled it from my wallet and forced it back in. I wonder if and when the money arrived, the money I swiped from the truck stop in Eau Claire. I wonder if she knew it was from me. She would have known I was in trouble when the money arrived, five hundred dollars or more crammed in an envelope with no return address.

I'm not one to be sentimental. I just need to know that she's okay.

It's not like she's alone. At least that's what I tell myself. The neighbor comes by once a week, gets the mail and checks on her. They'll see the money. When Sunday comes and goes and I don't show, they'll know. If they haven't already seen my face on the TV. If Valerie hasn't already seen my face on TV and gone to check on her, to make sure she's okay. I try and convince myself: Valerie is there. Everything is okay.

I almost believe it.

Later that night, we're outside. I'm attempting to grill fish for dinner. Except there's no charcoal so I'm seeing what else I can burn to start a fire. The girl's sitting on the porch, wrapped in a blanket that she snagged from inside. Her eyes scan the land below. She's wondering where the damn cat is. She hasn't seen it in two days and she's worried. It's getting colder out all the time. Sooner or later, the thing won't survive.

"I take it you're not a bank teller," she says.

"What do you think?" I ask.

She takes it as a no.

"What do you do then?" she asks. "*Do* you work?"

"I work."

"Anything legal?"

"I do what I need to do to survive. Just like you."

"I don't think so," she says.

"And why's that?"

"I earn an honest living. I pay taxes."

"How do you know I don't pay taxes?"

"*Do* you pay taxes?" she asks.

"I work," I say. "I earn an *honest living*. I pay taxes. I've mopped the floors of the john at some Realtor's office. Washed dishes. Loaded crates into a truck. You know what they pay these days? Minimum wage. Do you have a fucking clue what it's like to survive on minimum wage? I work two jobs at a time, thirteen or fourteen hours a day. That pays the rent, buys some food. Someone like you works—what? Eight hours a day plus summer vacation."

"I teach summer school," she says. It's a stupid thing to say. She knows it's a stupid thing to say before I give her the look.

She doesn't know what it's like. She can't even imagine.

I look up at the sky, at the dark clouds that threaten us. Not rain, but snow. It will be here soon. She pulls the blanket tighter around herself. She shudders from the cold.

She knows that I would never let her leave. I have more to lose than she does.

"You've done this kind of thing before," she says.

"Done what?"

"Kidnapping. Holding a gun to someone's head." It isn't a question.

"Maybe. Maybe not."

"You didn't snatch me with the hands of a virgin."

I've started a fire. I drop the fish on the grill pan and they begin to sear.

"I've never bothered someone who didn't need to be bothered."

But even I know that isn't true.

I flip the fish. They're cooking faster than I want. I move them to the edge of the grill so they won't burn.

"It could be worse," I assure her. "It could be much worse."

We eat outside. She sits on the floor, her back pressed to the wooden planks of the deck rail. I offer her a chair. She says no thanks. She spreads her legs out before herself and crosses them at the ankles.

The wind blows through the trees. We both turn to watch the leaves lose their hold on the branches and fall to the ground.

And that's when we hear it: footsteps on the shriveled leaves that cover the earth. It's the cat, I think, at first, but then know that the footsteps are too heavy for the scrawny little cat, too deliberate. The girl and I exchange a look, and I put a finger to my lips and whisper, "Shhh." And then I rise to my feet and feel the seat of my pants for a gun that isn't there.

GABE

BEFOЯE

I was waiting to talk to the Dennetts until I had some hard facts, but it doesn't work out that way. I'm chomping down a greasy Italian beef sandwich at my desk when Eve Dennett comes into the station and asks the receptionist if she can speak to me. I'm still wiping the au jus from my face with a stack of napkins when she approaches my desk.

This is the first time she's ever been down to the station, and boy does she look out of place here. Much different than the drunken losers we usually have walking around.

I smell her perfume before she ever arrives at my desk. She walks demurely as every sick bastard eyes her from across the room, jealous when her high heels come to a stop before me. Every cop knows I'm working the Dennett case and they have an ongoing bet as to if and when I screw the whole thing up. I even saw the sergeant putting money on it; he said he'd need the pot when he and I both found ourselves out of a job.

"Hello, Detective."

"Mrs. Dennett."

"I haven't heard from you in a few days," she says. "I was just wondering if there's any...news."

She carries an umbrella, which drips water on the linoleum floor. Her hair is matted down and windblown from the fury outside. It's a horrible day, windy and cold. Not a day to be outside. "You could have called," I say.

"I was out, running errands," she says, but I know she's lying. No one would be out today if they didn't have to be. It's just one of those days, a day to lie around in pajamas and watch TV.

I lead her to an interrogation room and ask her to have a seat. It's a dingy room, poorly lit, with a big table in the middle and a couple of folding chairs. She lays the umbrella on the ground, but clutches her purse. I offer to take her coat; she says no thanks. It's cold in here, one of those damp colds that chills you straight to the bone.

I sit down across from her and lay the Dennett file on the table. I see her eye the manila folder.

I look at her, at her delicate blue eyes. They've already begun to swell with tears. As the days pass by, all I can think is, what if I never find Mia? It's apparent that Mrs. Dennett breaks a little more with each passing hour. Her eyes are heavy and bloated, as if she no longer sleeps. I can't imagine what would become of her if Mia never came home. I think about Mrs. Dennett at all hours of the day and night; I imagine her lost and alone inside that mansion of a home, dreaming up all the horrific things that might have happened to her child. I feel this consummate need to protect her, to answer those burning questions that keep her awake at night: who and where and why?

"I was going to call you," I say quietly. "I was just waiting for some good news."

"Something has happened," Mrs. Dennett says. It isn't a question. It's as if she knew all along that something had happened and that's what brought her down to the station today. "Something bad." She lays her purse on the table and digs inside for a tissue.

"There's news. But that's all right now. I haven't quite figured out what it all means." If Judge Dennett was here he would rip me a new one for not having all the answers. "We think we know who Mia was with before she disappeared," I say. "Someone identified the photo that's been on the news, and when we went to his apartment, we found some of Mia's belongings—her purse and a coat." I open the file and lay some photos across the table, ones taken of the apartment by the rookie who accompanied me the other day. Mrs. Dennett picks up the photo of the purse, one of those messenger-bag types that you sling across your body. The bag is laying on the floor, a pair of sunglasses and a green wallet falling out onto the parquet floor. Mrs. Dennett brings a tissue to her eyes.

"You recognize something?" I ask.

"I picked it out, that bag. I bought that for her. Who is he?" she asks, not pausing between thoughts. She glances at the other photos, one at a time, then sets them down in a row. She folds her hands on the table.

"Colin Thatcher," I say. We ran the fingerprints we pulled from the apartment building in Uptown and came up with the man's true identity, every other name in the apartment—on the mail, the cell phone, etc.—a pseudonym, a charade. We pulled mug shots from previous arrests and compared with the forensic sketch. Bingo.

I watch how Mrs. Dennett's hands shake before me and how she tries, and fails, to control the trembling. It's without thought that I feel my own hand reach out and find hers, ice-cold hands that melt in mine. I do it before she can hide them in her lap, hoping to disguise the terror she feels inside.

"There's some footage from the security cameras. Colin and Mia entering the apartment, around eleven o'clock at night, then again later leaving the building."

"I want to see it," she says to my surprise. Her response is definite, not the kind of indecision I'm used to from her.

"I don't think that's a good idea," I say. The last thing Eve needs to see right now is the way Colin Thatcher hurled her daughter out of the building and the distress in the girl's eyes.

"It's bad," she concludes.

"It's inconclusive," I lie. "I don't want you to get the wrong impression." But there's nothing mistakable about the vigilant way the man hurries from the elevator, making certain no one sees, or the fear in the girl's eyes. She's crying. He mouths something that I'm certain contains the f-word. Something happened inside that apartment. The earlier footage couldn't be any different. Two lovebirds heading up for a quickie.

"But she was alive?"

"Yes."

"Who is he?" she asks. "This Colin..."

"Colin Thatcher." I release Mrs. Dennett's hand and reach inside the manila folder. I pull out the man's rap sheet. "He's been arrested for a number of misdemeanors—petty theft, trespassing, possession of marijuana. He served time for selling and is wanted for questioning in an ongoing racketeering case. According to his last probation officer, he went MIA a few years back and is essentially a wanted man."

I couldn't begin to explain the horror in the woman's blue eyes. As a detective I'm used to words like *trespassing* and *racketeering* and *probation officer*. But Mrs. Dennett has only heard these words on reruns of *Law & Order*. She couldn't begin to understand what it all means; the words themselves are elusive and hard to grasp. She's terrified that a man like this has her daughter.

"What would he want with Mia?" Mrs. Dennett asks. I've asked myself this very question a thousand times. Random crime is relatively rare. Most victims know their assailant.

"I don't know," I say. "I have no idea, but I promise you I'm going to find out."

COLIN

BEFORE

The girl sets her plate on the wooden deck beside her. And then she rises beside me and we both stare, over the wooden railing, into the dense forest as a woman emerges. A fifty-something woman with short brunette, hair in jeans and a flannel shirt, pudgy hiking boots, and she's waving to us, like she knows us, and a new thought crosses my mind: it's a trap.

"Oh, thank heaven," the woman says as she welcomes herself onto our property.

She's trespassing. This is our space. No one was supposed to be here. I feel suffocated, smothered. She's got a water jug in a hand. She looks like she's walked a hundred miles.

"Can we help you?" The words eject from my mouth before I can figure out what's happening, what I'm going to do. My first thought: get the gun and shoot her. Drop her body in the lake and run. I don't have the gun anymore, don't know where the girl is keeping it. But I could tie her up while I ransack the cabin for its hiding place. Under the mattress, in the bedroom, or along some crevice in the log walls.

"I've got a flat. About a half mile down the road," she says. "You're the first cabin that wasn't deserted. I've been walk-

ing...." she says, and then stops, to catch her breath. "Mind
if I sit?" she asks, and when the girl manages a nod, she drops
to the bottom step and guzzles from the water jug like someone who's been stranded in the desert for days. I feel my hand
reach out and clutch the girl's, feel myself crush the bones of
her hand until she lets out a whine.

We forget all about our dinner. But the woman reminds
us. "I'm sorry to interrupt," she says, motioning to the plates
on the floor. "I was just wondering if you might be able to
help me fix the tire. Or call someone, maybe. My phone has
no reception around here," she says, holding it up for the girl
and me to see. She says again that she's so sorry to interrupt.
Little does she know what she's intruding on. It's not just our
dinner she's disturbing.

My eyes drift to the girl. Now's her chance, I think. She
could tell the woman. Tell her how this crazy person kidnapped her, how he's holding her captive in this cabin. I hold
my breath, waiting for any number of things to go wrong.
For the girl to tell, for the lady to be part of a ploy to catch
me. She's working undercover, maybe. Or for Dalmar. Or
maybe she's just some lady who watches the news and sooner
or later she's gonna realize that *that* girl is the one she's been
seeing on TV.

"We don't have a phone," I say, remembering how I dropped
the girl's cell in the garbage can in Janesville, how I cut the
phone lines when we arrived at the cabin. Not that I can have
her stepping foot inside our cabin, seeing the way we've been
living for weeks: like two convicts on the run. "But I can help
you," I say begrudgingly.

"I don't mean to be a bother," the woman says, and the girl,
simultaneously, says, "I'll just stay here and do the dishes," as
she squats to the ground to retrieve our plates.

No chance in hell that's gonna happen.

"You better come with," I say to her. "We might need your help."

But the old lady says, "Oh, please. I don't want to drag you both out tonight," and she pulls her flannel shirt around herself and says that it's cold.

But of course I can't leave her alone, though the woman promises to be an excellent assistant. She begs me not to drag my *girlfriend* out on a night like tonight. It's cold out, she says. Nightfall is coming soon.

But I can't leave her. If I leave her here, she might just run. I picture her, tearing through the woods as fast as she can, a mile or so away by the time I manage to fix the flat and get back. It would be dark by then, and there'd be no chance in hell I'd be able to search the woods in the dark and find her.

The woman apologizes for doing this, for being such an inconvenience. I picture my hands, closing in around her neck, compressing the jugular vein to stop the flow of oxygen to the brain. Maybe that's what I should do.

"I'm just going to do the dishes," the girl objects, quietly, "so we don't have to worry about it later," and she gives me a playful look, as if implying intimate plans later tonight.

"I think you should come," I say gently, laying a hand on her arm as if I can't possibly stand the idea of being apart.

"Romantic getaway?" the woman asks.

I say, "Yeah, something like that," and then turn to the girl and whisper roughly, "You're coming—" I lean closer and add, "Or that lady doesn't leave here alive." She's deathly still for a split second. Then she sets the plates on the ground and we head for the truck and climb in, the woman and me in the front seat, the girl smashed in back. I swipe remnants of rope and duct tape from the passenger's seat, hoping the woman didn't see. I thrust them in the glove compartment and slam the door, and then turn to her and smile. "Where to?"

In the truck the woman tells us how she's from southern Illinois. How she and some girlfriends stayed at some lodge and went canoeing in the Boundary Waters. She pulls out a camera from her purse and shows us digital images of the four old ladies: in the canoe, with sun hats on, drinking wine around a fire. This makes me feel better: not a trap, I think. Here's the proof, the pictures. She was canoeing with girlfriends in the Boundary Waters.

But she, she tells us—like I give a shit—decided to stay an extra couple days. She's a recent divorcée, in no rush to return to an abandoned home. A recent divorcée, I think. No one at home waiting for her return. There would be time before she was reported missing—days, if not more. Enough time for me to run, to be far enough away when someone stumbled upon her body.

"And then, there I was," she says, "making my way back to civilization when I got a flat. Must've hit a rock," she says, "or a nail."

The girl responds impassively. "Must have," she says. But I can hardly listen. We pull up behind a compact car. But before we get out, my eyes survey the thick woods that surround us. I peer through the tangle of trees for cops, binoculars, rifles. I check to make sure the tire is flat. It is. If this was an ambush, no one would go to such elaborate measures to trap me. By now, as I step from the truck and approach the abandoned car, I'd be facedown on the ground, someone on top of me with a pair of cuffs.

I see the woman, watching me, as I grab some tools out of the bed of the truck, and remove the hubcap and loosen the nuts, as I jack up the car and switch the tires. The ladies are talking, about canoeing and the northern Minnesota woods. About red wine and a moose, which the lady saw on her trip, a male with enormous antlers strolling through the trees. I make believe she's trying hard to connect the dots, trying to remember whether or not she saw us on TV. But I remind myself that she's been in the middle of nowhere with girlfriends. She was canoeing, sitting around a campfire, drinking wine. She wasn't watching TV.

I thrust a flashlight in the girl's hands and tell her to hold it. It's getting dark out by now, and there isn't a streetlight around. My eyes threaten her when they meet, reminding her to avoid words like *gun* and *kidnap* and *help*. I'll kill them both. I know it. I wonder if she does.

When the woman asks about our trip, I see the girl turn to stone.

"How long are you staying?" the woman asks.

When the girl can't answer, I say, "Just about another week."

"Where are you all from?" she asks.

"Green Bay," I say.

"Is that right?" she asks. "I saw the Illinois plates and thought—"

"Just haven't gotten around to changing them, is all," I say, cursing myself for the mistake.

"You're from Illinois," she asks, "originally?"

"Yep," I say. But I don't tell her where we're from.

"I've got a cousin in Green Bay. Just outside, actually. In Suamico." I've never heard of the damn place. But still, she's talking. How her cousin is a principal at one of the middle schools. She's got this dull brown hair, short like an old lady's hair. She laughs when the conversation goes quiet. Nervous laughter. Then looks for something else to say. Anything else. "Are you all Packers fans?" she asks and I lie and say that I am.

I thrust on the spare as fast as I possibly can, then lower the car and tighten the lug nuts and stand, looking at the woman, wondering if I can just let her go—back to civilization where she might just figure out who we are and call the cops—or if I need to smash her head in with the wrench and leave her in the woods for good.

"I can't tell you how much I appreciate it," she says, and I think of my own mother, lying in the abandoned woods to be eaten by bears and I nod and say it was okay. It's dark enough out that I can barely see her and she can barely see me. I grip the wrench in my hand, wondering how hard I'd have to hit her to kill her. How many times? Wondering if she'd have it in her to fight or if she'd just drop to the ground and die.

"I don't know what I would have done if I hadn't found you." And she steps forward to shake my hand and says, "I don't think I caught your names."

I clutch that wrench in my hand. I can feel it shake. It's far better than killing her with my bare hands. Much less personal. I don't have to stare into her eyes while she struggles. One good hit and it will all be done.

"Owen," I say, clutching her cold veiny hand in mine, "and this is Chloe," and she says that she's Beth. I don't know how long we all stand there, on the dark street in silence. My heart is beating fast as I eye a hammer in the toolbox. Maybe a hammer would be better.

But then I feel the girl's hand on my arm, and she says to me, "We should go." I turn to her and know she sees what I'm thinking, sees the way I've got that wrench gripped in my hand, ready to strike. "Let's go," she says again, her nails digging into my skin.

I drop the wrench into a toolbox and set it in the bed of the truck. I watch as the woman climbs into her car and drives away, slowly, headlights swerving through the thick trees.

I'm gasping for air, my hands a sweaty mess as I open the truck door and step inside and try to catch my breath.

EVE

AFTER

We sit in the waiting room, James, Mia and me, Mia sandwiched in the middle like the cream filling of an Oreo cookie.
I sit in silence with my legs crossed and my hands folded on
my lap. I stare at a painting on the wall opposite her—one of
many Norman Rockwells in the room—of an old man holding a stethoscope to a little girl's doll. James sits with his legs
crossed as well, ankle to knee, flipping through the pages of
a *Parents* magazine. His breathing is loud and impatient; I ask
him to please stop. We've been waiting more than thirty minutes to see the doctor, the wife of a judge friend of James's. I
wonder if Mia considers it odd that every magazine cover in
the entire room is cloaked with babies.

People size her up. There are whispers and we hear Mia's
hushed name escape from the tongue of strangers. I pat her
hand and tell her not to worry; just ignore them, I say, but it's
hard for either of us to do. James asks reception if they can
hurry things along, and a short, redheaded woman disappears
to see what is taking so long.

We haven't told Mia the real reason why she's here today.
We didn't discuss my suspicions. Instead we told her that we

were worried that she hasn't been feeling well lately and James suggested a doctor, one whose Russian name is nearly impossible to pronounce.

Mia told us she had her own doctor, one in the city who she's been seeing for a half dozen years, but James shook his head and said no, Dr. Wakhrukov is the best. It never occurs to her that the woman is an ObGyn.

The nurse calls her name, though of course she says *Mia* and it takes an elbow from James to get her attention. She sets her magazine on the chair and I look at her with indulgent eyes and ask if she wants me to keep her company. "If you want," she says, and I wait for James to disapprove but he is silent.

The nurse stares strangely at Mia as she weighs her and gets a height. She eyes poor Mia like she's a celebrity of some sort, instead of the victim of a horrible crime. "I saw you on TV," she says. The words come out sheepishly, as if she isn't quite sure whether she said them aloud or managed to keep them in her head. "I read about you in the paper."

Neither Mia nor I am quite sure what to say. Mia has seen the collection of newspaper articles I clipped during the time she was away. I tried to hide them in a place where she wouldn't see, but she did anyway when she was looking for a needle and thread in my dresser drawer, to replace a button that had fallen from a blouse. I didn't want Mia to see the articles for fear of what they might do to her. But she did nonetheless, reading each and every one until I interrupted her, reading about her own disappearance, about how the police had a suspect, about how, as time went on, it was feared she might be dead.

The nurse sends her to the bathroom to urinate in a cup. Moments later, I meet her in the examination room, where the nurse takes Mia's blood pressure and pulse then asks that she undress and put on a gown. She says that Dr. Wakhrukov

will be with us in a few minutes and as Mia begins to undress, I turn my back.

Dr. Wakhrukov is a somber, subdued woman who must be
approaching sixty. She comes into the room quite abruptly and
says to Mia, "When was your last menstrual period?"

Mia must find the question terribly odd. "I...I have no
idea," she says, and the doctor nods, remembering only then,
perhaps, of Mia's amnesia.

She says that she is going to perform a transvaginal ultrasound and covers a probe with a condom and some sort of gel.
She asks that Mia sticks her feet into the stirrups and without
an explanation, she plunges the device into her. Mia winces
and begs to know what she's doing, wondering what this has
to do with her overwhelming fatigue, with the listlessness that
makes it nearly impossible to rise from sleep in the morning.

I remain silent. I long to be in the waiting room, beside
James, but I remind myself that Mia needs me here and let my
eyes wander around the room, anything to avoid the doctor's
very intrusive examination and Mia's obvious confusion and
discomfort. I decide then that I should have told Mia about
my suspicions. I should have explained that the fatigue and
the morning sickness are not symptoms of acute stress disorder. But perhaps she wouldn't have believed me.

The exam room, I find, is as sterile as the doctor. It's cold
enough in here to kill germs. Perhaps that is the intention.
Mia's bare flesh is coated with goose bumps. I'm certain it
doesn't help that she's completely nude with the exception of
a paper robe. Bright fluorescent lights line the ceiling, revealing every graying hair on the middle-aged doctor's head. She
doesn't smile. She looks Russian: high cheekbones, a slender
nose.

But when she speaks, she doesn't sound Russian. "Con-
firming the pregnancy," the doctor states, as if this is common

knowledge, something Mia should know. My legs become anesthetized and I sink my way into an extra chair, one placed here for elated men who are soon to be fathers.

Not me, I think. This chair is not meant for me.

"Babies develop a heartbeat twenty-two days after conception. You can't always see it this early, but there is one here. It's tiny, hardly noticeable. See?" she asks as she turns the monitor to Mia. "That little flicker of movement?" she asks as she points a finger at a dark blob that is practically still.

"What?" Mia asks.

"Here, let me see if I can get a better look," the doctor says and she presses on the probe, which delves farther into Mia's vagina. Mia squirms in apparent pain and discomfort, and the doctor asks her to hold still.

But Mia's question was something other than what the doctor interpreted it to be. It wasn't that Mia couldn't see where her finger was pointing. I watch as Mia lets a hand fall to her abdomen.

"It just can't be."

"Here," the doctor says as she removes the probe and hands Mia a tiny piece of paper, a whimsy of blacks and whites and grays like a lovely piece of abstract art. It's a photograph, much like the one of Mia herself long before she became a child. I clutch my purse in my shaking hands, ravaging its insides for a tissue.

"What's this?" Mia asks.

"It's the baby. A printout from the ultrasound." She tells Mia to go ahead and sit up, and pulls a latex glove from her hand, which she tosses into the garbage can. Her words are lifeless as if she's given this lecture a thousand times: Mia is to come back every four weeks until she reaches thirty-two weeks; then biweekly and a few weeks later, every week. There are tests they need to run: blood tests and an amniocentesis if she wants, a glucose tolerance test, a test for Group B Strep.

At twenty weeks, Dr. Wakhrukov tells Mia, she can find out the sex of the baby if she's interested. "Is that something you might want to do?"

"I don't know" is all Mia manages to say.

The doctor asks if Mia has any questions. She has only one, but she can barely find her voice. She tries, and then, clearing her throat, tries again. It's spineless and faint, little more than a whisper. "I'm pregnant?" she asks.

This is every little girl's dream. They begin thinking about it when they're too young to know where babies come from. They carry around their baby dolls and mother them and dream of baby names. When Mia was a girl it was always overtly flowery names that flowed off the tip of a tongue: Isabella and Samantha and Savannah. Then there was that phase where she thought everything should end in *i*: Jenni, Dani and Lori. It never crossed her mind that she might have a boy.

"You are. About five weeks."

This is not the way it's supposed to be.

She rubs a hand against her uterus and hopes to feel something: a heartbeat or a small kick. Of course it would be too early and yet she hopes to feel the flutter of movement inside her. But she feels nothing. I can see it in her eyes when she turns and finds me weeping. She feels empty. She feels hollow inside.

She confides to me, "It can't be. I can't be pregnant."

Dr. Wakhrukov pulls up a swivel stool and sits down. She drapes the gown over Mia's legs and then says, her voice softer now, "You don't remember this happening?"

Mia shakes my head no. "Jason," she says. But she's shaking her head. "It's been months since I've been with Jason." She counts them on her fingers. September. October. November.

December. January. "Five months," she concludes. The math simply does not add up.

But of course I know Jason is not the father of that child.

"You have time to decide what you'd like to do. There are options." The doctor is producing pamphlets for Mia: adoption and abortion, and the words are coming at her so fast that she can't possibly keep up.

The doctor sends for James, allowing Mia a few minutes to get dressed before the nurse brings him in. While we're waiting, I ask Mia if I can see the ultrasound. She hands it to me, her lifeless words repeating...*it just can't be*. It's then, taking that photograph in my hands and laying eyes on my grandchild, my own flesh and blood, that I begin to cry. As James enters the room, the crying turns into a moan. I try to suppress the tears but simply can't. I yank paper towels from a dispenser on the wall and blot my eyes. It's just as Dr. Wakhrukov returns that I can no longer hold it inside and I wail, "He raped you. That bastard raped you."

But still, Mia feels nothing.

COLIN

BEFORE

Winter has arrived. It was snowing when we woke and the temperature in the cabin had dropped by what felt like twenty degrees.

There's no warm water. She layers on all the clothes she can find. She puts on two pairs of long johns and that gangly maroon sweatshirt. She slips on a pair of socks, complaining that she hates to wear socks, but without them her feet would freeze. She says that she's always hated socks, even when she was a baby. She would rip them from her feet and throw them to the floor beside her crib.

I haven't admitted to being cold before, but it's fucking freezing. I started a fire the moment I woke up. I've already had three cups of coffee. I'm sitting with an old, torn U.S. map spread across the table. I found it in the glove compartment, along with an all but dried-up pen and I'm circling the best routes to get us the hell out of here. I've got my mind set on the desert, somewhere between Las Vegas and Baker, California. Somewhere warm. I'm wondering how to make a detour to Gary, Indiana, first, without highway patrol spotting the truck. I figure we'd have to ditch the truck and swipe a new one, somehow, and hope it doesn't ever get reported. That or hop a freight train. Assuming people are looking for us there could be roadblocks in our honor, especially around Gary, just in case I have the nerve to go home. Maybe the police are using her as bait. Maybe they've got a surveillance team lined up around the old Gary home, waiting for me to call or make a stupid move.

Damn.

"Going somewhere?" the girl asks, looking at the map as I fold it up and push it away.

I don't answer her question. "Want some coffee?" I ask instead, knowing we couldn't stay in the desert for long. Squatting in the desert nixes any chance of a quasinormal life. It would all be about survival. We can't go to the desert, I decide, then and there. The only chance we stand is somewhere abroad. We don't have enough cash for a flight anymore, so the way I see it, there's two choices: up or down. North or south. Canada or Mexico.

But of course to get out of the country, we need passports. And that's when it hits me: what I have to do.

She shakes her head no.

"You don't drink coffee?"

"No."

"You don't like it?"

"I don't drink caffeine."

She tells me that she did drink caffeine, for a long time, but it made her agitated and jittery. She couldn't sit still. Eventually the caffeine high would fade, only to be replaced by extreme fatigue. So she'd have another cup of coffee. A vicious circle. "And when I tried to avoid caffeine," she says, "I'd succumb to debilitating headaches, only to be soothed with Mountain Dew."

But I pour her a cup anyway. She takes the warm mug into

her hands and presses her face to the rim. The steam rises up to meet her. She knows she shouldn't but she does it anyway. She raises the mug to her lips and allows it to sit there. Then she takes a sip, burning every bit of her esophagus on the way down.

She chokes. "Be careful," I say too late. "It's hot."

There isn't a damn thing to do but sit and stare at each other. So when she said she wanted to draw me I said okay. There isn't anything else to do.

To be straight, I don't want to do it. At first it's not a big deal, but then she wants me to *hold still* and *look straight* and *smile.*

"Forget it," I say. "I'm done." I stand up. I'll be damned if I'm going to sit here and smile at her for the next half hour.

"Okay," she concedes, "don't smile. Don't even look at me. Just sit still."

She places me beside the fire. She presses her frigid hands to my chest. She lowers me into place, on the floor. My back all but touches the stove. The flame nearly burns a hole in my shirt and I begin to sweat.

I think of the last time she touched me. The desperation of her hands as she tried to undress me. And the last time I touched her, smacking her across the face.

The room is gloomy, the dark pine logs of the walls and ceiling blocking any light. I count the log walls, stacked fifteen high. There is no sun to pass through the small windows.

I look at her. She isn't all that bad to look at.

She was beautiful that first night, in my apartment. She watched me with these unsuspecting blue eyes, never thinking for a minute that I had it in me to do this.

She sits on the floor and leans against the couch. She pulls her legs into her and rests the notebook on her knees. She takes a pencil from the pack, extracts the lead. She tilts her head and her hair falls clumsily to one side. Her eyes trace the shape of my face, the curve of my nose.

I don't know why, but I feel the urge to knock the guy who was with her before me.

"I paid him off," I confess. "Your boyfriend. I gave him a hundred bucks to make himself busy for the night."

He didn't ask why and I didn't say. The coward just grabbed the money from my hand and disappeared into thin air. I don't tell her I confronted him in the john with my gun.

A hundred bucks can buy a lot these days.

"He had to work," she says.

"That's what he told you."

"Jason works late all the time."

"Or so he says."

"It's the truth."

"Sometimes. Maybe."

"He's very successful."

"At lying."

"So you paid him off. So what?" she snaps.

"Why'd you come home with me?" I ask.

"What?"

"Why did you come home with me that night?" She forces a swallow and doesn't respond. She pretends to be lost in her work, the fury of her lines as she sketches manically across the page. "I didn't realize it was a hard question," I say.

Her eyes well up. A vein in her forehead protrudes through the skin. Her skin becomes clammy and her hands shake. She's mad.

"I was drunk."

"Drunk."

"Yes. I was drunk."

"Because that's the only reason someone like you would come home with someone like me, right?"

"Because that's the only reason *I* would go home with *you*."

She's watching me and I wonder what it is she sees. What she believes she sees. She thinks I'm numb to her indifference, but she's wrong.

I take off my sweatshirt and drop it to the floor beside my clamorous boots. I've got on an undershirt and jeans that she's probably never seen me without. She scribbles my face on the page, delirious lines and shadows to describe the demon she sees before the fire.

She had a few drinks that night, but she was lucid enough to know what she was doing, to welcome my hands on her. Of course, that was long before she knew who I really was.

I don't know how long we're silent. I hear her breathe, the sound of lead striking the paper's surface. I can almost hear her thoughts in my mind. The hostility and anger.

"It's like cigarettes or smoking pot," I finally say to her.

The words startle her and she tries to catch her breath. "What is?"

She doesn't stop drawing. She pretends, almost, like she's not listening. But she is.

"My life. What I do. You know they're bad for you the first time you try. Cigarettes. Pot. But you convince yourself it's okay—you can handle it. One time, that's it, just to see what it's like. And then all of a sudden, you're sucked in—you can't get out if you want to. It wasn't because I needed the money so bad—which I did. It was because if I tried to get out I'd be killed. Someone would rat me out and I'd end up in jail. There was never the option of saying no."

She stops drawing. I wonder what she's going to say. Some smart-ass comment, I'm sure. But she doesn't. She doesn't say anything. But the vein in her forehead fades away, her hands stand still. Her eyes soften. And she looks at me and nods.

EVE

AFTEЯ

I watch from the hall as James thrusts himself into Mia's bed-room with great gusto. The sound of his footsteps outside the door, loud and clamorous, approaching quickly, startles her from sleep. She jumps upright in the bed, her eyes wide with fear, her heart likely thrashing about inside her chest as happens when one is scared. It takes a second for her to become aware of her surroundings: remnants of her high school wardrobe that still hang in the closet, the jute rug, a poster of Leonardo DiCaprio she hung when she was fourteen. And then it set-tles. She remembers where she is. She's home. She's safe. She drops her head into her hands and begins to cry.

"You need to get dressed," James says. "We're going to see the shrink."

I enter the bedroom once he leaves and help Mia pick a matching outfit from the closet. I try to appease her fears, to remind her that here, in our home, she is perfectly safe. "No one can hurt you," I promise, but even I am not sure.

Mia eats in the car, just a piece of dry toast I brought along for the trip. She doesn't want a thing to do with it, but from the passenger's seat, I turn around every few minutes and say to her, "Take another bite, Mia," as if she is four years old again. "Just one more bite."

I thank Dr. Rhodes for squeezing us in so early in the morning. James pulls the doctor aside for a private word, as I help Mia out of her coat, and then I watch as Mia and Dr. Rhodes disappear behind closed doors.

Dr. Rhodes will be speaking to Mia this morning about the baby. Mia is in denial about the fetus growing in her womb, and I suppose I am as well. She is hardly able to say the word. *Baby.* It gets lost in her throat and every time James or I breach the subject, she swears that it can't possibly be real.

But we thought it would be helpful for Mia to talk with Dr. Rhodes, as both a professional and as an impartial third person. Dr. Rhodes will be discussing Mia's options with her this morning, and already I can imagine Mia's response. "My options about what?" she will ask and Dr. Rhodes will again have to remind her of the baby.

"Let me make this clear, Eve," James says to me once Mia and the doctor have left the room. "The last thing we need is for Mia to be carrying the illegitimate child of *that man.* She will have an abortion and she will do it soon." He waits, thinking his way through the logistics. "We'll say the baby didn't make it, when people ask. The stress of this *situation,"* he says. "It didn't survive."

I don't comment. I simply cannot I watch James, with a *motion in limine* spread across his lap. His eyes scan through the motion with more regard than he gives our daughter and her unborn child.

I try to convince myself that his heart is in the right place. But I wonder if it is.

It wasn't always this way. James was not always this disinterested regarding his family life. In the quiet afternoons, when James is at work and Mia napping, I find myself unearthing fond memories of James and the girls: old photographs of him holding baby Grace or baby Mia in their swaddling blankets. I watch home videos of James with the girls when they were babies. I listen to him—to a different James—sing them lullabies. I reminisce on first days of school and birthday parties, special days that James chose not to miss. I excavate photographs of James teaching Mia and Grace to ride their bikes without training wheels, of them swimming together in a lovely hotel pool or seeing the fish at the aquarium for the first time.

James comes from a very wealthy family. His father is a lawyer, as was his grandfather and perhaps his great-grandfather; I honestly don't know. His brother Marty is a state representative, and Brian is one of the best anesthesiologists in the city. Marty's daughters, Jennifer and Elizabeth, are lawyers, corporate and intellectual property, respectively. Brian was bestowed sons, three of them, a corporate lawyer, a dentist and a neurologist.

There is an image for James to maintain. Though he wouldn't dare say the words aloud, he's always been in competition with his brothers: who is the most affluent, the most powerful, the preeminent Dennett in the land.

For James, second best was never an option.

In the afternoons I slip into the basement and sift through old shoeboxes of photographs to prove to myself that it was real, those twinkling moments of fatherly love. I didn't imagine it. I find a picture that five-year-old Mia drew with an inelegant hand, her childish block letters adorning the illustration: I LOVE YOU DADDY. There's a taller figure and a shorter figure and it appears that their fingerless hands are clasped. Their faces are embellished with enormous smiles and all around the periphery of the paper she's placed stickers, nearly three dozen red and pink heart-shaped stickers. I showed it to him one evening after he'd come home from work. He stared at it for I don't know how long, a minute or more, and then took it into his office and placed it, with a magnet, on the black filing cabinet.

"It's for Mia's own good," he says, breaking the earsplitting silence. "She needs the time to heal."

But I wonder if that's truly the case.

I want to tell him there are other ways. Adoption, for example. Mia could give the child to a family who is unable to have their own child. She could make some unfortunate family very happy. But James would never see it that way. There would always be what-ifs: what if the adoption fell through, what if the adoptive parents chose not to take the child, what if the baby was born with a birth defect, or what if, when the baby turned into a young adult, it searched for Mia, ruining her life all over again.

Abortion, on the other hand, is quick and easy. That's what James has said. Never mind the guilt that will haunt Mia for the rest of her life.

When Dr. Rhodes finishes her session with Mia, she walks her into the waiting room and before we leave, she lays a hand on Mia's arm and says, "It's not like you have to decide today. You have plenty of time."

But I see in James's eyes that he has already decided.

COLIN

BEFORE

I can't sleep, and this isn't the first time. I tried counting sheep, pigs, whatever, and now I'm pacing the room. Every night is hard. Every night I'm thinking about her. But tonight it's worse because the date on my watch reminds me that it's her birthday. And I'm thinking about her all alone back home.

It's pitch-black, when all of a sudden my feet aren't the only ones in the room.

"You scared the shit out of me," I say. I barely make out her profile, my eyes not accustomed to the dark.

"Sorry," she lies. "What are you doing?" she asks. My mom always nagged me about how heavy I walked. She said I could wake the dead.

We don't turn on a light. In the dark we run into each other. Neither of us offers an apology. We shy away and retreat in our own direction.

"I couldn't sleep," I say. "Trying to clear my head."

"About what?" she asks and at first I'm silent. At first I'm not going to tell her. She doesn't need to know.

But then I do. It's dark enough in the room that I pretend she's not there. But that's not it. That's not why. It's something about the way she says, *Never mind,* and her footsteps start to leave the room that makes me want to tell her. Makes me want her to stay.

I say that my father left when I was a kid, but it didn't matter anyway. It's not like he was ever there to begin with. He drank. Went to bars and gambled. Money was already tight without him wasting it away. I say that he was a womanizer and a cheat. I tell her that I learned about life the hard way: how there wasn't always food on the table or warm water for a bath. Not that there was anyone to give me a bath anyway. I was three, maybe four years old.

I tell her how my father had a temper. I say that he scared the shit out of me when I was a kid. With me it was a lot of screaming and not a lot more. But he hit my mother. More than once.

He worked, sometimes, but he was usually *between jobs.* He was always getting fired for not showing up. For showing up drunk. For telling off the boss.

My mother, she worked all the time. She was never home because she'd work twelve hours in the grocery store bakery, up at 5:00 a.m., then moonlight as a bartender where men hit on her and touched her and called her names like *sweetie* and *doll.* My dad called her a slut. That's what he said: *You good-for-nothing slut.*

I say that my mom got my clothes from resale shops, that we'd drive around town on garbage day loading Ma's station wagon with whatever we could find. We got evicted more than once. We'd sleep in the car. We used to run to the gas station before school so I could sneak into the bathroom and brush my teeth. Eventually the attendants got the idea. They said they'd call the cops.

I tell her about all the times, in the grocery store. Mom would have twenty bucks and we'd fill a basket with stuff we needed: milk and bananas, a box of cereal. At the register, it always totaled more than twenty bucks, though we tried to do the math in our head. And there, we'd have to pick—the cereal or bananas—while some prick in line sighed and told us to hurry up. I remember one time, some asshole from school was in line behind us. I heard about it for the next two weeks. About how Thatcher's mom didn't have enough money for fucking bananas.

I'm quiet and she doesn't say a thing. Any other girl would offer sympathy. She'd say she was *so sorry*. She'd say how it must have been *so hard*. But this girl doesn't. Not because she isn't empathetic, but because she knows it's not compassion that I want or need.

I never told anyone else about my father.

I never told anyone about my mother. But I do. Maybe it's the boredom, I don't know. We've run out of things to say. But somehow I think it's more than that, something about this girl that makes it easy to talk, makes me want to tell her, makes me want to get it off my chest. Because then maybe I'll be able to sleep.

"When I was five or six, she started to shake," I say. Her hands first. She started having trouble at work. She kept dropping things, spilling shit. Within a year she was shuffling around. She couldn't walk right. She'd barely move her feet, didn't move her arms. People would fucking stare, tell her to hurry up. She stopped smiling, stopped blinking. She became depressed. She couldn't hold a job. She was too slow, too clumsy.

"Parkinson's disease," the girl says, and I nod, though of course she can't see. Her voice is close enough to touch, but I can't see the expression on her face. I can't make out the sensitivity in her blue eyes.

"That's what the doctors said." By the time I was in junior

high I had to help my mom get her clothes on, always sweats because she couldn't handle a zipper. By high school I had to help her pee. She couldn't cut her own food. She couldn't write her name.

She took drugs to help with the symptoms but they all had side effects. Nausea. Insomnia. Nightmares. So she stopped. I started working when I was fourteen. I made as much money as I could. It was never enough. My dad was gone by then. As soon as she got sick he took off. I turned eighteen, dropped out of high school and left home. I thought I could make more money in the city. I sent her everything I made to pay the medical bills and have food to eat. So she wouldn't wind up on the street. But there was never enough money.

And then one day, I was washing dishes in a restaurant. I asked if I could get some extra hours, said I was tight on cash. My boss said to me, "Aren't we all." Business was slow, but he knew somewhere I could get a loan.

And the rest is history.

GABE

BEFORE

I track down a next of kin in Gary: Kathryn Thatcher, Colin Thatcher's mother. We had found a cell phone stashed in a drawer in Thatcher's kitchen—registered to a Steve Moss, a.k.a. Colin Thatcher—and pulled the records. There were many calls, almost every day, to the middle-aged woman in Gary, Indiana. The other thing that caught my attention were three calls made to a prepaid cell phone on the evening that Mia disappeared as well as about ten missed calls from the same number in the early hours of the following morning. I have the techies dump the voice mail and when they do, we all hover around and listen to the messages. Some guy wanting to know where the hell the girl is, the judge's daughter, and why Thatcher missed the drop-off. He doesn't sound happy. In fact he sounds really, really unhappy. He's pissed.

It's then that I realize Colin Thatcher is working for someone else.

But who?

I try and track down the owner of this prepaid cell phone. I know it was purchased at a convenient store in Hyde Park. But the owner of the store, an Indian man who barely speaks three words of English, doesn't have a clue who bought it. Apparently it was paid for with cash. Just my luck.

I decide to question the mother myself. The sergeant wants to use his clout to have a guy in Gary do it; I say no way. I'll do it myself.

In Chicago, Gary, Indiana, isn't spoken of highly. We like to think of it as a hellhole. Much of the population is poor. There is a large African-American population, and it's home to massive steel mills that sit along Lake Michigan and puff obnoxious smoke into the air.

The sergeant wants to go with me, but I talk him out of it and go by myself. We don't want to frighten the poor woman into silence, after all. I made the mistake of telling Mrs. Dennett that this was on my schedule for today. She didn't ask to go, but she did hint. I laid a cautious hand on her arm and promised, "You'll be the first one I call."

It takes about two hours. Only fifty some miles, but for the mass amounts of semis along I-90, I lollygag around at about thirty miles per hour. I make the mistake of picking up coffee at a drive-through, and have to nearly piss my pants by the time I arrive. I run into a gas station in Gary, grateful for the arsenal hiding beneath my clothes.

Kathryn Thatcher lives in a pale blue ranch. The home is dated, straight out of the '50s. The lawn is overrun, the shrubbery overgrown. Potted plants lie dead.

I knock on the screen door and wait on a concrete stoop that desperately needs repair. The day is dreary, a typical November day in the midwest. It's just blah, the forty degrees feeling cold, though I know in a month or two, we'll pray for a forty-degree day. When there's no answer, I open the screen door and knock on the wood door, beside a wreath that hangs from a rusting nail. The door is open. It gives with the slightest touch of my hand. *Damn it,* I think to myself. Maybe I should have brought the sergeant. I reach for my gun, tiptoe in and call, "Mrs. Thatcher."

I walk into the front room, so outdated I have to remind myself I'm not in the home of my grandmother: shag carpeting, wood paneling on the walls, peeling wallpaper and the furniture—everything mismatching, torn taupe leather beside flowered upholstery.

The dull sound of off-tune humming from the kitchen puts me at ease. I slide the gun back into its harness so I don't scare the shit out of the lady. And then my eyes come to a standstill on the image of Colin Thatcher, and what I presume to be Kathryn, dressed to the nines, in a small frame atop a 27-inch TV. The TV is on and muted, a soap opera filling the screen.

"Mrs. Thatcher," I call again but there is no response. I follow the humming to the kitchen and knock on the frame of the open doorway, only after watching for a moment as her trembling fingers try once, twice, three times to peel back the plastic covering from a TV dinner. The woman herself looks old enough to be the grandmother of Colin Thatcher and I wonder if we've made a mistake. She wears a robe and fuzzy slippers on her feet; her legs are bare and I'm trying not to believe that there's nothing on beneath the robe.

"Ma'am," I say, my feet crossing onto the vinyl floor. This time when she turns, nearly jumping out of her skin at the sound of my voice and the presence of a complete stranger in her home, I hold out my badge to reassure her she's not about to be killed.

"Good Lord," she stutters, a shaky hand finding its way to her heart. "Colin?"

"No, ma'am," I say, stepping closer. "If I may," I say, reaching across her fragile frame to pull the plastic from the TV dinner. I drop the moist wrapper into an overflowing wastebasket beside the back door. It's a child's microwave dinner with chicken nuggets and corn and a brownie.

I hold out a hand to steady Mrs. Thatcher. To my surprise, she accepts. There's very little stability whether walking or standing still. She moves with painstaking movements, her face void of expression. She stands stooped, her feet shuffling before her; I'm certain at any moment she might fall. Saliva drips from her mouth.

"My name is Detective Gabe Hoffman. I'm a policeman with the—"

"Colin?" she asks again. This time she begs.

"Mrs. Thatcher," I say, "ma'am, please sit." I help her to a nearby breakfast nook, where she sits down. I carry the TV dinner to her and fish a fork out of a drawer, but her hand shakes so persistently she can't get the food to her mouth. She gropes the nugget with a bare hand.

The woman looks old enough to be seventy, but if she's Colin Thatcher's mother, chances are she's only fifty or so. Her hair is gray, though in the not-so-outdated photo in the front room, it's a chestnut-brown. She appears to have dropped a dress size or two as her robe hangs around her like a garment bag and the flesh I can see is all sticks and bones. There's a display of medicine bottles across the countertop, and rotten fruit in a basket. And of course there are the bumps and bruises scattered here and there across Mrs. Thatcher's skin, reminders, I'm assuming, of recent falls.

I know there's a name for this. It's on the tip of my tongue.

"Have you seen Colin?" I ask.

She says that she hasn't. I ask her when she last saw him. She doesn't know.

"How often do you see Colin?" I ask.

"Every week. He mows the lawn."

I peer out the kitchen window at a yard covered in shriveled leaves.

"He takes care of you?" I ask. "Mows the lawn, gets the groceries…" She says that he does. I see the fruit rotting on the counter, swarming with an abundance of fruit flies. I allow myself to peek inside the refrigerator/freezer and find a bag of frozen peas, a carton of expired milk, a couple of TV dinners. The pantry is as inadequate: a few cans of soup that Mrs. Thatcher likely can't open by herself, and crackers.

"Does he take out the garbage?" I ask.

"Yes."

"How long has he been helping you? A year? Two years?"

"He was a child. When I got sick. His dad…" Her voice trails off.

"Left," I finish.

She nods.

"And now Colin…lives with you?"

She shakes her head. "He comes. To visit."

"But not this week?"

"No."

"Or last?"

She doesn't know. There are very few dishes in the sink, but the garbage is an abundance of paper plates. He encouraged her to use paper—easier than cleaning up after herself—and takes the trash to the curb every week he comes.

"But he does the shopping and the cleaning and the—"

"Everything."

"He does everything. But he hasn't been here for a while, has he, Mrs. Thatcher?"

A calendar on the wall points to September. The milk in the fridge expired on October seventh.

"Would it be okay if I took out the garbage for you?" I ask. "I see that it's full."

"Okay," she says.

The tremors are hard to watch. It makes me uncomfortable, to be honest.

I grab the wretched bag of trash and lift it from the bin and head out a back door. It reeks. I jog down three steps and toss the garbage into the trunk of my car to deal with later. I make sure no one's looking, and I peek into the mailbox and grab what's there, a stack so high it practically overflows onto the road. There's a slip tucked inside from the USPS, requesting the resident pick up additional mail from the post office. The mailman crammed in what he could until there was no more room.

Back inside Mrs. Thatcher is fighting with the corn. I can't take it. Nobody should have to work so hard to eat a damn TV dinner. I slide into the nook across from the gaunt woman and say, "Let me help." I take the fork and serve her a bite. There's a moment of hesitation. God knows the day someone has to spoon-feed me is the day I'd rather be dead.

"Where's Colin?" she asks.

I offer the food slowly, only a few kernels at a time.

"I don't know, ma'am. I'm afraid Colin might be in trouble. We need your help." I find a photograph of Mia Dennett and show it to the woman. I ask if she's ever seen her before.

She shuts her eyes. "TV," she utters. "I saw her on TV...she's the... Oh, God, Colin. Oh, Colin." And she begins to sob.

I try to assure her that we know nothing. It's only speculation. Mia Dennett may or may not be with Colin. But I know she is.

I explain that I need her help to find Colin. I say that we want to make sure that he and Mia are okay, that he isn't in trouble, but she doesn't buy it.

She's lost all interest in her dinner. Her deformed body

droops before the table and over and over and over again, she says, "Colin," an out-of-place answer to every question I ask.

"Mrs. Thatcher, can you tell me if there's any place Colin might go if he needed to hide?"

Colin.

"Can you provide me with contact information for family or friends? Anyone he might have contacted if he was in trouble. His father? Do you own a Rolodex, an address book?"

Colin.

"Please try and remember the last time you spoke. Have you talked to him since he was here last? By phone, perhaps?"

Colin.

I can't take it. I'm getting nowhere.

"Ma'am, is it okay if I look around? I'm just going to see if there's something here that might help me find your son."

It's like taking candy from a baby. Another mother would lawyer up and demand a warrant. But not Mrs. Thatcher. She knows what will happen to her if Colin doesn't come home.

I leave her crying on the breakfast nook and excuse myself.

I pass a dining room, a half bath, the master bedroom, and end up in the bedroom of seventeen-year-old Colin Thatcher, the navy walls and White Sox—egad—pennants and high school textbooks that were never returned. In the closet still hang some clothes: a football jersey and a pair of ripped jeans, and on the floor a pair of dirty cleats. There are posters of 1980s athletes thumb-tacked to the walls, and hanging in the closet, a discreet pullout of Cindy Crawford where his mother won't see. There's an afghan Kathryn likely crocheted when her hands still could, folded across the end of the bed, and a hole in the wall where, in a fit of rage, Colin might have thrown a punch. There's a radiator lining the wall beneath the window and in a small frame beside the bed, a very young

Colin, a beautiful Kathryn and a quarter inch of a man's head, the rest ripped off and tossed.

I take the scenic route on the way back. I mosey into the master bedroom, the unmade bed reeking of BO. There are dirty clothes in a pile. The blinds are shut, the room dark. I flip on a light, but the bulb has burnt out. I yank a cord in the closet and a scant amount of light enters the room. There are photographs of Colin Thatcher in every stage of his life. He doesn't look that different than me. Just your typical bundle of baby fat, turned football jock, turned *America's Most Wanted*. There are dandelions pressed behind glass; he might have collected those for her when he was a child. There's a stick figure drawing. His? And a cordless phone that's been knocked to the floor. I pick it up and return it to the base. It's dead. It will take hours for the battery to charge.

I make a mental note to get telephone records. I consider a phone tap.

In the front room, I run my fingers across the keys of a dusty piano. It's out of tune, but the sound beckons Mrs. Thatcher, who hobbles into the room. There is corn on her chin. She misses her footing on the way and somehow I manage to catch her in my arms.

"Colin," she says for the umpteenth time as I lower her onto the couch. I encourage her to lie down and prop a pillow behind her head. I find the remote and click on the volume to the TV. God knows how long she's been watching on mute.

There are scrapbooks lining an oak shelf, one for every single year of Colin Thatcher's life until the age of thirteen. I take one and fall into a leather armchair. I flip through the pages. Boy Scouts. Schoolwork and progress reports. There are leaf collections, picked up on afternoon walks and pressed in the pages of a massive encyclopedia. Newspaper clippings. Miniature golf scores. A Christmas list. A postcard to Ms. Kathryn Thatcher from Grand Marais, Minnesota, a fifteen-cent stamp stuck crookedly in the corner. The date *1989* is printed on the card; the image is of a forest, a lake, nature. There's a simple inscription: *Dad sucks. Miss you.*

There are photographs up the wazoo, mostly older ones that are yellowing and beginning to bend.

I stay with Kathryn Thatcher as long as I can. She needs the company. But she needs much more than that; she needs something I can't provide. I've said my goodbyes and promised to be in touch, but I don't go. The TV dinners will be gone in no time, and all it takes is one good fall to give her a concussion that will end her life.

"Ma'am, I can't leave you here," I admit.

"Colin," she whispers.

"I know," I say. "Colin takes care of you. But Colin isn't here now, and you can't be alone. Do you have family, Mrs. Thatcher? Anyone I can call?"

I take her silence as a no.

This makes me wonder. If Colin had been taking care of his ailing mother for so long, what would make him leave her?

I remove a few things from Mrs. Thatcher's closet and place them in a bag. I collect the medicine bottles. There's a nursing home in Gary. For now that will have to do.

I tell Mrs. Thatcher that we're going to go for a ride. "Please. No," she begs as I lead her to the car. "Please. I want to stay here. I don't want to go."

I have a coat draped over Mrs. Thatcher's robe. On her feet remain fuzzy slippers.

She's protesting as vehemently as she possibly can, which isn't much. I know that she doesn't want to go. She doesn't want to leave her home, but I can't leave her here.

A neighbor steps onto a front porch to see what the fuss is

about. I hold out a hand and say, "It's okay." I show him my badge.

I help her into the car and reach across her to secure the seat belt. She's crying. I drive as fast as I possibly can. In a few minutes this will all be through.

I think of my own mother.

An attendant meets me in the parking lot with a wheelchair and lifts Mrs. Thatcher from the car like a stuffed animal in a child's arms. After I watch him drive the wheelchair into the building, I peel out of the parking lot.

Later I search through the wretched garbage bag with a pair of latex gloves. It's a bunch of junk with the exception of a gas receipt dated September 29—I can only assume Mrs. Thatcher's license has been revoked—and a grocery store receipt with the same date, totaling thirty-two dollars. Enough to last a week. Colin Thatcher planned on returning in a week. He didn't plan to disappear.

I sort through the mail. Bills, bills and more bills. Past-due notices. But that's about all.

I think of that postcard, of all the trees. I think that maybe Grand Marais would be an amazing place to visit in the fall.

COLIN

BEFOЯE

I tell her that my mother's name is Kathryn. I show her a picture I keep in my wallet for safekeeping. It's an outdated photo, taken a decade or so ago. She says she can see my eyes on her, the seriousness and the mystery. My mother's smile is forced, revealing a crooked eyetooth that drives her crazy.

"When you talk about her," she says to me, "you actually smile." My mother's hair is dark, like mine. It's straight as an arrow. I say that my father's is, too. My own curls are a mystery, the result of some recessive gene, I guess. I never knew my grandparents to know if they had curly hair.

I can't go home for a number of reasons, but the one I never mention is the fact that the police want me behind bars. I was twenty-three when I broke the law for the first time. That was eight years ago. I tried to live the right way. I tried to follow the rules, but life just didn't work out that way. I robbed a gas station and sent every dollar I snatched to my mom to pay for her prescriptions. A few months later I did it again to pay the doctor bills. I figured out how much money I could make selling dope and did that for a while until I was caught by an undercover cop and spent a few months in jail. After that, I tried to play it straight again, but when my mother received an eviction notice, I became desperate.

I don't know why luck has been on my side. I don't understand why I've gone so long without getting nailed by the cops, really nailed. Part of me wishes it would happen, so I don't have to go on like this, on the run, hiding behind fake names.

"Then—" she begins. We're outside, walking through the vast trees. It's a milder November day, temperatures lingering in the upper 40s, and she's wearing my coat, sinking into it and burying her hands in the pockets. The hood envelops her head. I have no idea how long we've been walking, but I can no longer see the cabin. We step over fallen logs and I push aside the branches of an evergreen so she can sneak by without having to wrestle the sixty-foot balsam fir. We hike up hills and nearly fall down gulleys. We kick aside pinecones and listen to the call of birds. We lean against a western hemlock, in the midst of dozen similar trees, to catch our breath.
"Then you're not Owen."

"No."

"And you're not from Toledo."

"I'm not."

But I don't tell her who I am.

I say that my dad brought me here once, to Minnesota, to the Gunflint Trail. I tell her that he owns the cabin, that it's been in his family for as long as anyone can remember. He'd met some lady. "What she saw in the bastard, I don't know," I say. "I know it didn't last." We hadn't spoken in years and I'd all but forgotten about him. Then one day he invited me on this trip. We'd rent an RV. We'd drive from the home he owned in Gary, Indiana, to Minnesota. This was long before he moved to Winona to work for the D.O.T. I didn't want to go, but my mom said I had to. She had some naive idea my father wanted to fix things with me, but she was wrong.

"The lady had some prick kid about the same age as me. So he planned some big vacation, as if this was something we *did*. The lady, her kid and me. He wanted to impress her. He promised me a bike if I didn't do anything to screw it up. I kept my mouth shut the whole time. Never saw the bike." I tell her that I haven't spoken to him since. But still, I keep tabs on him. Just in case.

She says that she doesn't know how I maneuver my way through the woods. I say that it's second nature. Boy Scouts, for one, and this innate ability to know which way is north and which way is south. That and a lot of time spent roaming the woods—anything to get away from fighting parents— when I was a kid.

She keeps up with me as I hike through the woods. She doesn't get tired.

How does a girl who grew up in the city know all the names of the trees? She points them out to me—balsam fir and spruce and pine—as if it's a fucking biology lesson. She knows that acorns belong to oak trees, and those stupid little helicopters fall from maple trees.

I guess it doesn't take a genius to know that. It's just that I never cared—not until I watched her hands release the seeds and then watched her eyes as she stared in awe as they spun their way to the ground.

She teaches without meaning to. She points out that those helicopters are samaras and the red cardinal is the male. She's offended that all the showy animals are male and the females are drab. Cardinals, ducks, peacocks, lions. I'd never noticed the difference. She wouldn't be so offended if she hadn't been screwed over by every man in her life.

She says that she could never wrap the words around it, about how her father makes her feel. She says I wouldn't un- derstand anyway because he'd never hit her and never let her spend one night cold. He never let her go to sleep without dinner.

She has a student named Romain, this black kid who spends most of his nights in a homeless shelter on the north side. He chooses to go to school though no one's making him. He's eighteen, working on a high school diploma because he won't settle for a GED. He spends his days studying his ass off in school and spends his afternoons cleaning city streets. He spends his nights begging for money under the "L." She volunteered in a homeless shelter to see what it was like. "For two hours I pulled moldy cheese off prepackaged sandwiches," she says. The rest of the sandwich was salvaged for the tenants to eat.

Maybe she isn't all that wrapped up in herself as I expected her to be.

I know the feel of dismissive eyes, eyes that look without really seeing a thing. I know the sound of contempt in a voice. I know how betrayal and disillusionment feel, when someone who could give you the world refuses even a tiny piece of it.

Maybe we aren't so different after all.

GABE

BEFOЯE

I check the phone records for Kathryn Thatcher. Not a questionable call in sight. The last time she spoke to her son was when he called from a cell phone registered to Steve Moss at the end of September. The rest were telemarketers, collection agencies, reminders for doctor appointments to which she never went.

I put a call into the nursing home in Gary. The attendant asks if I'm family. I say no, I'm not, and they won't pay me the time of day. I can hear an elderly man screaming in the background. I try not to imagine Mrs. Thatcher listening to his roar. I know it would make her upset. I remind myself that she's being fed, bathed, cared for.

I remind myself that I am not her son. This is not my responsibility.

But still I can't get this picture out of my mind: my mother sitting in her bathrobe at the end of a sunken bed, staring vacantly out a dirty window, hopeless and alone, while an elderly toothless man shouts in the hall. Underpaid nurses ignore her. The only thing to look forward to is the day she will die.

The case of Mia Dennett runs nightly on the evening news,

thanks to pressure on the part of Judge Dennett, but still no leads.

I checked with the DMV and there are no vehicles registered to a Colin Thatcher or Steve Moss, or a Kathryn Thatcher for that matter. We've been in contact with anyone who knew Colin Thatcher that we can possibly find. Friends are few, only a couple high school pals who haven't spoken to him in years. There's an ex-girlfriend in Chicago who I can't be entirely certain he wasn't paying for sex. She doesn't have one nice thing to say about him. She's a woman scorned; she offers nothing valuable to me other than a quick lay if I'm interested, which I'm not. Some schoolteachers say he was a boy who got the short end of the stick. Others describe him as a misfit. Mrs. Thatcher's neighbors can only say he visits frequently, he takes out the trash and mows the lawn. Big deal. The neighbors don't know what goes on inside the home. But they can tell me he drives a truck. Color? Make? Model? No one seems to know. The answers all conflict. I don't bother with a license plate number.

My mind drifts to the postcard of Grand Marais from time to time. I find myself researching the harbor town on the internet, and ordering travel brochures online. I track the mileage from Chicago to Grand Marais and go so far as to request footage from traffic cams along the route, even though I haven't a clue what I'm looking for.

I'm at a dead end. There's nothing to do now but wait.

COLIN

BEFORE

Just my luck, the girl's still sleeping when I hear a scratch on the front door. It about scares the shit out of me. I jump from my bed on the flabby couch and realize I don't have the gun. It's dawn, the sun just beginning to rise. I pull aside the curtains for a look but I see nothing. What the hell, I think. I open the front door to discover that the damn cat has brought us a dead mouse. He's been MIA for days. He looks like hell, almost as bad as the nearly decapitated rodent beside his bloody feet.

I scoop the cat into my hands. I'll deal with the mouse later. For now, the damn cat is my ransom, divine intervention, if I actually believed in that kind of shit. The cabinets have been cleared out. No food left. If I don't get to the store soon, we'll starve.

I don't wait until she's awake. I let myself into the bedroom and say, "I'm going to town."

She sits up at the sound of my voice. She's confused by sleep and rubs at her eyes.

"What time is it?" she asks, but I ignore the question.

"He's coming with me." The cat lets out a cry. This gets

her attention. She's alert. She reaches her hands out to him, but I step back. The little bastard claws my arm.

"How did you—"

"If you're still here when we get back, I won't have to kill him." And then I leave.

I race to town. I go over seventy in a fifty-mile-per-hour zone. I'd bet my life the girl wouldn't do anything stupid, but then again, I can't get the image out of my mind: the cabin swarmed by cops waiting for me when I return.

I pass a couple outfitters on the way to Grand Marais. I always try to mix it up. I can't say I've been to the same place twice. Last thing I need is for someone to recognize me.

But right now, food isn't the only thing on my mind.

I know a guy who specializes in fake IDs, manufactured identities, the works. I find a payphone outside the hardware store and dig a couple of quarters from my pocket. I pray to God I'm not making a mistake. It doesn't take three minutes or whatever they claim on TV to trace a call. The damn operators can do that the second the line connects. Soon as I dial the number. All it takes is for Dan to tell the cops he got a call from me and by tomorrow, they're clustered around Hardware Sam looking for me.

It comes down to options. Try our best to survive the rest of the winter—and then what? Then we're screwed. If we're still alive come spring, there'll be nowhere to hide.

And so I drop in the quarters and dial the number.

When I come back, she's running down the snow-covered steps to whisk the damn cat from my hands.

She's yelling about how she wouldn't have left. She's cursing me for threatening the cat. "How the hell would I know?" I ask. I take the paper bags of canned food from the backseat of the truck. There must be a dozen bags, each one piled high with ten or fifteen cans of food. This is it, I tell myself. The last trip to town. Until the passports are ready, we'll get by on condensed soup and baked beans and stewed tomatoes. That and whatever I pull out of the frozen lake.

She grabs me by the arm and forces me to look at her. Her grip is firm. "I wouldn't have left," she says again.

I duck away and say to her, "I wasn't about to take any chances." I head up the stairs, leaving the cat and her alone outside.

She convinces me to let the cat stay inside. It gets colder every day. He won't survive all winter.

"No way," I say.

But she insists. "He stays." Just like that.

Something is changing.

I tell her about working with my uncle when I was a kid. It's with reluctance that I talk at all. But there's only so much silence a person can take.

I started working for my mother's brother when I was fourteen. This beer-bellied bum who taught me how to do all his handyman services so that, at the end of the day, I could do all the work and he could take home 90 percent of the pay.

No one in my family went to college. No one. Maybe some distant cousin or something, I say, but no one I know. Everyone is blue collar. Most people work in Gary's steel industry. I grew up in a world where I, as a white boy, was a minority and where nearly a quarter of the population lived below the poverty line.

"The difference between you and me," I tell her, "is that I grew up with nothing. I didn't hope for more. I knew I wouldn't get it."

"But you must have dreamed of becoming *something*?"

"I dreamed of maintaining the status quo. Of not stooping any lower than I already was. But then I did."

My uncle, Louis, taught me to fix leaky faucets and install hot-water heaters. How to paint bedrooms and fish a toothbrush out of a toilet. How to edge a lawn, fix a garage door and change the lock on someone's house after they'd kicked out their ex. Louis charged a flat twenty dollars an hour. At the end of the day, he sent me home with about thirty dollars to my name. I knew I was getting ripped off. By the time I was sixteen I was working on my own. But the work was unstable. I needed something I could depend on. Unemployment in Gary is high.

She asks me how often I visit my mother. I stiffen at the mention of her and am quiet.

"You're worried about her," she says.

"I can't help her when I'm here."

And then it hits her.

"The money," she says. "The five grand—"

I sigh. I tell her that it was for her. She won't take her medicine anymore, not unless I force her to. She says that she forgets. But the reality is that she doesn't want to deal with the side effects. I tell her that I would go to her home in Gary every Sunday. Organize the medicine into a pill dispenser, take her grocery shopping, clean the house. But she needed more. She needed someone who could take care of her all the time, not just on Sundays.

"A nursing home," she says. I wanted to put my mother in a nursing home, and I planned to use the five grand to get her in. But of course now there is no money, because in one impulsive moment I chose to save the girl and ended up screwing over my mother and myself at the same time.

But in the back of my mind, I know why I did it. And it wasn't about the girl. If my mother found out that I'd been the one to snatch the judge's daughter, later, when it was all over the news that she'd been found somewhere slain, it would have killed her. The five grand wouldn't have mattered anymore. She'd be dead. And if not dead, she'd want to be. She didn't raise me to be like this.

I just didn't think about all that before the girl was in my truck. When the dollar signs gave way to reality: the girl, crying beside me, the image of Dalmar's guys tearing her from the truck, the thirty years in prison. My mother would be dead before I was ever released. What good would that do?

I begin to pace the room. I'm mad. Not at her. At myself. I ask, "What kind of person wants to put their mother in a nursing home because they're so fucking sick and tired of caring for them?"

It's the first time I let myself be unguarded. I stand at an angle against the pine walls, and I press my hand to a lingering headache. I look at her receptive eyes and ask again, "Seriously, what kind of person would put their mother in a nursing home because they don't want to take care of them anymore?"

"There's only so much you can do."

"I can do more," I snap. She's standing before the front door, watching the snow fall. Beside her feet the damn cat roams in circles, begging to be let out. She won't let him. Not tonight.

"Can you?"

I tell her that some Sundays, when I arrive, I'm surprised she's still alive. The place is trashed. She hasn't eaten. The meals I've left in the freezer are still there. Sometimes the door is unlocked. Sometimes the oven is on. I asked her to come live with me, but she said no. This was her home. She didn't want to leave Gary. She'd been there her entire life. She grew up there.

"There are neighbors," I say. "One lady checks on her once a week, gets the mail, makes sure there's enough food. She's seventy-five but she gets along better than my own mom. But everyone has their own life. I can't expect them to babysit a grown woman for me." I tell her that there's also my aunt, Valerie, who lives nearby in Griffith. She helps out, from time to time. I'm hoping that Valerie has figured it out somehow: a call from the neighbor, seeing me on TV. I'm hoping she's figured out that my mother's alone and that she's doing something, *anything,* to fix the situation.

My mother didn't know about the nursing home, but she never wanted to be an inconvenience. This was the best I could do. A compromise.

But I know that a nursing home is a shitty compromise. Nobody wants to live in a nursing home. But there wasn't a better option.

I grab my coat from the arm of a chair. I'm upset with myself. I've let my mother down. I force my shoes onto my feet, slam my arms into the coat. I won't look at her. I nearly run her over to get at the door.

"It's snowing," she says. She's not quick to move. She lays her hand on my arm and tries to stop me but I shrug her off. "No one belongs outside on a night like tonight."

"I don't care." I push past her and open the door. She hoists the cat into her hands so it won't run away. "I need some fucking air," I say, slamming the door.

EVE

BEFORE

In the days after Thanksgiving a woman microwaves her three-week-old infant and another slashes her three-year-old's throat. It's not fair. Why have these ungrateful women been blessed with children when mine has been taken from me? Have I been that bad of a mother?

The weather on Thanksgiving was like spring: temperatures in the sixties, plenty of sun. Friday, Saturday and Sunday were more of the same, though even as we ate the last bites of leftover mashed potatoes and stuffing, the makings of a typical Chicago winter were in the works. The weathermen warn us for days of the impending snowstorm that's to arrive Thursday night. The grocery stores have run out of bottled water as people prepare to take shelter in their homes; my God, I think, it's winter, an annual certainty, not the atomic bomb.

I take advantage of the warm weather to decorate the home. I'm certainly not in the cheery holiday spirit, but I do it nonetheless—to stave off boredom and the dreadful thoughts that fill my mind. To enliven the home, not that James or I will notice, but just in case. Just in case Mia is here for Christmas to enjoy it, the tree and the lights and her aging, childhood stocking with the embroidered angel whose hair is beginning to fall off.

There's a knock at the door. I start, as I always do, and a thought crosses my mind: Mia?

I'm entangled in white Italian lights, testing them in the electric socket and attempting to unravel twelve months of knots. I'm never quite sure how the knots are able to form inside the plastic bins in the attic, and yet every year, as certain as the unmerciful Chicago winter, they do. Celtic Christmas music spews forth from the stereo: "Carol of the Bells." I'm still in my pajamas, a striped silk set—a button-front shirt and drawstring pants. It's approaching ten o'clock and so the pajamas, in my mind, are considered acceptable though my coffee has gone lukewarm, the milk drifting toward sour. The home is a mess: red and green plastic storage bins sprinkled here and there, lids removed and tossed where they won't be in the way. There are branches of the artificial Christmas tree we've assembled every year since James and I rented an apartment in Evanston while he was finishing up his law degree. They're stacked in piles across the living room. I've looked through the boxes of ornaments we've collected over the years, everything from Baby's 1st Christmas to those beaded candy canes the girls made in third grade. But these are the ornaments that rarely make it to the tree, forced to remain in the box and collect dust. I was always insistent upon a lavish tree for others to admire at holiday parties. I hated the chintzy clutter that filled other homes on Christmas, the snowmen and bric-a-brac that people collected over the years.

But this year, I vow, the girls' ornaments will be the first I hang.

I rise from the floor, leaving the lights behind. I can see Detective Hoffman peering through the beveled glass. I open the door and welcome a gust of cool air that rushes in to greet me.

"Good morning, Mrs. Dennett," he says, welcoming himself into my home.

"Good morning, Detective." I run a hand though my un-combed hair.

His eyes peek around the house. "Doing some decorating, I see," he says.

"Trying to," I respond, "but the lights are all tangled."

"Well," he begins, removing a light jacket and setting it on the floor beside his shoes, "I am an expert at untangling Christmas lights. Do you mind?" he asks and with a sweep-ing hand I tell him to help himself, grateful that someone is here to finish the burdensome task.

I offer the detective coffee, knowing he will accept because he always does, certain that he takes his with cream and sugar and a lot of it. I rinse out my own cup and refill it, returning to the living room with a mug in each hand. He's kneeling on the floor, delicately prying the string of lights apart with the tips of his fingers. I set his coffee on a coaster on the end table and sit on the floor to give him a hand. He's come to talk about Mia. He's asking about some town in Minnesota: Have I been there, or Mia? I tell him no.

"Why?" I ask and he shrugs.

"Just curious." He says that he saw some photographs of the town; it looks beautiful. A harbor town about forty miles from the Canadian border.

"Does it have something to do with Mia?" I ask and though he tries to elude the question, he finds he can't. "What is it?" I persist.

"Just a hunch," he says, and then admits, "I don't know anything. But I'm looking into it," and when my eyes beg desperately for more information, he vows, "You'll be the first to know."

"Okay," I concede after a moment of hesitation, knowing that Detective Hoffman is the only one who cares about my daughter nearly as much as me.

It's been nearly two months since Gabe Hoffman started showing up unexpectedly at my home. He comes whenever he has the urge: a quick question about Mia, some thought that hit him in the middle of the night. He hates it when I call him *Detective* just as I hate it when he calls me *Mrs. Dennett* and yet we keep up the semblance of formality when, after weeks of discussing the private details of Mia's life, first names should be routine. He's a master at the art of small talk and beating around the bush. James isn't yet convinced that the man is not an idiot. But I think he's sweet.

He pauses in his work, reaches for the mug of coffee and takes a sip. "They say we're supposed to get a lot of snow," he responds, changing the subject. But still, my mind is lost on this harbor town. Grand Marais.

"A foot," I agree. "Maybe more."

"It would be nice if we had snow on Christmas."

"It would," I say, "but it never happens. Maybe it should be a blessing. With all the travel and errands that we have to do around Christmastime, maybe it's a good thing it doesn't snow."

"I'm sure you'll have all your shopping done long before Christmas."

"You think so?" I ask, a bit surprised by the assumption, adding, "I don't have many people to shop for. Just James and Grace and—" I hesitate "—Mia."

He pauses and between us a moment of silence passes in respect for Mia. It could be uncomfortable and yet it's happened nearly a million times in the past few months, anytime her name is so much as mentioned. "You don't seem like a procrastinator," the detective says after a moment.

I laugh. "I have too much time on my hands to procrastinate," I say and it's true. With James at work all day, what else do I have to do besides shop for holiday gifts?

"Have you always been a homemaker?" he asks then and,

sitting up straighter, uncomfortable, I have to wonder, how did we get from Christmas décor and the weather to this? I hate the word *homemaker*. It's very 1950s and outdated. It has a negative connotation now, something that it didn't neccssarily have fifty-some years ago.

"And by homemaker you mean?" I ask, adding, "We have a cleaning lady, you know. And I cook, sometimes, but usually James is late and I end up eating by myself. So I don't think you can really say I *make* the home. If you mean have I always been *unemployed*—"

"I didn't mean to offend you," he interrupts. He looks embarrassed, sitting beside me on the floor, prying the lights apart. He is making significant headway, much better than me. A strand of lights lies nearly untangled before him and as he leans over to test them in the socket, I'm astonished that they all work.

"Bravo," I say, and then a lie: "I'm not offended." I pat his hand, which is something I've never done before, any sort of gesture that intruded upon our three feet of physical space.

"I worked in interior design for a while," I say.

He eyes the room, taking in the details. I did decorate our home myself, one of the few things I'm proud of, my job as a mother falling short. It was something that made me feel accomplished, something I hadn't experienced in a long, long time, since before the girls were born and my life became equated with changing soaked diapers and wiping tossed mashed potatoes off my hardwood floors.

"You didn't like it?" Detective Hoffman asks.

"Oh, no. I loved it."

"What happened? If you don't mind me prying…" I think to myself: he has a handsome smile. It's sweet, juvenile.

"Children happened, Detective," I say casually. "They change everything."

"Did you always want kids?"

"I guess so. I dreamed of children since I was a child—it's something every woman thinks about."

"Is motherhood a calling, as they say? Something a woman is instinctively programmed to do?"

"I'd be lying if I said I wasn't ecstatic when I found out I was carrying Grace. I loved being pregnant, feeling her move inside me." He blushes, embarrassed with this sudden personal revelation.

"When she was born, it was a wake-up call. I had dreamed of rocking my child to sleep, soothing her with the sound of my voice. What I faced was sleepless nights, utter delirium from lack of sleep, intense crying that couldn't be soothed by anything. There were food fights and temper tantrums and for years I didn't have the time to file my own nails or wear makeup. James stayed at the office late and when he did come home, he wanted little to do with Grace anyway—he wiped his hands of any child-rearing. That was my job—the all-day, all-night, exhausting, thankless job, and at the end of the day he always seemed confused when I didn't have time to pick up his dry cleaning or fold a load of laundry."

There's silence. This time, uncomfortable silence. I've said too much, been too candid. I stand from my perch, begin poking Christmas-tree branches into their place on the center pole. The detective attempts to ignore my admission, laying the finished strands of lights in parallel rows. There's more than enough to decorate the tree and so he asks if I'd like a hand and I say sure.

We're nearly halfway finished with the tree when he says to me, "But then you had Mia. You must have got the knack of motherhood somewhere along the way."

I know he means well, a compliment, but I'm struck by the fact that what he's taken from my earlier admission was not that motherhood is a tough job, but that I didn't have what it took to be a good mother.

"We tried for years to conceive Grace. We nearly gave up. Afterwards, well, I guess we were naive. We thought Grace was our miracle baby. Certainly it wouldn't happen again. And so we weren't cautious with Mia. And then, one day it happened—the morning sickness, the fatigue. I knew right away that I was pregnant. I didn't tell James for days. I wasn't sure how he'd react."

"How did he react?"

I take the next branch from the detective's hand, thrust it into the tree. "Denial, I suppose. He thought I was wrong, that I misread the signs."

"He didn't want another child?"

"I don't think he wanted the first one," I admit.

Gabe Hoffman stands before me in a camel-hair blazer that I'm certain cost him an arm and a leg. He wears a sweater beneath that and a dress shirt beneath that and it's beyond me how he's not sweating. "You're very formal today," I say, standing before the Christmas tree, sporting my silk pajamas. I can taste morning breath on my tongue. In that moment, the sunlight pouring in the living room windows and obscuring my view, he looks chic and suave.

"Court. This afternoon" is all he manages to say and then we silently stare.

"I love my daughter," I say to the detective.

"I know you do," he responds. "And your husband? Does he love her, too?"

I'm overcome by the brashness. But what should offend and turn me away, somehow pulls me closer. I'm fascinated by this no-nonsense Gabe Hoffman, one who doesn't beat around the bush.

He stares and my eyes drop to the ground. "James loves

James," I admit. On the far wall is a framed photograph: James and me on our wedding day. We were married in an old cathedral in the city. James's parents covered the extravagant cost, though according to tradition, it should have been my father who footed the bill. The Dennetts wouldn't have it. Not because they were trying to be nice; rather, they believed James and my wedding might be chintzy otherwise, a humiliation in front of their affluent friends.

"This just isn't the life I envisioned when I was a child." I let the Christmas tree branches drop to the ground. "Who am I kidding? We'll have no Christmas this year. James will maintain he has to work, though I'm certain work is not what he'll be doing, and Grace will be with the parents of this man she's apparently begun to date, though we have yet to meet. We'll have a meal, James and me, Christmas day, as we do many other days of the year, and it will be as mundane as it can possibly be. We'll sit in silence and choke down a meal so we can retire to separate rooms for the night. I'll call my parents but James will encourage me to *hurry up* because of the cost of the international call. It doesn't matter anyway," I conclude. "All they'd want to know about was Mia, and I'd be reminded as I am every waking minute of every single day..." I try to catch my breath. I hold up a hand: enough. I shake my head, turn my back to the man who is staring with such pity in his eyes, I'm ashamed. I can't go on. I can't finish.

I feel my heart race. My flesh is clammy; my arms begin to perspire. I can't breathe. There's an overwhelming need to scream.

Is this what a panic attack feels like?

But as Detective Hoffman's arms close around me, every bit of it fades. His arms wrap around me from behind, and my heart rhythm slows to a steady jog. His chin rests on the top of my head, and my breath comes back to me, oxygen filling my lungs.

He doesn't say that it's going to be okay, because maybe it's not.

He doesn't promise to find Mia, because maybe he won't.

But he holds me so tightly that for a moment, the emotions are at bay. The sadness and fear, the regret and the loathing. He bottles them up inside his arms so that for a split second I don't have to be the one carrying the weight of them. For this moment, the burden is his.

I turn to him and bury my face against his chest. His arms hesitate, and then they wrap around my silk pajamas. He smells of shaving cream.

I find my feet rising to my tiptoes and my arms reaching up to pull his face to me.

"Mrs. Dennett," he protests gently. I tell myself that he doesn't mean it as I press my lips to his. It's new and exciting and desperate, all at the same time.

He clenches a fistful of my pajamas in a hand, and draws me to him. I wrap my arms around his neck, and run my fingers through his hair. I taste his coffee.

For a moment he returns the kiss. Only a moment.

"Mrs. Dennett," he whispers again, his hands moving to my waist to gently pry my body from his.

"Eve. Please," I say, and as he steps back, he wipes at his mouth with the back of his hand. I make a final, failed attempt, pulling him into me with the shirttails of his blazer in my hands.

But he won't have me.

"Mrs. Dennett. I can't."

The silence lasts a lifetime.

My eyes are lost on the floor. "What have I done?" I whisper. This isn't something I do. I've never done this before. I am the one who's wholesome and virtuous. This…this is the behavior that James specializes in.

There was a time in my life when the eyes of men followed me. When men thought I was beautiful. When I passed through a room on the arm of James Dennett and every man and his covetous wife turned to stare.

I feel the detective's arms around me still, the reassurance and compassion, the warmth of his flesh. But now he stands feet away and I find myself staring at the floor.

His hand comes to my chin. He lifts my face, forces me to see him. "Mrs. Dennett," he says, and then he starts again, knowing I'm not quite looking. I can't. I'm too ashamed to see what's in his eyes. "Eve." I look and there's no anger, no scorn. "There isn't anything in the world that I'd rather do. It's just that…under the circumstances…"

I nod. I know. "You're an honorable man," I say. "Or a good liar."

He runs a hand along the top of my hair. I close my eyes and lean into his touch. I curl myself into him and let his arms fold around me. He holds me close. He presses his lips to the top of my head and kisses my hair, and then runs a hand down the length of it.

"No one makes me come see you two, three times a week. I do that. Because I want to see you. I could call. But I come to see *you*."

We stand like that for a minute or so and then he says that he needs to head down to the courthouse in the city. I walk him to the door and watch him leave and then stand, in front of the cold glass, staring down the tree-lined street until I can no longer see his car.

COLIN

BEFOⱤE

It's called an Alberta clipper. It's an area of fast-moving low
pressure that happens when warm air from the Pacific Ocean
collides with the mountains of British Columbia. It forms into
something called a Chinook, strong hurricane-like winds,
bringing arctic air south. I didn't have a clue what they were
two days ago. Not until the temperature in the cabin plunged
so low we decided to blast the heat in the truck for a few minutes. We needed to thaw out. We pushed our way through the
biting wind to the truck. She walked on my heels, used me
for wind resistance. The doors were practically frozen shut.
In the truck, I found a station on the radio and the weatherman was talking about this Alberta clipper. It had just arrived
in the area. It was busy pummeling us with snow and plung-
ing the wind chill into what I could only describe as unbear-
able. The temperature must have dropped by twenty degrees
since morning.

I didn't think the truck would start. I let out a few fuck-
yous while she said a few Hail Marys, but in the end, something worked. It took a while for warm air to come out of

the vent, and when it did, we blasted the heat and just sat. I
don't think she ever stopped shivering.

"How long have you had this truck?" she asks. She says
my truck must be older than some of her students. The front
speakers don't work. The vinyl seat is torn.

"Too long," I say. The weatherman breaks for commercial.
I spin the dial on the radio, flipping from country music to
Beethoven's *Für Elise*. No chance in hell. I try again and find
a classic rock station. I leave it there and turn the volume low.
Outside, the wind shrieks. It pitches the truck back and forth.
It must be going sixty miles an hour.

I have a cough and a runny nose. She told me it's from walking around in the cold the other night, but I tell her you can't
get sick from being in the cold. And then I turn my head and
cough. My eyes are tired. I feel like shit.

We watch, out the window. The trees lurch back and forth
in the wind. A branch snaps off a nearby oak and hits the
truck. She jumps and looks at me. I say, "It's okay." It will be
over soon.

She asks me what my plan is, how long I intend for us to
hide out in this cabin. I tell her that I don't know. "There
are some things I need to figure out," I say, "before we can
go," well aware that when I go, she's coming with me. It's all
I can think about these days: when and where we're going.
The dropping temperatures make clear that we can no longer stay here. I've got Dan working on phony passports, but
he said it would take time. *How much?* I asked, from the payphone outside Hardware Sam, making sure he knew we didn't
have much time. *Call me in a couple weeks,* he said. *I'll see what
I can do.*

So for now we wait. But I don't tell her that. For now I let
her think I don't have a clue.

The Beatles come on the radio. She says that they remind

her of her mom. "She used to listen to their records when Grace and I were kids," she says. "She liked the music, but more than anything, it was a link to her English heritage. She cherished all things English—tea and Shakespeare and the Beatles."

"Why don't you ever talk about your mom?" I ask.

She says she's sure she's mentioned her. "But I probably only mentioned her in passing. That's the way my mother is," she tells me. "Never in the spotlight. There's just never anything to say. She's quiet, submissive. Malleable."

My hands hover before the vent, trying to absorb as much heat as I can. "What does she think happened to you?" I ask.

I can smell the way our soap clings to her skin like it never does mine. A subtle smell. Like apples.

"I don't know," she says. "I haven't thought about it."

"But she knows you're gone."

"Maybe."

"And she's worried."

"I don't know," she says.

"Why's that?"

She thinks about it. "In the last year, she's called. Maybe once or twice. But then I didn't call back, and she didn't want to be a bother. So she let it go."

But she says she wonders. She says the thought has crossed her mind a number of times. What did people think when her birthday passed. When she wasn't at Thanksgiving dinner. She wonders if people are looking for her. If they realize she's gone. "I wonder if the police are involved or if it's just gossip. Did I lose my job to another teacher? Was my apartment taken from me when I didn't pay the rent?"

I tell her that I don't know. Maybe. But does it matter anyway? It's not like she can go home. It's not like she'll ever return to that job, that apartment. "But she loves you," I say. "Your mother."

"Sure," she says. "She's my mother." And then she tells me about her.

"My mother is an only child," she says. "She grew up in Gloucestershire, in this sleepy little village with old stone cottages, the ones with the steep sloping roofs, with homes that are hundreds of years old. It's where my grandparents live. Theirs is nothing special, an outdated cottage with so much clutter it always drove me crazy. My grandmother is a pack rat, my grandfather the kind of man who will be drinking beer until he's a hundred and two. He reeks of it, in an endearing sort of way—his kisses are always slobbery kisses that taste of beer. They're your typical grandparents—she can bake like no one else in the world, he has hours and hours of fascinating stories about fighting in *the war*. My grandmother writes me letters, these long letters on sheets of notebook paper, with the most perfect penmanship, this fluent cursive that dances on the page, and in the summer she slips in pressed flowers from a climbing hydrangea I always adored, this amazing vine that's climbed along the stone wall and now covers the roof of her home."

She tells me that her mother used to sing "Lavender's Blue" to her when she was a kid. I've never heard of it. I tell her that

She remembers growing up with her sister, a game of hide-and-seek. After her sister closed her eyes and counted to twenty, she disappeared into her bedroom and put some headphones on. "I was in a closet," she tells me. "A small, cramped linen closet. Just waiting for her to find me." She says she sat there for over an hour. She was four years old.

It was her mother who found her in the end, who searched the house from top to bottom when she finally noticed Mia was missing. She remembers the squeak of that closet door sliding open and she, on the floor, half asleep. She remembers her mother's eyes, deeply apologetic, and the way she cradled her on the floor, saying over and over again, "You're my good girl, Mia," letting her mind wonder about that which wasn't said.

She remembers that her sister was hardly reprimanded. "She had to apologize," she tells me, "which she did. Albeit like a snob." She remembers, even at the age of four, wondering what the advantage was of being good. But she wanted to be good. That's what she tells me. She tried hard to be the good girl.

She says that when she was the only one at home, her sister at school or playing, and her father *out,* she and her mother would share afternoon tea. "It was our secret," she says. "She'd warm apple cider for me, and brew herself a cup of tea that she kept hidden for this. We'd share a PB and J that she sliced to finger sandwiches. We'd drink with pinkies raised, and call each other names like *dearie* and *love,* and she'd tell me all about life in this magical British kingdom, as if princesses and princes roamed freely down every cobblestone street."

But she says that her father hated it there. He forced her mother to assimilate. He forced her to become American. To lose any sense of her own culture. She tells me that it's called imperialism: a relationship based on dominance and subordination.

She grimaces when she says her father's name. I don't think she means to. I don't think she knows she's doing it, but she does. I think her parents' relationship isn't the only imperialistic one.

It's dark outside, pitch-black without the moon. The truck's interior lights help us see, but still, there's just the contour of her skin, the reflection of light off her eyes. She says, "She's nearly devoid of her English upbringing, having been in the United States since she was younger than me. My father made her stop using words like *lorry* and *lift* and *flat* in place of *truck* and *elevator* and *apartment*. I don't know when it happened, when chips became French fries to her or when she stopped slipping the word *bloody* into angry snipes, but somewhere over the course of my childhood it happened."

I ask who's looking for her. Certainly someone has figured out she's gone.

"I don't know," she says. But she can assume. "My coworkers are worried, my students confused. But my family? I honestly don't know. And you?" she asks. "Who is looking for you?"

I shrug. "No one gives a damn that I'm gone."

"Your mother," she says.

I turn and look at her. I say nothing. Neither of us is sure if it's a question or not. What I know is that I feel something change inside me every time she looks at me. Her eyes no longer look through me. Now, when she talks, she looks at me. The anger and hate are gone.

I reach out and run a hand toasted by the heating vent across her cheek. I tuck a strand of hair behind her ear. I feel her cheek press against my hand and linger there awhile. She doesn't object.

And then I say to her, "We should get inside. It's only going to get harder the longer we stay out here."

She isn't quick to move. She hesitates. I think she's gonna say something. She looks like she wants to, like she's got something on the tip of her tongue.

And then she mentions Dalmar.

"What about Dalmar?" I ask, but she doesn't tell me. She's mute, ruminating on something or other. Like how it is that she ended up here. At least that's what I guess she's thinking about. How is it that the daughter of a rich judge ends up hiding out in a shitty little cabin with me?

"Never mind," she says. She's reconsidered. She doesn't want to talk about it.

I could sweat it out of her, but I don't. The last thing I want to talk about right now is Dalmar.

"Let's go inside," I say instead.

She nods her head slowly and says, "Okay. Let's go." And then we push the doors open against the weight of the wind. We retrace our steps back into the cold, dark cabin, where inside, we listen to the wind moan.

GABE

AFTER

I'm flipping through the sketch pad, desperate for clues, when it comes to me: that damn cat. I personally hate cats. Their elasticity scares the shit out of me. They have a tendency to become cozy on my lap, most certainly because they know it pisses me off. Their fur sheds and they make that bizarre purring noise.

My boss is all over me to wrap this thing up. He keeps reminding me that it's been weeks since the Dennett girl came home and I'm not one step closer to finding out who did this to her. My problem is simple: Mia is the only one who can help. And Mia can hardly remember her own name, much less the details of the last few months of her life. I need to trigger her memory.

And so I stumble upon the picture of the cat. My mom tells my dad all the time she'd keep the schnauzer over him. I personally have been dumped over a parrot. I see my neighbor smooching her poodle all the damn time. People have a funny relationship with their pets. Not me personally. The last pet I had I ended up flushing down the john.

And so I call a guy up in Minnesota and ask him to do me

a favor. I fax him the drawing and tell him we're looking for a gray-and-white mackerel tabby cat, maybe about ten pounds. He sends a trooper from Grand Marais out to the cabin to have a look around.

No cat, but there are animal prints in the snow. At my suggestion—it didn't seem like rocket science—he leaves a bowl of food and some water that will probably freeze overnight. Better than nothing. I ask him to check back in the morning and see if the cat ate the food. Can't be much worth hunting this time of year, and the damn thing has to be cold. My pal suggests that finding stray cats isn't their sole priority.

"What is?" I ask. "Arresting folks who exceed their daily limit of trout?" I remind him that this is a kidnapping case that's made national headlines.

"All right, all right," he says to me. "I'll get back to you in the morning."

COLIN

BEFORE

I tell her that my middle name is Michael, after my dad. She still doesn't know my real name. She calls me Owen when she calls me anything at all. Generally I don't call her anything. There's no need. I have a scar near the bottom of my back that she's seen when I'm coming out of the bathroom after a bath. She asks about it. I tell her it's from a dog bite as a kid. But the scar on my shoulder I won't talk about. I tell her I've broken three bones in my body: a collarbone in a car accident when I was a kid; my wrist playing football; and my nose in a fight.

I rub my facial hair when I'm thinking. I pace when I'm mad. I do anything to keep busy. I never like to sit for more than a few minutes, and only ever with a purpose: feeding the fire, eating dinner, sleeping.

I tell her how this all started. How some man offered me five grand to find and deliver her to Lower Wacker Drive. I knew nothing about her at the time. I'd seen a photo and for days I followed her around. It wasn't something I wanted to do. I didn't know the plan until that night. Until they called me on the phone and told me what I was supposed to do. That's the way it is; the less I know the better. This wasn't like the other times. But this was more money than I'd ever been offered. The first time was only for repayment of a loan, I tell her. "So I didn't get my ass kicked." After that it was a few hundred dollars, sometimes a grand. I say that Dalmar is only a go-between. The others are all hidden behind a smoke screen. "I don't have a damn clue who pays the bills," I say.

"Does that bother you?" she asks.

I shrug. "That's just the way it is."

She could hate me for doing this to her. She could hate me for bringing her here. But she's coming to see that what I did may have saved her life.

My first job was to find a man named Thomas Ferguson. I was supposed to make him cough up a substantial debt. He was some rich, eccentric man. Some technological genius who made it big in the '90s. He had a fancy for gambling. He'd taken out a reverse mortgage and gambled away nearly all the equity in his home. Then a child's college fund. Then he moved onto funds his in-laws had left to his wife and him when they died. When his wife found out, she threatened to leave him. He got his hands on more money and headed out to the casino in Joliet to earn it all back. Ironically Thomas Ferguson did make a small fortune at the casino. But he didn't repay his debt.

Finding Thomas Ferguson was easy.

I remember the way my hands shook when I walked up the steps of the home in Chicago's Streeterville neighborhood. I just didn't want to get in trouble. I rang the doorbell. When a teenage girl peeked through the opening, I forced it open. It was after 8:00 p.m. on a fall night and I remember that it was cold. The house was dim. The girl started screaming. Her mother ran into the room and they took cover beneath an old desk when I showed my gun. I told the woman to call for her husband. It took a good five minutes for the coward to show his face. He'd been upstairs hiding. All the necessary precautions had been made: cutting phone lines and blocking the back door. He wasn't going to get away. And yet Thomas Ferguson waited long enough for me to tie up the wife and girl and stand, with the gun to the wife's head, when he finally appeared. He said he had no money. Not a penny to his name. But of course that couldn't be true. Parked outside was a brand-new Cadillac SUV that he'd just given to his wife.

I tell her that I never killed anyone. Not that time, not ever. We make small talk, to pass the time.

I tell her that she snores when she sleeps. She says, "I wouldn't know. I can't remember the last time someone watched me sleep."

I always wear shoes, even when we know there's nowhere to go. Even when the temperature plummets into negative degrees and we know we won't move an inch from the fire.

I leave the water at a trickle in all the faucets. I tell her not to turn it off. If the water freezes, the pipes will burst. She asks me if we'll freeze to death. I say no, but I'm not so sure.

When I'm really bored I ask if she can show me how to draw. I yank them out page by page because they look like shit. I drop them into the fire. I try to draw a picture of her. She shows me how the eyes go toward the center. "The eyes are generally aligned with the top of the ear, the nose with the bottom," she says. Then she makes me look at her. She dissects her own face with her hands. She's a good teacher. I think of the kids, in her school. They must like her. I never liked a single one of my teachers.

I try again. When I'm through she says that she's a perfect replica of Mrs. Potato Head. I yank it from the spiral notebook, but when I try to torch the page, she takes it from my hands.

"In case you're famous one day," she says.

Later, she hides it where I won't find it. She knows that if I do, it'll become food for the fire.

EVE

AFTEя

He worked on it all weekend, dropping subtle hints here and there, about how fat she would get and about the sinful child who was growing in her womb. He ignored my pleas to stop. Mia has yet to accept the notion that there is life inside her, though I heard her in the bathroom, vomiting, and knew morning sickness had arrived. I knocked on the door to ask if she was okay; James pushed me aside. I caught the door frame so I didn't fall, staring at him in dismay.

"Don't you have errands to run?" he asked. "A manicure? Pedicure? *Something?*"

I'm opposed to abortion. To me, it's murder. That's a child inside Mia, no matter what kind of madman helped create it. A child with a heartbeat and budding arms and legs, with blood that runs through its tiny body, through my grandchild's body.

James wouldn't leave me alone with Mia. He kept her confined to the bedroom for most of the weekend, filling her mind with literature on the pro-choice movement: pamphlets he'd picked up from clinics in the city and articles he'd printed from the internet. He knows my opinion on abortion. We're generally both conservative in our views, but now that there's an illegitimate child inside our daughter's womb, he tossed all rational thinking aside. There's only one thing that matters: getting rid of the child. He promised to pay for the abortion. He told me that much, or at least muttered it under his breath as if he was talking to himself. He said he'd pay for it because he didn't want the bills submitted to the insurance company for coverage; he wanted no record that *this* had ever happened.

"You can't make her do this, James," I said Sunday night. Mia wasn't feeling well. James had brought crackers into the bedroom. He'd never paid her this much attention in her entire life. She didn't join us for dinner. It was no coincidence. I was certain James had locked her in the bedroom so she couldn't be influenced by me.

"She wants to do it."

"Because you told her she has to."

"She's a *child,* Eve, who doesn't have the slightest memory of creating the bastard. She's sick—she's been through enough. She's not capable of making this decision right now."

"Then we'll wait," I suggested, "until she is ready. There's time."

There is time. We could wait weeks, even more. But James doesn't think so. He wants this done now.

"Damn it, Eve," he snapped, skidding his chair out from the kitchen table and standing up. He walked out of the room. He hadn't finished his soup.

This morning he had Mia up and out of bed before I'd finished a cup of coffee. I'm sitting at the kitchen table when he all but pulls her down the stairs. She dressed in a mismatching outfit I'm certain James has ripped from her closet and forced her to put on.

"What are you doing?" I demand as he yanks her coat from the front closet and insists she get it on. I hurry into the foyer, my coffee cup slipping from the edge of the table and shattering into a thousand pieces on the hardwood floor.

"We've talked about this," he says. "We're in agreement. All of us." He stares at me, compelling me to agree.

He had called his judge friend and asked that the man's wife, Dr. Wakhrukov, do him a favor. I heard him on the phone early this morning, before 7:00 a.m., and the word *disbarred* stopped me outside his office door midstride. Abortions are done at clinics throughout the city, not reputable obstetricians' offices. Dr. Wakhrukov is in the practice of bringing babies into this world, not taking them out. But the last thing James needs is for someone to catch him walking into an abortion clinic with his daughter in tow.

They will sedate Mia until she's so calm and content, she can't say no if she wants to. They'll dilate her cervix and reach in to suction the baby out of its mother's womb, like a vacuum.

"Mia, honey," I say, reaching out for her hand. It's as cold as ice. She's in a fog, not yet awake from sleep, not yet herself. She hasn't been herself since before her disappearance. The Mia I know is outspoken and forthright and strong in her convictions. She knows what she wants and she gets what she wants. She never listens to her father because she finds him cold and reprehensible. But she's numb and emotionless and he has used this to his advantage. He has her entranced. She's under his spell. She cannot be allowed to make this decision. This decision will remain with her the rest of her life. "I'm coming," I say.

James backs me against a wall. With a finger pointed at me, he orders, "You're not."

I push him away and reach for my coat. "I am."

But he won't let me get in the way.

He rips the coat from my hands and throws it to the floor. He's clinging to Mia with one hand, dragging her through the front door. The Chicago wind rushes into the foyer and grips my bare arms and legs, twirling my nightgown around me. I try to pick up the coat, calling out, "You don't have to do this. Mia, you don't have to do this," but he's holding me back and when I don't stop, he pushes me hard enough that I fall to the ground. He slams the front door closed before I can catch my breath and rise to my feet. I get the strength to stand and peer out the window as the car pulls out of the drive. "You don't have to do this, Mia," I still say, though I know she can no longer hear me.

My eyes drift to the cast-iron key holder to see that my keys are missing, that James has taken them in an attempt to keep me at bay.

COLIN

BEFORE

It only took a day or two and the damn cold was gone. I felt like shit the first day. But around the time I started to feel sorry for myself, my nose opened up and I could breathe. That's me. For her it's something different. I can tell by the cough.

She started coughing shortly after me. Not a dry cough like mine, but something much deeper. I'm forcing her to drink tap water. I don't know much—I'm not a doctor—but it might help.

She feels like shit. I can see it in her face. Her eyes droop. They water. Her nose is raw and red from wiping it with scraps of toilet paper. She's freezing her ass off all the time. She sits before the fire with her head pooled over the arm of a chair, and she sinks to a place where she hasn't been before. Not even when I held that gun to her head.

"You want to go home?" I ask. She tries to hide it. But I know that she's been crying. I can see the tears run their course down the length of her cheeks. They drip to the floor.

She lifts her head. She wipes at her face with the back of a sleeve. "I just don't feel good," she lies. Of course she wants to go home. That cat doesn't leave her lap. I don't know if it's the warm afghan she has or the fact that she's cooking before the fire. Or maybe it's pure devotion. How the hell would I know?

I picture myself holding that gun to her head. I imagine her lying on the rocky earth surrounded by leaves. These days I can't get that image out of my head.

I press a hand to her head and tell her that it's hot.

She says she's so tired all the time. She can barely keep her eyes open, and when she comes to, I'm always there with a glass of water for her to drink.

She tells me that she dreams of her mother, of lying on their family room sofa as a kid, when she was sick. She dreams of being huddled under a blanket she carried around all the time. Sometimes her mom would toss it in the dryer for a few minutes to heat it up. She'd make her cinnamon toast. She'd wait on her while they watched cartoons and when the soap operas came on, they'd watch them together. There was always a glass of juice to drink. Fluids, her mother would remind her. Drink your fluids.

She tells me that she's certain she sees her mom standing here in the cabin's kitchen in a silk nightgown, and slippers the shape of ballet shoes. There's Christmas music, she says: Ella Fitzgerald. Her mother is humming. The scent of cinnamon fills the air. She calls out for her mommy, but when she turns, she sees me and starts crying.

"Mommy," she sobs. Her heart races. She was sure her mother was there.

I cross the room and press a hand to her head. She flinches. My hand is like ice. "You feel hot." And then I hand her a glass of lukewarm water.

I sit down beside her on the couch.

She presses the glass to her lips but doesn't drink. She lays sideways, her head set on a pillow I brought from the bed. It's as thin as paper. I wonder how many heads have been here before her. I reach for the blanket that fell to the floor and I drop it to her. The blanket is rough, like wool. It scratches her skin.

"If Grace was my father's favorite, then I was my mother's," she says suddenly. Like it hit her right there, a moment of clarity. She says that she sees her mother running into her bedroom when she'd had a nightmare. She feels her arms around her, protecting her from the unknown. She sees her pushing her on the swing when her sister was at school. "I see her smiling, I hear her laugh. She loved me," she says. "She just didn't know how to show it."

In the morning she complains that her head hurts and her throat and God knows she can't stop coughing. She doesn't bitch about it. She tells me because I ask.

There's pain in her back. At some point she moves to the couch, where she falls asleep facedown. She's as hot as hell when I touch her, though she shakes as if at any moment she might freeze into a chunk of ice. The cat moves onto her back until I shoo it away. Then it takes refuge on the back of the couch.

No one's ever loved me so much.

She mumbles in her sleep about things that aren't there: a man in a camouflage coat and graffiti on a brick wall, sprayed illegally with aerosol paint, wild-style, with an illegible tag. She describes it in her dreams. Black and yellow. Fat, interwoven letters in 3D.

I let her take over the couch. I sleep on a chair, two nights now. I'd be more comfortable on the bed but I don't want to be that far away. I'm kept awake half the night by that fucking cough, though somehow she manages to sleep through it. It's the stuffed-up nose that generally wakes her up, that terrifying inability to breathe.

I don't know what time it is when she says she has to use the bathroom. She sits up and when she thinks she can, she stands. I can tell from the way she moves that everything aches.

She's only gone a few steps when she starts to fall.

"Owen," she manages to whisper. She reaches a hand out to the wall, misses and tumbles toward the ground.

I don't think I've ever moved so fast in my life. I didn't catch her, but I did stop her head from hitting the hardwood floors.

She isn't out long, only a couple seconds at best. When she comes to she calls me Jason. She thinks that I am him. And I could get pissed, but instead I help her to her feet and together we go into the bathroom and I pull down her pants and help her pee. And then I carry her to the couch and tuck her in.

She asked once if I had a girlfriend. I told her no, that I tried it once and it wasn't for me.

I asked her about this boyfriend of hers. I met him in the bathroom stall and hated the guy the minute I laid eyes on him. He's the kind of bastard that acts tough. He thinks he's better than everyone else but inside he's a coward. He's the kind of Thomas Ferguson that would let a man hold a gun to her head.

I watch her sleep. I hear the cough rattle from her lungs. I listen to the shallow breathing and watch as her chest rises and falls irregularly with each breath.

"What do you want to know?" she'd said when I asked her about the boyfriend.

Suddenly I didn't want to talk about it.

"Nothing," I said. "Never mind."

"Because," she said, "I believe what you said."

"What?"

"About paying him off I believe you."

"You do?"

"It doesn't surprise me."

"Why do you say that?"

She shrugged. "I don't know. It just doesn't."

I know that I can't let this go on. I know that every day she gets worse. I know that she needs an antibiotic, that without it she could die. I just don't know what to do.

EVE

AFTER

She certainly can't be alone. I leave the house as soon as James arrives home without Mia in tow. There's nothing more important than Mia. I am positive she's standing alone on a street corner, deserted by her own father, and certainly lacking the resources to get back home.

I'm screaming at him. How could he do this to our child?

He let her walk out of that doctor's office alone, into the cold January day, knowing full well she isn't able to make herself breakfast, much less find her way home.

And he told me that *she's* the one who's being stubborn. That Mia is the one being unreasonable about this *damn baby*. He said that she refused the abortion, that she walked out of the obstetrician's office just as the nurse called her name.

James stomps into his office and slams the door, unaware of the suitcase I pack and quietly walk down the stairs before I leave.

I don't give her enough credit. By the time I pry my car keys out of James's hands and circle the doctor's office many, many times, she's tucked safely in her apartment with a can of soup warming on the stove for lunch.

She opens the door and I fall into her and hold her as tight as I possibly can. She's standing in the small apartment she used to call home. It's been a long time since she was here. Her houseplants hold on to life by a thread, and there's dust everywhere. It smells like a new home, that scent that says no one's been here for quite some time. The calendar on the kitchen refrigerator is stuck on October, the image ablaze with red-and-orange leaves. The answering machine beeps; there must be a thousand messages waiting for her.

She's cold, frozen from all that time walking and waiting for a cab. She says that she didn't have a dime on her for the fare. It's freezing cold in the apartment. She's slipped her favorite hooded sweatshirt over a thin blouse.

"I'm so, so sorry," I say over and over again. But she has it all together. She holds me at an arm's length and asks what happened and I tell her about James. It's me who's losing it, who's falling apart. She takes the suitcase from my hands and brings it into the bedroom.

"Then you'll stay here," she says. She sits me down on the couch and covers me up with a blanket, and then walks into the kitchen to finish the soup—chicken noodle, she says, because it reminds her of home.

We eat our soup, and then she tells me what happened at the obstetrician's office. She runs a hand across her abdomen and curls into a ball on a chair

Everything was going as planned. She said that she had talked herself into it and it was only a matter of time before it was all going to be through. James was sitting there, reading from some law journal and waiting for the appointment. In just a few minutes the Russian doctor was going to get rid of the baby.

"But," she tells me, "there was a little boy and his mother. He was barely four." She tells me about the woman, with her belly the size of a basketball. The boy played with his Matchbox cars up and down the legs of the stiff waiting room chairs. *Vroom, vroom, vroom...* He dropped one at James's feet and the bastard had the nerve to push it away with his Italian loafers, his nose never rising from the book. "And then I heard his mother," Mia says, "dressed in these cute denim overalls and looking as uncomfortable as could possibly be, say to the boy, 'Come here, Owen,' and he ran for her and zoomed a car over her protruding belly and climbed into her lap, saying, 'Hi, baby,' to the unborn child."

She stops to catch her breath, and then admits to me, "Owen. I didn't know what it meant, but it meant something. I couldn't take my eyes off the little boy. 'Owen,' I heard myself say aloud and both the boy and his mother looked at me."

James asked Mia what she was doing and she related the feeling to déjà vu. It was as if she'd been there before. But what did it mean?

Mia says that she leaned forward in her seat and told the little boy that she liked his cars. He offered to show Mia one, but his mother laughed and said, *Oh, Owen, I don't think she wants to see them,* but Mia did. James scolded her and told her to give the kid his toys back. But she wanted to do anything to be close to the boy. She says that the sound of his name made it hard to breathe. Owen.

"I took one of the cars in my hand, a purple van, and told him how much I liked it, and then drove it over the top of his head and he laughed. He said that he was going to have a baby brother soon. Oliver."

And then the nurse was there in the doorway calling her name. James rose to his feet and when she didn't he told her that it was her turn.

The nurse called her name again. She looked right at Mia; she knew who she was. James said her name more than once.

He tried pulling on her arm and got in her face to discipline her as only James would do. He reminded her again that it was their turn.

Mia tells me, "Owen's mother called to him and I saw myself reach out and stroke that curly hair and I don't know who was the most aghast, the boy's mother or Dad, but the boy liked it and smiled and I smiled back. I placed the two Matchbox cars back in the boy's hands and stood from my seat." She tells me that James sighed: *Thank God—it's about time.* But it wasn't time. She reached for her coat and whispered to him, "I can't do this."

She slipped out into the hall. He ran after her, of course, full of condemnation and criticism and threats. He urged her to reconsider, but she couldn't. She didn't know what any of it meant. Owen. She didn't know why that name meant so much to her. All she knew was that it wasn't time for her baby to die.

COLIN

BEFORE

It's 2:00 a.m. when I'm woken up by her scream. I stand from the chair and see her pointing across the pitch-black room at something that isn't there.

"Mia," I say. But I can't get her eyes off it. "Mia," I snap again. My voice is firm. I must look at the spot five times because she's scaring the shit out of me. Her eyes, filled with tears, are locked in place on *something*. I reach for the light and turn it on, only to reassure myself that we're alone. Then I drop to my knees before the couch. I take her head into my hands, and force her to look at me. "Mia," I say and she snaps out of it.

She tells me that there was a man at the door with a machete and a red bandana tied around his head. She's hysterical. Delirious. She can describe everything about him down to a hole in the right thigh of his jeans. A black man with a cigarette pinched between his lips. But what concerns me the most is the heat coming off her face when I press my hands to it. The glazed-over look of her eyes when she finally looks at me and her head drops to my shoulder and she begins to cry.

I run the water in the bathtub and let it fill to the top. I have no medicine. I have nothing to bring the temperature down. It's the first time I'm grateful that the water refuses to warm beyond lukewarm. Warm enough to keep her from becoming hypothermic. Cool enough that she doesn't begin to seize.

I help her rise to her feet. She leans on me and I carry the weight of her into the bathroom. She sits on the toilet seat as I peel the socks off her feet. She flinches when her bare feet touch the bitter tile. "No," she begs.

"It will be okay," I coax. It's a lie.

I turn off the water and say that I'll give her privacy, but she reaches out and clenches my hand. She says to me, "Don't go."

I watch as a convulsing hand attempts to undo the button of her khaki pants. She becomes weak and reaches for the sink to steady herself before she can finish. I step forward and unclasp the button. I lower her onto the toilet seat and pull her pants to the ground. I peel a pair of long johns from her legs and throw a sweatshirt over her head.

She's crying as she sinks into the bathtub. She lets the water rise up to her knees as she pulls them into her chest. She drops her head to them and her hair falls one way, the last few inches swimming in the water. I kneel beside the bathtub. With my hands, I cup the water and drop it where it doesn't reach. I soak a washcloth, drape it over the back of her neck. She doesn't stop shaking.

I try not to look at her. I try not to look below the eyes as she begs me to keep talking, anything to avoid the freezing cold. I try not to imagine the things I can't see. I try not to think about the color of her pale skin or the curvature of her spine. I try not to stare at her hair, bobbing on the surface of the bath.

I tell her about a lady who lives down the hall from me. This seventy-year-old lady who always manages to lock herself out of her apartment when she takes the trash to the chute down the hall.

I tell her how my mother cut my father out of all our early family photos. All their wedding photos she stuck in the shredder. She let me keep one photo of him. But after we stopped talking I used it for target practice.

I tell her that as a kid I wanted to play in the NFL. Wide receiver, just like Tommy Waddle.

I tell her that I can fox-trot because my mother taught me. But it isn't the kind of thing I'd ever let anyone see. On the Sundays when she's having a good day, she plays Frank Sinatra on the radio and we limp around the room. These days I'm better than her, by a long shot. She learned it from her own parents. There was nothing better to do, growing up when times were tough. Really tough. She always told me I knew nothing about being poor, even on those nights that I snuggled up with a sleeping bag in the backseat of our car.

I tell her that if it were up to me I'd live somewhere like this, in the middle of God knows where. The city isn't for me, all those damn people.

What I don't tell her is how beautiful she looked that first night. How I watched her sitting alone at the bar, masked by the faded lights and cigarette smoke. I watched her longer than I needed to for the pure pleasure of it. I don't tell her how the candle made her face glow, how the photograph I was given didn't do her justice. I don't tell her any of it. I don't tell her the way she makes me feel when she looks at me, or how I hear her voice at night, in my dreams, forgiving me. I don't tell her I'm sorry, though I am. I don't tell her that I think she's beautiful, even when I see her look in a mirror and hate the image she sees.

She tires from shaking. I see her eyes close as she begins to fall asleep. I press a hand to her forehead, and I convince

myself the fever has gone down. I wake her. And then I help
her stand in the bath. I wrap a rough towel around her and
help her step over the side of the tub. I help her dress into the
warmest clothes I can find, and then I towel-dry the ends of
her hair. She lies on the couch before the fire. It's beginning
to die, so I lay a branch across the logs. Before I can cover her
with a blanket, she's asleep, but she continues to hack. I sit
beside her and will myself not to sleep. I watch the rise and
fall of her chest so I know that she's alive.

There's a doctor in Grand Marais. I tell her we need to go.
She tries to object. *We can't,* she says. But I tell her we need to.

I remind her that her name is Chloe. I do everything I can
to disguise us. I tell her to pull her hair back, which she never
does. On the way, I run into a grocery store for a pair of reading glasses. I tell her to put them on. Not perfect, but it will
have to do. I wear my Sox hat.

I tell her we're paying in cash. No insurance. I tell her not
to talk more than she has to. Let me do the talking.

All we need is a prescription.

I drive around Grand Marais for a good thirty minutes before deciding on a doctor. I do this by their names. Kenneth
Levine sounds too formal. Bastard probably falls asleep every
night to the news. There's a clinic, but I keep driving—too
many people. There's a dentist, an ObGyn. I decide on some
broad named Kayla Lee, a family practitioner with an empty
parking lot. Her little sports car is parked out back. Not very
practical for the snow on the ground. I tell Mia we don't want
the best doctor in town, just one who knows how to write a
prescription.

I help her cross the parking lot. "Be careful," I say. There's
a layer of ice on the ground. We skate across it to the door.

She can't get rid of the damn cough, though she lied and said she was feeling better.

The office is on the second floor, above a copy shop. We enter and head straight up the narrow stairway. She says that it's heaven to be somewhere warm. Heaven. I wonder if she really believes in that kind of shit.

There's a lady sitting behind the desk, this woman who's humming Christmas crap. I usher Mia into a seat. She buries her nose into a tissue and blows. The receptionist looks up. "Poor thing," she says.

I get the paperwork from her and sit down in the bariatric chair. I watch Mia fill out the forms. She manages to remember Chloe, but when she comes to *last name* her hand becomes still.

"Why don't I do it for you?" I ask. I slide the pen from her hand. She watches me write Romain. I make up an address. I leave the insurance information blank. I bring the paperwork up front and tell the lady we'll be paying cash. Then I sit beside her and ask if she's okay. I take her by the hand. My fingers slip between hers and I squeeze lightly and say to her, "Everything's gonna be okay."

She thinks it's all a ruse for the receptionist's benefit, but what she doesn't know is that I suck at acting.

The lady leads us to a back room and takes Mia's vitals. The room is small and there's an animal mural painted across the walls. "Low blood pressure," the lady says. Increased respiration rate and pulse, temperature of 104. "Poor thing," she says again. She says the doctor will be in soon. I don't know how long we wait. She sits on the edge of the table staring at whimsical lions and tigers while I pace back and forth across the room. I want to get the hell out of here. I say it at least three times.

Dr. Kayla Lee knocks and then lets herself in. She's chipper—brunette, not blonde as I expected. A blonde bimbo was what we were hoping for.

The doctor is loud and she talks to Mia like she's three. She sits on a swivel stool and pulls it close to Mia. Mia tries to clear her throat. She coughs. She's a fucking mess. But maybe feeling like shit helps disguise the fact that she's scared half to death.

The doctor asks if she's seen us before. Mia can't come up with the words so I step in. I'm surprisingly calm. "No," I say. "New patients."

"So what's going on—" she peeks down at the file "—Chloe?"

Mia is growing exhausted from this trip. She can't hold the doctor's stare. I'm certain the doctor smells the BO on both our clothes, clothes we've worn almost every day so that we no longer smell the stink. She's hacking up a lung. There's a barking cough that sounds like a dozen terriers fighting inside her. Her voice is hoarse. It threatens to disappear.

"She's been coughing like this for about four days," I say. "Fever. Chills. I told her we needed to get in to see you Friday afternoon. But she said no, it was only a cold."

"Fatigue?"

Mia nods. I tell her that Mia is lethargic, that she passed out at home. She writes this down in her notes.

"Any vomiting?"

"No."

"Diarrhea?"

"No."

"Let me take a look," the doctor says and quickly shines a light in Mia's eye, up her nose, into her ears. She tells her to say *ahhhh* and feels her glands. And then the stethoscope finds its way to Mia's lungs. "Take a deep breath for me," Dr. Lee says. Behind her I continue to pace. She moves the stethoscope around Mia's back and chest. She has her lie down. Then sit up again as she taps on her chest and listens.

"My suspicion is pneumonia. Do you smoke?"

"No."

"History of asthma?"

"No."

I take in the artwork: a polka-dot giraffe. A lion whose mane looks like one of those damn cones dogs wear when they can't stop licking themselves. A baby-blue elephant that looks like it just crawled out of the delivery ward.

"I hear a lot of junk in your lungs, in layman's terms. Pneumonia is inflammation of the lungs, caused by an infection. Fluid blocks and narrows your airways. What starts as a cold might decide to settle in your lungs for whatever reason and what you get is this," she says, sweeping her hand across Mia's perimeters.

The doctor reeks of perfume. She doesn't shut up when Mia's hacking, though we all know she hears.

"We treat it with antibiotics," she continues. She lists the possibilities. Just give us a prescription. "But first I'd like to confirm with a chest X—"

The color fades from Mia's face, as if there was any there to begin with. There's no way we're stepping foot into a hospital.

"I appreciate your diligence," I interrupt. I step forward, close enough to touch the doctor. I'm bigger than both of them, but I don't use my size to change her mind. We'd run into dozens of people in a hospital. Maybe more.

I plaster a fucking smile on my face and confess that I'm between jobs. We're uninsured. We can't afford the two or three hundred dollars that a chest X-ray will cost us.

And then Mia starts coughing until we all think she might puke. The doctor fills a little plastic cup with water and hands it to her. And then she stands back to watch her patient gasp for air.

"Okay," she says. She writes out the damn prescription and leaves the room.

We pass her in the hall on the way out. She's bent over a countertop, writing notes in Chloe Romain's file. Her smock hangs low, to the top of leather cowboy boots. There's an ugly dress beneath. Her stethoscope is wrapped around her neck.

We're almost to the door when she stops and says, "Are you sure I haven't seen you before? You just look so darn familiar." But she isn't looking at Mia. She's looking at me.

"No," I say dismissively. No need to be kind. I got what I need.

We make a follow-up appointment for Chloe Romain, one she'll never keep.

"Thank you for your help," Mia says as I gently shove her out the door.

In the parking lot I tell her that we did good. We have the prescription. That's all we need. We swing by a pharmacy on the way back to the cabin. Mia waits in the truck while I run inside, grateful to find a sixteen-year-old pothead working the register and the pharmacist, tucked in back, never raising his head. I give Mia a pill before we pull out of the parking lot and I watch, out of the corner of my eye, as she falls asleep on the way home. I slip out of my coat and lay it over her so she doesn't get cold.

GABE

BEFORE

I spend many days visiting Kathryn Thatcher in her new abode. The first time I showed up I said I was her son. The receptionist said to me, "Oh, thank goodness—she talks about you all the time," and led me to the woman's room. I could tell in her eyes that she was disappointed to see me, but so relieved to have company she didn't bother to tell them I'd lied. She's well-medicated now and can function minimally on her own. Mrs. Thatcher shares a room with an eighty-two-year-old woman on hospice care; it's only a matter of time before she dies. She's so doped up on morphine she doesn't have a damn clue where she is, and she's certain Mrs. Thatcher is a lady named Rory McGuire. No one comes to visit the woman. No one comes to visit Mrs. Thatcher but me.

Turns out Mrs. Thatcher likes true crime novels. I go to the bookstore and pick up every bestseller I can find. I sit in on the edge of her bed and read them to her. I suck at reading aloud. I suck at reading at all; I don't think I quite mastered that in the first grade. Turns out I like true crime novels as well.

I sneak chicken nuggets into her room. As often as we can, we share a ten-piece and a large fry.

I bring an old CD player of mine and borrow Christmas CDs from the library. She says that it doesn't feel like Christmas in the nursing home; she can see the snow out the window, but inside everything feels the same. When I leave at night, I turn on music so she doesn't have to listen to her roommate's troubled breathing.

The days off I don't spend with Kathryn Thatcher, I spend with Eve. I find some asinine reason to repeatedly show up at her door. As December sets in and winter descends upon us, a fog comes over her. She chalks it up to seasonal affective disorder, whatever the hell that is. I can see that she's tired all the time. She's sad. She sits and stares out the window at the falling snow.

I try and devise one small scrap of information—real or not—about the case that will give the impression I'm not at a dead end.

I teach her to make my mother's lasagna. I'm not trying to turn her into a chef. I'm just not sure there's any other way to make her eat.

She says her husband is coming home less and less. He works even later, sometimes until ten or eleven at night. Last night he didn't come home. He claims to have worked all night catching up on motions, something that Eve attests he's never ever done.

"What do you think?" I ask.

"He looked tired this morning. He passed through to change his clothes."

I'm trying to hone my great detective skills to figure out why she doesn't leave her husband. So far, no luck.

"So he *was* working," I conclude.

Fat chance in hell he was working. But if it makes Eve feel better, so be it.

We never allude to the kiss. But every time I see her, I

imagine Eve's lips pressed to mine. When I close my eyes, I taste her, and smell everything from her hand soap to her perfume.

She calls me Gabe and I call her Eve. We stand closer than we used to.

Now when she opens the front door, there's a flicker of happiness and not just a letdown because I'm not the long-lost daughter; there's a flicker of happiness for *me*.

Eve begs me to bring her to the nursing home, but I know it would be more than she can handle. She wants to talk to Mrs. Thatcher, mother to mother. She thinks there's something Mrs. Thatcher might tell her that she wouldn't tell me. But still, I tell her no. She asks what Kathryn is like and I tell her that she's a strong woman and defiant. Eve tells me she used to be strong; fine china and haute couture have made her weak.

As soon as Mrs. Thatcher is fully stabilized, she'll go to live with a sister nearby, a woman who, apparently, hasn't so much as turned on the evening news for the past few months. I phoned her the other day at Kathryn's request. She had no idea her nephew had gone AWOL, had never heard a word about the search for Mia Dennett.

I've been assigned to other cases. A fire in an apartment building that's possible arson. Complaints from numerous teenyboppers against a high school teacher.

But at night when I retire to my own apartment, I drink to help me sleep, and when I do, I fall asleep to the image of Mia Dennett on video surveillance, being shepherded from an elevator by the abrasive Colin Thatcher. I imagine a bleak Eve crying herself to sleep. And I remind myself that I'm the only one who can stop it.

I'm visiting the nursing home one snowy Tuesday afternoon when Kathryn Thatcher turns to me and asks about her neighbor, Ruth Baker. "Does Ruthie know I'm here?" she asks and I shrug and say that I don't know. I've never heard of this Ruth—aka Ruthie—Baker. But she tells me how Ruthie checks on her every week, during the week when Colin can't be there. She says that she collects the mail every day and brings it with her, to Mrs. Thatcher's home. I envision the mail in the mailbox nearly tumbling to the ground, stuffed to the point it was impossible to close the door. There was so much mail I needed to drive to the Gary Post Office with a warrant to collect what the mailman couldn't stuff into the box. I spoke to the neighbors, but there was no Ruth or Ruthie, no Mrs. Baker. Mrs. Thatcher tells me that Ruth lives in the white Cape Cod across the street, and it's then that I remember the For Sale sign out front. No one answered the door.

I do my research and stumble upon an obituary from the first week of October. I pull up the death records and find that Mrs. Ruth Baker had a stroke and died at 5:18 p.m. on October 7th. Mrs. Thatcher has no idea. Mrs. Baker was supposed to be keeping an eye on Kathryn Thatcher while Colin was away. I'm guessing that wherever he is, he doesn't have a clue the seventy-five-year-old woman he left in charge of his mother is dead.

My mind reverts to the mail. I pull out the stack of mail I swiped from Mrs. Thatcher's box and collected from the post office, and sort it by postmark date. Sure enough, there is a gap, from Mia's disappearance until the bills and past due notices begin. About five days. I wonder who the hell has Mrs. Thatcher's missing mail. I return to the home of Ruthie Baker and knock on the door. Again, no answer, and so I track down a next of kin, a woman about my own age, Ruthie's daughter, who lives in Hammond with her husband and kids. One day I knock on her door.

"Can I help you?" she asks, startled when I show her my badge.

"Is your mother Ruth Baker?" I ask before I ever say my name.

She says that she is. Anytime a cop shows up at your door, the first thing you wonder is: *What's wrong?*

I forget to tell her that I'm sorry for her loss. I jump right in, with only one thought on my mind: finding Mia. "I believe your mother might have been collecting the mail from a neighbor of hers. Kathryn Thatcher," I say and a wave of guilt and embarrassment washes over the woman. She begins to apologize up and down. I know she's sorry, but I think she's also worried she might be in trouble. Mail theft is, after all, a felony, and here I am, a cop standing at her front door.

"It's just...it's been so busy," she says. "With all the arrangements...the funeral and packing up her home." She saw the mail. In fact she's walked past it about a million times, every time she goes into or comes out of her mother's home, stacked on a wooden end table beside the front door. She just never got around to returning it to its rightful owner.

I follow the lady in her minivan back to the street on which Kathryn Thatcher lives. We pull into the drive of Ruth Baker's house and the woman runs in to retrieve the mail. I thank her and snatch it from her hand, and there, in the driveway, I scramble through the mail. Chinese takeout menu, a water bill, grocery store ad, more bills and a pudgy envelope made out to Kathryn Thatcher with no return address. The handwriting is sloppy. I rip open the envelope and find, tucked inside, a crapload of cash. No note, no return address. I turn it over and over in my hands. I read the postmark. Eau Claire, WI. I toss the mail in the passenger seat of my car and speed away. Back at the station I pull up a map online. I track the route from Chicago to Grand Marais. Sure enough. Right where

I-94 heads west to St. Paul/Minneapolis and U.S. Highway
53 heads north and then west into northern Minnesota is the
Wisconsin town of Eau Claire, just about five hours shy of
Grand Marais.

I contact an Officer Roger something-or-other from northeastern Minnesota. He assures me I'm barking up the wrong
tree, but he says he'll look into it nonetheless. I tell him that
I'm faxing a sketch, just in case. Colin Thatcher's face has made
the news only in the tri-state area. TV stations throughout
Minnesota and the rest of the world don't have a clue who he
is. But they will.

COLIN

BEFORE

The antibiotic kicks in and she starts to feel better overnight. While the cough continues to rage, the fever drops significantly. She looks alive, no longer a zombie.

But as she feels better, something begins to change. I tell myself that it has to do with the antibiotic. But even I know that's not true. She's quiet. I ask if she's okay and she says she still doesn't feel good. She doesn't want to eat. I try and convince her to take a few bites, but she sits and stares out the window. Silence fills the cabin, uncomfortable silence, bringing us back to a place we used to be.

I try to make small talk, but her only responses are one-word answers. *Yes, no, I don't know.* She says we're going to freeze to death. She says she hates the snow, that if she has to eat chicken noodle soup again she'll vomit.

Generally I'd get pissed. I'd tell her to shut up. I'd remind her how I saved her life. I'd tell her to eat the damn soup before I shove it down her throat.

She wants nothing to do with drawing. I ask if she wants to go outside—the day is nicer than we've seen for a while—

but she says no. I go anyway and she doesn't move an inch while I'm gone.

She can't make a decision. She doesn't want the chicken noodle soup. I know that. So for dinner I give her the option. I rattle off the name of everything in the cabinet. She says she doesn't care. She's not hungry anyway.

She says she's tired of shaking all the time. She's tired of the crap we eat, cans of glop masquerading as food. Just the scent of it makes her want to vomit.

She's tired of the boredom. She's tired of having absolutely nothing to do for hours on end, day after day after unending day. She doesn't want to go for another walk in the godforsaken cold. She doesn't want to draw another picture.

Her nails are a jagged mess. Her hair is greasy from the inside out, a tangle that will never come undone. We can't escape our own smell, though we force ourselves to bathe nearly every day in that dirty tub.

I tell her that they'd send me to jail if I was ever caught. I don't know how long. Thirty years? Life? It's not about *this*, I tell her. But the number of years mean nothing. They're pointless. I'd never live to see them. Every criminal knows someone on the inside. I'm as good as dead inside the pen. They'd make sure of it.

It isn't a threat. I'm not trying to make her feel guilty. That's just the way it is.

I don't want to be here, either. I spend every waking moment wondering when Dan is gonna come through with the passports, how I'm gonna get them without the cops finding me. The food is always sparse, the nights getting colder so that one morning we won't wake up. I know that *now* is the time to go. Before the food runs out, before the money runs out. Before we freeze to death.

She lets me be the one to worry. She says there's never been someone to worry about her before.

I think of all the things that could go wrong. Starving. Freezing. Being found by Dalmar. Being found by the police. There's danger in returning home. There's danger in staying here. I know it. She knows it. But my bigger concern now is not having her with me.

GABE

AFTEЯ

Believe it or not, they find the damn cat. The poor little guy was hiding out in some shed behind the cabin, freezing his little ass to the verge of death. There wasn't a thing to eat so he was quite taken with the Kibbles 'n Bits the cops brought. But he sure as hell didn't like their cage, or so they said, and fought tooth and nail to get out of it before they fastened the lock. The feline took a turbo prop down to Minneapolis, then a commercial airliner into O'Hare. Little guy gets around more than me! I picked him up this morning and took him over to the Dennetts when—lo and behold—I find out Eve and Mia have moved out.

I make the jaunt to Wrigleyville and surprise the women at 10:00 a.m. with a dozen donuts, café mochas and a malnourished tabby cat. They're both in their pajamas, watching TV.

I catch the door as someone is leaving so I don't have to wait to be buzzed in. I like the surprise of it.

"Good morning," I say when Mia opens the door.

She wasn't expecting me. Eve rises from the couch and pats at her untidy hair. "Gabe," she says. She pulls on her robe to make sure nothing is exposed.

I attempt to leave the cat in the hall but so help me, all it takes is a "thank you" from Mia, in response to my "I brought some donuts and coffee," and the cat goes absolutely berserk, clawing at the bars of the cage and making noises I've never heard a cat make before. So much for my grand entrance.

Eve turns white. "What is that noise?" she asks and so I bring the little guy in and close the door.

According to research, people who live with animals have decreased anxiety and lower blood pressure. They have lower cholesterol. They are more relaxed and less stressed and are, overall, in better health. Unless of course you have a dog who pees uncontrollably wherever it wishes or eats your furniture to shreds.

"What are you doing with that cat?" Eve asks. She's clearly at a loss and thinks I'm off my rocker.

"This little guy?" I ask. I play dumb. I squat down and open the cage and take the cat into my arms. He claws me with his back claws. *Shit!* "I'm watching him for a friend of mine. I hope you don't mind. Is anyone allergic to cats?" I ask, setting him on the ground and standing to meet Mia in the eye.

The fur-ball jaunts over to her and does about a thousand figure eights around her legs. He's meowing. His insides purr.

Eve laughs. She runs a hand through her hair. "Looks like you have a friend, Mia," she says.

The girl is muttering something under her breath, as if trying a new word on for size before she blurts it out and astounds us all. She lets that cat grope her for I don't know how long as we listen to Eve go on and on about how taken the little guy is with Mia's feet.

"What's that you said?" I ask, stepping forward as she leans down and scoops the cat into her arms. He doesn't scratch *her.* They nuzzle noses and he bumps into her face with his head.

"I always told her she should get a cat," Eve continues to babble.

"Mia?" I say.

She looks at me with tears in her eyes. She knows that I know and that I did this for a reason. "Canoe," she whispers to me. "I said Canoe."

"Canoe?"

"It's his name."

What ever happened to Max or Fido? Canoe? What kind of name is that?

"Mia, honey..." Eve comes to her side, aware, for the first time, that something is happening here. "Whose name is Canoe?" she asks. Her voice is dumbed down, as if she's talking to a mentally challenged child. She's certain Mia is talking gibberish, a side effect of the ASD. Except this is the first time I've ever seen Mia say something that makes sense.

"Eve," I say, ever so gently prying her hand off Mia's arm. I reach into my coat pocket and pull out the fax I sent to the cops in Grand Marais and unfold it to reveal a perfectly sketched image of little Canoe. "This," I say, holding it out to her, "is Canoe."

"Then he isn't..."

"There was a shed," Mia is saying. She doesn't look at us. Her eyes are lost on the cat. Eve takes the drawing from my hand. She knows now. She's seen the sketchbook, every last image down to the drawing of Colin Thatcher that she told me kept her awake at night. But she had forgotten the cat. Eve sinks into the couch. "There was a shed behind the cabin. He was living in there. I found him sleeping in an old rusty canoe. I scared him the first time. I just threw open the door to have a look around and scared him half to death. He ran away, out a small hole in the shed, and flew like a bat out of hell through the woods. I never thought he'd come back. But he was hungry, and I'd left out food. He said there was no way in hell a cat was staying with us. No way in hell."

"Who said that, Mia?" I ask. *Of course* I know. I should have been the damn shrink. But her answer is unexpected.

"Owen," she says and then she begins to sob, laying a hand on the wall to steady herself.

"Mia, honey, who is Owen? There is no Owen. The man in the cabin? That man? That man is Colin Thatcher."

"Eve," I say. My self-worth is increasing by the second. I managed to do what a Ph.D. couldn't. I've got Mia placing herself in the cabin with a man named Owen and a cat named Canoe. "He went by a number of aliases. Owen is probably just another one of them.

"Is there anything else you remember?" I ask. "Can you tell me anything else about him?"

"We should call Dr. Rhodes," Eve interrupts. I know she means well—she has Mia's best interest at heart—but I can't let that happen. She reaches into her purse and I say her name. Enough has passed between us that Eve knows she can trust me. I won't let anything happen to Mia. She looks at me and I shake my head. Not now. This is getting good.

"He said that he hated cats. And that if he saw it in the cabin he'd shoot it. He didn't mean it. Of course he didn't or I wouldn't have let the cat in."

"Did he have a gun?"

"Yes."

Of course he did. I know he did.

"Were you afraid of him, Mia? Did you think he might shoot you?"

She's nodding. "Yes." But then she stops. "No." She shakes her head. "I don't know. I don't think so."

"Well, of course you were, honey—he had a gun. He kidnapped you."

"Did he threaten you with the gun?"

"Yes." She's thinking. She wakes up from a dream and tries to remember the details. She gets bits and pieces, but never the whole thing. We've all been there. In a dream, your house is a house but it's not your house. Some lady doesn't look like your mother, but you know that she is your mother. In the daytime, it doesn't quite make as much sense as it did during the night. "He held me down. Outside. In the woods. He pointed the gun at me. He was so mad. He was screaming." She's shaking her head vigorously. Tears fall freely down her cheeks. It's making Eve a nervous wreck. I have to step between the women to keep Eve back.

"Why?" I ask. My voice is calm, subdued. Maybe I was a shrink in a former life.

"It's my fault. It's all my fault."

"What's your fault, Mia?"

"I tried to tell him."

"Tried to tell him what?"

"He wouldn't listen. He had the gun. He kept pointing it at me. I knew if anything went wrong, he was going to kill me."

"He told you that?" I ask. "He said if anything went wrong, he would kill you?"

No, no, she shakes her head. She looks me right in the eye. "I could see it in his eyes." She says that she was scared that day in the bar. She tried not to be, but she was scared. My mind does an about-face to the jazz bar in Uptown, the balding proprietor and fancy green candle. This is where Mia first encountered Colin Thatcher, aka Owen. From the waitress's testimony, Mia left in a hurry, of her own free will. I think back to the waitress's words: *Seemed to me she couldn't wait to get out of here.* Doesn't sound like fear to me.

"And then," Mia cries, "everything was going wrong. I tried to tell him. I should have just told him. But I was scared.

He had the gun. And I knew that if anything went wrong he'd kill me. I tried to—"

"Colin Thatcher," I interrupt, "*Owen*. Owen would kill you if anything went wrong?"

She nods, then quickly shakes her head. "Yes. No." She's frustrated. "I don't know," she splutters.

"What did you try to tell him?" I ask instead but her mind does a 180 and she shakes her head, stymied, frustrated; she can no longer remember what she was about to say.

Most people think there are two natural responses to fear: fight or flight. But there's a third reaction to a bad situation: freeze. Like a deer in headlights. Play dead. Mia's words—*I was scared; I tried to tell him*—prove just that. There was no fight-or-flight response. She froze. There she was: on high alert, adrenaline pumping, but unable to do anything to save her life.

"It's all my fault," she says again.

"What's your fault?" I ask, expecting a replay of the same conversation.

But this time she says, "I tried to run away."

"And he caught you?"

She's nodding.

I recall her earlier admission. "Outside, in the woods?" I ask. "And he was mad at you for trying to run away. So he pointed the gun at you. And told you that if you ever tried that again…"

"That he would kill me."

Eve gasps. She covers a gaping mouth with her hand. Of course he threatened to kill her. That's what they do. I'm sure it happened many times.

"What else did he say?" I query. "What can you remember?" She's shaking her head; she comes up with nothing. "Canoe," I prompt, "you said he'd shoot him if he saw him in the cabin but he didn't. You remember that the cat was in the cabin?"

She strokes the cat's fur. She doesn't look at me. "He said he laid by me for days. He never left my side."

"Who didn't?" I ask.

"He said no one had ever loved him as much in his life. No one had ever been as devoted."

"As who?"

She looks at me. *Duh,* her eyes say. "Canoe."

And that's when it hits me: if seeing the cat brought this much back to life, what memories could we exhume if we placed Mia back in the homely log cabin? I have to find the person that did this to her, before I know for sure that she, and Eve, are safe.

COLIN

BEFORE

I tell her we're going for a walk. It's dark outside, after 10:00 p.m.

"Now?" she asks. As if we have something better to do.

"Now."

She tries to argue but I won't have it. Not this time.

I help her into my coat and we head outside. The snow is falling lightly and the temperature hovers right around thirty-two degrees. The snow is light. It's perfect for a snowball fight. It brings me back to the trailer park, tossing snowballs with the other trailer trash kids before Ma bought a home that wasn't mobile.

She follows me down the steps. At the bottom she stops to take it all in. The sky is black. The lake is lost to oblivion. It would be dark—too dark—without the brilliance of the snow. She catches it into her hands and the snow collects in her hair and on her eyelashes. I stick out my tongue to taste it.

The night is silent.

Out here, the snow makes everything glow. It's brisk outside, not cold. One of those nights that the snow somehow makes you feel warm. She's standing at the bottom of the steps. The snow is up to her ankles.

"Come here," I say. We trudge through the snow for the crappy little shed out back. I pry the door open. I have to force the damn thing through the snow to get inside. It isn't easy.

She helps me pull, and then says, "What are you looking for?" when we're inside.

"This," I say, holding up an ax. I thought I'd seen it in here before. Two months ago she would have thought the ax was meant for her.

"What's that for?" she asks. She isn't scared.

I have a plan.

"You'll see."

The snow must be four inches by now, maybe more. Our feet slosh in it and the legs of our pants become soaked. We walk for a while, until the cabin is no longer in sight. We're on a mission, and that in itself is vitalizing.

"Ever cut your own Christmas tree?" I ask.

She looks at me like I'm nuts, like only some crazy hick would cut their own Christmas tree. But then I see that hesitation flee. She says to me, "I've always wanted to cut my own Christmas tree." Her eyes light up like a child's.

She says that at her home, it was always fake. Real trees were messy. Her mother would never go for it. There was nothing fun about Christmas in her home. It was all for appearance's sake. The tree was decked out with all these breakable crystal ornaments. She'd get yelled at for coming within three feet of the thing.

I tell her to pick it out, whichever one she wants. She points to a sixty-foot fir.

"Try again," I say. But for a moment I stare it down and wonder if I could.

I convince myself that she's having fun. She doesn't mind the cold or the way the snow gets caught in the ankle of her sock. She says that her hands are freezing. She presses them to my cheeks to feel, but I can't feel a thing. My own cheeks are numb.

I tell her that as a kid, my mother and I forgot about Christmas. She'd drag me to mass, but as for the presents and trees and all that shit—well, we didn't have the money. And I never wanted my mother to feel guilty about it. So I just let December 25th come and go like it was any other day. Back in school the kids would all brag about what they'd gotten. I'd always make something up. I didn't feel sorry for myself. I wasn't one to feel sorry for myself.

I tell her that I never believed in Santa Claus. Not one day of my life.

"What did you want?" she asks.

What I wanted was a dad. Someone to take care of my mother and me, so I didn't have to do it myself. But what I tell her is Atari.

She finds a tree. It's about five feet tall. "You want to try?" I ask and hand her the ax. Holding it in her hands, she laughs. It's a sound I've never heard before. She gives the tree a whack.

After four or five tries she hands me the ax. I examine the base. She's made a dent but not much more. It's not like it's easy. I tell her to stand back as I whack the hell out of it. She's watching with the wide eyes of a five-year-old child. I'll be damned if I don't cut down this tree.

The entire world is quiet. Everything is at peace. I'm sure I've never experienced a night as perfect as this before. She tells me that it's impossible to believe that somewhere out there, the world is at war. People are starving. Children are being abused. We're removed from civilization, she says, "Two tiny figurines in a snow globe that some child has turned over." I picture it: us trudging across ceramic mounds while glittery snow encircles us in our own bubble.

In the distance I'm certain I hear an owl hoot. I stop her

and say, "Shhh," and for a moment we listen. This is where the snowy owl migrates in the winter. We're freezing to death, but he comes here to keep warm. We listen. It's quiet. She looks toward the sky and watches the clouds burst at the seams. They shower us with snow.

The tree is heavy. We haul it in together, her in the front, me in the back. We slide it across the snow, and four or five times one or both of us slides on the snow and falls. Our hands are so cold, they're hardly able to grasp the trunk of the tree.

When we get to the cabin, I take the base of the tree. Moving backward, I heave it up the steps. She stands at the bottom. She pretends to help, but we both know that she does nothing.

We force it through the front door and prop it against a wall. I collapse. The tree must weigh a hundred and fifty pounds, sopping wet and overflowing with heavy snow.

I kick off my wet shoes and gulp water right from the kitchen faucet. She lets her hands wander across the juvenile leaves, still filled with snow. She smells the pine. It's the first time neither of us complains of being cold. Our hands are raw, our noses and cheeks red. But under layers of clothes we sweat. I stare at her, her skin alive from the cold.

I go into the bathroom to clean up and change my clothes. She wipes the moisture from the floor, from under the tree and where our shoes pooled snow. I can smell the pine on my hands. I feel the sticky sap, I breathe hard, trying to catch my breath. I drop to the couch when I return.

She heads into the bathroom to strip the wet clothes from her skin. She sinks into an extra pair of long johns that had been drying on the window curtain, and when she comes out she says, "No one's ever given me a tree before."

I'm rekindling the fire as she passes through the room. She watches my calculating hands manipulate the wood just right, bringing the fire to life. She says that I do everything that way, with a certain expertise I pretend doesn't exist. I don't say a thing.

I sit back on the couch and drape a blanket over my legs. My feet rest on a coffee table. I'm still breathing hard.

"What I would give for a beer," I say.

She watches me sitting there for I don't know how long. I can feel her eyes on me.

"You, too?" I ask after a minute.

"A beer?"

"Yeah."

"Yeah," she says.

I remember the two of us sitting side by side, drinking beer in that bar. I ask her if she remembers and she says yes. She says it seems like a million years ago, long before someone glued us to the lid of an empty baby food jar and filled our world with glitter.

"What time is it?" she asks.

My watch rests on the table beside my feet. I lean forward for a look. I say that it's 2:00 a.m.

"Are you tired?" she asks.

"Getting there."

"Thank you for the tree," she says. "Thank you for getting *us* a tree," she adds. She doesn't want to be presumptuous.

I stare at the tree, leaning against the log wall. It's misshapen. Homely. But she says it's perfect.

"No," I say. "It's for you. So you stop looking so damn sad."

I promise to find lights for it. I don't know how, but I promise I'll do it. She tells me not to worry about it. "It's perfect the way it is," she says. But I say I'll find the lights.

She asks if I ever ride the "L." I give her a dumb look. I say yes, of course I do. You can hardly get around Chicago without riding the "L," the city's rapid transit system. She says that she rides the Red Line most of the time, *flying under the city as if all that commotion aboveground doesn't exist.*

"Do you ever ride the bus?" she asks.

I wonder where the hell she's going with this. "Sometimes."

"Go out. To bars. Stuff like that."

"Sometimes." I shrug. "It's not really my crowd."

"But you do?"

"I guess. Sometimes."

"You ever go by the lake?"

"I know a guy who's got a boat at Belmont Harbor." And by that I mean some lowlife like me. Some guy working for Dalmar who lives in a boat, a used cruiser he keeps gassed and docked, in case he needs to run. He's got enough provisions on that boat that he could last for at least a month, traveling up the Great Lakes to Canada. This is how people like us live. Always ready to run.

She nods. Belmont Harbor. Of course. She says she runs by there all the time.

"I could have seen you before. We might have passed on the street, ridden together on the bus. Maybe waited underground for the same 'L'?"

"Millions of people live in Chicago."

"But maybe?"

"I guess. Maybe. What are you getting at?"

"I'm just wondering…" Her voice trails off.

"What?" I ask.

"If we would have ever met. If it wasn't for…"

"This?" I shake my head. I'm not trying to be an ass. It's just the truth. "Probably not."

"You don't think so?"

"We wouldn't have met," I say again.

"How do you know?"

"We wouldn't have met."

I look away, draw the blanket to my neck and lie down on my side.

I ask her to turn off the light, and when she hovers in the kitchen, I say, "Aren't you going to bed?"

"How can you be sure?" she asks instead.

I don't like where this conversation is headed.

"What difference does it make?" I ask.

"Would you have talked to me if we did meet? That night, would you have ever talked to me if you didn't have to?"

"I wouldn't have been in that bar in the first place."

"But—*if* you were."

"No."

"No?"

"I wouldn't have talked to you."

The rejection slaps her across the face.

"Oh."

She crosses the room and turns off the light. But I can't leave it like that. I can't let her go to bed pissed.

In the darkness I admit, "It's not what you think."

She's defensive. I've hurt her feelings. "What do I think?"

"It has nothing to do with you."

"Of course it does."

"Mia—"

"Then what?"

"Mia."

"*What?*"

"It has nothing to do with you. It doesn't mean anything."

But it does. It does to her. She's walking toward the bedroom when I admit, "The first time I saw you, you were coming out of your apartment. I was across the street sitting on the steps of some four flat, just waiting. I'd seen a picture. I called from a payphone on the corner. You answered and I hung up. I knew you were there. I don't know how long

I waited, forty-five minutes, maybe an hour. I had to know what I'd gotten myself into.

"And then I saw you through the little windows on the side of the front door. I saw you jog down the steps with your headphones on. You opened the door and sat down outside to tie a shoe. I memorized your hair, the way it fell over your shoulders before you took these long arms and tied it back. A woman passed by with like four or five dogs. She said something to you and you smiled and I thought to myself that I'd never seen anything so... I don't know... I'd never seen anything so *beautiful* in my life. You went off running down the road and I waited. I watched cabs drive by and hordes of people walk home from the bus stop at the corner. It was six, maybe seven o'clock. It started to get dark. The sky was one of those dramatic fall skies. You were walking when you returned. You passed right in front of me and then jogged across the street, waving to a cab that slowed down to let you pass. I was almost certain you saw me. You dug in your shoe for a key and let yourself in, up the steps where I couldn't see you. I saw the light in your window and your silhouette. I imagined what you might be doing inside. I imagined myself in there with you, what it would be like if it didn't have to be like this."

She's quiet. And then she says that she remembers the night. She says she remembers the sky, so vibrant, as the sunlight was scattered by particles in the sky. She says that the sky was the color of persimmon and sangria, shades of red only God could make. She says, "I remember the dogs, three black Labs and a golden retriever, and the woman, all ninety-some pounds of her, swept away in a tangle of leashes." She says she remembers the call, though at the time it left her unfazed. She remembers sitting inside feeling alone because that damn boyfriend of hers was working but, more so, because she was glad he was.

"I didn't see you," she whispers. "If I did I'd remember."

She lowers herself onto the couch beside me. I open the blanket for her and she slides in. She presses her back into me, a vacuum seal. I can feel the rhythm of her heart pressing against me. I can feel the blood pulsing through my own ears. It's loud enough I'm sure she hears. I wrap the blanket over her. I reach across her, find her hand, and our fingers lace together. Her grasp is reassuring. In time, mine stops to shake. I slide my bottom arm under the crevice of her neck. She falls into every gap there is until we become one. I rest my head onto a mat of dirty blond hair, close enough that she can feel the exhalation of air on her skin, reassuring her that we're alive though inside, we can hardly breathe.

We fall into oblivion this way, into a world where nothing matters. Nothing but us.

She's gone when I wake up. I no longer feel her pressed into me. Something is missing, though it wasn't that long ago that there was nothing there.

I see her outside, sitting on the porch step. She's freezing her ass off. It doesn't appear that she minds.

The blanket is wrapped around her shoulders and she's wearing my shoes on her feet. They're huge. She's kicked the snow off the step, though the ends of the blanket lie in it and get wet.

I don't go out right away.

I make coffee. I find my coat. I take my time.

"Hey," I offer as I step outside in my bare feet. I hand her a mug of coffee. "Thought this would warm you up."

"Oh." She's startled. She eyes my bare feet and says, "Your shoes," but before she can get them off, I stop her. I say that I don't mind. I like the look of it, her in my shoes. Her lying beside me in bed. I could get used to this.

"It's cold out here," I say. It's fucking cold. Maybe twenty degrees.

"It is?" she asks.

I don't answer.

"I'll leave you alone," I say. Seems to me someone who chooses to freeze their ass off on a day like today wants to be alone.

It's not as though anything happened, but lying beside her for all those hours just for the hell of it, just to be *close* to her, to feel the softness of her skin and the way her chest rattled when she snored, *that* happened.

"Your feet must be freezing."

I glance at my feet. They stand on a thin layer of snow and ice. "They are," I say. I turn to go inside.

"Thanks for the coffee."

I don't know what I expect her to say, but I expect her to say something.

"Yep," I say and let the door slam closed.

I don't know how much time passes—enough that I start to get pissed. Pissed at myself for being pissed at her. I shouldn't care. I shouldn't give a shit.

But then she appears. Her cheeks are ruby-red from the cold. Her hair cascades around her. "I don't want to be alone," she says.

She drops the blanket at the door.

"I can't remember the last time anyone told me I was beautiful," she says.

Beautiful doesn't do her justice.

We stare at each other across the room, taking it all in. Reminding ourselves to breathe.

When she comes to me, she moves humbly. Her hands touch with caution. The last time I pushed her away, but the last time was different.

She was a different woman.

I was a different man.

I run my hand the length of her hair. My hands move down her arms. They memorize her fingers and the shape of her back. She stares at me with this look I've never seen before, not on her or any other woman. Trust. Respect. Desire. I commit to memory every freckle, every blemish on her face. I learn the shape of her ears and run a finger across the arch of her lips.

She takes my hand and leads me to the bedroom. "You don't have to do this," I say. God knows she's no longer my prisoner. What I want is for her to want to be here.

We pause in the doorway. Her lips find their way to mine, and I hold her head in my hands. My fingers stroke her hair. Her arms are locked behind my back. She doesn't let go.

What changes is the way we touch. There's contact, something that we used to avoid. We graze past each other when we enter a room. She runs her fingers through my hair. I let my hand linger on her back. She traces the lines of my face. We share the same bed.

Our hands and fingers memorize what our eyes could not. An uneven scalp. Patches of dry skin.

There is nothing frivolous about it. We don't flirt. We're beyond that. We don't dredge up past relationships. We don't try and make the other jealous. We don't create pet names. We don't mention the word *love*.

We kill time. We talk. We list all the crazy things you see in the city. The homeless pushing shopping carts around. Jesus freaks walking around with crucifixes on their backs. Pigeons.

She asks my favorite color. I say I don't have one. She asks my favorite food. I let a spoonful of slop drop into a bowl. "Anything other than this," I say.

She asks what would have happened to her if we didn't come here. If I'd handed her over and collected my reward.

"I don't know," I say.

"Would I be dead?"

We learn things we didn't know before. That skin-to-skin contact helps keep us warm. That SpaghettiOs and baked beans do mix. That two can fit on the shaky armchair.

We're eating some meal. What it is, I don't know. We eat out of necessity. There's no such thing as breakfast, lunch or dinner. It's all the same. It all tastes like shit.

She's staring at me with those eyes of hers. They demand an answer. "I don't know," I say again. I see her being ripped from my car and tossed into the van. Her hands bound and her eyes blindfolded. I hear her cry.

I push my bowl away. I'm not hungry. I've lost my appetite.

She stands and reaches for my bowl. She says she'll do the dishes tonight, but I gently clench her wrist when it comes within reach and say to her, "Leave it."

We settle by the window where we watch the moon, a sliver in the sky. The clouds flicker by and sometimes we see the moon, sometimes we don't.

"Look at all the stars," she says. She knows the names of the constellations. Aries. Fornax. Perseus. She says that in Chicago she used to wish on airplanes because there were far more of those floating around in the night sky than stars.

There are times she's too far away, even when she's in the same room.

She teaches me to count to a hundred in Spanish. I teach her the fox-trot. When the lake freezes completely over, we ice fish. We never stay out long. She doesn't like to watch. So she walks on the lake as if Moses has parted the waters for her. She likes the newly fallen snow. Sometimes there are animal prints. Sometimes we hear snowmobiles in the distance. When she's frozen solid she goes in. And then I feel alone.

I take her outside. I bring the gun with me. We walk through the woods for a while, to a place so desolate I'm sure no one will hear the sound of a bullet exploding from the muzzle.

I tell her that I want her to know how to shoot the gun. I give it to her flat, on both hands, like a piece of fine jewelry. She doesn't want to touch the damn thing.

"Take it," I say lightly.

"Why?" she asks.

"Just in case."

I want her to learn to shoot it so she can protect herself.

"That's what you're here for."

"What if one day I'm not?" I ask. I tuck a strand of her hair behind a raw ear. I watch as the wind frees it again. "It isn't loaded."

She loops her thumb and forefinger through the trigger guard. She lifts it from my hands. It's heavy, the metal cold in the freezing temperatures. The ground is coated with snow.

I place her finger on the trigger, wrap her palm around the grip. I move her thumb downward. I pull her left hand up to meet the right. My hand on hers assures her that she will be all right. That this will be all right. Her hands are cold, like mine. But they come to me without reserve like they used to, pulling away when we touched.

I tell her about the parts of the gun: the barrel and muzzle and trigger guard. I pull a magazine from the pocket of my jeans and show her how to attach it to the gun. I tell her about the kinds of guns there are: rifles and handguns and semiautomatics. This is a semiautomatic. When one round is fired, another round is loaded from the magazine into the chamber. All with the pull of the trigger.

I tell her never to aim the gun at something she doesn't intend to kill.

"I learned this the hard way," I say, "when I was seven. Maybe eight. Some kid in the neighborhood. His old man owned a gun. He used to brag about it all the fucking time. I called him a liar. He wanted to prove it to me, so we went to his house after school. No one was home. His dad kept the thing in a bedside table, unlocked and loaded. I grabbed it from the drawer like it was a toy. We played a round of cops and robbers. He was the cop but I had the gun. The kid said, 'Hands up,' and I turned and shot him."

And then we stand there in the freezing cold. We remember the times she stared down the barrel of the gun. There's guilt. And sorrow. I'm sure she sees it in my eyes. I'm sure she can hear it in my voice when I say, "I wouldn't have killed you."

I'm clutching blindly to her hand.

"But you might have," she says. We both know it's the truth.

"Yeah," I admit. I'm not one to say I'm sorry. But I'm sure the look on my face says it all.

"But that was different," she says.

"How so?" I ask.

She lets me shadow her from behind. I raise her arms and together we aim at a nearby tree. I part her legs and show her how to stand, and then we cock the hammer and pull the trigger. The sound is deafening. The release of the bullet nearly knocks her off her feet. Bark explodes from the tree.

"Because if I'd have had the chance, I would have killed you, too," she says.

This is how we settle all those things that happened between us in the early days. This is how we make up for all the mean words that we said, for the horrible thoughts that ran through our minds. This is how we annul the violence and the hate of our first days and weeks in the cabin, inside the log walls that have now become our home.

"And your friend?" she asks. I'm nodding to the gun in her hands. This time, I want her to try by herself.

"Luckily for him, I had no aim when I was a kid. The bullet grazed the outside of his arm. A scratch."

EVE

CHRISTMAS EVE

Gabe called early in the morning to tell me he was on his way. It was just after 5:30 a.m. when my cell phone rang, and unlike James, who slept like a baby, I'd been awake for hours, plagued by another sleepless night. I don't bother to wake him. I find my robe and slippers and step outside.

There's news. I stand on the front step, shivering from the cold, waiting for Gabe's car to pull into our snow-covered drive. It's after six o'clock and still dark outside. Neighbors' Christmas décor lights the night sky: decorated trees glittering through bay windows, icicle lights hanging from gutters, candles flickering in every single double-hung window that faces the street. From the chimneys, clouds of smoke swirl into the frosty air.

I pull my robe tight around me and wait. I hear a train in the distance, rumbling through town. No one waits beside its tracks, before dawn on a Sunday morning, Christmas Eve.

"What is it?" I ask when he parks his car and climbs out. He comes right up to me. He doesn't shut the door.

"Let's go inside." He takes my hands and leads me where it's warm.

We sit on the plush white sofa, pressed close together. We're hardly aware that our legs touch. It's dark in the house; only the stove light in the kitchen is turned on. I don't want to wake James. We whisper.

There's a look in his eye. Something new.

"She's dead," I concede.

"No," he says, but then he revises his statement and, staring down into his own hands, humbly admits, "I don't know."

"There's a doctor in a tiny town in northeastern Minnesota, a Dr. Kayla Lee. I didn't want to get your hopes up. We received a call a week or so ago—she saw Mia's picture on the news and recognized her as a patient. It had been weeks, maybe a month since Mia was in. But she's sure it's her. Mia was using a pseudonym: Chloe Romain."

"A doctor?"

"Dr. Lee said that she was with a man. Colin Thatcher. She said that Mia was sick."

"Sick?"

"Pneumonia."

"Pneumonia."

Without treatment, pneumonia can lead to blood poisoning. It can lead to respiratory distress, the inability to breathe. Without treatment, a person can die.

"She was given a prescription and sent home. The doctor asked to see her back in a week; Mia never returned for the appointment."

Gabe said he had a nagging feeling about this Grand Marais. Something in his gut told him she might be there.

"What made you think of Grand Marais?" I ask, remembering the day he showed up at my home, asking if I'd ever heard of it.

"A postcard I came across at the Thatcher home. Sent by

Colin to his mother. For a boy who rarely left home, it caught my eye. A good place to hide.

"There's more," he says.

"What?" I beg.

She was given a prescription, but that doesn't mean it was ever filled. That doesn't mean the pills were ever taken.

"I've been talking to Kathryn Thatcher and doing some research into the Thatcher family. Turns out there's a cabin up in Grand Marais that's been in the family for years. Kathryn says she doesn't know much about it. She's never been there. But her ex brought Colin there when he was a boy. It's a summer home, so to speak, inhabited only for a few months of the year. I sent an officer to check on the home and when he did, he found a red truck with Illinois plates parked outside."

"A red truck," I repeat. Gabe reminds me that Mrs. Thatcher's neighbors were sure Colin drove a truck.

"And?" I ask anxiously.

He stands to his feet. "I'm on my way. Driving there. This morning. I was going to take a flight, but there's no good way, no direct routes and between layovers and connections—"

I rise up to meet him. "I'm coming. Let me pack a—"

I try to step past him. His hands seize me by the shoulders.

"You can't come," he says in a gentle voice. He says this is only a hunch. There's no proof. The home is under surveillance right now. He's not even certain that Mia is there. Colin Thatcher is a dangerous man, wanted for much more than this.

"I can," I cry. "She's my daughter."

"Eve."

My voice is uneven. My hands shake. I've waited for months for this moment, and now that it has arrived, I'm not certain I'm ready. There's so much that could go wrong. "She needs me right now. I'm her mother, Gabe. It's *my* duty to protect her."

He embraces me, a burly bear hug. "It's my duty to protect *you*," he says. "Trust me. If she's there, I will bring her home."

"I can't lose her now," I cry.

My eyes stray to a family photograph we had done years ago: James, Grace, Mia and me. Everyone else looks as if they were forced to be there, with artificial smiles plastered to furrowed brows and rolling eyes. Even me. But Mia simply looks happy. Why? I wonder. We never gave her a reason to be happy.

Gabe lowers his lips to my forehead and holds them there, pressed tightly against the creased skin.

This is how we stand when James comes hobbling down the steps, dressed in a pair of tight-fitting tartan pajamas.

"What the hell is this?" he demands.

I'm the first to pull away. "James," I say, hurrying to meet him in the foyer. "They found Mia."

But his eyes brush past me and he evades my greeting. "And this is how you break the news?" he challenges, deriding Gabe. "By putting the moves on my wife?"

"James," I say again, reaching for his hand so that he'll understand: our daughter is coming home. "They found Mia."

But James replies with a patronizing look in Gabe's direction. He doesn't look at me. "I'll believe it when I see it," he says, and walks out of the room.

COLIN

BEFOЯE

There are lights on the Christmas tree. I won't tell her how they got there. I said she wouldn't like it. I said that someone else's loss is our gain.

She says they look absolutely gorgeous at night when we turn off the lights and lay side by side in the dark, with just the lights from the Christmas tree and the fire.

"This is perfect," she says.

"This isn't good enough," I say.

"What do you mean?" she asks. "It's perfect."

But we both know it's far from perfect.

What is perfect is the way she looks at me, and the way she says my name. The way her hand strokes my hair, though I don't think she knows she's doing it. The way we lay together night after night. The way I feel: complete. What is perfect is the way she sometimes smiles and she sometimes laughs. The way we can say anything that comes to mind, or sit together for hours in absolute silence.

The cat lies by us during the day. He sleeps with us at night, on her pillow where there's an ounce of warmth. I tell her to shoo him away, but she won't. So she moves closer to me. She shares mine instead. She feeds the cat table scraps, which he devours. But we both know that as the cabinets empty, she will have to decide: us or him.

We talk about where we would go if we had the chance.

I list everywhere I can possibly think of that's warm. "Mexico. Costa Rica. Egypt. The Sudan."

"The *Sudan?*"

"Why not? It gets hot."

"You're that cold?" she asks. I pull her on top of me.

"I'm getting warmer," I say.

I ask where she'd want to go—if we ever got out of *here.*

"There's a town in Italy," she says. "A ghost town—it's all but abandoned, lost in olive trees, a nearly nonexistent town of only a couple hundred people, with a medieval castle and an old church."

"This is where you want to go?" I'm surprised. I expected Machu Picchu or Hawaii. Something along those lines.

But I can tell she's been thinking about it.

"It's the kind of place we could slip in. It's a world apart from TVs and technology. It's in Liguria, this part of Italy that borders the south of France—we'd be only miles from the Italian Riviera. We could live off the land, and grow our own food. We wouldn't have to rely on others. We wouldn't have to worry about being caught or found or…" I'm giving her a look. "You think it's stupid," she says.

"I think fresh vegetables would be a nice change from stewed tomatoes."

"I hate stewed tomatoes," she admits.

I say that I hate them, too. I only got them because I was in a rush.

"We could find a rustic old home, one of those granite monstrosities, one, I don't know, maybe two hundred years old. We'd have breathtaking views of the mountains, maybe the coastline if we're lucky. We could raise animals, grow our own food."

"Grapes?"

"We could have a vineyard. And change our names, get a new start."

I sit up on my elbows. "Who would you be?"

"What do you mean?"

"Your new name."

The answer seems obvious. "Chloe."

"Chloe. Then that's who you'll be," I say. I consider the name. Chloe. I remember the day, months ago, when we're driving in the truck back to Grand Marais. I forced her to pick a name, and she came up with Chloe. "Why Chloe?" I ask.

"What do you mean?"

"That day. When I told you you couldn't be Mia anymore. And you said Chloe."

"Oh," she says and she sits up straight. There are creases on her face from my shirt. Her hair is long. It goes halfway down her back. Maybe more. I'm waiting for a simple answer. *I just like it,* something like that. But what I get is more. "Just some girl I saw on TV."

"What do you mean?"

She closes her eyes. I know she doesn't want to tell me. But she does anyway. "I was six or seven years old. My mother was in the kitchen, but she left the TV on, the news. I was coloring. She didn't know I was paying attention. There was a story, a high school band trip from some school, Kansas or Oklahoma, something like that. There was a group of kids in a bus traveling to a competition or something. I don't know. I wasn't really paying attention to that. The bus skidded off the road and went down a ravine. Half a dozen kids were killed, the driver.

"Then this family appears, a mom, a dad and two older

boys, maybe eighteen or nineteen. I can still see them—the dad gaunt with a receding hairline, the boys, both of them, tall and lanky like basketball players, with burnt-orange hair. The mother looked like she'd been run over by an eighteen-wheeler. They're crying, every single one of them, standing before this little white house. That's what made me pay attention. The crying. They were heartbroken. Destroyed. I watched the father, mostly, but all of them really, the way they openly wept for their dead daughter. Their dead sister. She'd been killed in the accident, plunged down the ravine when the driver fell asleep at the wheel. She was fifteen but I remember her father gushing about his baby girl. He went on and on about how amazing she was, though the things he said—that she was kind and silly and born to play the flute—were not necessarily *amazing*. But to him they were. He kept saying, 'my Chloe,' or 'my baby Chloe.' That was her name. Chloe Frost.

"All I could think about was Chloe Frost. I wanted to *be* her, to have someone long for me the way her family longed for her. I cried for Chloe, for days on end. I spoke to her, when I was alone. I carried on conversations with my dead friend, Chloe. I drew pictures of her. Dozens of them, with her own burnt-orange hair and coffee-colored eyes." She runs her hands through her hair and looks away, in a sheepish sort of way. Embarrassed.

Then she admits, "I was jealous of her, really. Jealous that she was dead, jealous that somewhere, out there, someone loved her more than they loved me." She hesitates, then says, "It's crazy. I know."

But I shake my head and say, "No," because I know it's what she wants to hear. But I think how lonely she must have been growing up. Longing for a dead friend she didn't even know. Things weren't so grand for Ma and me, but at least we weren't alone.

She changes the subject. She doesn't want to talk about Chloe Frost anymore.

"Who will you be?" she asks.

"John?" I say. I couldn't be further from a John.

"No," she says, the answer almost as obvious as Chloe had been. "You'll be Owen. Because it doesn't matter anyway, does it? That's not your real name."

"Do you want to know?" I ask. I bet she's thought about it a million times. I bet she's guessed to herself what my real name might be. I wonder if she ever thought about asking.

"No," she says, "because this is who you are to me. You're Owen." She says that whoever I was before this doesn't matter.

"And you'll be Chloe."

"I'll be Chloe."

And in that moment, Mia ceased to exist.

EVE

AFTER

I consult with Dr. Rhodes. She agrees under one condition: that she is allowed to go along, too. I purchase the three airplane tickets with a credit card that James and I share. The police department pays Gabe's fare.

We will be revisiting the cabin in which Mia was held prisoner all that time. The hope is that being there will help jog her memory and make her remember something about her time in captivity. If the cat alone can trigger memories of Colin Thatcher, then I wonder what that cabin will do.

Mia and I pack one bag. Between us, we don't have much. I never mention to James where we are going. Mia asks Ayanna to watch Canoe for a few days, and the woman agrees without reservation. Her nine-year-old son, Ronnie, is thrilled to have a cat to keep company. We ask the taxi to drive us to her apartment on the way to O'Hare. It's with great difficulty that Mia is able to part with Canoe for the second time. I wonder what happened the first time she said goodbye.

The airport is a horrendous place for a person in Mia's condition. The noise is deafening: thousands of people, loudspeakers, airplanes soaring overhead. Mia is on edge; we all see it, though she's tucked between Dr. Rhodes and me, and I have her arm looped through mine. Dr. Rhodes suggests a dose of Valium, which she has brought along in her suitcase just in case.

Gabe peers over. "What else have you got in there?" he asks. The four of us are sitting in a row at our terminal.

"Other sedatives," she replies. "Stronger sedatives."

He sits back and reaches for a newspaper that someone has left behind.

"Is it safe?" I ask. "For the..."

"For the baby," Mia finishes impassively. I can't bring myself to say the word.

"Yes," I say, humbled that she was able to.

"It's safe," the doctor assures us, "this once. I wouldn't suggest using it frequently during pregnancy."

Mia takes the pills with a sip of water, and then we wait. By the time our flight is announced, she is nearly asleep.

We will fly to Minneapolis/St. Paul for a forty-five-minute layover, before continuing onto Duluth, Minnesota. There, a so-called friend of Gabe's, Detective Roger Hammill, will meet and drive us to Grand Marais. He refers to him as his friend, but even I can hear the disdain in his voice when he speaks of this man. Our flight is early, 9:00 a.m., and as the airplane ascends into the dreadfully cold sky, we know it will be a long day. Our only saving grace is that Mia is asleep.

Mia and I sit side by side. She has the window seat, and me the aisle. Gabe sits opposite the slender aisle and once or twice brushes a hand against my arm and asks if I'm okay. Beside him Dr. Rhodes is lost in an audiobook, the headphones covering her ears. The rest of the plane is oblivious to our situation. They jabber on and on about the weather, skiing conditions and their connecting flights. A woman loses herself in the "Our Father" as the plane takes off, praying we land in one piece. She grips a rosary in her trembling hands. The pilot warns of a bumpy flight and asks that we remain in our seats.

By the time we land in Minneapolis, Mia has come to and is upset once again by the commotion. I ask the doctor when she is due for more medicine, but Dr. Rhodes assures me that we must wait; we need Mia to be lucid for this afternoon. As we wait for our connection, Gabe offers up an iPod for Mia, and finds the least offensive music he can possibly find to drown out the sound.

I wonder what will happen when we arrive. The thought of it is enough to make me sick. I think of Mia's reaction to the cat. What will her reaction be when we see the place where she was held prisoner all this time? I think of the progress we've made since she returned home. Will it be lost?

I excuse myself to use the bathroom and Dr. Rhodes takes my seat beside Mia so that she won't be alone. When I come out of the bathroom, Gabe is waiting for me. I walk into him so that he collects me in his arms, and says, "Soon, this will all be through. Trust me."

I do.

In Duluth, we're escorted to a police department SUV by a man who introduces himself as Detective Hammill. Gabe calls him Roger. Mia says it's nice to meet him, though Gabe reminds me that it isn't the first time they've met.

He's a big-bellied man, about my age but to me he looks much older, and I'm made aware than I am getting older by the day. There's a photograph of his wife taped to the inside of the SUV: an overweight blonde woman, with a circle of children huddled around them. There are six children, each as burly and plump as the next.

Mia, Dr. Rhodes and I slide into the backseat while Gabe takes the front. He offered it to me, but I happily refused, not up to the burdensome task of small talk.

The drive is over two hours. Gabe and Detective Hammill lose themselves in idle banter about police work. They try to one-up one another, and I can tell that Gabe does not like the man. Gabe's voice is not overly friendly, and at times he is short, though for the benefit of us women, he remains civil. He tries to speak to Mia and me more than our chauffeur, and for much of the drive, the rest of us sit in silence while Detective Hammill gives a soliloquy on two Tiberwolves wins this season against the Chicago Bulls. I have no knowledge of professional sports.

We travel along Highway 61 for the bulk of the journey, riding, in part, along the shores of Lake Superior. Mia's eyes are steadfast on the waters. I wonder if she's seen them before.

"Anything look familiar?" Gabe asks more than once. He asks all the questions I don't have the courage to.

Earlier, Dr. Rhodes made it clear that Gabe should not pry too hard. Gabe made it clear that he had a job to do; hers was to pick up the pieces when they fell.

"Assuming the shortest distance between two points is a straight line," Detective Hammill says, peering at Mia in the rearview mirror, "you would have traveled this path."

We pass through Grand Marais and take a path known as the Gunflint Trail. Detective Hammill is a wealth of information, although little he has to offer is new to me, having memorized every detail of the scenic byway in the sleepless nights since Mia returned. We travel along a two-lane road, through the Superior National Forest, surrounded by more vegetation than I believe I've ever seen in my entire life. Much of the greenery is dead now, buried under mounds of snow; it will not be unearthed until spring. The evergreen trees embrace the snow in their needles, where they lie heavy from the weight.

What I see in Mia as we continue along our journey is a

straighter posture, her eyes more attuned to the outdoors, not a glassy-eyed look like I've seen in the past, but an awareness and an interest.

Dr. Rhodes is instructing Mia in visualization and repetitive affirmations: *I can do this.* I can hear James now, mocking the woman for her irrational techniques.

"Do you recognize anything now?" Gabe asks. He's turned around in his seat, and she shakes her head. It's late afternoon, three, maybe four o'clock, and already the sky is becoming dark. Clouds fill the sky, and though the heat runs steady, my hands and toes begin to numb. The heater cannot compete with the subzero temperatures outside.

"Damn good thing you got out when you did," Detective Hammill says to Mia. "You never would have survived the winter."

The thought sends a chill through me. Had Colin Thatcher not killed her, Mother Nature would have done the job herself.

"Ah," Gabe says to lighten the mood. He sees something pass through me that he doesn't like. "You'd be surprised. Mia is quite a fighter. Isn't that right?" he asks with a wink. And then he mouths the words that only she and I see: *you can do this,* as the tires of the SUV hit a mound of snow and we all turn and find ourselves face-to-face with a bleak log cabin.

She's seen the pictures. There were so many times I found her sitting lethargically, staring at images of this very cabin, or staring into the vacant eyes of Colin Thatcher and seeing nothing. But now she sees something. Detective Hammill opens the door, and like a magnetic force, Mia emerges from the car, and I have to stop her. "Mia, your hat," I say, "your scarf," because it's so cold out here the very air will freeze her flesh. But Mia seems completely unaware of the cold and I have to force the gloves onto her hands like she's a five-year-old child. Her eyes are lost on this cabin, on the stack of steps that lead from the snow-covered drive to a door that's been barred with yellow caution tape. Snow covers the steps, though footprints remain, and tire tracks in the drive suggest that someone has been here since the last snowfall. The snow is everywhere: on the roof, the porch, the uninhabited world around the home. I wonder how Mia felt arriving at this home, so remote one might believe they are the last inhabitants on earth. I shiver at the thought of it.

There's the lake that I've seen in Mia's pictures, frozen over a thousand times, unlikely to thaw before spring.

I'm overwhelmed with such feelings of loneliness and despair that I don't see Mia making her way up the steps with comfort and familiarity. Gabe reaches her first and offers to help. The steps are slick and more than once her feet slip.

At the top they wait for Detective Hammill to unlock the door. Dr. Rhodes and I follow close behind.

The detective presses the door open, and it creaks. The rest of us fight for a look inside, but it's Gabe, with his general decorum, who says to Mia, "Ladies first," though he follows close behind.

GABE

CHRISTMAS EVE

Somewhere in Minnesota it begins to snow. I drive as fast as I can, which isn't fast enough. It's hard to see through the windshield though the wipers go as fast as they can. This is every six-year-old's dream: snow on Christmas Eve. Tonight Santa will come, his sleigh loaded with gifts for every girl and boy.

Detective Hammill calls. He's got a couple of guys keeping the cabin under surveillance. He told me about it, a little cabin lost out in the woods. But they haven't seen anyone come or go; they haven't gotten a visual of anyone on the inside.

By the time I arrive he plans to have a team assembled: ten or so of his best guys. This is a big deal around here. It's not every day that this kind of thing happens.

I think of Eve. I go over it a thousand times in my mind: what I will say, the words I will use, to convey the good news. And then I consider the possibility that there isn't good news: that Mia isn't in the cabin, or that she doesn't survive the rescue. There are a million things that could go wrong.

By the time I make my way up the coast of Lake Superior, Roger's guys are getting antsy. He's got a half dozen of them headed out to the woods. They set up a perimeter. They're armed with the department's best firepower.

Detective Hammill is a man on a mission. Seems he has something to prove.

"No one takes a shot until I get there," I say as I gun the engine along a narrow, snow-covered road. The tires skid and I struggle to regain control. Scares the shit out of me. But what worries me more is the brassiness in the detective's voice. Even more than me, he's a guy led into the line of duty by the prospect of carrying a gun.

"It's Christmas Eve, Hoffman. My guys have families to see."

"I'm doing the best that I can."

The sun sets and it's dark out here. I floor it. I fly through the narrow pass, nearly decapitating myself on branches that hang low from the weight of the snow. I don't know how many times I come to a near standstill, the tires kicking up snow and going absolutely nowhere. This piece-of-shit car is going to get me killed.

I'm going as fast as I can, knowing I need to get to Thatcher before Detective Hammill does. There's no telling what that guy might do.

COLIN

CHRISTMAS EVE

This afternoon I returned to town and put in a call to Dan. Everything's ready to go. He says he'll meet us on the 26th in Milwaukee. It's the best he could do. The guy wasn't about to drive all the fucking way to Grand Marais. He made that clear.

It's my Christmas present for her, a surprise for tomorrow. We'll leave by sundown and drive all night. It's the safest way. I suggest we meet at the zoo. Nice public place. Open Christmas day. I've gone through it in my mind a thousand times. We'll park in the lot. She'll hide out in the primate house. I'll meet Dan by the wolves. I'll find her when he's gone, when I'm sure we aren't being trailed. From there, the quickest way to Canada is in Windsor, Ontario. We'll drive into Windsor, and then as far as we can get on the gas money we have. I have enough cash to get us there. And then it will be gone. We'll live under pseudonyms. I'll get a job.

I've got Dan working on a fake ID for Ma, too, and when I can, I'll get it to her, somehow. When I figure that part out.

I know this is my last night in this shitty old cabin. She doesn't. I'm secretly saying my goodbyes.

Tomorrow is Christmas day. I remember that when I was a

kid I'd leave the house early on Christmas day. I'd count out a dollar and two cents from a change jar we kept. I'd walk to the bakery at the corner. They were open until noon on Christmas. We pretended it was a surprise, though it never was. Ma would lie in bed long enough to hear me sneak out the front door.

I never went straight to the bakery. I'd be a Peeping Tom, staring through the open windows of the other kids in the neighborhood, just to see what they got on Christmas. I'd stare for a while at their happy, smiling faces, then think *fuck them* as I trudged through the snow the rest of the way.

The reindeer bells on the bakery door would announce my arrival to the same old lady who'd worked there a hundred years. She wore a Santa hat on Christmas and would say *Ho, ho, ho.* I'd ask for two fifty-one-cent chocolate long johns that she'd slip into a white paper lunch sack. I'd return home where Ma would be waiting with two cups of hot chocolate. We'd eat our breakfast and pretend that it wasn't Christmas day.

This time I'm staring out the window. I'm thinking of Ma, wondering if she's okay. Tomorrow will be the first time in thirty some years we haven't shared a long john on Christmas day.

When I can get my hands on paper and a pen I'll write her a note and drop it in a mailbox in Milwaukee. I'll tell her that I'm okay. I'll tell her that Chloe is okay, just to give her useless parents some peace of mind, if they give a shit. By the time the letter makes it to Ma, we'll be out of the country. And as soon as I can figure out how, I'll get Ma out of the country as well.

Chloe comes up behind me and wraps her arms around me. She asks if I'm waiting for Santa Claus.

I think of what I'd change if I could, but I wouldn't change a thing. The only regret is that Ma isn't here. But I can't fix

that without ruining *this*. One day it'll all be right. That's how
I satisfy the guilt. I don't know how or when. I don't know
how I'll get the fake ID to Ma without being found, or how
to send her enough money for a flight. But someday...

I turn and gather her into me, all hundred-and-some
pounds. She's lost weight. Her pants no longer rest on her
hips. She's always yanking on them to keep them from falling. Her cheeks are hollow. Her eyes have begun to dull. This
can't go on forever.

"You know what I want this year for Christmas?" I ask.

"What?"

"A razor," I say. I comb the mustache and beard with my
fingers. I hate it. It feels disgusting. I think of all the things
that will be better when we get out of the country. We won't
be so fucking cold. We can shower with real soap. I can shave
this woolly face. We can go out into the world together. We
won't have to hide, though it will take until all eternity for
us to feel safe.

"I like it," she mocks, smiling. When she smiles I see all
the pieces fall into place.

"Liar," I say.

"Then we'll ask for two," she says. She lets me feel the soft
hair on her legs.

"What would you ask Santa for?" I ask.

"Nothing," she says without thought. "I have everything
I want." She rests her head against my chest.

"Liar," I repeat.

She pulls back and looks at me. What she wants, she says,
is to look pretty. For me. To take a shower. To wear perfume.

"You look beautiful," I say and she does. But she reiter-
ates in a whisper: *Liar*. She says she's never felt so revolting
in her life.

I settle my hands on the sides of her face. She's embarrassed and tries to look away, but I force her to look at me. "You look beautiful," I say again.

She nods. "Okay, okay," she says. Then she fingers my beard and says, "And I like the beard."

We stare for a moment before calling a truce.

"One day," I promise, "you'll wear perfume and all that."

"Okay."

We list the things that we'll do *one day*. Go out to dinner. Watch a movie. Things the rest of the world does every damn day.

She says that she's tired and disappears to the bedroom. I know she's sad. We talk about a future, but in her mind she's convinced no such thing exists.

I gather our things, trying to be sly. I set them aside on the counter: her drawing pad and pencils, what's left of the cash. It takes all of two minutes to gather the things that are of importance. She is the only thing I need.

Then, out of boredom, I carve the words *We Were Here* into the countertop with a sharp knife. The words are serrated, not a masterpiece by any means. I drape my coat over the engraving so she won't see it until it's time to leave.

I remember that first night in the cabin. I remember the fear in her eyes. *We Were Here,* I think, but it's someone else who leaves.

I watch the sun set. The temperature in the cabin drops. I add wood to the fire. I watch the minutes on my watch tick by. When I think the boredom is certain to kill me, I start dinner. Chicken noodle soup. This, I tell myself, is the last time in my life I'll ever eat chicken noodle soup.

And then I hear it.

EVE

AFTEЯ

She's been here before. She gathers that immediately.

Mia says that there used to be a Christmas tree, but now it's gone. There used to be a fire constantly roaring in the stove, but now it's silent. There used to be a smell much different than this; now all there is, is the piercing odor of bleach.

She says that she sees excerpts of what may have happened: cans of soup lying on the countertops, though they are no longer there. She hears the sound of water running from a faucet, and the ruckus of heavy shoes on the hardwood floors, though the rest of us remain still, watching Mia like a hawk, our backs pressed against the log wall.

"I hear rainfall on the cabin's roof," she says, "and see Canoe scurry from room to room." Her eyes follow an imaginary path from the family room to the bedroom, as if, in that moment she actually sees the cat, though we all know he is tucked safely away with Ayanna and her son.

And then she says that she hears the sound of her name.

"Mia?" I ask, my voice barely audible, but she shakes her head. No.

"Chloe," she reminds me, her hand settling on an earlobe, her body pacified for the first time in a long time and she smiles.

But the smile doesn't last long.

COLIN

CHRISTMAS EVE

Ma always told me I have ears like a bat. I can hear anything. I don't know what the sound is, but it forces me from my seat. I flip off the light and the cabin goes black. Chloe starts to stir in the bedroom. Her eyes fight through the darkness. She calls my name. When I don't answer right away, she calls again. This time she's scared.

I peel the curtains back from the window. The faint glow of the moon helps me see. There must be a half dozen of them: police cars, with twice as many cops.

"Shit."

I let the curtain drop. I run through the cabin.

"Chloe. Chloe," I snap. She jumps from the bed. The adrenaline rushes through her body as she fights off sleep. I pull her from the bedroom to a windowless section of the hall.

She's coming to. She grips my hand, her nails digging into the skin. I can feel her hands shake. "What's wrong?" she asks. Her voice trembles. Tears fall from her eyes. She knows what's wrong.

"They're here," I say.

"Oh, my God," she wails. "We have to run!" She slides

away from me and into the bathroom. She thinks we'll get out the window, somehow, and escape. She thinks we can run.

"It won't work," I tell her. The window is jammed shut. It'll never open. She tries anyway. I put my hands on her, lure her away from the window. My voice is calm. "There's nowhere to go. You can't run."

"Then we'll fight," she says. She pushes past me. I try to avoid the windows, though I bet the blackness in the cabin makes us invisible. But I do it anyway.

She's crying that she doesn't want to die. I try to tell her it's the cops. The damn cops, I want to say, but she can't hear a word I'm saying. She keeps saying over and over again that she doesn't want to die. The tears run from her eyes.

She thinks it's Dalmar.

I can't think straight. I peer out the window, and I tell her that there's nowhere to go. We can't fight. There's too many of them. It'll never work. It will only make things worse.

But she finds the gun in the drawer. She knows how to shoot it. She grasps it in her shaking hands. She attaches the magazine.

"Chloe," I say softly. My voice is a whisper. "It won't do any good."

But she sets her finger on the trigger anyway. She puts her left hand and right hand together. She holds firmly, like I told her to. She leaves no space between her hands and the grip.

"Chloe," I say. "It's through."

"Please," she cries. "We have to fight. We can't let it end this way." She's crazed, wild and demented. Hysterical. But for some strange reason I'm calm.

Maybe because I knew all along that sooner or later it would come to this.

A moment passes between us. I watch her eyes. They're

crushed and defeated. She's crying. Her nose runs. I don't know how much time passes. Ten seconds. Ten minutes.

"I'll do it myself," she says then, incensed. She's pissed that I won't do it for her. I watch the way the gun shudders in her hands. She can't do this. And if she tries, she'll get herself killed. And then under her breath, she says, "But your aim..."

She lets the words hang in the air. I read her expression: hopelessness. Desperation.

"Never mind," she says after time passes. "I'll do it myself."

But I don't let her. I nod. "Okay," I say. I reach out and take the gun from her hands.

I can't let it end like this. Not with her begging me to save her life. And me refusing.

Floodlights pour into the cabin. They blind us. We're standing before the window, completely exposed. I stand with the gun in my hands. My eyes are composed though hers are wide with fear. The light makes her jump and she falls into me. I step before her to hide her from view. I raise a hand to shield the light.

The hand with the gun.

GABE

CHRISTMAS EVE

Hammill calls to say his guys have been made.

"What do you mean?" I snap.

"He heard us."

"You get a good look?" I ask.

"It's him, all right," he says. "It's Thatcher."

"No one shoots," I say. "No one moves until I get there. You hear?" He says okay, but deep down I know he doesn't give a shit.

"I need him alive," I say, but he doesn't hear. There's a lot of commotion on the other end of the line. Hammill sounds like he's a mile away. He says he's got his best sniper here. *Sniper?*

"No one shoots," I say over and over again. Getting my hands on Thatcher is only half the job; finding out who hired him the other. "Hold your fire. Tell your guys to hold their fire."

But Hammill's too busy listening to the sound of his own voice, he doesn't hear me. He says it's dark in there. But they've got night vision. They got a visual on the girl. She looks terrified. There's a pause, then Hammill says, "There's a gun," and I feel my heart drop.

"No one shoots," I say as I make out the cabin, buried in the midst of trees. There are a gazillion cop cars parked outside. No wonder Thatcher heard.

"He's got the girl."

I skid up the drive, throwing the car into Park when it becomes apparent I'm not going to get any farther in this snow. "I'm here!" I'm screaming into the phone. My feet sink in the snow.

"He's got the gun."

I drop my phone and keep running. I see them, lined behind their vehicles, every single one of them waiting for a shot. "No one shoots," I say when the distinct sound of gunfire stops me in my tracks.

EVE

AFTEЯ

I'm not sure what I had expected to happen upon our return to the cabin. At the airport, I had listed for Gabe all of the worst-case scenarios I could possibly conceive in my mind: that Mia would remember nothing, that weeks of therapy would be undone, that *this* would throw Mia over the edge.

We're all watching Mia as she eyes the inside of the tiny cabin, a shanty in the middle of the Minnesota woods. Mia gives the place a once-over. It doesn't take long for her memories to come flooding back, and as Gabe asks for the umpteenth time, "Mia, do you remember anything?" we realize that we should be careful what we ask for.

The sound that emerges from my daughter is one I've never heard before, a sound akin to an animal dying. Mia falls to her knees in the middle of the room. She is screaming, an incomprehensible language I've never heard before. She is sobbing, a wild outburst I never knew my Mia was capable of, and I, too, begin to cry. "Mia. Honey," I murmur, wanting to gather her in my arms and hold her.

But Dr. Rhodes warns me to be careful. She holds a hand out, refusing to let me console Mia. Gabe leans in close and whispers to the doctor and me that this, this spot on the floor where Mia has collapsed in hysteria, is where, less than a month ago, a bloody corpse had been.

Mia turns to Gabe with anguish in her pretty blue eyes, barking, "You killed him. You killed him," over and over and over again. She's crying, delirious, saying that she sees the blood, pouring from his lifeless body, seeping into the cracks of the floors. She sees the cat running away, tracking bloody footprints across the room.

She hears the shot piercing through the silent room—and she jumps, reliving the moment right then and there, hearing the breaking glass as it shattered to the ground.

She says that she sees him fall. She sees his limbs become flaccid, and plummet to the ground. She remembers that his eyes failed, his body jerked in ways beyond his control. There was blood on her hands, her clothes. "There's blood everywhere," she sobs desperately, groping at the ground. Dr. Rhodes says that Mia is experiencing an episode of psychosis. I push the doctor's hands away from me, wanting nothing more than to soothe my daughter. I am making my way to her, to Mia, when Gabe reaches for my arm and stops me.

"Everywhere. Red blood everywhere. Wake up!" Mia smacks her hands against the ground and then pulls her knees into herself and begins to rock, furiously. "Wake up! Oh, God, please wake up. *Don't leave me.*"

GABE

CHRISTMAS EVE

I'm not the first one into the cabin. I spot Hammill's fat face in the crowd. I grab him by the collar and ask what the fuck that was all about. On a normal day he could kick my ass if he wanted to. But this isn't a normal day; today I'm a man possessed.

"He was gonna kill her."

He claims Thatcher didn't leave them a choice.

"Or so you say."

"This isn't your jurisdiction, asshole."

Some wannabe—looking no more than nineteen, maybe twenty years old—comes from the cabin and says, "Bastard's dead," and Hammill responds with a thumbs-up. Someone claps. This is apparently the sniper, a kid too stupid to know better. I remember when I was nineteen. The only thing in the world I wanted was to get my hands on a gun. Now the very thought of using it scares the shit out of me.

"What's your problem, Hoffman?"

"I needed him *alive*."

They're all making their way inside. An ambulance makes its way through the snow, sirens blaring. I watch the red and blue, red and blue, screaming through the dark night. EMTs unload, trying their damndest to steer a stretcher through the snow.

Hammill follows his guys in. They all hike up the stairs and into the cabin. There's a floodlight illuminating the inside until someone has the common sense to flip on a lamp. I hold my breath.

I've never met Mia Dennett before in my life. I doubt that she's ever heard my name. She doesn't have a clue that for three months now, she's been the only thought on my mind, the face I see when I wake up in the morning, the face I see when I go to bed.

She emerges from the cabin, marshaled by Hammill, his grip tight enough she might as well be cuffed. She's covered in blood, her hands and clothing, even her hair. It stains the strands of blond hair red. Her skin is a frightening white, translucent in the obnoxious glow of the floodlight, which no one has the courtesy to turn off. She's a ghost, a phantom, with an empty expression on her face; the lights are on but no one's home. Tears freeze to her cheeks as she slips down the stairs and Hammill jerks her back to her feet.

"Me first," Hammill vows as he leads Mia away from me. Her eyes graze over my face. What I see in her is Eve, thirty years ago, before James Dennett, before Grace and Mia, before me.

Son of a bitch.

I'd kick his fucking ass if I wasn't so worried about frightening Mia. I don't like the way he touches her.

Inside I find the corpse of Colin Thatcher sprawled awkwardly across the floor. Once or twice as a street cop, I helped pull a stiff from a wreck. There's nothing like it in the world. The feel of dead flesh: hard and cold the instant the soul leaves it. The eyes, whether open or closed, lose their life. His eyes are open. His flesh is cold. There's more blood than I've ever seen. I force the lids down and say, "It's nice to finally meet you, Colin Thatcher."

I think of Kathryn Thatcher in that shitty nursing home. I see the look on her deteriorating face when I break the news.

Hammill's guys have already gotten to work: crime scene photos, fingerprinting, gathering evidence.

I don't know what to make of the place. It's an inadequate living, at best. The place reeks. I don't know what I had expected. A medieval head crusher and knee splitter? Chains and flails? Handcuffs, if nothing more? What I see is an ugly little place with a gosh-darn Christmas tree. My own apartment is more dreadful than this.

"Check this out," someone says, letting a parka drop to the floor. I stand, my legs cramping. Into the Formica someone has carved the words *We Were Here*. "What do you make of it?"

I let my fingers run over the words. "I don't know."

Hammill comes into the cabin. His voice is loud enough to wake the dead. "She's all yours," he says to me as he gives Thatcher a little kick—just in case.

"What'd she say?" I ask for conversation's sake. I don't really give a shit what she told *him*.

"See for yourself," he says. There's something in his tone that perks my interest. He shows off this arrogant smile—*I know something you don't know*—and adds, "It's good."

I lean over Colin Thatcher for a last look. He lies dead-as-a-doorknob on the wooden floors. "What did you do?" I ask discreetly, then head outside.

She's sitting in the back of the open ambulance, being attended to by an EMT. They've got a wool blanket wrapped around her. They're trying to make sure none of that blood is hers. The ambulance is quiet now, the lights and siren silenced. There's the sound of people talking, someone laughing.

I saunter up to her. She's staring off into space, letting the EMT take a look, though she flinches with every touch.

"It's cold out here," I say, getting her attention. Her hair is long, falling over her face and clouding her eyes. There's an indistinguishable look on her; I don't know what it means. Dried—frozen?—blood clings to her skin. Her nose runs. I pull a handkerchief from my pocket and set it in her hand.

I've never cared this much about someone I didn't know.

"You must be exhausted. This has been quite an ordeal. We'll get you home. Soon. I promise. I know someone who can't wait to hear your voice.

"I'm Detective Gabe Hoffman. We've been looking for you."

I find it impossible to believe this is the first time we've met. Seems to me I know her more than I know half my friends.

Her eyes lift up to mine for a split second, and then find their way to an empty body bag that's heading in. "You don't need to look," I say.

But it isn't the body bag, per se. It's the space. She's looking off into space. The vicinity is crowded with people who come and go. They're mostly men, only one woman. They mention Christmas plans in passing: church and dinner with in-laws; staying up late to assemble some toy the wife bought online. All in the line of duty.

Any other case I'd be slapping high fives for a job well done. But this isn't any other case.

"Detective Hammill asked you some questions. I have questions, too, but they can wait. I know this hasn't been…easy… for you."

It crosses my mind to stroke her hair or pat her hand, some simple gesture that might bring her to life. Her eyes are lost. She rests her head on bent knees and doesn't say a word. She doesn't cry. None of this surprises me; she's a woman in shock.

"I know this has been a nightmare for you. For your family. So many people have been worried. We'll have you home in time for Christmas. I promise," I say. "I'll bring you there myself." As soon as I'm given the okay, Mia and I will make the long drive home, where Eve will be waiting with open arms in front of their home. But first we'll need to stop by the local hospital for a full examination. I'm hoping reporters haven't caught on to this, that they won't be lining the hospital parking lot with video cameras and microphones and a whole slew of questions.

She doesn't say a word.

I consider calling Eve on my phone and letting Mia be the one to deliver the good news. I dive my hands into my pockets; where the hell is my phone? Oh, well. Probably too much, too soon. She isn't ready. But Eve waits on pins and needles for my call. Soon.

"What happened?" her soft voice finally asks.

Of course, I think. It all happened so quickly. She's struggling to make sense of it all.

"They got him," I say. "It's all over."

"All over." She lets the words slip from her tongue and fall to the snow.

Her eyes do a 360. She takes in the view as if this is the first time she's seen it. Is it possible that this is the first time she's been let outdoors?

"Where am I?" she whispers.

I exchange a look with the EMT, who shrugs. Well, hell, I think, this is more up your alley than mine. I get the bad guys. You take care of the good.

"Mia," I say. I hear a cell phone ring in the distance. Sounds a hell of a lot like mine. "Mia," I begin again.

She looks addled the second time I say her name. I say it a third time because I can't think of any words to come after it. What happened? Where am I? These are the questions I planned to ask *her.*

"That's not my name," she says in a low voice.

The EMT is packing his things. He wants her checked out by a doctor, but for now she's okay. There are signs of malnutrition. Wounds healing. But nothing of immediate concern.

I swallow. "Sure it is. You're Mia Dennett. Don't you remember?"

"No." She shakes her head. It's not that she doesn't remember. It's that she's certain I'm wrong. She leans in close, as if divulging a secret, and says to me, "My name is Chloe."

Detective Hammill passes by and lets out an obnoxious sound. "Told you it was good." He sneers as he barks out to his guys, "Hurry up so we can call it a day."

GABE

AFTEЯ

In the town of Grand Marais, we check into a hotel, a traditional little inn on Lake Superior, with a sign boasting Free Continental Breakfast that catches my eye. Our return flight is not until morning.

Dr. Rhodes has given Mia a tranquilizer that knocked her out. I carried her to the double bed in a room she shares with Eve. The rest of us stand in the hallway and talk.

Eve is a jumble of nerves. She knew this whole thing was a mistake. She goes almost as far as to blame me, but stops short. "Sooner or later it would have all come out," she decides, but I can't tell if she believes it or if she's only trying to appease me.

Later I will remind her of the case, that Colin Thatcher was not the one who ordered a hit on Mia. There *is* someone out there looking for her, and we need Mia as cognizant as possible to track this *someone* down. He must have told her something. Colin must have told her what this was all about.

Eve leans against a hallway wall covered in pastel wallpaper. The doctor has changed into a pair of lounge pants and slippers. Her hair is tied into a stringent bun that makes her forehead look huge. She stands with her arms crossed and says to us, "It's called Stockholm syndrome. It's when victims become emotionally attached to their captors. They bond with them in captivity and when it's all said and done, they defend their captors and become fearful of the police who came to their rescue. It's not unusual. We see it all the time. In domestic abuse situations, abused children, incest. I'm sure you can relate, Detective. A woman calls the police department to say her husband is beating her, but when the police arrive at her door, she turns on them and comes to the defense of her spouse.

"There are a number of conditions that aid in the development of Stockholm syndrome. Mia would have needed to feel threatened by her aggressor, as we know she did. She would have needed to feel isolated from others besides her aggressor. We know this to be the case, too. She needed to feel an inability to escape the situation. This goes without saying. And finally, Mr. Thatcher would have needed to show a minimal amount of humanity to her, such as—"

"Not letting Mia starve to death," I offer.

"Precisely."

"Giving her clothes to wear. Shelter." I could go on and on. It makes perfect sense to me.

But not Eve. She waits until Dr. Rhodes has said good-night and retreats down the hall—out of hearing range—before uttering, "She loved him," in that mother-knows-best tone.

"Eve, I think—"

"She loved him."

I've never seen Eve so sure of anything as she is this. She stands in the doorway watching Mia sleep on the bed. She watches her like a new mother might watch her infant child.

Eve sleeps in the bed beside Mia. I sleep in the second double bed though I have my own room. Eve begs me not to leave.

Who am I to talk, I think as I slide between the sheets. I don't know a damn thing about being in love.

Neither of us sleeps.

"I didn't kill him," I remind Eve, but it doesn't matter because someone did.

EVE

AFTER

The entire flight home, she's lost. She takes the window seat and presses her forehead against the cold glass. She's unresponsive when we try to speak to her, and at times I hear her cry. I see the tears she sheds drip down her cheeks and fall to her hands. I try to console her, but she pulls away.

I was in love once, so long ago that I can barely remember. I was enraptured by this handsome man I'd met in a restaurant in the city, this alluring man who made me feel like I walked on air. Now he's gone and all that remains in the space between us are hurt feelings and despicable words. He wasn't taken from me. I drifted away, far enough that I can no longer see that youthful face or persuasive smile. And still it hurts.

Dr. Rhodes leaves us at the airport. She wants to see Mia in the morning. The doctor and I decided amongst ourselves that we would increase her sessions to two times per week. Acute stress disorder is one thing, grief another.

"This is a lot for someone to handle," she says to me, and we look over to watch as Mia's hand drops to her abdomen. This baby is no longer a burden, but a last trace of him, something to hold on to.

I think what it would have done to Mia if she'd had the abortion. It would have pushed her over the edge.

We find Gabe's car in long-term parking. He has offered to drive us home. He tries awkwardly to manage all of our bags; he won't let me help. Mia walks faster than the rest of us so that we struggle to keep up. She does it so she won't see the uneasy countenance on my face, or have to look into the eyes of the man she believes shot her lover.

She rides the entire trip in the backseat in silence.

Gabe asks if she's hungry; she doesn't respond.

I ask if she's warm enough; she ignores me.

The traffic is light. It's a frigid Sunday, the kind you long to spend in bed. The radio is turned on, the volume low. Mia lies down in the backseat and, in time, she falls asleep. I watch the clumsy hair fall across her rosy cheeks, numb still from the winter air. Her eyes flutter, her body asleep while images fill her mind. I try to make sense of it all: how someone like Mia could fall for someone like Colin Thatcher.

And then my eyes wander to the man sitting beside me, a man so unlike James it's almost comical.

"I'm leaving him," I disclose, my eyes never rising from the road ahead. Gabe says nothing. But when his hand closes over mine, he says everything he needs to say.

Gabe drops us off at the door. He offers to help us up, but I decline, telling him we can manage.

Mia is making her way inside the building without me. In silence, we watch her go. Gabe says that he'll be back in the morning. He has something for her.

And then, when the heavy door closes and she is no longer in view, he leans in to kiss me, altogether ignoring the commuters who walk home along the busy sidewalks, the cabs passing by on the boisterous street. I place my hands on his chest and stop him. "I can't," I say. This pains me more than it will Gabe and I watch as he studies me for an explanation, his soft eyes wondering why, and then gradually he begins to nod. It has nothing to do with him. But it's time to get my priorities in order. They've been out of sync for so long.

Mia tells me that there is the sound of breaking glass. She watches him struggle for breath. There's blood, everywhere, as he reaches out his hands and she can do nothing but watch him fall.

She wakes up in her own bed, screaming. By the time I make my way in, she's fallen from the bed and to the floor, poised above someone who isn't there. She whispers his name. "Please don't leave me," she says, and then proceeds to tear apart the bedding, looking for him. She tosses aside the blanket and rips sheets from the bed. "Owen," she cries. And then she pushes past me where I'm standing in the doorway watching the heartbreaking scene, barely making it to the toilet before she throws up.

It's like this every day.

Some days the morning sickness isn't so bad. But those days, Mia says, are the hardest. When she's not preoccupied with the constant sense of nausea, then she's constantly reminded that Owen is dead.

I hover in the doorway. "Mia," I say. I'm willing to do anything to make the pain go away. But there's nothing I can do.

When she's ready, she tells me about the last moments inside the cabin, the way the gunshots sounded like fireworks, the way the window broke, glass shattering to the floor, the winter air welcoming itself in. "The noise terrified me, my eyes darting outside before I heard Owen begin to wheeze. He whispered my name. *Chloe*. He struggled to come up with enough breath. His legs began to collapse. I didn't know what had happened," she cries, shaking her head, reliving the moment as she does a hundred times a day in her head, and I lay a hand on her leg to stop her. There's no need to go on. But she does. She does because she has to, because her mind can no longer keep the flashbacks contained. They lay dormant in her mind, like a volcano about to burst.

"*Owen?*" she utters aloud, trapped in a moment that isn't the present time. "The gun dropped from his hands. It dented the floor. He reached his hands out to me. There was blood, everywhere. He'd been shot. His legs began to give. I tried to catch him, I did, but the weight was too much. He crumbled to the floor.

"I fell to him. '*Owen! Oh, my God. Owen,*'" she sobs.

She says that she envisioned the jagged coastline of the Italian Riviera. In that last moment, that's what she saw. The boats floating lazily in the Ligurian Sea, and the abrupt peaks of the Maritime Alps and the Apennines Mountains. She saw a rustic stone cottage lost in the hillside, where they toiled in the lush green countryside until their backs broke. She and the man known as Owen. She imagined that they were no longer on the run. They were home. In that last moment, Mia saw children running through the thick grass, dodging between rows of unvarying grape trees. They had dark hair like his and dark eyes like his and they inserted Italian words into their departing English. *Bambino* and *allegro* and *vero amore*.

She tells me how the blood spilled from his body. How it spread across the floor, how the cat ran through the room, his tiny paws spreading bloody prints across the floor. And again, her eyes dart through the room, as if it's happening here, in this moment, though the cat sits perched on the bedroom windowsill like a porcelain statue.

She says that his breathing was slow, that he took shallow breaths with great effort. There was blood everywhere. "His eyes became still. His chest still. 'Wake up. Wake up.' I shook

him. 'Oh, God, please wake up. Please don't leave me,'" she
sobs into the sheets of her bed. She tells me that his limbs
stopped fighting as the front door pushed open. There was a
blinding light and a masculine voice telling her to step away
from the body.

"Please don't leave me," she cries.

She wakes up every morning screaming his name.

She sleeps in the bedroom; I roll out the futon and sleep in
the family room. She refuses to open the curtains and accept
the world into the room. She likes it dark, where she can believe it's nighttime twenty-four hours a day and succumb to
her depression. I can barely get her to eat anymore. "If not
for you," I advise, "then do it for the baby." She says it's the
only reason she has to live anymore.

She admits to me in confidence that she can't go on. She
doesn't say it when she's lucid, but when she's sobbing, lost in
despair. She thinks about death, of all the ways to kill herself. She lists them for me. I tell myself that I'll never leave
her alone.

Monday morning Gabe showed up with a box of things
he'd brought from the cabin. He'd been saving them as evidence. "I planned to return them to Colin's mother," he said,
"but thought maybe you'd like to have a look."

He was hoping for a ceasefire. What he got was a reproach-
ful look as she muttered, *"Owen,"* under her breath.

When I drag her from her bedroom, she sits and stares
mindlessly at the TV. I have to mind what she watches. The
evening news tears her apart, words like *death* and *murder* and
convict.

I tell Mia that Gabe was not the one to shoot *Owen* but she
says it doesn't matter. It means nothing. He's dead. She doesn't
hate Gabe for this. She feels nothing. There's a vast emptiness
filling her soul. I justify what he did—what we *all* did. I try

to make her understand that the police were there to protect her. That what they saw was an armed convict and his prey.

More than anything, Mia blames herself. She says that she put the gun in his hand. She sobs at night that she's sorry. Dr. Rhodes talks to her about the stages of grief: denial and anger. One day, she promises, there will be an acceptance of the loss.

Mia opened the box Gabe had brought for her and raised a gray hooded sweatshirt from the cardboard. She brought it to her face; she closed her eyes and smelled the cotton. It was clear that she planned to keep it. "Mia, honey," I said, "let me wash it." There was a horrible stench to it, but she refused to let me take it from her hands.

"Don't," she insisted.

She sleeps with it every night, pretending that it's his arms that hold her tight.

She sees him everywhere: in her dreams, when she's awake. Yesterday I insisted on a walk. It was a bearable day for January. We needed fresh air. We'd been cooped up in this apartment for days. I cleaned the apartment, scouring a bathtub that hadn't been used in months. I snipped at her plants with a pair of pinking shears, dropping the dead foliage into a trash can. Ayanna offered to pick up some items for us at the market—milk and orange juice and, at my request, fresh flowers, something to remind Mia of all the things in the world that are *alive*.

Yesterday Mia sunk into the wide arms of a jacket she collected from the same cardboard box, and we went outside. At the bottom of the steps, she paused and stared at an imaginary place on the opposite side of the street. I don't know how long she stared, until I pulled her gently by the arm, and said, "Let's walk." I couldn't quite figure out what she was staring at; there was nothing there, only a four-flat brick building with scaffolding out front.

The Chicago winter is harsh. But every now and then God blesses us with a thirty- or forty-degree day to remind us that misery comes and goes. It must be thirty-eight, thirty-nine degrees, when we head out for our walk, the kind of day that teenagers foolishly rush out in shorts and T-shirts, forgetting that in October we were aghast at temperatures like this.

We stayed on the residential streets because I thought there would be less noise. We could hear the city not so far away. It was the middle of the day. She dragged her feet. Rounding the corner onto Waveland, she and a young man ran right into one another. I may have prevented it had I not been staring at outdated Christmas décor on a nearby balcony, out of place beside puddles of snow that melted on the sidewalk, reminding me of spring. The man was handsome with a baseball cap pulled low, his eyes gazing at the ground. Mia wasn't paying attention. She nearly doubled over in disbelief.

He couldn't make sense of the crying. "I'm sorry. I'm so sorry," he said. I begged him not to worry.

It's the same baseball cap Mia took from the box, the one that sits beside her bed.

The grief and the morning sickness send her running to the bathroom three, sometimes four times a day.

Gabe arrived this afternoon, fully intent on getting to the bottom of this. Until today, he was content with small visits, with the sole purpose of reconciliation. But he reminds me that there's a lingering threat out there, and the policemen parked outside her building for security will not be there forever. He set Mia down on the futon.

"Tell me about his mother," she says. This is called give-and-take.

Mia's apartment is approximately a four-hundred-square-foot box. There's the family room with the futon and tiny TV; she pulls out the futon when company comes to stay. I've polished the bathroom many times, and still it doesn't feel clean. The bathtub fills with water every time I shower. The kitchen is only large enough for one person; you cannot stand behind the refrigerator when the door is open without being shoved into the stove. There is no dishwasher. The radiator rarely warms the room, and when it does, the temperature soars to ninety degrees. We eat dinner on the futon, which we don't often bother to sit up, since night after night I use it for a bed.

"Kathryn," Gabe replies. He's perched awkwardly on the edge of the futon. For days now, Mia has been asking about Colin's mother. I didn't know what to say, other than that Gabe would know more about Ms. Thatcher than me. I've never met the woman, though in a matter of months we will be grandmothers to the same child. "She's a sick woman," he says, "with advanced stages of Parkinson's disease."

I disappear into the kitchen and pretend to wash dishes.

"I know."

"She's as well as to be expected. Ms. Thatcher had been living in a nursing home—she wasn't fit to care for herself."

Mia asks how the woman came to be living at a nursing home. As far as Colin—*Owen*—was concerned, the woman was living at home.

"I brought her there."

"You brought her there?" she asks.

"I did," Gabe confesses. "Ms Thatcher needed constant care."

This earns Gabe brownie points in Mia's eyes.

"He was worried about her."

"He had good reason to be. But she's fine," Gabe reassures. "I drove Ms. Thatcher to the funeral." He pauses long enough to let it settle. Gabe told me about the funeral. It was only days after Mia returned home. We were absorbed in first appointments with Dr. Rhodes and discovering that the hum of the refrigerator scared the living daylights out of our child. Gabe clipped an obituary from a Gary paper and brought it to me. He brought me a program from the funeral, with this polished photograph on the front, a black-and-white set amidst ivory paper. At the time I'd been incensed that Colin Thatcher had such a civil burial. I discarded the program in the fireplace, watching his face go up in flames. I prayed the same thing happen to the real man, that he burn in hell.

I stop what I'm doing and wait for the sound of weeping; it doesn't come. Mia is still.

"You went to the funeral?"

"I did. It was nice. As nice as to be expected."

Gabe's image is growing by leaps and bounds. I hear a change in Mia's voice, no longer seeping with abhorrence. It softens, and loses a bit of the defensiveness. I, on the other hand, stand in the kitchen, clutching a ceramic plate, imagining Colin burning in hell, and try desperately to recant.

"Was the casket—"

"Closed. But there were pictures. And a lot of people. More people loved him than he'll ever know."

"I know," she whispers.

There's silence. More silence than I can take. I dry my hands on the seat of my pants. When I peer into the family room, I see that Gabe is sitting close, right beside Mia, and that she has allowed her head to droop to his shoulder. His arm is draped around her back and she cries.

I want to intrude, to be the one whose shoulder she cries upon, but I don't dare.

"Ms. Thatcher is living with her sister Valerie now. She's fully medicated and better able to manage the *disease*."

I hide in the kitchen pretending not to listen.

"The last time I saw her," Gabe says, "there was...hope."

"Tell me how you ended up in that cabin," Gabe asks.

She says that these are the things that are easy to explain.

I hold my breath. I don't know if I want to hear this. She tells Gabe what she knows, that he was hired to find her and turn her over to a man she'd never heard of. But he couldn't do it, and so he brought her to a place where he believed she would be safe. I take a deep breath. He brought her to a place where he believed she would be safe. Maybe he wasn't a madman after all.

She says something about a ransom. She says that it has something to do with James.

I've stepped into the family room, where I can listen. At the mention of James's name, Gabe stands heatedly from the futon and begins to pace the room. "I knew it," he says over and over again. I watch my baby sitting on the futon and think that her father had the ability to protect her from this. I leave the apartment, finding solace in the freezing winter day. Gabe watches me leave, knowing he cannot console us all at once.

When she goes to bed at night, I hear her toss and turn. I hear her cry and call his name. I stand outside her bedroom door, wanting to make it go away, but knowing I cannot. Gabe says that there isn't anything I can do. *Just be there for her,* he says.

She says she could drown herself in the bathtub.

She could slice an artery with a kitchen knife.

She could stick her head into the stove.

She could jump from the fire escape.

She could walk onto the "L" platform at night.

GABE

AFTEЯ

I get a warrant and conduct a search of the judge's chambers. He's beside himself. The sergeant comes along and tries to smooth things over, but Judge Dennett doesn't give a crap. He says when we turn up empty-handed, we're both going to find ourselves out of a job.

But we don't come up empty-handed. As it turns out, we find three threatening letters hidden among Judge Dennett's locked, personal files. All ransom demands. The letters say that they have Mia. In return for her release, they demand a shitload of money, or they'll disclose the fact that Judge Dennett accepted $350,000 in bribes in 2001 for a lenient sentence in a racketeering case. Blackmail.

It takes some time, interviews and my superior detective work, but we're able to identify key players in the failed ransom plot including Dalmar Osoma, a Somali man who helped carry out the plan. We have a task force assigned to tracking Osoma down.

I'd pat my own back if I could reach that far. But I can't. I let the sergeant do it for me.

As for Judge Dennett, he's the one who finds himself out

of a job. He's disbarred. But that's the least of his concerns. He has evidence tampering and obstruction of justice to think about while he awaits his own trial. An inquest is made into the bribery charges to see if there's any merit there. I'd bet my life there is. Why else would Judge Dennett sandwich the letters between file folders, never imagining someone would see?

I question him before he's sent to prison. "You knew," I say with utter disbelief. "All along. You knew she'd been abducted."

What kind of man would do that to his own child?

His voice still brims with egotism, but for the first time ever, there's an ounce of shame mixed in. "At first, no," he says. He's in a holding cell at the precinct. Judge Dennett behind bars: an image I've dreamed of since our paths first crossed. He sits on the edge of the bed staring at the public toilet, knowing that sooner or later he'll have to piss in front of us all.

It's the first time I'm sure Judge Dennett is being sincere.

He says that at first, he was certain Mia was off doing something stupid. It was in her nature. "She'd run off before." And then the letters began to arrive. He didn't want anyone to know he was corrupt, that he'd accepted the bribes all those years ago. He would have been disbarred. But, he admits and for a split second, I believe him: he didn't want anything to happen to Mia. He was going to pay the ransom to free her, but also so they'd shut up. He demanded proof of life; there was none.

"Because," I say, "*they* didn't have her." Colin Thatcher had her. Colin Thatcher had presumably saved her life.

"I assumed she was dead," he says.

"And?"

"If she was dead, then no one needed to know what I'd

done," he admits with a modesty I never ever expected from Judge Dennett.

Modesty *and* remorse? Was he sorry for what he'd done?

I think of all the days that he sat in the same room with Eve, of all the nights he shared the same bed, believing that their daughter was dead.

Eve files for divorce, and when it's granted, she'll take half of everything Judge Dennett owns. That's enough money to buy a new life for her and Mia.

EPILOGUE

MIA

AFTER

I sit in the opaque office across from Dr. Rhodes and tell her about that night. The rain was pouring down, thick and heavy, and Owen and I sat in the dark room listening to it batter the roof of the log cabin. I tell the doctor how we'd been outside, collecting firewood, and how the rain saturated us before we could make it inside. "That," I tell her, "was the night something changed between Owen and me. That was the night I understood why I was there, in that cabin, with him. He wasn't trying to hurt me," I explain, recalling the way he looked at me with those dark, austere eyes and said, *No one knows we're here. If they did, they'd kill us. Me and you,* and suddenly I was part of something, no longer alone as I'd been my entire life. "He was *saving* me," I say. And that's when everything changed.

It was then that I wasn't scared anymore. That's when I understood.

There are things I tell Dr. Rhodes, about the cabin, about our lives there, about Owen. "Did you love him?" she asks, and I say that I did. My eyes fill with sadness and the doctor stretches a tissue across the coffee table that separates us, and I hold it to my face and cry.

"Tell me what you're feeling, Mia," she prompts, and I tell her how I miss him, how I wish the memories hadn't returned so that I could remain in the dark, completely unaware of Owen's passing.

But, of course, it is much more than that.

There are things I can never tell the doctor.

I can tell her how the sadness haunts me day in and day out, but I can never tell her about the blame. The knowledge that I put Owen in that cabin, that I put the gun in his hands. If I had told him the truth, we could have come up with a plan. We could have figured it out together. But in those first minutes, in those first days, I was too terrified to tell him the truth for fear of what he might do to me, and later, I couldn't tell him the truth for fear of how it would change things.

He wouldn't be the one protecting me from my father and Dalmar, even if it was all bogus, all a sham.

I spent my entire life desperate for someone to take care of me. And there he was.

I wasn't about to let that go.

I rub a hand over an ever-growing midsection and feel the baby kick. Out the hazy windows, summer has come, the heat and humidity that make it hard to breathe. Soon the baby will arrive, a keepsake from Owen, and I will no longer be alone.

There's an image I carry in my mind. I'm in junior high when I proudly carry home an A-book report that my mother hangs to the refrigerator door with a lame Bee Happy magnet I'd gotten her for Christmas that year. My father comes home and sees the assignment. He gives it a quick once-over, and then says to my mother, "That English teacher should be fired. Mia is old enough to know the difference between *there* and *their,* don't you think, Eve?" He uses the paper as a coaster, and before escaping the room, I watch the water stain seep into the fibers of the report.

I was twelve years old.

I think back to that September day, as I walked into the gloomy bar. It was a beautiful Indian summer day but inside the bar it was dark, nearly vacant, as a bar should be at two in the afternoon, just a handful of patrons sitting quietly at their own tables, drowning their sorrows in straight-up bourbon and whiskey shots. The place was a hole in the wall, the corner unit of a brick building with graffiti on the side. Music played in the background. Johnny Cash. I wasn't in my own neighborhood, but farther south and west, in Lawndale, and as I looked around the bar, I saw that I was the only one who was white. There were wooden barstools pulled up to the bar, some cracked along the seat or missing spindles, glass shelves of alcohol lining the back wall. Smoke infused the air, drifted to the ceiling, making the place hazy, opaque. The front door was propped open with a chair, but even the fresh fall day— the sunlight and warm air—was hesitant to enter. The bartender, a bald man with a goatee, nodded to me and asked what he could get me to drink.

I asked for a beer and made my way to the back of the bar, to a table closest to the men's bathroom, where he told me he'd be. When I saw him, my throat rose up inside me and I found it hard to breathe. His eyes were black, like coal, his skin dark and rubbery, like tires. He was sunken in a slat-back chair, leaned over a beer. He wore a camouflage coat, which he didn't need on a day such as that, my own coat removed and tied around my waist.

I asked if he was Dalmar and he watched me for a minute, those anthracite eyes perusing my wayward hair, the conclusiveness in my eyes. They drifted down my body, down an

oxford shirt and jeans; they appraised a black bag crisscross-
ing my body, the parka tied around my waist.

I'd never been so sure about anything as I was of this.

He didn't say if he was or wasn't Dalmar, but asked what I
had for him instead. When he spoke, his voice was a low, bass
voice, one which held on to its African enunciation for dear
life. I invited myself into the chair opposite him and noted
that he was big, much bigger than me, each of his hands, as
he groped the envelope that I removed from my bag and set
on the table, twice as big as my own. He was black, like the
blackest of black bears, like the blubbery skin of the killer
whale, an alpha predator with no predators of their own. He
knew, as he sat across from me at the unpretentious table, that
he was at the top of the food chain and I was mere algae.

He asked why he should trust me, how he could know for
certain he wouldn't be played for a fool. I gathered what courage I could possibly muster, and replied, unblinkingly, "How
do I know that *you* won't play *me* for a fool?"

He laughed audaciously and in a somewhat deranged man-
ner, and said, "Ah, yes. But there's a difference here, you see.
Nobody plays Dalmar for a fool."

And I knew then, that if anything went wrong, he would
end my life.

But I would not let myself be scared.

He removed papers from the envelope: the proof, which
I'd had in my possession for six weeks or more, until I knew
what to do with it. Telling my mother or going to the police
seemed too easy, too mundane. There needed to be something more, a gruesome punishment to fit a gruesome crime.
Disbarment does not offset being a lousy father, but the loss
of a hefty sum of cash, the shattering of his splendid reputation, that came close. Closer at least.

It wasn't easy to find. That's for sure. I stumbled across

some papers in a locked filing cabinet, late one night when he dragged my mother to a benefit dinner at Navy Pier, paying $500 a piece to support a nonprofit organization whose mission is to improve the educational opportunities for children living in poverty, which I found to be absolutely absurd—ludicrous—seeing as how he felt about my own career path.

I came to their home that night, took the Purple Line out to Linden and, from there, a cab. I came under the guise of a crashed computer. My mother, offering her own old, slow one, suggested I pack a bag and stay for the night, and I said okay, but of course I wouldn't stay. I packed a bag anyway, for appearance's sake, the perfect way to stow away the evidence, hours later, after a complete dissection of my father's office, as I called for a cab and returned home to my own apartment, to a fully functioning computer where I researched private investigators to turn my suspicion into full-fledged proof.

It wasn't extortion I was looking for. Not exactly. I was searching for anything. Tax evasion, forgery, perjury, harassment, whatever. But it was extortion that I found. Evidence of a $350,000 transfer into an offshore account that my father kept in a sealed envelope in a locked file cabinet and I, as luck would have it, found the key, tucked inside an antique tea tin given to my father by a Chinese businessman a dozen years ago, lost in the midst of loose tea leaves. Small and silver and sublime.

"How does this work?" I asked the man across from me. Dalmar. I didn't know exactly what to call him. A hitman. A contract killer. That is, after all, what he does. I was given his name by a shady neighbor who's had more than one run-in with the law, police showing up at his apartment in the middle of the night. He's a braggart, the kind of man who just loves to ramble on about his faux pas while climbing the stairs to the third floor. The first time Dalmar and I spoke

on the phone—a brief call from the payphone on the corner
to arrange this meeting—he asked how I wanted him to kill
my father. I said no; we weren't going to kill him. What I
planned for my father was far worse. Being of ill repute, vili-
fied, his reputation blackened, living amongst the lowlifes he
sentenced to jail; that, for my father, would be worse, like
purgatory: hell on earth.

Dalmar would take sixty percent. I would take forty. I nodded, because I wasn't in the position to negotiate. And forty
percent of the ransom demand was a lot of money. Eighty
thousand dollars to be exact. An anonymous donation to my
school was what I had in mind, what I planned to do with
my share of the money. I'd outlined the details in my mind,
made preparations in advance. For the sake of authenticity, I
would not simply disappear. There needed to be proof, in the
event of an ensuing investigation: witnesses, fingerprints, vid-
eotapes and such. I wouldn't ask who, what or when. There
needed be a surprise factor so that, in the moment, my own
behavior was legit: a terrified woman in a kidnapping plot. I
discovered a derelict studio apartment on the northwest side,
in Albany Park. This is where I would hide while the professionals, Dalmar and his associates, did the rest. This was the
plan, at least. I paid, in advance, three months of rent from
a cash advance I received from Dalmar, and squirreled away
bottles of water, canned fruit, frozen meats and breads, so that
I would never need to leave. I purchased paper towel and toilet
paper, art supplies en masse so that I wouldn't risk being seen.
Once the ransom was paid, and yet, my father's dirty deeds
discovered, it would be from this crippled little apartment in
Albany Park where my rescue would ensue, where the police
would find me, bound and gagged, my abductor still at large.

Dalmar wanted to know who he was to take hostage, who
he was to hold for ransom. I looked into his black serpentine

eyes, at the shaven head and a scar, three inches or more, running vertically down the length of his cheek, a rivet in his skin where I imagined some kind of blade—a switchblade or a machete—sliced through the vulnerable exterior, creating a man untouchable on the inside.

My eyes circled the bar, to make sure we were alone. Nearly everyone there, except for a twentysomething waitress in jeans and a too-tight shirt, was male; all, besides me, were black. A man perched at a barstool before the bar slipped clumsily, drunkenly, from the stool and fishtailed his way into the men's room. I watched him pass, watched him push his way through a bulky wooden door, and then my eyes returned to Dalmar's serious, unforgiving black eyes.

And I said, "Me."

★ ★ ★ ★ ★

ACKNOWLEDGMENTS

First and foremost, a huge thank-you to my amazing literary agent, Rachael Dillon Fried, who had enough faith in *The Good Girl* for the both of us. I can never thank you enough, Rachael, for all the hard work and unending support, but most of all, for your firm belief that *The Good Girl* would be more than just another file on my computer. If it wasn't for you none of this would have happened!

My editor, Erika Imranyi, has been absolutely incredible throughout this process. I could not ask for a more perfect editor. Erika, your brilliant ideas have shaped *The Good Girl* into what it is today, and I'm so proud of the finished product. Thank you for this amazing opportunity, and for encouraging me to do my absolute best.

Thanks to all at Greenburger Associates and Harlequin MIRA for helping along the way.

Thanks to family and friends—especially those who had no idea I'd written a novel, and responded with nothing but pride and support, especially Mom and Dad, the Shemanek, Kahlenberg and Kyrychenko families, and to Beth Schillen for the honest feedback.

And finally, thank you to my husband, Pete, for giving me the opportunity to live my dream, and to my children, who are perhaps the most excited that their mommy wrote a book!

THE
GOOD
GIRL

MARY KUBICA

Reader's Guide

1. Initially Detective Hoffman wishes that he had not been assigned the case of the missing Mia Dennett, and yet later, he finds himself completely preoccupied by it. Are his motives fueled more by professional or personal desire? Do you feel that his character evolved during the course of the novel, or did he remain true to himself throughout?

2. In the early pages of the novel, Colin Thatcher comes across as a hardened criminal carrying out a kidnapping plot for his own financial benefit. What would make a man like Colin decide to save Mia from her assumed fate? Did your perception of him change at all during the course of the novel?

3. Do you think it was admirable for Colin to forsake his own and his mother's well-being for a stranger, or should he have carried out the kidnapping plot as planned? Were his actions entirely selfless, or did his decision to save Mia also serve a selfish purpose?

4. Imagine for a moment that Mia went through with the abortion at her father's request. How would this have

affected her once she learned of Colin's death? Do you think it would have been easier or harder for her to accept his death if she was not carrying his child?

5. Mia Dennett is portrayed in many different lights: the devoted teacher, the neglected daughter, a kidnapping victim, an underhanded conspirator and more. Which of these do you feel accurately portray the character, or is Mia truly a conglomeration of all personas? Are any of these portrayals merely an act on Mia's part to fill some self-seeking need and, if so, how does this behavior differ from that of her father?

6. Eve Dennett exhibits a strong emotional attachment toward Detective Gabe Hoffman throughout *The Good Girl*, and yet, at the end of the novel, she chooses to forsake that relationship for the benefit of her daughter. Do you feel that Eve's feelings for the detective were genuine, or rather an instance of being caught up in the moment? In your opinion, was Eve appropriate in ending the relationship, or should she have continued on with Detective Hoffman regardless of Mia's mental state and emotional needs?

7. Dr. Avery Rhodes suggests that Mia's feelings for Colin Thatcher were an example of Stockholm syndrome, a psychological situation in which a kidnapping victim forms a bond with his or her captor. Do you feel that Mia was suffering from Stockholm syndrome, or that the relationship she developed with Colin was authentic?

8. Mia suffers from amnesia throughout the pages of *The Good Girl*. It's only in the last few chapters that her memory comes back and she is able to recall her days inside the Minnesota cabin. Knowing, however, that Mia staged her own kidnapping, is it also possible to imagine that she faked the amnesia throughout the novel? Was Mia truly suffering

from acute stress disorder, or was this another act from a
capable and conniving performer?

9. At the end of the novel we learn that Mia arranged her
own kidnapping to seek vengeance against her father for a
neglectful upbringing. Do you feel that Mia was justified in
this behavior? What other actions could she have taken to
get even with her father? Was his conduct as awful as Mia
perceived in her mind for it to be?

10. After reading *The Good Girl*, who do you feel was the true
victim, or victims, and the true conspirator? Have your
opinions changed since beginning the novel, and if so, how?

The Good Girl is a gripping story of an abduction where nothing is exactly what it seems. What was your inspiration for the story and characters?

An atypical kidnapping plot was my inspiration, the first trace of a story I began to craft in my mind, a kidnapping plot that is not exactly what it seems. Add to it characters that appear one way but turn out to be far different than imagined. My hope was not only to keep the reader wondering, but also for them to fall in love with the characters and to feel pulled into the story, into the cold Minnesota cabin with Mia and Colin, and into the loneliness and despair Eve Dennett feels when her daughter disappears.

When you began the novel, did you have Mia's journey already mapped out? How did she surprise you along the way, and how did her story evolve over the course of writing and editing the novel?

In all honesty, when I began writing The Good Girl, I had very little mapped out. As someone has since suggested to me, it was Mia and Colin who told me their story rather than the other way around. Mia certainly evolved over the course of writing and editing the novel, becoming someone I couldn't have predicted in the early days of writing The Good Girl. She became a much stronger persona, not only the victim, but so much more.

The Good Girl is told in alternating first-person perspectives, both before and after Mia is recovered. Why did you choose to narrate the story this way, and why did you choose the perspectives of Colin, Eve and Detective Hoffman?

Mia is the character that is central to this novel, and yet, Mia's voice is rarely heard. For this reason, I wanted to make certain the other characters fully encapsulated Mia Dennett in their narratives, and I chose those characters that were closest to both Mia and to the investigation to portray her life and tell her story.

Alternating first-person perspectives told a more comprehensive story than other points of view, leaving no stone of Mia's life unturned. It was important to me that the reader sees her from all angles: the neglected daughter, the powerless victim and the many more personas she exhibits throughout the novel.

What was your toughest challenge writing The Good Girl? Your greatest pleasure?

My toughest challenge in writing The Good Girl was simply finding the time to write. My daughter was just a year old when I began writing the novel, and my son had yet to be born. As parents know, finding the time to do just about anything with little ones around is oftentimes a daunting task. To this, I thank my children excessively for sleeping "in" every morning (as if 6:30 a.m. counts as sleeping in), and for reliable daily naps that gave me the time I needed to write.

I wrote The Good Girl in complete secrecy, not telling anyone, other than my husband, of the work in progress. I sent the manuscript off to literary agents without so much as having a friend proofread for grammar. I waited alone on pins and needles for the many months it took to acquire an agent, and then later, to sell the novel to MIRA Books. The greatest pleasure of the entire process was finally telling family and friends that not only did I write a book but that it was going to be published!

Can you describe your writing process? Do you write scenes consecutively or jump around? Do you have a schedule or a routine? A lucky charm?

My absolutely favorite time to write is around 5:00 a.m. every day, with my first cup of coffee, when the house is still quiet and quality writing time has yet to be hampered by dirty laundry and grocery shopping, endless games of Chutes and Ladders, and all those other daily tasks that otherwise occupy my time. As an animal lover, I'll gladly admit that I wrote the majority of The Good Girl *with Maggie, a little orange tabby cat, on my lap, and I'm certain she was my lucky charm.*

I chose to write The Good Girl *in three different segments, merging them together upon completion: Eve and Gabe in the Before chapters, Eve and Gabe After, and finally, Colin Before. I found that I was able to empathize with each of the characters and all of their complications when focused on a single, or in some cases dual, perspective and a single time frame. Merging them together was such fun, as the three sections I had been working on individually finally became one, telling a story altogether different than the individual parts.*

How did you know you wanted to be a writer, and how did you come to write *The Good Girl*?

I remember it exactly, the moment I knew I wanted to write: I was around eleven or twelve years old, with a cousin at a sleepover at our grandparents' home. My cousin Carrie was about the same age as me when she produced her first manuscript for me to read, and I remember holding the crisp computer paper (the continuous feed paper with perforated edges) and thinking: this is where books come from. It was then that I knew I wanted to be a writer.

Writing for me, however, was always more of a dream or hobby and less of a career, the kind of thing I did as a girl when I stole away with the family's typewriter and hurried off to my bedroom to write in private. More practically I dreamed of becoming a high school history teacher, and did just that after graduating from college. But though I loved teaching, that urge to write— the need to write—never disappeared, and I would find myself brainstorming plotlines when writing lesson plans, pillaging student names for characters. After giving birth to my daughter, and taking time off to raise her, I was able to refocus on my dreams of writing professionally. In the quiet early mornings and sleepy afternoons that she napped, The Good Girl was born.

Can you tell us something about your next book?

Pretty Baby is another suspenseful tale, a story of a Chicago woman who stumbles upon a young homeless girl waiting with a baby in the rain, beside the Chicago "L." The woman becomes fixated on both the young girl and her baby, going to great lengths to discover who she is and why she's come to be there, digging into a past she'll soon wish she hadn't chosen to uncover.

Read on for a thrilling excerpt from Mary Kubica's next novel,
PRETTY BABY, coming soon.

HEIDI

The first time I see her, she is standing at the Fullerton Station, on the train platform, clutching an infant in her arms. She braces herself and the baby as the purple line express soars past and out to Linden. It's the 8th of April, forty-eight degrees and raining. The rain lurches down from the sky, here, there and everywhere, the wind untamed and angry. A bad day for hair.

The girl is dressed in a pair of jeans, torn at the knee. Her coat is thin and nylon, an army green. She has no hood, no umbrella. She tucks her chin into the coat and stares straight ahead while the rain saturates her. Those around her cower beneath umbrellas, no one offering to share. The baby is quiet, stuffed inside the mother's coat like a joey in a kangaroo pouch. Tufts of slimy pink fleece sneak out from the coat and I convince myself that the baby, sound asleep in what feels to me like utter bedlam—chilled to the bone, the thunderous sound of the "L" soaring past—is a girl.

There's a suitcase beside her feet, vintage leather, brown and worn, beside a pair of lace-up boots, soaked thoroughly through.

She can't be older than sixteen.

She's thin. Malnourished, I tell myself, but maybe she's just thin. Her clothes droop. Her jeans are baggy, her coat too big.

A CTA announcement signals a train approaching, and the brown line pulls into the station. A cluster of morning rush hour commuters crowd into the warmer, drier train, but the girl does not move. I hesitate for a moment—feeling the need to do *something*—but then board the train like the other do-nothings and, slinking into a seat, watch out the window as the doors close and we slide away, leaving the girl and her baby in the rain.

But she stays with me all day.

I ride the train into the Loop, to the Adams/Wabash Station, and inch my way out, down the steps and onto the waterlogged street below, into the acrid sewage smell that hovers at the corners of the city streets, where the pigeons amble along in staggering circles, beside garbage bins and homeless men and millions of city dwellers rushing from point A to point B in the rain.

I spend whole chunks of time—between meetings on adult literacy and GED preparation and tutoring a man from Mumbai in ESL—imagining the girl and child wasting the better part of the day on the train's platform, watching the "L" come and go. I invent stories in my mind. The baby is colicky and only sleeps in flux. The vibration of approaching trains is the key to keeping the baby asleep. The woman's umbrella—I picture it, bright red with flamboyant golden daisies—was man-handled by a great gust of wind, turned inside out, as they tend to do, on days like this. It broke. The umbrella, the baby, the suitcase: it was more than her two arms could carry. Of course she couldn't leave the baby behind. And the suitcase? What was inside that suitcase that was of more importance than an umbrella on a day like this? Maybe she stood there all day, waiting. Maybe she was waiting for an arrival rather than a departure. Or maybe she hopped on the red line seconds after the brown line disappeared from view.

When I come home that night, she's gone. I don't tell Chris about this because I know what he would say: who cares?

I help Zoe with her math homework at the kitchen table. Zoe says that she hates math. This comes as no surprise to me. These days Zoe hates most everything. She's twelve. I can't be certain, but I remember my "I hate everything" days coming much later than that: sixteen or seventeen. But these days everything comes sooner. I went to kindergarten to play, to learn my ABCs; Zoe went to kindergarten to learn to read, to become more technologically savvy than me. Boys and girls are entering puberty sooner, up to two years sooner in some cases, than my own generation. Ten-year-olds have cell phones; seven- and eight-year-old girls have breasts.

Chris eats dinner and then disappears to the office, as he always does, to pour over sleepy, coma-inducing spreadsheets until after Zoe and I have gone to bed.

The next day she's there again. The girl. And again it's raining. Only the second week of April, and already the meteorologists are predicting record rainfall for the month. The wettest April on record, they say. The day before, O'Hare reported 0.6 inches of rain for a single day. It's begun to creep into basements, collect in the pleats of low-lying city streets. Airport flights have been cancelled and delayed. I remind myself, *April showers bring May flowers*, tuck myself into a creamy waterproof parka and sink my feet into a pair of rubber boots for the trek to work.

She wears the same torn jeans, the same army-green jacket, the same lace-up boots. The vintage suitcase rests beside her feet. She shivers in the raw air, the baby writhing and upset.

She bounces the baby up and down, up and down, and I read her lips—*shh*. I hear women beside me, drinking their piping hot coffee beneath oversize golf umbrellas: *she shouldn't have that baby outside. On a day like today?* they sneer. *What's wrong with that girl? Where is the baby's hat?*

The purple line express soars past; the brown line rolls in and stops and the do-nothings file their way in like the moving products of an assembly line.

I linger, again, wanting to *do something*, but not wanting to seem intrusive or offensive. There's a fine line between helpful and disrespectful, one which I don't want to cross. There could be a million reasons why she's standing with the suitcase, holding the baby in the rain, a million reasons other than the one nagging thought that dawdles at the back of my brain: she's homeless.

I work with people who are often poverty stricken, mostly immigrants. Literacy statistics in Chicago are bleak. About a third of adults have a low level of literacy, which means they can't fill out job applications; they can't read directions or know which stop along the "L" track is theirs. They can't help their children with their homework.

The faces of poverty are grim: elderly women curled into balls on benches in the city's parks, their life's worth pushed around in a shopping cart as they scavenge the garbage for food; men pressed against high-rise buildings on the coldest of January days, sound asleep, a cardboard sign leaned against their inert body: Please Help. Hungry. God Bless. The victims of poverty live in substandard housing, in dangerous neighborhoods; their food supply is inadequate at best; they often go hungry. They have little or no access to health care, to proper immunization; their children go to underfunded schools, develop behavioral problems, witness violence. They have a greater risk of engaging in sexual activity, among other things, at a young age and thus, the cycle repeats itself. Teenage girls give birth to infants with low birth weights, they have little access to health care, they cannot be properly immunized, the children get sick. They go hungry.

Poverty, in Chicago, is highest among blacks and Hispanics, but that doesn't negate the fact that a white girl can be poor.

All this scuttles through my mind in the split second I wonder what to do. Help the girl. Get on the train. Help the girl. Get on the train. Help the girl.

But then, to my surprise, the girl boards the train. She slips through the doors seconds before the automated announcement—*bing, bong, doors closing*—and I follow along, wondering where it is that we're going, the girl, her baby and me.

The car is crowded. A man rises from his seat, which he graciously offers to the girl; without a word, she accepts, scooting into the metal pew beside a wheeler-dealer in a long black coat, a man who looks at the baby as if it might just be from Mars. Passengers lose themselves in the morning commute—they're on their cell phones, on their laptops and other technological gadgets, they're reading novels, the newspaper, the morning's briefing; they sip their coffee and stare out the window at the city skyline, lost in the gloomy day. The girl carefully removes the baby from her kangaroo pouch. She unfolds the pink fleece blanket, and miraculously, beneath that blanket, the baby appears dry. The train lurches toward the Armitage station, soaring behind brick buildings and three and four flats, so close to people's homes I imagine the way they shake as the "L" passes by, glasses rattling in cabinets, TVs silenced by the reverberation of the train, every few minutes of the live long day and long into the night. We leave Lincoln Park, and head into Old Town, and somewhere along the way the baby settles down, her wailing reduced to a quiet whimper to the obvious relief of those on the train.

I'm forced to stand farther away from the girl than I'd like to be. Bracing myself for the unpredictability of the train's movements, I peer past bodies and briefcases for the occasional glimpse—flawless ivory skin, patchy red from crying—the mother's hollow cheeks—a white Onesies jumpsuit—the desperate, hungry suction on a pacifier—vacant eyes. A woman walks by and says, "Cute baby." The girl forces a smile.

Smiling does not come naturally to the girl. I imagine her beside Zoe and know that she is older: the hopelessness in her eyes, for one, the lack of Zoe's raw vulnerability, another. And of course, there is the baby (I have myself convinced that Zoe still believes babies are delivered by storks), though beside the businessman the girl is diminutive, like a child. Her hair is disproportional: cut blunt on one side, shoulder length the other. It's drab, like an old sepia photograph, yellowing with time. There are streaks of red, not her natural hue. She wears dark, heavy eye makeup, smeared from the rain, hidden behind a screen of long, protective bangs.

The train slows its way into the Loop, careening around twists and turns. I watch as the baby is swaddled once again in the pink fleece and stuffed into the nylon coat and prepare myself for their departure. She gets off before I do, at State/Van Buren, and I watch through the window, trying not to lose her in the heavy congestion that fills the city streets at this time of day.

But I do anyway, and just like that, she's gone.